WICKED WIND

A Solsti Prophecy Novel

Sharon Kay

This is a work of fiction. Any actual places are used in a fictional context. Other names of places and people are the product of the author's imagination, and any resemblance to actual places or people is purely coincidental.

Edited by Janet Michelson
Cover art by Amanda Simpson at Pixel Mischief
Interior design by Ink Slinger Editorial Services

FIRST EDITION

BOOKS BY SHARON KAY

The Solsti Prophecy series
WICKED WIND
WICKED WAVES
WICKED FLAMES
ON WICKED GROUND

Companion to the series
KISSED BY A DEMON SPY: A NOVELLA

ACKNOWLEDGEMENTS

To my husband, for supporting my out-of-the-blue idea to write a novel, for giving me time to write, for proofreading, and for putting up with all my quirks. I love you!

To my son. I'll always be here to "hug you and kiss you for one hundred days."

To my local chapter of NaNoWriMo, for hammering the mantra of JUST WRITE, and write until the novel is done. Editing comes LATER.

To my critique partners - I adore each of you. Thank you for falling for my characters, but keeping enough perspective to let me know when they stepped out of line.

Kaci and Claudia - thank you for the words of encouragement and for slogging through my unpolished first drafts!

Cam - thank you for sharing your thoughts and asking me the tough questions.

Racquel - You've been there for me since the newbie stage, since the first chapter of the first draft. You were one of the first to make me see that my little novel could take flight. You dissected my early attempts with TLC and you've been in my corner ever since.

Amy - thanks for the mornings in the coffee shop, talking about our novels and everything else. I'm grateful for your insight and words of encouragement, whether about writing or life.

Victoria - You're an amazing writer and an amazing

woman. Your strength and grace are as much an inspiration to me as your plucky heroines. I'm excited to watch you take the publishing world by storm! And my fight scenes kick serious bad-guy booty thanks to you!

To my SW's, Jamie and Cristin – Name a subject and I'll bet we have talked about it. I will be forever grateful for the straight talk, the silly talk, the smart-ass talk and the supportive talk, for the late night "we're-so-tired-but-just-have-to-say-one-more-thing" pep talks. You both inspire me to stretch my "wordology" and improve my writing!

Jamie (SFAM) – I admire how you jumped feet first into the indie publishing world and am so proud of your success!

Cristin (Spice) – Your stories are breathtaking. I can't wait to see them on Kindles and bookshelves!

To my brother David and my sister Diana – thanks for just being awesomely supportive. And Di, thanks for the last minute read-throughs!

Thank you to my parents and my in-laws, for your love, support, and encouraging my creativity.

PROLOGUE

"THAT CONCERT WAS AWESOME." NICOLE Bonham raked a hand through her hair, pulling the blond strands into a bunch at one shoulder.

The warm air of the summer night swirled around Nicole and her sister Brooke, a refreshing change from the stuffy venue they'd left. Their heeled boots clicked on the sidewalk as they walked a few blocks down Madison Street toward the bus stop. Traffic around the United Center was a bitch, especially after a sold-out show, so they used public transportation whenever possible.

"Their drummer is so hot," Brooke murmured.

"You just like him because he's blond." Nicole shot her a smirk.

As they crossed the street and turned south, a muffled cry carried on the wind. Startled, the sisters exchanged a look before tip-toeing in the direction of the sound. From an alley up ahead, more noises filtered out: a thud, then a low chuckle and the sound of tearing cloth. A sick feeling formed in Nicole's gut as the sounds coalesced in her mind, giving her a good idea of what was taking place mere feet away.

She peeked around the edge of the building. Ice shot through her veins. A woman was held down by one man, while another guy stood next to them, hands at his zipper. In the dim light from the lone streetlamp, a knife flashed silver at her throat.

Nicole turned back to Brooke in horror. "Shit, she's being attacked!"

Brooke's eyes widened, reflecting Nicole's terror and outrage. "We have to help her."

Nicole reached for her phone.

"No, that'll take too long." Brooke put a hand on her sister's arm and gave her a piercing look. "We haven't taken years of Tae Kwan Do for nothing."

Nicole nodded, indignation replacing any lingering fear. These scumbags weren't going to commit any crimes tonight. Side by side, she and Brooke stepped into the narrow mouth of the alley.

"Hey!" Brooke yelled. "Leave her alone!"

The man who was standing spun around and snarled, "What the fuck?"

The man holding the woman shoved her aside and darted toward them, knife in hand.

Brooke reacted in a heartbeat. When he got close, she stepped to the side and hooked his neck with her arm. Spinning him, she used his own momentum to knock him off balance. As his feet faltered, she extended her right leg and tripped him. She grabbed his knife hand at the wrist, and his weapon clattered to the ground.

He shot to his feet and lunged for Brooke's throat. As she drew her hand back to drive the heel of her palm into his chin, the second man delivered a sharp kick to the back of her knee.

Fury ignited in Nicole's brain. She glanced around for any hard object and spied an empty beer bottle. She lunged, snagging it in a fluid dip, and kept moving toward the second man. Stretching her arm back, she smashed the bottle over his head with all her strength. He cursed loudly and turned, cocking his arm for a punch.

How obvious. Years of training kicked in. When his fist shot forward, she dodged to the side, and then grabbed his wrist on the recoil. She brought her free hand up to push hard against his elbow, pitting all her strength against the pressure point. He howled and swayed to the side.

Brooke had stumbled at the blow to her leg, but regained

her balance with innate grace. She hovered in front of her opponent, whose pants were still undone.

"You pretty, bitch," he slurred. "Too bad I gotta fuck you up."

He charged, but Brooke was ready. She whirled her leg into a high arc, her foot slamming his jaw again. A satisfying crack filled the dark alley. As he slumped to the ground she turned to Nicole. "You okay?"

"Yeah." Nicole eyed the second man.

He backed up a step. "Fuck this shit." With a look of wariness he dashed around them and took off down the street.

Ignoring the unconscious loser on the ground, the sisters turned to the woman. Tears streamed down her face and one eye was already swollen shut. A large purple bruise marred her face and dirt covered her torn blouse, but she managed to sit up. "Thank you," she said hoarsely. "You...you're angels."

Brooke slid her arm around the woman's shoulders and helped her stand. "Are you okay?" She studied the woman's face.

"Yes, thanks to you. Now I gotta get home to my little girls." Her voice broke on the last word.

"Do you want us to call someone?" Nicole asked.

"No. I'm gonna catch my bus, right over there." She pointed to the mouth of the alley and shivered in the temperate night air, her rapid breaths slowing to shaky sighs.

"Can we take you to a hospital?" Nicole's gaze swept up and down the woman's form. She didn't seem to have any serious injuries; then again, Nicole and Brooke hadn't seen the entire incident.

"No. No hospitals. I'm not usually out this late, but I had to work a double. Another waitress was sick, and I took her hours because I need the money." She wiped the last of the tears from her face.

After more insistence from the woman that she was fine, the sisters walked her to the bus stop and waited until she safely boarded. Then they walked one more block to catch their own bus.

"Whoa," was all Nicole could say afterward. She and Brooke sat at opposite ends of the five-seat sectional that made up the last row of every CTA bus, their legs stretched out across the worn fabric. Her head reeled at what they'd just done. "We just beat up two guys."

"Two guys who are lower than dirt and totally deserved it. Let's do that again!" When Nicole gave her an incredulous look, Brooke added, "It's not like we did much of anything to them. They'll have a few bruises. And that woman is safe because of us."

"Yeah, it did feel great to help someone." Nicole frowned. "But what if they had guns?"

"We could learn to work around that. You're right, we need to be careful–but most of these guys only know how to throw one kind of punch, or pull a trigger. We can take them down long enough to help their victims. And we could get our own weapons, just in case."

Nicole folded her arms and waited for Part Two of her sister's opinion. *She should've been the lawyer in the family.*

"Think about it. This could be why we have our gifts. What if a strong gust of wind blows debris into some pimp's eyes? Or what if he got soaked in a sudden rain and lost his grip on his gun?" Brooke's gray eyes sparkled.

Nicole stared at her for several moments, thoughts swirling around her head. The chance to find a purpose behind the unusual talents she and her younger sister had been born with was too tempting to pass up. A slow grin spread across her face as she reached forward to slap Brooke's raised hand in a high-five that echoed throughout the bus.

CHAPTER 1

Three months later

NICOLE STRETCHED HER LEGS UNDER her desk, kicked off her shoes, and wiggled her toes. It was five PM on a sunny Friday afternoon, a long Labor Day weekend ahead of her. And she was using personal time off for the rest of the week. *Yes!* She smiled and swiveled her chair around to take in the view of Lake Michigan from her office high above Chicago's bustling downtown streets. She loved the energy of the city as much as she loved the ever-changing moods of the lake.

"Nicole, are you heading out soon?" Her thoughts were interrupted by her friend Julie, the other staff attorney at the large insurance company. "Geez, I thought that meeting would never end."

"Most meetings here are never-ending." Nicole shook her head. "I have to bring the Perkins and Hansen files home with me. I'm almost ready. Let me just gather a few things together and I'll walk out with you."

"Cool." Julie plopped down in the chair across from Nicole. "Bryce and I are going to that new club that just opened in Bucktown. You should come with us."

"I'm too old for clubs." Nicole clicked the icon that would copy the files to her flash drive.

"You did not just say that! Twenty-eight is most definitely

5

not too old. C'mon, it'll be fun. And you never know who you might meet." Julie grinned. She and Bryce had met in a club several months ago and now were practically engaged. Nicole couldn't fault her friend's enthusiasm, but she had other plans for tonight. Plans that involved pounding the pavement, not a dance floor. Plans she didn't share with her friends.

Copying finished, Nicole opted to avoid the invitation. She dropped the flash drive into her bag and slid her feet back into her heeled sandals. "Ready."

Julie grabbed a piece of candy from the dish on Nicole's desk before turning to follow her to the elevators. "I just think you need to have some fun. You're always working, or working out."

The brushed metal doors slid open, revealing several people already inside the small space. The women squeezed into the front. Nicole shrugged at Julie, silently invoking the rule of not continuing the conversation if there were other people in the elevator.

"So?" Julie asked when they reached the lobby and walked out into the early September heat.

The blast of humid, late-summer air relaxed Nicole's muscles better than any massage. It felt like a warm smiling breath waiting for her, surrounding her. In spring and fall, the brisk wind would lift her hair slightly as if in greeting. And in winter, the chilled air served to remind her of its power, and her own.

The weather swings in the Chicago area provided a visceral reminder that everything changed. She was constantly aware of the wind and different patterns in the air, and it made her uneasy because it somehow *responded* to her. With only a thought, she could summon a gentle breeze or a forceful gale. No one knew about her mysterious ability except her sisters, who had similar gifts.

"Are you even listening to me, Nic?" Julie's voice broke through Nicole's reflections. "Really, when was the last time you went out?"

"I know, it's been awhile," Nicole acknowledged.

"Remember all the crazy times we had at China Club?"

"Yeah." Nicole couldn't stop the grin from spreading across her face.

"You danced on that bar so many times I thought they'd name the place after you. Remember staying out so late on weekdays–"

"That we didn't have time to go home before work?"

"Sleeping under our desks sucked."

"Yeah." Nicole laughed. "That's one thing I can cross off the bucket list. Don't need to do that again. Look, how about I try to meet you later? I need to work out when I get home."

"All right, but I'm going to keep checking on you until you show up. I'll text you the address." Julie turned in the direction of her condo. "See ya."

Nicole waved, knowing her friend would hold her to her words, walked the few blocks to the L station, and caught the next Red Line train. Julie could text her all night long, but Nicole's phone would be set to silent mode. Stealth and the element of surprise would be on her agenda tonight.

After a short ride she arrived at the Lincoln Park condo that she shared with Brooke. Dropping her bag in the living room, she went to her bedroom and changed into yoga pants and a tank top. She pulled her long blond hair into a ponytail and grabbed a water bottle. She hadn't been kidding about the workout, and Friday nights were her favorite times to go. The gym in her building would be deserted at this hour.

Nicole grinned as she pulled open the heavy glass door to the fitness center. A bright pink sign announcing a new aerobic dance class reminded her of her youngest sister Ginny. Gin, as she preferred to be called, was wrapping up a graduate program at the University of Illinois downstate, and taught aerobics in her spare time. The three sisters had spoken last night via video chat. Always the funny one, Gin had them doubled over laughing in front of the computer monitor. She happened to be great at doing impressions, and last night's antics had Gin in full *Golden*

Girls mode.

"You know this will be us someday, all of us with white hair and living together," Nicole said, wiping a tear from the corner of her eye.

"Whatever!" Gin hooted. "You'll be the one with all the gentleman friends coming over."

The three of them were the only family they had, and no matter what life had thrown at them, their tight knot of support endured. Nicole hoped that Gin would find work in the city when her studies were done. It would be nice to have those laugh-until-we-cry chats in person.

She began a set of walking lunges to warm up her legs. Nicole credited martial arts with helping her cope with the losses in her life. The workouts kept her body strong, while the focus and meditation eased her mind. She and her sisters had loved the karate lessons they'd taken as kids. Then later, she and Brooke eagerly pursued the different disciplines of judo and Tae Kwan Do. They still made martial arts their main workout, sometimes sparring with each other, and sometimes refining techniques alone. Their skills and fierce loyalty were what grounded them. She visualized their bond as a strong knot of three ropes, and the more stress put upon it, the tighter it got. The strength of their sisterhood flowed into her muscles as she moved with practiced ease.

Two hours later, she had showered and was devouring leftover Chinese food when Brooke came home. "Remind me not to complain about having to work late," Nicole murmured as her sister grabbed her own leftovers and put them in the microwave.

"I was almost finished with my project. You know I can't leave any loose ends." Brooke's work as a graphic designer occasionally involved some crazy hours. "And I am more than ready to hit the streets tonight."

"Me, too. Where do you want to start?"

"Englewood." Brooke's eyes gleamed as she named one of

the city's toughest areas.

Nicole nodded. "Never a dull night over there."

The microwave beeped. With a grin, Brooke took out her food. "Thank goodness we found a Chinese place that can make decent egg rolls. They usually have way too much ginger."

When she was done they dressed in black T-shirts, black jeans, and Doc Martens with knives concealed, in case things got ugly. They headed to the parking garage to retrieve their plain gray Honda sedan. Brooke slid behind the wheel and they pulled out, turning south on Damen Avenue. "I got an email from Ray yesterday," she drawled. "He wonders where we've been. He misses you."

Nicole rolled her eyes. "Yeah, right. He's such a flirt."

Over the summer, they had spent a lot of time at the local shooting club Ray managed, making sure their firearm skills were top-notch. The guys they encountered on their searches weren't always the best combatants, but they had a never-ending supply of guns. Nicole and Brooke needed to be prepared for anything. The best part of their routine was the element of surprise. No one expected two young white women to deliberately get involved in a street fight.

While Nicole refined her talent, Brooke worked just as hard on her affinity with water. The two of them regularly drove to rural areas, intent on exploring their abilities where they had space and privacy. If the weather forecast ever called for rain, Nicole knew what they'd be doing. More than once, she watched her sister derive a huge sense of satisfaction from seeing a gang member distracted by a puddle of dirty, oil-slicked rainwater strategically directed into his eyes. Their method was vigilante justice, but they both felt a gratifying sense of purpose in it.

This night would be no different. They parked on a side street near the expressway and exited the car, slipping down the cracked sidewalks with all senses on high alert. It didn't take long to find trouble. As they rounded a corner, they heard the unmistakable sounds of a struggle drifting from an old brick building. There in the doorway was a young woman, looking like she was still in her teens, trying to fight off a barrel-chested man twice her size.

"Hey, why don't you leave her alone?" Nicole shot a chilled breeze past the man's head.

"What the—" He turned and saw Nicole and Brooke. Then his grimy face broke into a lewd grin that revealed a couple of missing teeth. "Hey, double the fun. This is my lucky day!"

"Actually, I'd say it's her lucky day," Brooke said. "Step away from her."

"You bitches be next, when I'm done with her," he grunted, and started to turn back to the frightened teen.

"Wrong answer," Nicole called out in a sweetly sarcastic voice, as she directed a breeze to swoop upward from the dirty street and into his face.

Brooke, already at a dead run, yanked his shoulder to pull him off the girl. He managed to stay on his feet as she delivered a kick right below his ribs, and when he swayed slightly, Brooke bent at the knees to shift her center of gravity. She side-stepped his punch, and then struck a hard punch to his solar plexus. Nicole heard him exhale sharply and double over as he reached for the gun that was in his waistband, but Brooke kicked him in the back of his head with her boot and he slumped on the ground.

"Wh-who are you?" the young woman asked, gaping, as Brooke straightened and dusted off her hands.

"No one. Just helping out a sister in trouble," Nicole said. "Do you have somewhere you can go? Parents?"

"I live with friends." She kicked a pebble and shifted her weight from one stiletto-heeled foot to the other.

"We should call the police," Brooke said.

"No! No police. I'm fine."

"At least take this. I know some of the people there. They're cool." Nicole handed her the business card for an organization that helped disadvantaged women and children.

The teenager eyed it skeptically but took it, and managed a small smile. "Thank you."

"You're welcome. And it would be a good idea to go to your friend's house now, before more assholes like him show up."

Nicole and Brooke watched her walk up the block and start talking to another young woman, then the sisters walked in the opposite direction. Keeping to the shadows, they made their way to their little Honda. They were almost there when two men stumbled out of a rundown building and right into their path. "Hey baby, let's party," one of them drawled, strung out of his mind on whatever hit he had just taken. The other was in the same sad shape. Nicole shoved them against the building. As she turned, her skin tingled with awareness. *Someone's watching.*

She looked farther down the length of the building, and spotted the figure of a man. He loomed large, well over six feet tall, and wide as a door. His body was draped in shadows except for a sliver of light from the streetlamp. The pale beam illuminated his right side, revealing a chiseled jaw and shoulder. His eyes glinted and locked on her.

She turned and jumped into the car that Brooke had already started. "Go," she directed. "There's someone watching us."

As Brooke peeled out, tires screeching, Nicole looked back. A rat scurried along the base of the building. No one else was there.

She shook her head to clear it. "I really thought I saw someone."

"Well, if anyone was hanging around, all he saw was those crack-heads falling down in front of us. That's not much to talk about," Brooke said. "Let's find another loser to take down."

They drove west to another dilapidated neighborhood. Stealing along the side streets next to Brooke, Nicole scrutinized every dark shape and whisper of noise. They passed a drunk sitting next to a dumpster. Empty cardboard fast food containers spilled over the edge, the scents of old food and dirty diapers thickening the warm air. An addict sat in a doorway, hugging her knees to her chest, staring blankly into the night. Angry words from a male voice carried on the breeze, growing louder as the sisters neared.

"Here we go," Brooke murmured. They slowly rounded a corner and found a pissed-off drug dealer arguing with his client.

"You didn't pay up for last week's prime merchandise," growled the thin, shaggy-haired dealer. He gripped the T-shirt of a young woman in one hand, and a gun in the other. "What makes you think you're gonna get any more today?"

"Please, just a little more," the woman begged. "I can get you the money tomorrow. I just need a little bit right now."

"What are you gonna do to get it?" He tightened his hold, grabbing more thin fabric in his grimy fist.

"You don't need anything he's got." Nicole crossed her arms over her chest.

"Who the fuck are you?" the dealer spat out. He turned toward the sisters but didn't relinquish his hold on the woman.

"Doesn't matter who we are. You just need to let her go."

"Yeah, bitch? How 'bout you suck my dick?" he snarled.

"Save it for your boyfriend," Nicole snorted as she blew a gust of icy wind into his eyes. She spotted an empty plastic bag blowing down the street, grabbed it with an air current, and pushed it around his face. It distracted him long enough for her to kick the gun from his hand. He cursed and let go of the frightened woman, who took off running down the street.

"Wait, we can help you!" Nicole chased after her, but stopped when the woman reached an intersection and darted into oncoming traffic. Tires screeched and horns blared, but the woman charged forward, emerging unharmed on the opposite sidewalk. She kept running without looking back.

"Damn," Nicole muttered, and turned around and jogged to her sister.

Brooke stood behind the dealer, his neck snared in a choke hold. She leaned back, one arm around his throat, her gray eyes flashing as the blood flow to his head ceased. "Time to find another line of work, mister," she gritted. He groaned something unintelligible as his eyes slid shut and he went limp.

"Let's go." Brooke stepped away from his prone form. "He

won't be out for very long."

"Yeah," Nicole agreed as they started back to the car. When they reached it and climbed inside, she remembered Julie's club invitation and groaned. "Ah shoot, I told Julie I'd meet her and Bryce tonight." She pulled her phone from her pocket and switched the ringtone back on.

Brooke grinned at her. "You have fun with that, chica. All I've got left on my agenda is a long soak in the tub."

Nicole sighed. She'd rather soak in a bubble bath herself, but she had begged off several outings with friends lately, and couldn't do it again tonight. As they parked in the garage of their building, her cell trilled with Julie's number on the caller ID. "Hey," she answered. "I'll be there, I promise. Give me thirty minutes."

Chapter 2

GUNNAR BLEW OUT A BREATH. It seemed that tonight's search would come up empty. Skell demons had been seen around humans, mostly junkies, but hell if he and his comrades knew why. No citizens had turned up dead, just wounded. And the wounds were made to bleed but not necessarily kill. It looked sloppy—well, Skells *were* sloppy by nature—but there were too many to brush it off as a coincidence.

No Skells had shown their ugly faces tonight, but his curiosity meter jumped all over the evening's events. Looking for trouble in run-down neighborhoods, he'd found the unexpected. Astounding and impressive. And not much surprised him anymore.

As a Lash demon, he spent his life causing trouble, fighting trouble, or trying to get out of trouble. Tonight he had been prowling the city for the blasted Skells. The gray-skinned creatures usually tried to ally themselves with stronger demons in their quest for power. Happy to do someone else's dirty work in exchange for protection, an uptick in their numbers was a cause for concern.

Gunnar had gotten word of an increase in the Skells' activity in the run-down parts of the city. It was his responsibility to investigate the maggots. As he slipped like a ghost through alleys and past broken shells of buildings, he came upon a sight that stopped him in his tracks.

Two women interceded in a fight between a beefy man and a diminutive young woman. It didn't appear that they stumbled upon the scene unprepared; rather, it seemed that they were looking for it. Their speed and efficient grace were a marvel to watch; their martial skills unquestionable. But the jolt of power from the blond woman floored him. The lingering trace of it piqued his curiosity because he didn't recognize it. She wasn't a demon, vampire, or shifter.

But hell, she was drop-dead gorgeous. Tall for a woman, all lean curves and willowy limbs. He gazed in appreciation as she moved, dark jeans hugging her hips like a second skin, T-shirt clinging to her high, rounded breasts. She and her companion worked with confidence and accuracy. He could tell her senses detected him as he watched her dispatch the junkies that stumbled into their path a few minutes later. He'd allowed her to register his presence, even as he remained mostly hidden.

He tracked the women, too curious to let them disappear into the night. He travelled along the rooftops, a silent stealthy shadow. His suspicion that they actively sought out trouble had been confirmed by their second encounter with street scum. They'd efficiently nullified the drug dealer even as he felt another burst of power from the blonde. Their practiced ease told him they'd done this before, and not just the fighting. This wasn't the first time the blonde had used her energy to get what she wanted.

He followed them to their next stop, a four-story Lincoln Park condo building. *Her home?* He now stood in the shadows across the street, watching the front entrance, completely intrigued. Unfortunately, staking out a leggy blonde who may or may not be a supernatural creature was not on his agenda. She obviously wasn't a Skell demon.

And he hadn't caught any. Kai, his brother-in-arms, would give him hell for that, and for chasing a woman around. They had serious work to do, like keeping tabs on control-hungry demons and taking them down when necessary. Many creatures from their realm craved ruthless, dominating power. Some would kill for it.

For the last several months, Gunnar, Kai, and a few others

had been staying at the group's headquarters north of the city. The demons were able to move to different cities if they wanted, but Gunnar liked the fluid energy of Chicago's neighborhoods. He glanced down to check the time on his phone and realized he had spent a half-hour lost in his thoughts in the nice, leafy north-side neighborhood. He was about to leave and head to the tough, west-side Austin area when the door across the street opened.

Good Gods.

Gunnar felt his jaw slacken at the sight that emerged from the condo building. Blond hair loose around her face and shoulders, the female was no longer dressed for kicking drug dealers' asses, but for a night out on the town. Her perky backside and mile-long legs were poured into a pair of jeans even tighter than the previous ones. She wore knee-high black heeled boots and a clingy red top with a low V neck. She talked on her phone as she got into a waiting cab, pausing to give an address to the driver. An address Gunnar had no trouble overhearing, due to his heightened demon senses.

There was no way he was letting her out of his sight until he did a little more investigating into her identity. Was she going to meet up with friends, or a man? He had the sudden, irrational thought that he would rather see her meet friends. A woman as hot as she was wouldn't lack for male attention, though. Gunnar wondered why he even cared. Spending time with females, supernatural or human, wasn't a problem, and he'd never pursued a serious relationship. He couldn't wrap his head around the idea of anything long-term, not when his daily activities took him from one kind of danger right into another.

He followed her cab to a night club. Muffled music behind an unmarked gray metal door exploded into pounding sound as the entrance burst open to admit several chattering young women. The blond female was still on her phone as she exited the cab and walked inside, all sweet curves in those snug jeans.

From his position near the door, a muscular bouncer folded his arms across his chest. Gunnar approached with a fifty folded between two fingers, meeting the man's wary stare. The bouncer took it, his face breaking into a brief smile, and nodded at the door.

Inside, a deafening beat poured from huge speakers set up around a packed dance floor. Smoke hung in the air, illuminated by brightly colored flashing lights. Crowds surrounded the massive bar, and tables were scattered around the perimeter of the room. Gunnar scanned these first, noting a few supernatural creatures present but none that normally caused trouble. Two female fairies kissed each other, holding their human male companions enthralled. And one male Trant demon held court with a bevy of females in a corner. Since the Trant's purpose in life was seducing others, Gunnar dismissed him. Unless he tried to seduce the blond woman, Gunnar couldn't care less how many women went home with the Trant.

Looking across the crowd, he spotted her heading toward a table along the far wall. She greeted two brunette women and a man who had an arm wrapped around one of the women. Her friends had an amber-colored drink waiting for her, which she tossed back and grinned. Gods, she had a mega-watt smile. The unattached brunette took her hand and tugged her toward the dance floor. They wound their way into the sea of writhing bodies, stopping near the center to dance together.

Gunnar couldn't take his eyes off her, and neither could several human men. And no wonder. With her arms raised languidly above her head, her hips swaying to the pulsing beat, she was mesmerizing. She and her friend grinned at each other, letting their arms slide and tangle together as they moved. In just a few short minutes they were joined by two males in black leather pants and black T-shirts. They partnered off, and the man she was dancing with moved nearer to her. Gunnar narrowed his eyes as he watched them get as close as two people could get without touching, and when the man placed his hand on the small of her back to tug her against him, Gunnar's patience snapped.

Nicole's body hummed with energy. Fluid and free, her second wind coursed along her skin. She grinned to herself at the joke that only her sisters would get. She felt good about her accomplishments today, and being out with Julie, Bryce, and their other friend Alicia was a perfect way to top things off. The two guys dancing with her and Alicia were cute, although not tall enough for her taste, but it was only a dance. It wasn't as if she was looking for Mr. Right. She'd been in lots of short relationships, but nothing serious. It was kind of hard to explain her ability. "Oh by the way, I can manipulate air currents and temperature, but otherwise I'm just the girl next door" didn't tend to go over well. Not that she ever tried. She hadn't found a reason to.

She let her head tilt slightly to one side as she danced, just as her partner put his arm around her waist to pull her right up against him. Nicole took it in stride. This was a hot, just-opened club, advertised by word of mouth only. The wild energy in the room stoked the patrons to a kinetic level. All forms of dress paraded here tonight, including downright skimpy and dominatrix wanna-be. She wasn't about to sweat it if her cute-but-bland dance partner put his hand on her waist. And if he did try anything she didn't like, she could knock him on his ass in two seconds. She smiled at him as they moved to the pounding music.

Glancing to the side, her body ground to a screeching halt. Words fled her mind as her eyes locked onto a mountain of a man.

Dark strength radiated from his frame. He was tall, so tall that even in her boots she knew she'd have to look up at him. Built like the biggest linebacker in any football league, he parted the crowd as he stalked toward her. His eyes only left hers when he got up close, in order to glare at the man she'd been dancing with. He jerked his head to the side. Her partner gave her one last glance before melting away into the crowd. She raised an eyebrow at his boldness, but when he turned to her with a playful grin, any shred of resistance slipped away.

Nicole gazed up into hypnotic eyes that radiated Caribbean blue. She blinked. It might have been the funky lighting in the club, but she could have sworn his eyes actually glowed. His black hair hung sexy and disheveled—in a good way, with the longest layers just touching the neckline of his shirt. Her eyes drifted down to his sensual mouth and square jaw, then lower to the rippling muscles clearly visible beneath his black T-shirt. Mercy, he was fine. Mouth-watering. She swallowed, aware that she was staring. She started swaying to the music slowly, her eyes back on his. Her lips tugged into a small smile.

He smiled again, and—oh my god—he had *dimples*, on top of all his gorgeousness. He moved with her, boldly placing his big hands on her hips. Her lids grew heavy, wanting to slide shut so she could luxuriate in the sudden warmth flowing from those hands into her body. But she couldn't look away from those eyes. She smiled again, allowing his touch. Tracing her fingers lightly along his shoulders, she wound her arms around his neck. She couldn't remember the last time she flirted like this.

A tiny voice in the back of her mind needled her. *You don't know anything about him.* Maybe she should think twice about being so forward. But she never doubted her strength. Tonight, daring and power were her wingmen.

The tempo of the music picked up and she turned away from him, only to raise one arm up and back to wrap around his neck. She leaned back into him, until she felt their bodies press together, her back to his chest. For an instant, she thought she heard him groan. His hands found her hips again and locked her against his pelvis as they began a slow, dirty grind. One of his hands left her hip to travel up to her waist, then farther up to caress her ribs, stopping maddening short of her breast before moving all the way down her thigh and finally back to her hip. He did it again on her other side, turning her entire body into a live wire.

Then a tiny spark of reason emerged in her lust-fogged brain. She paused. God, she was so into him, she almost forgot they were in public. In a packed night club, in front of her friends. Nicole turned around to face him, touched his arm, and nodded toward the front door. He kept one hand at the small of her back as they made their way through the gyrating crowd.

He took her hand in his as they stepped through the entrance and out onto the sidewalk. They walked several feet away from the front door before Nicole stopped to lean against the brick wall of the building. The cool night air felt good against her skin as she looked up at him. "I'm Nicole."

"Gunnar," he murmured, his hand brushing a few stray strands of hair from her face. "I like dancing with you, Nicole."

She loved the way her name sounded on his lips. "Me, too. I just needed some fresh air."

"I'm glad you decided to take me along,"

"Of course. Maybe I'm not done dancing with you." She wasn't usually this bold. *Where had that come from?*

"Is that so?" He placed his hands against the wall on either side of her head. His body blocked everything else on the street as he slowly lowered his head toward hers. She knew he was giving her the chance to back out, but every nerve ending in her body screamed for his kiss. He smelled like leather and smoke and woods on a rainy night. She inhaled his scent, her body responding to the heat rolling off of his, the intensity making her feel like they were right back on the dance floor.

"Yes," was all she could manage to whisper before his mouth closed over hers.

Her lips were soft, sweet, and giving under his demands. Right now Gunnar didn't feel any need for teasing, gentle kisses. Oh, they had their time and place, but not following the round of hot dirty dancing that had just gone down inside. Her lips parted further, welcoming him as his tongue swept inside her mouth. She tasted delicious, a sweet mix of mint and Jack Daniels. Chest to chest, he felt her heart speed up, and damn, but he couldn't resist touching her. He took one hand off the brick wall behind her and slid his fingers into her soft blond hair. Her arms wrapped around his neck once more, keeping him close as she sighed into him. Every inch of her skin that he had touched was silky smooth, belying the strength of the sinewy muscles beneath.

He stifled a groan as she moved one hand down to his waistband, teased her fingers along the edge, and then found one front belt loop. She hooked a finger into it and tugged hard, pulling him flush against her lean curves. He couldn't resist pressing against her just a little more, making sure she felt the evidence of his arousal. He'd been hard for her ever since she first touched him on the dance floor, and when she rocked her perfect ass up against him, he nearly lost it. He broke away from her lush mouth to trail a line of kisses along her jaw and down her throat, reveling in the way she sighed his name.

He lifted his head to study her face. The bright emerald of her eyes darkened with desire as they flicked down to his mouth and back up. Her lips were slightly parted and swollen from his kiss. Still keeping one hand in her hair, he moved his other down her back to settle at her waist. His body roared for another taste of her. He bent to kiss her mouth again, then froze.

Nicole stiffened, too. They both looked toward the street corner, where a man was trying to snatch a woman's purse. Unfortunately, she tried to fight him off.

"You are *not* taking my Hermes, you freak!" she shrieked. He cuffed her head and she started to fall, but because she was wearing the purse across her body, he lost his balance as well.

Gunnar advanced on the pair as a zing of energy surged around his body. A sudden forceful gust of wind shot past him, lifting the hair at the back of his neck. The man lost his grip on the purse strap and crashed to the ground. Gunnar planted his knee in the man's back and looked for the woman, who was already being helped by Nicole.

"Are you okay? Do have someone you want to call?" Nicole asked her.

"I'm fine. I just live a block away, right over there." The woman clutched her over-priced purse with a white-knuckled grip. "Thanks for helping me."

Nicole leveled a stare at her. "I'm glad we were here. But be careful, okay? That bag is beautiful, but it's not worth you getting hurt."

After more assurances from the woman, they watched her walk across the street and into her building.

Only then did Gunnar let the man up, snarling, "I don't want to see your ugly fucking face around here again." The man ran down the dark sidewalk until he disappeared.

Gunnar turned to face Nicole, who stood with her arms wrapped around herself. "Wow," she said to him. "That was really something."

He quirked an eyebrow.

"How you helped that woman. That was incredible."

Gunnar shrugged it off, but wondered why she pretended that she had nothing to do with the outcome of the situation. She'd used her power again. Hadn't tried to mask it. She had to know what she was capable of. Why play coy now? And what the hell was she?

One thing he knew for sure was that he needed to talk to her somewhere else. He didn't want her to run back to her friends if she didn't like his questions. "Let's walk a bit." It wasn't a suggestion.

As if on cue, her cell phone chimed with a text message. "They saw me leave with you and now they're freaking out," she murmured. "Let me just tell them we're right out here and I'm fine."

Message sent, she walked beside him. "Have you ever done that before?"

"Grind with a hot woman in a club? Make out with said hot woman outside on the sidewalk? Or stop a thief?"

She grinned at him. "The last one."

"Wasn't I good at the first two?"

She huffed out a breath of air. "Yeah," she said softly as she looked up at him. "Real good." Her green eyes regarded him expectantly.

He considered his response. He had stopped thieves before,

but at this minute she didn't need to know they were dangerous demons who nabbed powerful artifacts that didn't belong in their evil hands. She also didn't need to know that he had been a thief himself. "May have broken up a few fights," he finally said.

She nodded. They walked in silence for a minute until they reached the end of the block. Crossing the street, they entered a small park. "How about you?" he continued. "Have you done that before?"

She flashed a mischievous smile and tilted her head to the side. "Which thing?" she whispered, reaching for his hand.

"How you helped that woman back there."

She froze. Surprise, then fear, flickered across her eyes before she managed to school her expression into one of simple confusion. "What do you mean?"

"I didn't do much to help her. You did."

"I didn't do anything. You're the one who tackled that guy."

"After you had already done something to knock him down."

"How could *I* have knocked him down?"

"That's what I want to know. I felt your power, Nicole. What did you do?"

"P-power?" she squeaked.

"Yes, power. Yours. What. Is. It?"

She stared at him, her expression wide-eyed terror. "I don't know what you're talking about." Her voice hovered between a breath and a whisper. "I have to go."

"No, you don't." He gripped her hand tightly. "You're not going anywhere until you tell me what you are."

Chapter 3

Oh, God. He knew. An arctic windstorm splintered Nicole's lungs. How could he connect a little gust to her? She had to protect her family's secrets. Had to get away from him. Unfortunately, they were alone in the small park, observed only by trees, manicured shrubs, and a few wooden benches. She mentally kicked herself for letting him lead her away from the club.

Adrenaline surged through her body as she debated her two options: fight or flight. Her eyes calculated. Her mind focused, her body readied to shift into familiar fight patterns. This man was muscle-on-muscle, but she had to try.

She shoved her free hand against his chest while hooking a leg behind his knees. He only gripped her hand tighter, and they both went down. As they fell, she broke his hold and rolled away from him. She spotted a large stick on the ground, scooped it up with a breeze and sent it flying toward his chest. He leapt up faster than she thought possible, and he *caught it.* Had been ready for it. Heck, he'd probably goaded her on purpose.

"I don't want to hurt you, Nicole." He dropped the stick and stepped closer, his expression neutral. "I just want to know what you are."

"I'm an attorney." She moved back.

"We both know that's not what I mean."

She stared at him. The warm night air stuck to her skin, pressing in on her, making it hard to breathe. All their lives, she and her sisters had kept their gifts to themselves, feeling like they were freaks of nature. Were there others like them in the world? Could she trust Gunnar? She had met him barely an hour ago. He could be a lunatic. Regret and shame slammed into her. *Why did I act like that in the club?* Had he put some kind of spell on her? She certainly didn't make a habit of public make-out sessions. She swallowed hard. "What are *you?*"

"Ah-ah, ladies first, Nicole. But I'll give you a small hint."

He lifted his hand. A tiny orange light popped into the air, dancing in the center of his upturned palm. The light grew bigger, until it was the size of an apple. It glowed and bobbed slightly, then went out as quickly as it had appeared.

She didn't even care that her mouth was hanging open. "What was *that?*"

"Demonfire."

"D-demon…fire?"

"It's a useful weapon."

"For who?"

"Well, it's particularly effective on the lesser demons, but–"

"What are you talking about?" she yelled. "You just made fire appear in your hand! And you're not hurt!"

"I created it. It won't hurt me."

"Okaaay. That was a very cool magic trick." She edged backward.

He was at her side in a flash. "Uh-uh."

"Gunnar, you're scaring me."

"I told you I won't hurt you. And from what I've seen, you're not entirely defenseless."

Completely unnerved, Nicole's legs shook. She felt like she had just fallen down the rabbit hole, and there was no climbing back up. Ever. She didn't know if it was real or not, but Gunnar made fire appear in his hand. She instinctively knew that if he wanted to, he could truly hurt her. The rip-her-to pieces kind of hurt. She had already tried to fight him, with no success—now it was time for flight.

Whirling, she ran in the direction of the club. She managed to get all of ten feet from him when he grabbed her around the waist and twisted them both in mid-air. They hit the ground. He absorbed most of the impact himself, then rolled and pinned her beneath him.

Seconds stretched out as he studied her. He relaxed his hold on her a fraction, but she still couldn't move under his massive bulk. "Nicole," he said softly. "There are many things I want to do to you, but hurting you is not on the list."

She sucked in a breath at his bold statement. *I don't want to die here, like this, with a fire-conjuring madman.* Fighting hadn't worked. Flight hadn't worked. She didn't want to end up dead in the park, so that left her with two options—distract him or start talking.

She gazed up at him with wary eyes. He was so handsome. A lock of dark hair fell over his forehead, and his lips looked way too kissable. *Dangerous.* She clenched her teeth and shoved the jumble of thoughts from her mind, disgusted with herself. He had her trapped, pinned on the ground, for heaven's sake. She had to figure out a way to get away from him, not closer to him, like her traitorous body wanted.

His blue eyes took on a soft turquoise luster, like in the club. Back then she thought she had imagined it. But now? "Why do your eyes look like they're glowing?"

"Certain situations cause it, like when I'm fighting someone. Or heightened emotions can cause it. Like anger." He paused, pinning her with blue heat. "Or lust."

She drew in a breath, feeling the lengths of their bodies pressed together on the ground. She had the sinking feeling that distraction wouldn't work. Yeah, maybe he was attracted to her, but he also seemed extremely determined. She may be able to briefly take his mind off of her power, but then she'd end up right back where she was.

"I intend to keep you here until you answer my question," he murmured, the sensual timbre of his voice sending little shivers down her arms. "I have all night. And I'm pretty comfortable right where I am."

Nicole let out a shaky breath. She swallowed hard. She was

really going to do this. After years of hiding her gift, years of being so careful, she was about to spill her secret to someone she barely knew. Dammit, she was trapped. Maybe she could get away with just telling him a few details. Maybe then she could get away. "I…," she began. "I don't know what I am."

If he was surprised, he didn't show it. His face revealed no reaction. Blue flames danced in his eyes, waiting, watching her.

Another shaky breath. "I just always thought I was a regular person who had a really weird talent." The words came a bit easier. "I've been this way as long as I can remember. I don't know anything about demons or supernatural beings. I just thought I was a freak. A human freak."

More silence as he gazed down at her. Shifting, he stretched his long body next to hers, head propped on an elbow, one big hand resting solidly on her hip. "What exactly can you do?"

"This," she said, summoning a breeze to gently lift his hair. "Or I call a stronger gust, like with the purse-snatcher tonight. I can manipulate air currents, make them stronger, change their direction, and cause them to move objects. I can affect air temperature a little bit, too."

He raised his eyebrows.

"Just a little–I'm still working on that part."

Blue eyes blinked and he gave a shake of his head, dark locks swishing across his forehead. "Nicole, those skills are powerful. Potentially lethal."

"I know. That's another reason why I always kept it secret. I was afraid I'd hurt someone. Or get myself locked up in the loony bin."

"Did your parents ever help you figure it out?"

She shook her head. "They were killed in a car accident when I was small. I don't know if they even knew. And my adoptive parents don't know about this."

"Who else knows about you?"

"Just my sisters." She would share her secret–and only hers, at least right now. She saw no reason to put her sisters in danger, in case Gunnar turned out to be a nut job.

"So, these skills of yours—you've just figured them out on your own?"

She nodded. No reason to spill that she and Brooke had worked long hours together, honing their gifts.

"Nicole," he began, and damn it, but she liked hearing him say her name. "You need to be very careful. If another being had seen you tonight, had felt your power like I did, you could be in danger."

"But you just said I'm not defenseless."

"No, but there are creatures out there that are worse than any nightmare. You could be kidnapped or tortured, manipulated for your power—and your sisters could be used as leverage. Not all supernaturals are honorable. Not all are above meddling for the sole reason of making someone else miserable. And some are just greedy for power."

"What kinds of other creatures are there?" Her curiosity was piqued. If he was making all this up, he was doing a good job. She wanted to see how far he would take it.

"Lots of them. You have the ones from pop culture stories, like vampires, werewolves, and fairies. Then there are imps, nymphs, sprites, shape shifters, and demons. Many different species of demons."

"And what are you?" she whispered. Part of her wanted to know what he was, and part of her didn't, but the words tumbled from her lips before she could think twice.

"I'm a Lash demon."

"You? A demon?" she sputtered, sitting up fast. She knew he let her. "But you're not—"

"Not what?"

"Not…hideous. Deformed. Scaly."

"My, you have a way with compliments," he said dryly. "That'll keep me going all week, knowing I'm not hideous."

"Sorry." She looked down. "I guess I had some pre-conceived notions."

"S'okay. There are some truly hideous, deformed, and scaly creatures out there."

"Do you have horns?"

"No."

"Do you bite people?"

He chuckled. "Only pretty girls, and only if they ask real nice."

A tiny smile she couldn't suppress tugged at the corner of her mouth. *That probably happens a lot.* She studied his strong, square jaw and full lower lip. For some strange reason, she didn't feel terrified anymore. His attitude oozed *don't-fuck-with-me*, but if he was on her side, she could handle it.

"Have you met anyone else like me?" she asked.

"No," he replied. "You, Nicole, are unlike anyone I have ever met."

She glanced down.

"But," he continued, "I know someone who may be able to help."

"Really? Who?"

"An Elder Lash demon."

Trepidation flared in her gut. Was she ready to meet more creatures who weren't supposed to exist? What if he wasn't friendly?

Gunnar seemed to sense her hesitation. "It'll be okay. He won't hurt you. He's one of the wisest creatures I've ever met. If he can't help you, he'll know someone who can. In fact, I bet we can talk to him tomorrow."

"You sound pretty sure of that."

"He lives with me and a few others. We have a house in Evanston," he replied.

"What do you mean, others?"

"Five of us are in Chicago right now."

"And you have a house in Evanston?" She inwardly cringed at her repeated words as her mind struggled to process the deluge of information. The picturesque north suburb contained many old-money mansions. *And one may be full of demons?*

He raised his eyebrows at the incredulity in her voice. "We don't live in caves, Nicole."

She rubbed her temple. "Sorry." She had managed to say the wrong thing again. Any hope of making a good first impression on him was gone. *But does it matter?* Now that she'd shared her secret with him, what mattered most was that she could trust him.

"Okay. Tomorrow." She gazed up at the clouds that obscured the stars, as mental and physical exhaustion rolled through her like a slow freight train. "I really should go now."

"Come home with me." He held her gaze.

"I can't do that!"

"Like I said, there are some pretty nasty creatures out there. If any of them noticed your power, they wouldn't hesitate to grab you. I can keep you safe. And I promise I'll be a complete gentleman." He raised both hands. "Even though it may kill me."

She couldn't hide another smile. Her gaze flicked down to his mouth, then back to his eyes. *It might kill me too.* "I share a condo with my sister, and she'll freak out if I don't come home. We look out for each other." Brooke would probably be furious with her for confiding in Gunnar. Nicole was not looking forward to that conversation, although Brooke's curiosity might outweigh her anger.

"You could call her."

"I could. But I also need some time to process all this. Alone. All the stuff you shared with me–it's a lot to take in."

He nodded. "You're right. It's a lot at once. And you may learn even more tomorrow. But I'll see you home safely."

She grinned. "You *are* being a gentleman."

"And it's killing me. Let's go before my resolve weakens and I have to toss you over my shoulder, caveman style."

"You wouldn't!"

"I most definitely would. But not tonight." He stood, straightening his long limbs.

She took his proffered hand and allowed him to tug her up and into his arms. For a minute, he simply held her, his jaw resting against her temple. She had the fleeting thought that this should be awkward. This huge man whose eyes glowed and who made fire appear in his hand, who claimed to not be human, embraced her in an empty park. But instead her mind was flooded with reassurance. And...heat. He slid a finger gently along her throat, tilting her head up. "I want to kiss you again."

Her heart skipped. *My, but this gentleman act is sensual.* Almost as much as the blatant, hungry contact between them back at the club. She looked up into the azure luster of his eyes as tangled thoughts swirled through her mind. He had just told her he wasn't human. He tackled her, then conjured fire. If those weren't red flags, she didn't know what was. Then again, he could've hurt her, but instead he'd only talked to her. Answered her questions. And hell, she wanted another kiss from his luscious lips. Done warring with herself, she whispered, "Then kiss me."

His hand moved from her jaw to her nape, angling her head just the way he wanted it, then he brushed his lips across hers. Slowly, tantalizingly, he did it again. His free hand slid to the small of her back and held her close. Desire uncurled deep in her belly, sending long tendrils of fire through her veins. "You're so beautiful," he murmured against her lips, before coaxing them apart with his tongue.

She sighed in delight, welcoming him. His masculine, woodsy scent wrapped around her as the heat from his body warmed every inch of her skin. A blast of pure need rocked her core, making her gasp. She clutched his broad shoulders as he explored her mouth gently, thoroughly. She tangled her tongue with his and pressed her breasts against the hard wall of his chest.

Too soon, he pulled away and touched his forehead to hers. "You still want to go home?" he rasped.

She nodded, knowing her voice would be ragged. "Then we should go." He guided her back toward the street. They caught a cab, and Nicole found herself amused at the thought of a demon riding in a taxi.

"Do you usually take cabs?" she asked.

"No, I usually fly."

She gaped at him.

"Just teasing." His smile dazzled as he chucked her under her chin. She elbowed him in the ribs.

The short ride passed in comfortable silence. She couldn't explain why she felt relaxed around him. *I should be totally weirded out.* Instead, the possibility of answers tantalized her mind. And being this close to Gunnar sent tingles across every inch of her skin.

Gunnar stood on the sidewalk with her after they exited the cab. "I'll pick you up tomorrow." He tucked a stray lock of hair behind her ear. "Try to get some sleep."

"I'll try." She walked to the door, turning to smile over her shoulder before pressing the security code into the keypad. "See you tomorrow."

Making a beeline for the stairwell, she jogged up to the fourth floor and tip-toed into the condo, doing her best not to wake Brooke. She walked into her bathroom and saw that Brooke had put a sticky note on the mirror, reminding her that Brooke was running an eight kilometer race tomorrow and would be out the door early. Nicole felt a twinge of guilt at her relief that she could delay the inevitable conversation with her sister until later in the day.

She stripped off her club clothes and washed her face, then pulled on a soft babydoll tee and bikini panties and crawled into bed. Her little world had flipped upside down. Muscles tired and mind racing, she stared at the ceiling. *What the heck am I getting myself into?*

Gunnar parked his Escalade a few blocks away from Nicole's building the next morning. *Nice area, but no damn parking.* Good thing he was early, and good thing coffee shops beckoned from every block.

It was also fortunate that he didn't require a lot of sleep. He only needed a few hours per night, and he could get by on no sleep for a few days if necessary. Last night his mind had been filled with thoughts of Nicole. Soft skin, gorgeous smile, long legs, mysterious power. Her courage impressed him, even as her losses sobered his thoughts. A large part of her life was a giant unknown, and yet she carved out time to help others.

And his hands had itched to explore her lean curves. He finally drifted off to sleep but woke just an hour later, hard as granite, dreaming of her lithe body beneath his in the park. Her sweet scent and full lips entranced him, as did the wicked smile that had played across her face more than once last night. He could guess the direction of her thoughts. Hoped like hell they were on the same track as his. And he intended to find out.

Striding down the smooth sidewalk, he passed a mix of brick buildings both old and new. Trendy stores displayed hip, tasteful merchandise, and restaurants set up outdoor tables to take advantage of the last warm weeks of fall. City ordinances prevented the condo buildings from being too tall, adding to the cozy neighborhood vibe.

In the midst of this urban idyll Gunnar paused, catching a familiar and thoroughly unpleasant scent. *Skells.* A frisson of unease crawled down his spine. They hadn't been found in a densely-populated, trendy area before. *Are they expanding their dirty work?*

Thanking the stars he had time to spare, he followed the Skell's odor of burning leaves down a wide alley between two restaurants. Ignoring the white delivery truck splashed with bright pictures of vegetables, he stalked to the end of the building and rounded the corner. The scent stopped.

Alone with the bricks and concrete, he inhaled. His heightened sense of smell teased apart the myriad odors in the air. Exhaust from the delivery truck, garbage from a nearby dumpster, wood and metallic smells from one of the new condo buildings. The Skell's scent was recent, but not recent enough to track. It had passed by within the last twelve hours, probably during the night. It could be anywhere by now.

Gunnar grimaced and made his way back to the busy street. A Skell demon this near to Nicole's home was too close for comfort. He picked up coffee and a muffin for her at a shop on her block, then walked to her door. Another resident dashed out, allowing Gunnar to walk right inside. He scowled at how easy it would be for anyone to do that. He followed her scent–ripe peaches, he decided–to a unit on the fourth floor, and knocked.

She opened the door and he sucked in a breath, temporarily forgetting about the Skell's scent. Nicole looked like sunshine and blue sky personified. She wore a bright turquoise sleeveless top that showed off her toned arms, and it managed to somehow fit loosely but still cling to her breasts. Her blond hair was pulled partially off her face. Bare feet with red painted toenails and another pair of tight jeans completed her look.

"Hi," she said. "I didn't hear the buzzer. Oh, wait, did you get in here with some special demon B & E skill?"

He scowled again. "No, I just walked in, and so could anyone else. This building isn't secure enough. Pack a bag so you can stay at my place tonight."

"Oh." She raised her perfectly arched brows. "Um, yeah. Not sure about that. I'm totally safe here, but I get the feeling that nothing will convince you. Come on in." Then she spotted the purchases he carried, and a huge grin lit her face. "Ooohh, you brought me coffee. Thanks!"

He handed her the cup and she took a slow sip, testing the temperature, before smiling again. She closed her eyes briefly, tilted her head back a little, and savored the bitter drink as if he had given her liquid gold. "Mmm, that's good." Emerald eyes met his. "The first sip is always the best."

Good gods, how was he going to survive the day with her, when she made a tiny act like drinking coffee look so erotic? "Glad I picked something you like." He dragged his eyes away. He needed to look anywhere but at her sweet body right now, so he glanced around her sunny condo.

"You know, this building has a nighttime security guy and cameras everywhere."

"That's not good enough."

"We've lived here for two years and there haven't been any problems."

Why did she have to be so stubborn? "I picked up the trail of a Skell demon not two blocks from here."

"Is that bad?"

"Hell yes, it's bad."

A tiny frown knit her brows together. "How did you know what it was?"

"Most species have a unique scent, and Lash demons can detect them all. The one that was here smells like burning leaves." He cursed softly. "It's gone now, and it's not the worst demon around. But the fact that it was in such a populated area isn't a good sign."

She narrowed her eyes. "Fine, I'll throw some things together. But I'm doing it to humor you. My sister and I have been practicing mixed martial arts for years."

He remembered that she didn't live alone. "Is your sister here? She should come with us."

"Oh, that idea will go over even better with her," Nicole drawled, rolling her eyes. "She was out the door early today. I haven't even gotten to talk to her yet." She disappeared into her bedroom.

Gunnar resisted the urge to follow her. He really did *not* need to see her bedroom. He did not need a visual of where she slept, cozy with bedding and pillows, all loose and soft and warm...He wrenched his thoughts into a different direction. He was anxious for her to meet the Elder.

No one knew exactly how old Rilan was. Gunnar guessed him to be well over a thousand years old. The old demon knew several languages and although not a sorcerer, he could cast many intermediate-level spells. His title came not just with his age, but also with the depth of knowledge that he possessed when it came to supernatural creatures. There were very few he hadn't encountered, and he was a walking encyclopedia of both fact and legend. If anyone could identify Nicole's species, Rilan was one of their best bets.

Gunnar looked around Nicole's living room as he waited. Vivid yellow paint decorated two of the walls, and the other two were a warm chocolate brown. Bright morning sun spilled through a window next to a bookshelf. All the shelves except one held dozens of books. He spotted fiction, biographies, and art books, crammed to the shelf's capacity.

The last shelf held roughly a dozen framed photographs. A smiling couple who looked to be a generation older than Nicole looked out from a silver frame, and most of the rest were snapshots of Nicole and two other women. The other two had brown hair and stood a bit shorter than her, but the family resemblance shone through. A smaller frame held a faded photo of a blond toddler girl, smiling but thin and pale, sitting on a blanket outdoors.

Nicole came to stand beside him. "Those are my sisters." She pointed to one of the frames of her with the two women. "Brooke and Gin." Gunnar recognized the sister she called Brooke as the woman he had seen her with last night, fighting in the run-down neighborhoods. "And these are our adoptive parents." She nodded at the older couple.

"Do they live nearby?"

"No." A trace of sadness flared in her smile. "They passed away a few years ago."

"I'm sorry to hear that."

"No need to apologize. They led full lives. I barely knew my birth parents, and my adoptive ones were awesome. Though I don't know if they realized what they were getting into, taking all four of us in."

"Four?" He turned to her, brows raised.

She pointed to the blond child in the smallest frame. "That's our youngest sister, Alina. She died when she was small. She was born with a heart defect."

Gunnar gazed at the shadows that flickered across her bright green eyes. "So much loss," he said softly. She had buried two sets of parents and a sister. Admiration flooded his mind. Others in her situation might simply withdraw from life. Not Nicole.

"Yeah," she murmured. "So Brooke, Gin, and I—we stick

together. We have to."

"It's good that you have them." Appreciation for her family welled in his gut. She hadn't been alone in life, and she had others who cared deeply for her. The slender blonde before him had love in her life to balance the grief. Unlike the two hundred years of his own existence, many of which had seen him living on the streets. For so many years he fought just to survive in the blighted, grimy underbelly of his city. Any other creatures he encountered were never friendly, just competition for food or shelter.

She nodded and a tiny smile tugged at her lush lips, pulling him from his thoughts. "Ready?"

They walked the few blocks to his Escalade. From steel sidewalk grates grew full, leafy trees that had yet to change color. Some people walked dogs and others pushed strollers. A few brave souls attempted to do both at the same time. Grocery delivery trucks double parked in front of the brick buildings.

"Where the hell do you park your car, anyway?" Gunnar glanced up and down the block.

"My condo has an underground garage for residents."

He snorted. "Another unguarded entrance."

"No, it's not. You have to punch in an access code."

"A good thief or hacker won't be stopped by that. Neither will an unfriendly demon." They got into his car and threaded their way through the busy Lincoln Park streets, toward a thoroughfare that would take them north and out of the city proper. Unable to shake the feeling that she wasn't safe, three words popped into his mind. *Protect her always.* He rubbed his chest as an odd, warm feeling bloomed behind his ribs. *What the hell?*

He blinked and focused on the road. Protection was his job. He stole a glance in her direction, and couldn't hold back a smile. Her luminous green eyes returned his gaze, studying him. *Damn.* As heat seeped from his chest into his limbs, the knowledge dawned that she was much more than a creature to safeguard. And that was unfamiliar territory.

Sharon Kay

CHAPTER 4

BITING INTO HER BLUEBERRY MUFFIN, Nicole peeked at the man sitting next to her. AC/DC's "Thunderstruck" churned from the satellite radio. Coffee, tender words, and eighties metal were the last things she expected from a demon. Not that she would have thought of them anyway, because she hadn't known demons existed until last night.

A little voice in her head told her this was all too strange to believe, but it was drowned out by the sheer presence of his steely, muscular body next to her. The SUV was big, but so was he, and he seemed to fill up all the space inside it. He didn't look particularly dangerous this morning, in a charcoal gray T-shirt and jeans, but she wondered if he had weapons concealed somewhere. *Would he even need any? He has demonfire.* And she was letting him drive her to his house. Oddly, no warning bells rang out in her mind. She somehow knew, deep down, that he wouldn't harm her.

He lived with four other Lash demons, one of whom was the Elder. *Will the other three demons be around? Will we all talk to the Elder together?* She wasn't sure how many others would be with them once they reached his house, so she used the time in the car to pepper him with questions. "Have you been in this area long?"

"A few months. We move around the country as needed. Monitor the larger cities, keep our ears open for signs of trouble."

"Where were you before Chicago?" She studied his profile,

surprised that she'd missed how long and dark his eyelashes were. They framed his azure eyes perfectly, making even the most casual glance seem sensual.

"I was in L.A. for a couple of years."

Great, the clubs there are full of petite, tanned, artificially curvy women who probably made a habit of throwing themselves at you. Ridiculous, unbidden jealousy burst like a firework in her mind. Were Gunnar-groupies waiting for him in every city? "Do you have a girlfriend?" she blurted.

He looked at her, eyes twinkling. "No."

"Are you married?"

This time he chuckled. "Again, no."

"Do demons even get married?"

"Not in the human sense of the word. Supernaturals sometimes find mates."

She frowned at the term. "How is a mate different from a spouse?"

"Mating is more permanent. It can only be broken with the death of one partner." He grinned. "Any more questions I can answer for you?"

"About a million, since you shifted my world off its axis last night," she replied, and then flushed at the twinkle that lit his eyes. "Um...I mean...you know what I mean."

His grin turned positively devilish. "Nicole, if last night shifted your world, you haven't seen anything yet." It was a good thing they were stopped at a traffic light, because heat rolled off his body as his blue eyes stared deeply into hers. He placed his big hand on her thigh and squeezed gently. "And there's a lot you need to know about the supernatural world, as well."

"Yeah," was all she could manage, as the warmth from his hand sent fluttering waves zinging through her body. The light turned green and she took a deep breath to clear her mind. "So you're like, on an assignment here in Chicago?"

"We're keeping an eye on something that may or may not be a problem."

She raised her eyebrows. "Guess you have to be vague

about it. I mean, you wouldn't want to give away secrets to the new girl." It came out more sarcastic than she intended.

He shot her a sideways glance. "If there's a chance you're able to help, you'll know more than you ever wanted to pretty soon."

The phrase *more than you ever wanted to know* had taken on a whole new meaning. Her thoughts bunched in a jumble of conflicts. Was she really putting faith in the tales he told her? Although it was a little late for second thoughts, considering she was in a car with him and on her way to meet his colleagues. And her own life was proof that, if nothing else, some people were just different. *Different enough to be supernatural creatures?* She had a feeling she was about to get a crash course in all things weird and wild.

She glanced down to where Gunnar's hand rested on her thigh. Her instincts told her to trust him. Focusing on the heat flowing from his body into hers, she pushed the jittery thoughts out of her head and looked out her window. Not even a mile to the east of them she caught glimpses of Lake Michigan, sparkling in the morning sun as they drove.

Soon they pulled into a private, gated lane that crossed a generous yard and led to a large two-story brick house. Tall trees and hedges shielded it from the road. Gunnar pulled around to the back of the house, where two more SUVs were parked. As they exited the car, Nicole prepared to be scrutinized within an inch of her life. Excitement and nerves ping-ponged in her belly. *It'll be worth it if I can get some answers.*

They walked into a large kitchen with gleaming black granite countertops. A coffee machine ticked and hummed quietly near the sink, releasing the aroma of strong, unflavored coffee. In the great room beyond, two muscular men sat playing video games in front of a large flat screen television. Nicole caught some of their running commentary, full of trash-talking insults, as they fired at computer generated aliens. They both looked up when Gunnar and Nicole entered the room.

"Hey man." One of them stood. He matched Gunnar's

height, but his hair was blond and his eyes sparked with watchful curiosity as he glanced at Nicole and back to Gunnar.

"Kai, this is Nicole," Gunnar said.

Kai drew in a breath and paused. Guarded brown eyes pierced her. "Fae?"

Nicole stared at him, unsure of what he was talking about. The game console had quieted when the two set down their controllers, and the raucous guitars of Iron Maiden's "Wasted Years" pounded from the stereo.

Gunnar stepped in without missing a beat. "No. Got any other ideas?"

Now the other guy got up and crossed over to them. "Since when do you fail to identify a female?" He spoke to Gunnar, but kept his eyes on Nicole. He had dark brown hair, cut short all over, and a relaxed attitude. But she couldn't tell if his grin was sincere or sarcastic.

"Shut up, Rhys, unless you want to offer a helpful suggestion."

I should say something. Too bad standing in close quarters with the three of them was a little intimidating. At five foot ten, she never felt petite. But the combined height and size of Gunnar and his friends made her feel like a tiny doll.

"I met Nicole last night. She has a unique ability." Gunnar went on to describe her talent while the other demons stared at her.

"How 'bout you show us." The unmistakable edge in Kai's low voice let her know it wasn't a request.

She hadn't planned on stirring any winds indoors. Nicole swallowed hard and focused on the air in the room. She manipulated it into a gentle breeze, lifting their hair as she had done last night in the park with Gunnar. They paused and looked at each other.

"That's it?" Rhys asked, eyebrows pinched.

"No, that's not it, but that's all I want to do inside your home," Nicole said, finding her voice.

"You really don't know what you are?" Kai folded his arms

across his chest.

Great. Now she felt intimidated and stupid. "No. I thought I was human until last night."

"We need to talk to Rilan," Gunnar muttered.

Kai raked a hand through his hair . "He's translating some old grimoires. It may be awhile before he's out of his study. You know how he gets into that old Demonish stuff."

"Yeah," Gunnar frowned. He turned to Nicole. "Looks like we've got some time to kill. Unless you're a fan of these Xbox role-playing games, I'll show you the rest of the house."

A grin tugged at her mouth. "I'll pass on the video game."

He flashed one of his devastating smiles and extended his arm in a sweeping motion. "This is the great room."

She studied the large high-ceilinged space. Brown leather couches and chairs sat near the television and a central stone fireplace. One side of the room held a long farm-style dining table with distressed white chairs. The other side of the room contained an enormous L-shaped computer desk outfitted with three large flat screen monitors. One of them displayed a map of the city, with little red dots that flashed intermittently.

Tall windows flanked the fireplace and the wood floor gleamed with a lustrous dark finish. The whole room was done in neutral colors: dark browns, grays, and the pale dining chairs. There wasn't a pop of color anywhere. *Brooke would have a fit*, she mused, thinking of her artistic sister.

Gunnar gestured toward the dining side of the room, which opened to reveal a hallway. "That leads to the front foyer and the staircase to the second floor. And here," he turned her back around toward the kitchen, "is the second staircase."

She noticed a closed door just inside the kitchen. Gunnar opened it for her, and they descended the steps to enter a long hallway with walls painted a dark gray. Reaching a glass door, Gunnar repeated his chivalrous gesture and opened it. She smiled and stepped into a giant workout room.

Besides free weights and a large treadmill, it held more weapons than she had ever seen. Short straight knives, wicked looking curved blades, and swords of all lengths were mounted on one wall. The area next to them opened to a wide space for practicing. Beyond that, a wall with a row of windows enclosed a firing range.

"Wow," she said as she took it all in. "You guys are well-stocked."

"Gotta be prepared."

Gingerly picking up a curved blade with a forked tip, she asked, "What do you use this for?"

"Carving the heart out of a Neshi demon."

Her jaw dropped.

"Sometimes they survive our demonfire, so that's one way to make sure they're truly dead."

She set the blade down and shook her head, almost sorry she asked. He sounded so casual about it. This was his world, and now it was hers as well. *Am I ready?*

Nicole crossed over to a table in the weapons area and touched a small silver dagger. Deeply carved lines circled the hilt, which was set with a small round sapphire. She picked it up and tested its weight in her hand, noting the intricate symbols carved on the blade. "May I?" She nodded at the far wall.

"Go for it." Gunnar grinned.

Eyeing one of the ragged wooden beams against the wall, obviously a well-worn target, she hurled the blade end over end and watched it sink with a resounding thunk into the wood.

"Not bad." Gunnar glanced at the rest of the weapons. "Try another."

"I've never used a sword. Only small knives and switchblades."

"You'll need to learn. Most supernaturals can only be killed by beheading or fire."

The thought of taking the head of a creature whose existence she probably wasn't even aware of was so far-fetched that Nicole only nodded. Her world had gone from weird to completely crazy in less than twenty-four hours. Here she stood in a room full of weapons, in a house full of demons, one of which was hopefully going to identify her odd ability. And she hadn't shared any of it with Brooke yet.

Gunnar broke through her musings. "Want to spar?"

Her eyebrows shot up. "Spar? With you?" She shook her head. "That didn't go so well for me last night. I ended up with my hair full of dirt." And with the delicious weight of his big body pressing hers to the ground. Nicole pushed the errant thought from her mind.

"Last night I didn't want you to run away. Today I want to see what you can do. And there's no dirt here." He spread his arms wide, gesturing to the large practice area covered in blue padded mats.

She stared at him with narrowed eyes. *Why not?* "Okay. I need to change clothes, though."

Gunnar went to get the bag she had left up in the kitchen, and when he returned she ducked into a small changing room off the main area. She emerged shoeless, in white Gi pants and a red workout tank. She walked to the center of the room where he was waiting for her.

She took a second to appreciate his sheer bulk, which made her stomach flutter in more ways than one. Last night he had pinned her so easily...but he didn't hurt her. She had sparred with the other students in her classes over the years, and she occasionally sparred with Brooke, but she had never taken on anyone as big as Gunnar. He was probably strong enough to snap her neck, though she knew she could move fast. *Faster than him?*

She booted her nerves with a mental drop kick. Focused on her muscles and her breathing. He watched her, waiting, a tower of coiled strength. A muscle twitched in his jaw.

In a blur of movement, she turned and whirled, kicking out to connect just below his ribs. He took a step back and reached for her ankle, as she expected. Without setting her foot on the ground she swiftly kicked him again, right in the indent of his waist, before she danced away.

He grinned as they circled one another, his eyes taking on

the blue luster she had seen last night. "Again."

She charged forward, darting to the side as she neared him. She quickly turned and moved to bring her foot down on his knee, a move that could shatter a man's kneecap. But Gunnar wasn't a man, and he moved just in time, catching her ankle with his foot.

The blue mats raced toward her eyes as she lost her balance, rolling away from him as she fell. She leapt to her feet and didn't even hesitate before running at him full speed and jumping onto his back. She brought her hand across his throat in a slicing motion.

He caught her wrist and yanked to the side, nearly pulling her over his shoulder. She went airborne. Before her brain even registered that she'd landed, he pounced, pinning her facedown to the mat.

She got the feeling he wasn't letting his full weight rest on her, but damn, he was heavy. She tried to twist away and couldn't. Tried to buck with her hips and couldn't. But that little motion only brought her rear right up against his pelvis.

She froze, fighting the urge to roll her hips against his. Her mind started to melt into a haze of lust as every inch of her reveled in the warm contact of their bodies, from shoulders to knees. He couldn't have known how much she loved lying just like this. And she wasn't about to share that bit of information with him. Not now. She found a tiny corner of her mind that was still rational, and rasped, "Again."

They continued until she was a sweaty mess and he, annoyingly, looked barely ruffled. Not once had she been able to bring him down. She guessed he was holding back, assessing her. And when he moved, it was faster than she could track. That's when she'd end up on the mat. Where she was at this very minute.

He had her face down again, her arms held behind her, when he gently touched his knee to her back. "This will hurt a lot more when a pissed-off Serus demon does it."

"Got it," she grunted, not wanting to know what a Serus

demon was. "I think I'm done for today."

He let her up and crossed the room to retrieve two water bottles from a small fridge. Nicole gulped as she leaned against the wall, still sitting on the floor.

Gunnar sat down next to her. "You didn't do so bad for your first time fighting a demon."

"Yeah, right. You could've killed me about five times."

"You didn't use your power."

"I thought you just wanted to see my fighting skills. Besides, I didn't want to wreck your house."

"These walls are reinforced with spells, so it would take a lot to bring this place down. But thanks anyway." He pushed a dark lock out of his eyes. "You have a good foundation of skills for battle."

She grimaced internally at the thought that something she had been doing her entire life was just a foundation, but on a deep level she knew he was right. Nodding, she glanced down at her tank top, now plastered to her chest. "I could use a shower."

"There's one over there." He pointed to another door across the room. "Towels, soap, and stuff are inside. While you do that, I'll see what's going on upstairs. And don't worry–none of the other guys will come down here."

Relieved at the chance to clean up, she walked into the bathroom. Like the rest of the house, it was large, with a closet stocked full of linens, toiletries, and even a hair dryer. It had two sinks, a full-size shower, and a small room at the far end that housed the commode. She pulled off her sweaty clothes, cranked the faucet, and stepped under the round silver sprayer. It was one of those fancy showerheads that simulated a gentle rainfall.

Images from her morning raced through her mind as she lathered her hair with a citrus-scented shampoo. *So demons aren't immune to the finer things in life.* This house had some nice features. And the nicest one was an immense dark-haired demon who had just bested her on the mats.

Gunnar climbed the steps from the lower level of the

house, trying his best not to think of Nicole's naked, svelte body in the shower. He tried not to imagine frothy suds and water droplets running down the bare skin of her long neck, between her pert breasts, and down her endless legs. He thoroughly enjoyed sparring with her. For someone raised human, she was a good opponent. No doubt her supernatural lineage boosted her fighting skills. Maybe he was a bastard, but he could feel his body fighting for every chance to press against hers, to hold her tightly, and to feel her lean curves next to him.

He entered the great room to find Rhys asleep on the couch and Kai searching the internet. "Cute female." Kai turned to face him. "Where'd you find her?"

Gunnar fought the urge to tell his friend to shut up. Nicole didn't belong to him. Hell, he barely knew her. "Englewood." He named the neighborhood where he had first seen her.

"No way she lives there."

"No, she doesn't live there. Would you believe she picks fights there?"

"Uh, no," Kai said. "No, I wouldn't." He leaned back in his chair. "This should be good."

Gunnar summed up the previous evening for his fellow warrior. "So she thinks you just happened to meet her at that club?" Kai asked. "Smooth, man. Hope that works for you. Because while you were chasing her tail, we found some maggots over on the west side."

Probably in one of the crime-ridden areas that Gunnar was supposed to be searching when Nicole walked out of her condo looking like a supermodel. His group constantly watched and investigated any suspicious supernatural activity. They were a loosely organized group called Watchers, with houses in several large American cities. They answered to Arawn, the powerful leader of the Lash demons. Like a general, he moved them around the country as needed.

Gunnar knew he should have been with his comrades last night. He blew out a breath. "How many?"

"Four. We took out three, but one got away. Weird thing

was, it was like they were trying to keep us occupied so the other one could escape. And even weirder was what they did before we jumped them."

Rhys stirred and sat up. "Dude, talk about bat-shit crazy. Skells are *not* that smart." Despite his laid-back surfer demeanor, Rhys was sharp as a tack and the most technologically savvy of the group.

Gunnar glanced between the two of them and waited.

"The Skells were as sloppy as ever," Kai continued. "Cut up some crackheads so they bled a lot, but the wounds weren't deep. Then they held up these, I don't know, container things–right under the cuts, and collected some of the blood. But not a lot of it, because that's when we joined their little party. When they realized they were being attacked, they all shoved the containers at the one Skell. He put them in a bag and took off while the rest stayed and fought."

"They just took a little blood instead of draining the victims?" Gunnar asked. "What could they do with a few drops of blood?"

"That's the big question." Kai shook his head. "That, and whatever species your female is."

Gunnar was about to tell them that Nicole wasn't his female, but decided to let them think it for the time being. Whatever she was to him, he wanted to figure it out with her on their own, preferably very soon and preferably very naked. And there was the other matter of determining her species. Rilan should be finishing up soon.

As if on cue, Nicole walked out of the kitchen and into the great room. They all turned to look at her. "Am I interrupting something?"

"No," was the only word Gunnar could manage as he drank her in. All sunshine and sweet peaches, her presence assaulted his senses in a sultry overload. Damp hair, radiant skin, and those tight jeans again. Blood rushed to his groin. She looked sexy as hell and didn't seem intimidated to be in the presence of three Lash demons. Maybe a bit wary, but he didn't sense any fear. Whether that was a good thing or a bad thing remained to be seen. She presented herself without hubris, just a calm confidence.

She raised her eyebrows, taking in his lingering stare. A smile tugged at the corner of her lush mouth. Gunnar cleared his throat, noticing Rhys and Kai exchanging eye rolls. He shot a glare over his shoulder at them, then nodded at Nicole. "Let's go check on Rilan."

He led her to the stairway in the foyer and up to the second floor of the house. They went into the first door, which opened to a large study crammed with books and other odd objects. There were two overstuffed armchairs and a couch arranged near some small tables, all piled with more books. Rilan sat at a huge desk, his back to them, hunched over an ancient tome. "Good timing, Gunnar," he grunted without turning around. "I've just finished."

Despite his years, the Elder didn't look a day over forty. He was short for a Lash demon, only about five and a half feet tall, with brown eyes and thick wavy brown hair that he never seemed to comb. He closed his book, rolled his shoulders, and drew a breath. He paused, then turned to face them. "You brought a friend." His eyes locked onto Nicole, his expression unreadable.

"This is Nicole. I thought you could answer some questions for her." A tinge of unease warred with his protective instincts as Rilan scrutinized the willowy woman before him. He honestly didn't know how the Elder would respond to her. Would he find her to be truly dangerous and a threat to their world, even if she didn't realize it herself? Or would he be able to identify her species at all? "Nicole was raised as a human, but she isn't one."

"No, she's not." Rilan stared intently at her. "You must have many questions." He reached for her hand and she hesitantly took it. Rilan could pick up clues about some people and objects with a simple touch, and Gunnar hoped it would work with Nicole.

"Until last night I thought I was just a regular human who

happened to have a weird talent."

"My dear girl. Let's sit down and talk about it, shall we?" The Elder muttered something under his breath, and the books cluttering the chairs and couch piled themselves in an orderly fashion on the floor. Releasing her hand, he gestured to the newly straightened seating area. "Please, tell me everything."

If Rilan asked her to explain, then either his touch hadn't shed any light on Nicole's species, or the Elder knew exactly what she was and wanted to see if she lied to them. Gunnar fervently hoped it wasn't the latter, because she was already under his skin. He listened as Nicole told Rilan the same things she had revealed to him last night, and used her talent to ruffle the Elder's hair, just as she had with him and the others. Rilan went completely motionless at the release of her power.

A stillness enveloped the room. An old mantle clock, which never told the correct time, ticked in the silence. The Elder closed his eyes, turned his hands palm up, and quietly recited something in a dialect of Demonish so ancient that Gunnar didn't recognize it. The air in the room swirled along the ceiling, as if a wind was trying to take hold. It wasn't Nicole's doing, though. She looked at him, uncertainty in her emerald eyes. Gunnar managed a tight smile which was probably not reassuring at all, and said quietly, "Just wait."

The Elder's eyes suddenly flew open, and instead of their usual chocolate brown, they had turned a solid, milky white. Gunnar had only seen Rilan's eyes this way a handful of times, and each time it was downright eerie. The elder had gone into a state that allowed him to see more and sense more than usual. He tapped into a deep, mystic, demonic energy that Gunnar couldn't even begin to explain.

Nicole jumped off the couch to stand by Gunnar as Rilan pinned her with that pale stare and slowly intoned one word. "Solsti."

Nicole turned confused eyes on Gunnar, as Rilan repeated louder, "Solsti."

Gunnar's mind filled with a mix of confusion tinged with

relief. *Solsti?* Had the Elder discerned that Nicole was one of the four mythical beings? "Rilan, the Solsti aren't real."

A chill crawled down his spine as the Elder ignored him and continued staring at Nicole. "You, Solsti. Where are the others?"

"What others?" Nicole whispered. "I'm the only one like me."

"There are three others. You are linked to them."

"No."

"Do not hide them, child. Their bond with you pulses strong in your blood."

"I don't understand," she protested.

Gunnar heard the slightest change in her voice, her confusion suddenly tinged with determination. Questions circled his mind as he looked at her and placed a hand at her elbow.

"You will bring them here, young one."

"No! I don't know what you're talking about!" She turned to leave, but Gunnar gripped her arm firmly. Cool resolve masked her face as she looked up at him. "I told you, there's no one else like me. What is he talking about?"

"His discernment is a gift, Nicole. He sees many things, especially in this state." Gunnar didn't want to scare her, but he needed to get rid of the niggling doubt that had crept into his mind. "Think hard about all the people you know. Do you remember anything unusual about anyone?"

Deflecting his question, she asked, "What's a Solsti?"

Gunnar didn't see how she could be a part of the ancient myth. "It's a well-known story among immortals," he said. "The Solsti were four females linked by blood. Each possessed an affinity to one of the four elements: air, water, fire, and earth. Each one individually was very powerful, but together the four could potentially bring about the destruction of the world. And they could also save the world.

"Several millennia ago, when the Solsti were alive, they maintained a balance between the good and evil forces. They united to defeat Saykon, a monster who had forcibly taken control of the underworld, the earth, and several different dimensions. After the Solsti had sent him to an excruciating death—one which involved his various body parts being taken to the different areas he controlled, and then burned to ash—they lived out their lives and then simply ceased to exist."

Nicole's ivory skin turned white as he relayed the legend. She swallowed hard. "I need to leave."

Gunnar's heart sank with disappointment, only to be replaced with anger. She had used the same words last night in the park, tried to run, and then ended up sharing one of her deepest secrets. *But not all of them.* He grasped her upper arms and turned her to face him. "What are you not telling us?"

Green, fear-filled eyes gazed up at him. So much for not scaring her. He needed to check the fury building inside him. With a monumental effort, he softened his voice. "Nicole, you're safe here. You can tell us."

She let out a shaky breath and looked at him as if she was gauging how much to trust him. *Good, let her guess.* He wasn't sure how much he trusted her either. She glanced back at Rilan, whose eyes had returned to their regular brown hue.

"My stars," the Elder breathed, gazing at her. "Many have stopped believing that the Solsti ever walked the realms." He stood and walked over to her, taking her hand. "My child, you will always have the protection of the Lash demons. But you need to bring the others to us. You are vulnerable while your powers are growing."

Nicole looked from Rilan to Gunnar, uncertainty written across her face. Gunnar's thoughts swept back to the earlier part of the morning, standing in her sunny condo, looking at her family photos...

"It's your sisters, isn't it?" he surmised.

Her eyes grew huge. "Please don't hurt them," she whispered.

Gunnar's simmering unease pricked his skin, unmitigated by her revelation. "Last night you told me that you were the only one. All you said about your sisters was that they knew about you."

She looked at the floor. "Technically, those are true statements."

His blood boiled. He wasn't a patient demon, and her little white lie pushed him toward a snapping point. "But not the whole truth," he growled.

"Gunnar." The Elder's voice sounded pleasant, but Gunnar recognized the warning in it. He dropped Nicole's arm and stepped away from her, knowing his eyes had to be flashing blue flames.

"But...you're wrong," Nicole said to Rilan. "I only have two living sisters. The youngest one died when we were small. If there are supposed to be four, how can we be these...Solsti?"

Two living sisters. The weight of her words sank in. They were all the family she had left. *Brooke, Gin, and I—we stick together.* He stared at her, seeing a mix of confusion and fear along with a dose of that stubborn resolve. She protected them. And gods alive, if he still had his sister, he would do the same. How could he fault her for that?

Rilan frowned. "I did not sense an incomplete circle." He walked back to his desk. "These two sisters, they have a talent like yours, but with other elements?"

She nodded.

The older demon gazed solemnly back at her. "Child, you and your sisters possess a very real and dangerous power. It is of the utmost importance for each of you to learn how to better control it, for we don't know why you were brought back to our world."

Her brow furrowed. "Brought back?"

"The myth of the Solsti also tells us that the four will return, when the time is right. When the world needs them."

Gunnar's head jerked away from the moody glare he had fixed on Nicole, and swiveled to Rilan in surprise. He had never heard that last detail before. *Good gods.* If she was one of the Solsti, then she was supposed to fight an enemy more powerful than he had ever seen. And she had just learned that she wasn't human. All of her beliefs about myths and reality, good and evil, had most likely been scattered like dust.

She exhaled sharply. "Okaaay, so I'm not human. And I'm supposed to somehow help the world. And the world contains a bunch of creatures that I thought were only stories until last night." She whirled and marched for the door. "I need some air."

CHAPTER 5

NICOLE'S HEAD SPUN AS SHE hurried down the stairs, through the gleaming kitchen, and out the back door of the house. She felt Kai's and Rhys's curious eyes on her as she swept past the great room, but she didn't stop.

Bursting into the warm fall sun in the huge back yard, she tried to wrap her head around Rilan's words. Her veins buzzed like a thousand tiny vibrating needles were pricking them.

I'm not human.

The questions she had harbored long ago about her birth parents roared back to life. Who were they? Had they known that their daughters would be gifted like this? To play a role in balancing good and evil in the world? Had their death truly been an accident? She felt sick with fear that she had put her family—the only family she had left—into danger, despite her efforts to protect them.

I'm not human. Brooke and Gin aren't either

She had always known she was different. But *this*?

The old demon had *known*, instantly and without a doubt, what she was. Knew that there were more like her, linked by blood. There was no possibility of keeping it from him. Not that she had thought about hiding her own skills, because she had come here for answers. Sharp dread and confusion caged her, a stomach-twisting contrast to the serenity of the lush green yard.

Heavy footfalls thudded behind her in the grass. She turned. *Gunnar.* The azure fury in his eyes a few minutes earlier had banked a bit, but she still took an instinctive step back. Not that it would do much good.

He stopped a mere foot away from her, glaring. "Why didn't you tell me about them last night?"

She returned the icy stare. "Why should I?"

"Because I asked you."

She made a feminine sound of disgust. "You're crazy if you think I'd instantly spill their secrets to a stranger." Her last word hung between them like a smoky cloud.

He shot a dark look at the branches above her, then raked a hand through his thick hair. "Nicole, you heard Rilan. You're all vulnerable while you're growing into your power."

"I would never put them in jeopardy."

"Neither would I. But telling half truths isn't going to cut it. Neither is staying in that building of yours, with its sorry-ass excuse for a security system."

"It's my home."

"Well, welcome to your new one." He jerked his head toward the house.

"Brooke and I have lived there for two years, and nothing has ever happened to us or anyone else in the building!"

"But you just recently started working on developing and controlling your powers."

"So?"

"So, that was before you two started running around the worst areas of the city, zinging power left and right, playing Thelma and Louise."

Her mouth dropped open. She narrowed her eyes at him. Her voice dipped to arctic depths. "What did you just say?"

"You heard me. And you should thank the stars that I found you before something else did."

"You *followed* me last night?" A tiny part of her acknowledged that maybe it wasn't a coincidence that she met him at the club—but hearing him say it so matter-of-factly stoked her anger.

He folded his muscular arms over his chest, still glaring at her. "I was patrolling Englewood last night, looking for Skells.

Instead, I found you."

A rush of recognition hit her. "You…you were the one standing in the shadows, when we got into the car."

He nodded. "The energy signature you leave is unique; if any other demons had seen–"

"You were stalking me and Brooke! It was no accident that you were at the club, was it? You followed me there, too. And then you found me on the dance floor." She looked away as a new wave of sickness rolled over her, the puzzle pieces of the last night clicking into place. God, she was so naïve. She was just some kind of pawn in his bizarre world, and he had played her expertly. "I'm leaving."

"I want you to stay."

"I don't think so." She brushed past him, knowing he'd allow it, and marched inside to grab her bag.

He followed her and started to speak, his voice softer. "Nicole, you caught me by surprise. You're not safe running around like that–"

"I said I'm leaving." She headed for the front door, opened it and stepped through, then slammed it with a resounding thud. She didn't care if it was childish.

She stomped down the driveway, little breezes dancing around her. Good thing the Central Street station was close. She mentally thanked the Chicago Public Transportation system that she had a way to get home other than with Gunnar. He hadn't followed her, although she couldn't take much comfort in that fact since he knew where she lived. He'd let her walk away. *Smart decision.* She was ready to rip the trees right out of that big yard of his.

As she stood on the platform, seething and waiting for the next train, her phone chimed with a text message from Julie. *Hey, girl. How's that guy?*

Nicole grimaced as several choice responses ran through her head. She finally settled on a simple one: *Total jerk.* Her emotions were a mess, and she didn't want to say anything more or even think about Gunnar at this point. A mix of anger at him and disappointment in herself roiled her stomach.

Sorry. Want 2 talk? Julie texted back.

No. Nicole typed rapidly. *4get him. Staying home w B 2nite.* As she pressed send, a silver CTA train pulled into the station. Nicole stepped through the automatic doors and settled into one of the worn blue seats. A huge sigh escaped her. She couldn't recall when she had ever been in such a big mess. And now, heaven help her, she had to go home and tell Brooke all about it.

Nicole winced as a coffee mug flew out of Brooke's hand to shatter against their stainless steel fridge. This was worse than she expected.

"What is *wrong* with you?" her sister shrieked. "You meet some guy who's tall and ripped, and you lose all sense of caution? What were you thinking? Oh, wait—you weren't thinking. You were acting like a guy who thinks with his dick!"

"Brooke, I am so sorry—"

"Sorry doesn't cut it! Did you even think about Gin and me?"

"Yes, like I said—"

"Oh, sure. Was it when you were grinding on him? Or when you let him into. Our. *Home?*"

"Brooke, stop! Gunnar might be a jerk, but Rilan understands what we are."

"How do you know that anything they told you is even true? It sounds like the craziest load of bullshit I've ever heard. Goddamn it, Nicole!" Brooke's gray eyes flared like a stormy sky, but Nicole didn't miss the hurt that flickered beneath her sister's anger.

"They're not human. There's no way they can be. They're different, like us. Except, they were raised with knowledge of their skills and limitations. They know about the other creatures out there."

With a grunt, Brooke took the chef's knife she twirled between her fingers and stabbed it into the wooden cutting board in front of her. "God*damn* it, Nicole," she repeated softly.

"I'm sorry. I really am. I should have told you right away. It's just that things happened so fast…"

"You don't say!" Brooke muttered.

"I jumped at the chance to get more information, after all these years of being in the dark. When Gunnar made that…that demonfire appear in his hand, I knew he was different too. It seemed like he was kind of a kindred spirit."

Brooke rolled her eyes and huffed out an angry breath. "I'm too pissed to talk to you. I'd love to wipe the gym floor with your ass. But instead, I'm going to take it out on some gang member. I'm leaving in five, whether you're with me or not."

"Yeah, I'll go with you." Nicole sighed with relief. If Brooke needed to hurt some criminals and was willing to do it with Nicole, they were going to be fine. They knew each other too well to sugar-coat anything. Brooke would accept that Nicole only wanted what they both did—to learn more about their talents.

Five minutes later the sisters walked out the door. There were several nearby neighborhoods that could use their special kind of help. Bad areas butted right up against nice ones; many gleaming new condo buildings loomed over dilapidated blocks in the name of "gentrification." Tonight they took a short cab ride and then walked the last few blocks on foot. Weeds sprouted in the endless sidewalk cracks beneath their feet.

They slipped quietly along a garbage-strewn street. Paper bags drifted along the gutter next to plastic ones, and empty cardboard beer cases were tossed against a dumpster. In the fading autumn light, children unsuccessfully begged their grandmothers to stay outside in their front yard for a few more minutes.

Nicole and Brooke paused near an alley, low male voices drifting out to them. Without passing the alley entrance, they stopped to listen to two rival gangs snarl at each other over turf and drugs.

Brooke turned to meet her sister's eyes. Arguments like this took place every day between one group and another, and as far as the women were concerned, they could fight it out themselves. They didn't jump into gang fights when they were outnumbered, especially when no innocents were involved.

The voices grew louder. The sisters stepped further back into the shadows as one gang's sentry walked out of the alley to stand in the middle of the broken sidewalk. Nicole glanced across the street at the children straggling slowly toward their front porch, willing them to walk faster.

She froze as the air erupted with the sounds of fighting in the alley. *Please don't open fire.* The sentry hadn't noticed her or Brooke, and he got distracted by another man tackling him to the ground. Two more men made their way out of the alley, circling each other with wary looks, knives in their hands.

Just then more gang members spilled into view. What had begun in the alley quickly turned into an all-out brawl, with shouts and the thuds of bodies slamming to the ground.

Brooke touched Nicole's arm in a silent command to wait, but at that moment a gunshot ripped through the early evening air. The women across the street screamed and tried to drag the last two wide-eyed children inside. Nicole assessed them. Still standing. Unharmed. *Thank God.*

"Shit. Here we go," Brooke muttered.

Nicole didn't hesitate as she sent a gale force wind tearing down the block and into the alley. Every last bit of garbage and debris lifted and swirled around the men. Some of them were distracted enough to stop fighting and look around in confusion as they staggered against the gust. Brooke's eyes locked on the gunman as she pulled a water bottle from her pocket and jerked it upward, sending a spray of droplets into the air. As she gazed at the airborne liquid, the round drops shifted into tiny marquis shapes. Nicole chilled the air temperature in front of them and directed the icy points straight into the man's eyes. He howled and clutched his face, dropping his weapon.

Some twenty men filled the street, many who fought with their rivals but, unfortunately, some had noticed the sisters.

Nicole guessed that more of them had guns, and she and Brooke needed to get out fast. They started to back away, Nicole continuing to work the wind and the debris.

Two burly, scarred men had drawn knives and advanced toward them, when a short slight figure darted out of nowhere to slash a blade across one of the men's calves. The man howled as his leg spurted blood, and as he fell to the pavement the figure pulled out a small bottle and held it close to the wound.

Nicole gasped. The figure had gray skin and an odd, long face ending in a pointy chin. It turned in her direction. What she initially thought was a short skinny human stared back at her from dull, red eyes beneath its bald head.

Frozen next to her, Brooke whispered, "What the—" but broke off as a second gray creature appeared and slashed the other man's arm. It then held a similar container to the fresh blood.

Nicole's unnatural gale helped scatter all but a handful of men. The remainder had noticed the gray figures, and pointed at them warily. The sisters stared at the creatures in horror as a third one dropped down directly in front of them. It leaned forward and *sniffed.*

Nicole grabbed Brooke's hand and turned to bolt, when a huge man landed behind the gray figure. *What else is going to jump off that roof?* She backed up against the side of the building and studied the man's dark close-cropped hair. *Where have I seen him before?*

Her eyes widened in wonder as he swung a sword horizontally and neatly separated the creature's head from its body. Smoke wafted from the remains, which disintegrated right in front of them.

A flash near the smoking pile caught her eye, and she extended her foot to draw the thing closer. Bending to pick it up, she saw it was a small silver disk, similar to a coin, with a symbol imprinted on it. She shoved it into her pocket and looked back at the man with the sword.

"Rhys?" Her memory clicked into place. *From Gunnar's house.*

"Stay back," he barked, as another massive demon emerged from the alley to send a fireball from his palm and into the other two gray creatures. They both disintegrated in the same manner as the first one.

"That's it. Only three tonight." The other demon looked around. The remaining gang members had taken off running when they'd seen Rhys' sword. He shot a questioning look at Nicole and Brooke.

"Nicole, right?" Rhys asked her.

"Friends of yours?" the other demon said as he took a step closer.

"Actually, she's a friend of Gunnar's. She was at the house today. You would have met her if you hadn't been...indisposed." Rhys smirked at his comrade, whose blond hair hung down to the middle of his back. With the weapons he had strapped on, he looked like a modern-day Viking. "Brenin," Rhys continued, "Meet Nicole, and..."

"Brooke. We're sisters."

"That's not all you are," the demon called Brenin said. "What kind of energy was that?"

Nicole bit her lip, debating her response. Before she could answer, Rhys interjected, "We should all head back to the house."

"We're not going to your house," Brooke declared.

"Most of those Skells can communicate telepathically, so, yeah, we're going to our house. Odds are that they've already told their friends about your unusual power, so unless you want to meet more of them, and some of their closest, ugliest buddies, you're coming with us. From what I hear, our place is a lot safer than yours anyway."

Brooke opened her mouth to protest, but Nicole stopped her. "I think we should go with them. How would we have fought that thing, anyway?"

"The way we usually do," Brooke retorted. When Nicole glared at her, she went on, "Obviously they have weaknesses."

"Yeah, but we don't walk around with swords and we can't

fling fireballs."

"I suggest we continue this scintillating conversation in our car," Brenin remarked dryly. "Let's go before we make any more new friends."

They walked a couple blocks to the demons' waiting Tahoe, Rhys muttering into his cell phone. "Kai's still out. Gunnar's going to meet us at the house." He ended the call.

Great. She was so not in the mood for a lecture tonight, and Gunnar was the last person she wanted to talk to. They reached the car, where she and Brooke climbed into the back seat. "What were those gray guys?"

"Those were Skell demons, also known as Nothing-But-Trouble," Rhys answered.

Nicole remembered that those were the demons Gunnar had mentioned earlier. "You guys are...um, observing them, right?"

Brenin snorted from the passenger seat. "That's one way to put it. Observe, then kill." He turned in his seat to look at her. "What the hell were you two doing in the middle of that gang war, anyway?"

"It's a long story," she sighed. "Might as well wait until we get to your house, if you don't mind."

Brenin shrugged and turned back around. Next to her, Brooke reached for Nicole's hand. "It doesn't sound like a load of crazy bullshit anymore," she whispered.

Nicole squeezed her sister's hand and smiled. "There's no going back now."

"I'm sorry I got so mad at you earlier. That seems like *days* ago."

"Don't worry about it. I probably would have reacted the same way if our roles were reversed." Nicole settled into her seat. "Can you believe we finally might get some answers?"

Brooke shook her head. "Whatever I may have thought about us, this...tonight... was *not* it." Nicole nodded and squeezed her hand again.

After a quick stop at their condo—over protests from the

men–to collect some clothes and other necessities, they got back on the road heading north out of the city. For the second time in less than twenty-four hours, she was riding toward someone who was going to be royally ticked at her.

Gunnar was a mystery. At times he seemed so gentle, even charming, and at other times it seemed he was barely holding back the blackest fury. She realized he hadn't told her anything about his life or his family, while she had babbled on about hers. Questions about his life bubbled in her mind. But how far would he let her in?

Nicole perched with Brooke on a couch in the great room, like a mouse trapped by a huge pacing cat. Or several cats, given that they sat in a room full of demons. Gunnar stopped in front of them and stood with his legs slightly spread, massive arms folded over his chest, blue eyes shooting sparks.

"What the hell were you thinking?" he growled.

Nicole gazed up at him, trying to keep her voice neutral. "We were just doing what we usually do. There were children in danger tonight."

She couldn't tell if his anger stemmed from concern, or if he was only pissed because she hadn't listened to him. Or both? She couldn't keep up with his mercurial moods. The story had been told multiple times tonight, from both the women's perspectives and the demons'. Through it all, Gunnar remained silent and glowering.

"It's admirable to help those less fortunate or weaker than you, but, shit, you gotta be more careful," Rhys said, from his position in one of the armchairs. "Skells are not the strongest bad guys out there. I say we start weapons training tomorrow with you two."

"We should start training regarding your specific talents as well," added Rilan. He'd stayed quiet for the summary of the evening's events. "We must assume that your anonymity has been compromised. You need to be ready to fend off creatures much more treacherous than Skell demons."

Even though the Elder had spoken of the Solsti's great powers, Nicole still felt weak in her newly discovered world of immortals. Resigned, she shoved her hands into her pockets and felt something cool and hard. "Oh, wait!" she exclaimed. "I found this." She pulled out the odd coin that had laid near the dying Skell.

Rilan took it, frowning, and closed his eyes. "I don't recognize it. But Rosa probably will."

Before Nicole could ask who Rosa was, Gunnar turned an incredulous look on Rilan. "You want her," He gestured to Nicole. "To go to Torth? To see Rosa?"

"You will go with her. She must go, since she found the object. It caught her eye for a reason."

"How do you know if Rosa will even speak to us?" Gunnar asked.

"She'll be intrigued, both by this item and by the emergence of the Solsti."

Hands on his hips, Gunnar blew out a breath. "If she doesn't singe us first."

"Um, who's Rosa and where is Torth?" Nicole asked. That down-the-rabbit-hole feeling washed over her again.

Gunnar closed his eyes and pinched the bridge of his nose. "You just had to get into trouble tonight. Well, congratulations, because tomorrow you get to travel to the demon realm and meet a witch who's literally as old as dust."

CHAPTER 6

NICOLE SPUTTERED. "D-DEMON REALM?" Silence hung in the room. "I'm guessing you don't hop on a plane to get there."

"Wherever it is, I'm going with you." Brooke turned to her sister.

"Only two can go at a time without attracting attention," Rilan cautioned. "You, child, will stay here and train with the rest of us."

Nicole felt her sister's distress at this new development, but on a deep level she knew that Gunnar would keep her safe. His colleagues would protect Brooke as well. Despite their glares and sarcasm, a sense of honor permeated the group.

Whether Gunnar wanted to go anywhere with her was the bigger question. She looked at him leaning against the wall, his strong arms crossed over his chest. A lock of black hair fell over his forehead, softening his grim expression.

"Nic?" Brooke said softly.

Nicole sighed. This part of the mess, at least, was her fault. Gunnar had warned her to be careful. Because she and Brooke had never encountered any immortal creatures before, she figured their luck would hold out. And Brooke had been itching for a fight this evening, another thing that was Nicole's fault.

She squeezed her sister's hand and hoped her voice sounded reassuring. "I'll be okay."

Brooke fixed her with a look that told her she saw right through Nicole's show of bravado. "I don't like this one bit."

"You should get some rest. It's too dangerous to open a

portal at night." Rilan's voice was quiet, but left no room for argument.

"P-portal?" Nicole sputtered again. *Ugh*. They were all going to think something was wrong with her.

"No planes leaving for Torth tomorrow," Rhys drawled sarcastically.

Tomorrow? "Hold on." Nicole narrowed her eyes at Rilan. She didn't care how stern he sounded. "You can't order us around like we're some of your guys."

"You might not be Lash, but you're part of our world," Brenin said from his sprawl in one of the oversized armchairs.

"We just found about *your world*." Brooke shot him a glare.

"Doesn't matter." Gunnar's voice was sharp. "You've known about your abilities. You've been using them with no idea what you could run up against."

"We use our talents to *help* people." Irritation simmered in Nicole's veins. How were they supposed to know demons, elves, and fairies were real?

Gunnar turned his scowl on her. "Yeah well, in the same neighborhoods where you like to help people, a couple hundred citizens have been attacked by Skell demons."

Nicole sucked in a breath.

"Hundreds?" Brooke whispered.

"Yeah. And that coin could be a clue to who's behind it." Gunnar's blue eyes pierced Nicole's. "We need your *help*."

Nicole stared at him, her mind reeling. *Hundreds?* All she and Brooke wanted was to use their skills in a positive way. Indignation turned to resolve as the scope of Gunnar's investigation settled over her. "Okay."

Gunnar nodded. "Enough discussion. It's late and you two had a crazy night. We can talk in the morning. Follow me."

More than you ever wanted to know echoed in her head, both a reminder and a prediction. She and Brooke walked behind Gunnar's towering figure to the foyer and up the stairs. They passed the first door. *Rilan's study*. Sconces lit the rest of the hall, spaced far apart and turned down to a dim glow. Dark mahogany wainscoting covered the lower half of the walls. Gunnar walked past another door and then gestured to two rooms.

The women exchanged a look, and Nicole knew her thoughts mirrored her sister's. "We'll share a room," she said.

He nodded and started to turn away. Brooke darted into the first room, muttering something about needing a shower.

"Wait," Nicole called to Gunnar. He paused and she stepped closer. "I...I owe you an apology."

He looked at her coolly, silently, one hand shoved into his pocket.

"For everything," she continued. "All of this has been so new, so surprising, so unexpected...and unbelievable. You tried to warn me about what could happen. You've been trying to help me, and I haven't–"

His mouth came down hard on hers. Gone was the gentleman who had kissed her tenderly in the park last night, replaced by a hardened fighter who took what he wanted. He eased her backward until she bumped the dark panels of the wall, his big hands gripping her upper arms.

The heat rolling off his body surrounded her, warming every fiber of her body. She breathed in his woodsy, masculine scent as his tongue swept across the seam of her lips. A soft feminine moan stole her breath and she opened to let him in, gripping his shoulders and pressing her body against his. She was engulfed by how incredibly *good* it felt to be in his arms. All the stress of the day dissipated like dust on the wind–the arguments, the knowledge of her true identity, the street fight, the Skell demons–as his talented tongue teased the roof of her mouth.

Loving the bulk of him pressing her against the wall, her fingers caressed their way up to his neck to wind in his thick black hair. She licked into his mouth, tangling her tongue with his, exploring, tasting, melting into a hot, delicious haze of desire. He angled her head to deepen the kiss as one hand settled at the small of her back, and she sighed her approval.

He pulled away from her hungry mouth, but before she could protest, he pressed a fiery line of kisses along her jaw and down her throat. His ragged breath seared her skin, sending shivers of white-hot need straight to her core. Reaching the sensitive spot where her neck met her shoulder, he grazed her skin with his teeth, making her gasp in pleasure. She remembered what he had told her about biting pretty girls, and wondered if it was true. And then, immediately and irrationally, wished for him never to do it to anyone else again.

He licked and nibbled his way across her shoulder until he reached the thin strap of her tank top. Pulling it between his teeth, he tugged and let it fall back in place. His mouth was velvety soft and oh-so-hot, destroying her defenses in a sensual onslaught. He grabbed her hips and pulled her flush against the hard ridge of his erection. Desire shot through her body, and she reflexively rocked into him.

He moved his hands slowly up her torso, pausing just below her breasts as he continued to nuzzle her overheated skin. She was infinitely thankful that in her haste to get dressed earlier in the evening, she had grabbed a tank top with a built-in bra. She ached with the unquenchable need to feel his hands all over her.

"Touch me," she breathed.

A low rumble escaped his throat as he cupped her breasts and squeezed gently. He drew his thumbs tantalizingly across her nipples, which hardened into stiff peaks. Liquid heat pooled between her thighs as her entire body went soft and pliable for him. He continued to tease her nipples through the soft fabric of her top until she wanted nothing more than to rip it off right there in the hallway.

Pulling back with a devilish grin, he untangled her hands from his neck and placed them at her sides, caressing her arms upward from wrists to shoulders. As if he knew just what she needed, he slipped her straps down to hang loosely against her biceps. He gently traced the gaping neckline, dragging his finger across the tops of her breasts slowly in one direction, and then the other.

Her muscles trembled. Every nerve ending screamed at his delicious torture. With each pass he pushed the cloth a little lower, until the pink tops of her nipples were visible above the fabric. His tender touch burned. She writhed against him—and her top slipped down to her waist.

For a moment he gazed reverently at her, his eyes glowing sapphires in the dim hall. "You're so beautiful," he whispered as he cupped her again, lifting and shaping the small weight of her breasts. He rolled her nipples between his thumb and forefinger as he lowered his head to kiss her throat, eliciting a soft, ragged moan from her mouth. With a gentle nudge, he turned her so her back was against his chest and she instinctively pressed her bottom into his hips, feeling his thick hardness against her soft curves.

She angled her head in invitation as he bent to kiss her neck, expertly using his teeth and tongue to send hot tendrils of fire racing through her body. Her knees weakened, her breath came in gasps, and she was grateful for his powerful strength holding her up. His hands were on her breasts, flicking his thumbs over the tight peaks slowly and then quickly, circling and tracing, tugging them gently. Need surged through her like a searing desert wind. *Oh, God.* Her eyes slid shut and she reached back to clutch his thighs. His name escaped her lips on a ragged moan.

He wrapped his arms across her chest and buried his face in her hair. "I'm furious with you."

She gasped and rubbed her backside against him. "I'll have to make you furious more often."

He nipped her ear and she sucked in a breath.

"Or maybe not," she added. "If this is furious, then I can't wait to get you in a good mood."

He stroked her arms, reaching for the straps of her tank and pulling them back up into place.

Confusion slammed into her. "What are you doing?"

"Covering you. You're half naked in the middle of the hallway."

"That didn't bother you ten seconds ago." Her body was still trying to process the loss of his touch.

"I shouldn't have pushed you that far. You've had an

exhausting day."

"I wasn't complaining." She turned to face him, a small frown on her face. "Are you punishing me?"

At his raised eyebrows, she went on. "For making you mad?"

He chuckled and she loved the smile that tugged at his gorgeous mouth. "Nicole, if I was punishing you," he brought his hand down hard against her bottom, the resounding *crack* echoing in the hall. "You'd know it."

She gasped and jumped, not because it had hurt, but because it *hadn't*. It hadn't even occurred to her that he might be into...that. Not that she was averse to domination games in the bedroom now and then. She realized again how little she knew of him. And his world. *Maybe stopping at second base is a good thing.* "Okay." Her breathing sawed unevenly. "Goodnight?"

"Goodnight, Nicole." He kissed her forehead.

She walked into the bedroom, closed the door, and leaned against it. Brooke came out of the bathroom then, her scrutinizing eyes sweeping over Nicole. "You look like you've been...busy."

Nicole smiled, nodded, and bit her lip. She hadn't planned to make out with Gunnar; in fact she hadn't even been certain that he would talk to her. But like last night, her body reacted so swiftly to his that her mind still hadn't caught up. She looked at her reflection in the mirror over the dresser, taking in her kiss-swollen lips and the side of her neck, reddened from his hungry mouth. The attraction between them was undeniable, but she didn't want to spend any more time on the wrong end of his Vesuvian temper. Nor was she going to let him order her around.

She ducked into the bathroom, washed her face, and climbed into bed next to Brooke. It brought back memories of sharing a bed when they were younger. "I still don't like this," her sister said.

"I don't think it's about whether or not we like it," Nicole murmured into the darkness. "This is bigger than anything we could have imagined." She wanted to reassure Brooke that she'd be fine, but her sister's mind was intractable. Excited and a little fearful about the upcoming day, she drifted into a fitful sleep.

Music pulsed through the smoky air of the club and bodies gyrated around Nicole and Gunnar. The lights flashed and streaked across the hard, chiseled granite of his bare chest. She hadn't had anything to drink, but her mind hazed over, her senses bombarded. Being that close to his raw masculinity intoxicated her. His hands stroked up and down her back, which she realized was bare.

A downward glance told her that she was dressed only in a black lace bra and panties, but no one else in the club seemed to notice. The other dancers moved in their own world, oblivious to Gunnar and Nicole. She looked back up at him. Blue eyes flared with undisguised heat. Stretching up on her tiptoes, she wound her arms around his neck. Goodness, he was tall. He made her feel small and safe and…

Her thoughts were broken by a surge of heat when he slid a hand down to cup her ass. A gasp wrenched from her throat as he hauled her tight against him, molding them as closely as possible. She scored his back with her fingernails. He hissed, nudged her legs apart with one of his muscular thighs, and kept it there. A delicious pressure built deep in her core.

She tugged him down to kiss her, needing his mouth on hers. He took over, nipping her lower lip and sweeping his tongue inside. Not teasing or gentle, but rough and possessive, and she craved him. His thumbs slid under the straps of her bra and he moved them down again, caressing the skin at the tops of her breasts. He kept up his maddening strokes until she was ready to tear the bra off herself, and then it disappeared.

No one in the club even glanced at them as Gunnar growled, tearing his mouth away from hers. Her nipples beaded into hard points as her breasts rubbed against his bare chest. Gunnar's nostrils flared at the surge of warmth between her legs.

He grabbed her ass and lifted her like she weighed nothing, holding her up in front of him so that her breasts were even with his mouth. He closed his lips around one of her nipples and her whole body jerked. Need tore through her. She couldn't hold back a moan as he laved and suckled one tight peak, and then drew her deeper into his mouth. She watched him release her, then flick his wicked tongue across her neglected nipple. Biting her lip, she writhed against the sweet ache he created.

Her feet brushed the floor as he set her down, his fingers trailing across her skin to circle her hips. One wicked hand moved around to squeeze her backside, then down to her panties. He fisted the fabric and yanked, and they were gone.

She stood before him, completely naked and trembling with need. The other dancers didn't even glance her way. She reached for the button of his leather pants, popping it open with urgent fingers. But before she had a chance to touch him, he took both her hands in his and guided them behind her. Gripping her wrists in one hand, he held them against her back, keeping her in place in front of him. He lowered his mouth to her aching breasts, seeking her nipples, kissing them so languidly that she let her head fall to the side in surrender. She melted into him, carried by a blazing need that was beyond her control.

With his free hand he traced a teasing line down her belly, across her hip, to slide beneath her and cup her intimately. Delicious shudders made her legs wobbly. His fingers curled upward to drift across her slick skin, coming forward to lightly circle her clit before moving back with drugging slowness. He stroked and teased her as she rolled her hips toward him, wanting more. He pushed one finger inside her, then two, stretching her as she arched into his hand. Her need grew to an unbearable intensity, her mouth barely capable of speech, and she simply whispered, "Please."

In a flash of movement so quick she couldn't track it, he tugged down the zipper of his pants to free himself, and lifted her up with his hands on her hips. The fire of his blue eyes locked with hers as he lowered her slowly onto his thick length.

She wrapped her legs around his waist, taking every long inch of him as she reveled in the way their bodies fit together. He had tortured her so deliciously and thoroughly that she was close, so close to losing control. He raised her hips, withdrawing almost all the way before plunging back inside. The sensations of his enormous cock stretching her sensitive tissues, and the tips of her breasts grazing his chest as he thrust beneath her, combined to destroy her completely. She cried his name as she shattered into a million fragments in his arms. He roared as his release followed hers, pumping into her until every last drop was wrung from each of them.

Nicole jerked awake, hot and trembling. She struggled to calm her heart, which raced from the single most erotic dream she'd ever had. Evidently her body was still processing the little interlude she and Gunnar had shared in the hallway. An interlude that left her needier than she realized.

She glanced over, relieved to find Brooke sleeping soundly next to her. Sure, they were close, but it would have been mortifying to explain herself if she had woken her sister during *that* dream. It had been so real, right down to the dampness she could still feel between her legs. Sighing, she stared at the ceiling. The gray light of dawn peeked along the edge of the window. She dragged herself from the bed and into the shower, wondering if there was any possible way to prepare for the day ahead.

An empty beer bottle had the misfortune to roll into Kai's path. Drawing his boot back, his kick sent it hurtling across the street to smash into a satisfying abundance of glass shards. Another night dragged on with no sign of those fucking Skells. After yesterday's encounter when he had deep-sixed of some of their sorry asses, he itched for a repeat. Especially since one of them managed to get away. He would find that one and make it wish it had never seen him.

And then the call came in from Rhys that Gunnar's perky new blonde had gotten into trouble with some Skells down on the south side and needed to be rescued. No way in hell he was going back to the house now. He so did not need to deal with any woman who thought she could play vigilante, and he didn't need to see Gunnar getting all pissy over a girl.

He shoved his hands in the pockets of his black fatigues and glared at a couple of drunks lolling on the sidewalk. He knew what he needed right now: a curvy warm female beneath him. Or on top of him. Or bent over in front of him. Whichever. It didn't matter, as long as he got laid.

He leapt up to the rooftop in order to travel faster. He knew where to find what he wanted. The trendy north side neighborhood near historic Wrigley Field was full of pretty young professional women, many having moved there from the suburbs, who thought they were hip because they lived in the city now.

Let 'em think so. Really, they were open books. He knew how to seem similar enough to the guys they usually met at the local bars, but just a little more rough, a little more edgy. With a sincere look on his face and understanding in his brown eyes— puppy dog eyes, he'd heard more than once—they fell for him every time.

Even at this early hour of the morning, people milled in the streets, wringing as much revelry as they could from the long holiday weekend. He entered a packed bar that had a beer garden and grabbed a glass of the piss that humans called light beer. He eyed the crowd, surveying the scene. He took note of a bachelorette party that had some possibilities, and then spotted three women moving toward the garden. They were all hot, but he decided he wanted the redheaded one.

As he made his way outside he noticed she was on her phone, standing a little bit apart from her friends. Good. He walked up to her, got into her personal space, and waited. She glanced up at him with a small frown on her pouty lips. She opened her mouth to say something. He smiled. She stared at him, blinked, and closed her phone. He brushed a lock of hair off her shoulder. "It's a nice night."

"It just got nicer," she purred.

The game was on. A little chit-chat, a little flirting, a touch on an arm or knee, a few drinks, and they were his. This one was no exception. Before long before she was sitting on his lap with an arm hooked around his neck, his hand on her hip. Her low cut top revealed full generous breasts and he was looking forward to spending lots of time playing with them. She giggled at something he said, and he leaned closer to suggest they find someplace more private, when he registered a blur on a rooftop across the street.

He froze as his keen night vision recognized the slight frame and grayish skin of a Skell. Oh, hell no. *Now* the miserable fuck had to make an appearance?

"Gotta go, babe." He peeled the confused redhead off his lap. "Hey, your friend over there wants to tell you something," he murmured, turning his would-be bed partner toward the women in her group. That goddamn Skell was really going to be sorry now.

Not bothering to make his way to the front door, he vaulted over the high fence that enclosed the beer garden. His movements were so swift that none of the patrons would notice, and their alcohol-fueled minds would only register a slight draft. The creature hadn't seen him. *Perfect.* He planned to track the bastard to his hiding place. The dumbshit Skells were up to something, and there was most likely a mastermind behind their activity.

Kai followed it silently along the rooftops of the leafy neighborhood. It hurried along in a southerly direction, and soon they were in an industrial area that flowed into a railyard. Kai opted to move along the tops of the boxcars instead of crunching on the gravel covered ground, although the Skell was so noisy and clumsy that it probably didn't matter.

They moved to a more desolate area on the south side, and Kai guessed the Skell had to be near its home base. But it kept going. Soon the urban streets gave way to suburban ones. If the thing had any intelligence, Kai would have thought it was taking him on a wild goose chase. When the smaller demon reached a highway overpass, it stopped and looked around.

The demon crept down a grassy embankment toward the underside of the bridge, where it stopped. Kai stopped as well, hidden behind some overgrown shrubs.

"Son of a bitch," he hissed as a beat-up Pontiac sedan pulled over to the shoulder, allowing the Skell to jump inside before the vehicle roared into the southbound lanes. Kai took off running along the shoulder.

Faster than a human, anyone who happened to see him

would only imagine a shadow crossing their vision. But the car cruised farther south without exiting, and Kai knew he couldn't keep up the high-speed chase for much longer. He stopped as the tidy suburbs gave way to open fields, cursing foully. Not only was he not going to get laid tonight, but that goddamn Skell had gotten away again. He broke into an easy jog, hoping to make it home before dawn.

Nicole stood transfixed by the shimmering circle that vibrated in the air before them. It was beautiful, like a giant iridescent ring, its center shining with ever-changing hues. She studied it, her skin tingling with anticipation and with the remnants of her dream. She was aware of Gunnar watching her reaction to the portal. Hell, this morning she was aware of everything about him, from his piercing blue gaze to his thick-soled black boots.

Nicole swallowed as she looked through the sheen of wavering light, peering at the trees on the far side of the lawn. Since Rilan wasn't going with them, he provided Gunnar with an amulet that would enable him to open a portal one time, allowing them to return. *Better not lose it.*

Brooke stood a few steps back with Rhys, Brenin, and Rilan. The sisters had hugged fiercely, each one nervous but resolved to see each other again soon.

"Ready?" Gunnar asked her.

"Yes." She forced more bravery into her voice than she truly felt.

They only planned to be gone for a day, but Nicole had stuffed extra clothes into her backpack just in case, as well as some throwing stars and additional knives. She also wore the small silver dagger with the sapphire hilt strapped to her thigh. Gunnar, however, was draped in weapons, mostly blades of different lengths. They hadn't brought any firearms, because he had explained that bullet wounds healed rapidly among the residents of Torth. He hadn't been kidding about dismemberment and burning being the best ways to harm someone over there.

"Going through this will feel a little disorienting. It's kind of like falling, but not actually harmful," Gunnar said. She nodded wordlessly and moved closer to him, letting his powerful hands grip her smaller ones.

Gunnar gave Rilan one last glance and was rewarded with an impatient, "Go, son." He took a breath and pulled Nicole into the pulsing entrance.

CHAPTER 7

GUNNAR HELD ON TO NICOLE as they spun through the portal. It was a feeling he could never quite get used to, having his stomach and heart hovering about a foot above his head. Of course, clasping her close had the added benefit of rekindling the sparks from the previous night. Part of him wished the ride could go on longer. His head swam with heated memories of her velvety skin, firm breasts, and nipples tightly puckered under his fingertips.

He never intended for things to go that far last night. When he learned of the altercation with the gang members and the Skell demons, he was infuriated, so much that he wasn't sure if a rational conversation with her was possible. But when she apologized, her emerald eyes full of contrition, his anger dissolved in a heartbeat. In its place came a burst of relief that she was unharmed. The need to kiss her and touch her had overwhelmed his senses.

With a thud onto soft earth, they landed on their feet in the middle of a dense forest. Nicole wobbled and dug her fingers into his T-shirt. His arms instinctively tightened around her slender frame until she took a deep, steadying breath. Stepping back, he looked her over. "You okay?"

"Yes. That was…exactly the way you described it. My insides were up here." She waved a hand above her head and grinned. "So this is an enchanted forest, huh?"

"Yeah, but there's not a lot to smile about. There are a lot of things out here besides us."

The canopy didn't allow much light to filter down to the carpet of pine needles, creating a lush dimness that pulsed with life. Chirping and buzzing sounds filled the air, punctuated by the rustle of leaves and the occasional squawk of a disgruntled bird.

Gunnar guided Nicole to a trail framed by tall trees and thick brush. They were surrounded by a mix of towering redwoods and conifers identical to their counterparts on Earth, along with the occasional mystical tree. Most of them contained wood nymphs, which were relatively harmless unless their tree came under attack.

Small wildflowers, in shades of palest pink to lush red, peppered the bushes on the forest floor. As far as Torthian forests went, this one didn't contain a majority of dangerous flora, but it was always wise to be cautious. As for the fauna, he hoped they wouldn't run into many of them, even if they were friendly. Forest creatures tended to be as gossipy as old women, and he didn't want any of them speculating about Nicole's heritage.

She walked ahead of him as they climbed a small hill, her peachy scent lingering in the air behind her. He had a hard time dragging his eyes away from her sweet, perky ass, clad in yet another pair of tight jeans. He gazed at the way her waist flared into slim hips, long legs tapering to tiny ankles hidden by her sturdy hiking boots. Her close-fitting green T-shirt matched her eyes, and she'd pulled her shiny blond hair up into a ponytail. Turning, she caught his stare. A smile twitched across her soft lips as she stopped and waited for him.

She took a swig of water from her bottle and pointed to a worn track that branched off to their left. "Do we keep climbing, or take that path?"

"Keep climbing." He watched her throat move as she swallowed, remembering the feel of her silky skin under his mouth.

"This place is beautiful. Did you grow up near here?"

Her question doused his heated thoughts with reality. Even

though he was well aware of the dangers hidden beneath the verdant beauty, he would have jumped at the chance to spend his early years here, instead of the gritty urban area where he had lived during most of his youth.

"No."

She shot him a glance, but didn't push for more. They continued for a minute more when she sucked in a breath and put her hand on his forearm. Pausing, he didn't sense any danger. He looked at her, eyebrows raised.

She pointed to a tree branch in front of them. "What is that?" she whispered in a horrified breath.

He followed her direction to a blue jay perched on the branch. "Surely you've seen blue jays before?"

"But it has…two heads."

"Welcome to Torth," he chuckled

She shook her head as if to clear it. "Oookay. Two-headed bird, check. Never thought I'd see that."

They walked for another hour, with Nicole pointing out everything new to her. He answered her questions, but he didn't want to get too chatty. The woods could hide many enemies and he couldn't afford to let his guard down. Walking behind her when the path narrowed again, he made a mental note to teach her to step more stealthily. He knew she wasn't trying to be noisy, and he had seen her move quietly in the city neighborhoods, but Torth was literally a whole new world. Most of its residents had enhanced senses like him. He frowned as she clambered over a tree that had fallen across the path.

A prickle at the back of his neck flooded him with foreboding, and in the same instant he heard the faintest rustle of leaves behind him. Nicole sensed the change in air pressure and whirled, wide-eyed, to face him.

"Get down!" he hissed as he vaulted toward her, easily clearing the fallen tree and pulling her to the soft dirt beside him. No sooner had they hit the ground when, with a soft thud, an arrow lodged in the bark in front of their heads. A sickly sweet smell emanated from the tree as the bark foamed and sizzled softly.

"Shit. Vipers." Gunnar cursed. Vipers were almost the worst things they could encounter out here. Their reptilian heads sat atop bodies that resembled the human form, but were covered in green scaly skin. Nicole was about to get a crash course in just how dangerous the forests could be.

Chancing a quick look over the log, he spotted the nearest Viper and hurled a fireball at it. The demonfire hit it square in its chest, incinerating it.

"One down," he said to Nicole. "I saw at least two more back there. You stay here."

She started to protest, but he ignored her as he rolled toward the cover of the dense shrubs that lined the path. Another arrow zinged past his ear. The poison in their arrows was the same toxin that dripped from their fangs; it wouldn't kill the stronger supernaturals, but it would incapacitate them for a while. Weaker ones wouldn't survive a direct hit. He didn't know how badly Nicole would be affected and didn't plan to find out.

From his vantage point, he saw the other two Vipers. They stood on his side of the path. One stalked toward him, and the other stared at the log which kept Nicole concealed. Tossing a fireball at the far one, Gunnar unsheathed his sword and charged toward the nearer one. He was the faster opponent, and his blade opened a long gash in the creature's thigh before he darted to the side.

The scaly green Viper swiveled to pin him with slitted snake eyes as it hissed in fury. Its head reared back, and Gunnar knew it was about to spit its venomous saliva at him. He dodged to one side, then ran at the beast to spear it under its rib cage. It howled, staggered, and turned toward him, but Gunnar was already raising his sword.

Before he could land the killing blow, an arrow flew past his raised arms, grazing his bicep. He cursed loudly. The wound was superficial but the poison was going to make his skin hurt like hell for a while, and for the first few minutes it could slow his reflexes. He broke off as he saw two more arrows fly past him, then dive straight into the ground. At the same time, a familiar burst of energy filled the air.

Nicole.

"I said stay down!" he roared at her, not taking his eyes off the injured Viper in front of him. It was determined but struggling, its reflexes sluggish as it charged. Gunnar lifted his sword and this time quickly severed its scaly head from its equally scaly body.

He turned to Nicole, still behind the log but standing in plain view of the third Viper. *Shit.* He spotted two more snake-heads moving through the trees, undoubtedly attracted by the commotion. *Double shit.*

He could fight the Vipers hand to hand, but their archery added a wrinkle that he didn't need. He also worried about Nicole trying to be a hero. Then the nearest one lunged for him.

Gunnar raised his sword arm to block the blow, but the poison made him move just a fraction slower, and the Viper's blade nicked his chest. It was another light wound, and it only stoked his fury higher. He let his rage build, drawing strength from it. He pushed forward savagely, landing blow after blow. More arrows flew, and he realized Nicole, who hadn't listened to him at all, guided the arrows toward the Viper. *Could they be harmed by their own poison?*

The beast howled as the arrows pierced its neck. Not a death blow, but enough to slow it down. Gunnar drew his sword up, slicing the Viper's belly open. It bellowed as it fell to the ground, and Gunnar severed its head with a fierce slash.

Nicole shrieked as he turned to locate the two remaining Vipers, one of which barreled toward her. The last one, its eyes locked on Gunnar, nocked an arrow. *Son of a bitch.* He jumped and rolled in her direction, grabbing the ankle of the Viper near her. It crashed down on top of him, but he kept rolling until he was on top of the thing. Mindful of its dripping fangs, he reached for one of the daggers strapped along his body and plunged it into the Viper's neck.

He was about to order Nicole to stay back when a ball of

demonfire erupted from behind the last Viper and blasted it to pieces. "Nice of you to keep them occupied for me, brother!" called a familiar voice.

"Showing up at the end of the party as usual, Raniero!" Gunnar shouted to his long-time friend. The other Lash demon's duties were similar to Gunnar's, but they kept him busy on Torth. The two had patrolled and fought together for decades before Gunnar had taken on the responsibilities of monitoring Earth cities. He climbed off the motionless but still very much living Viper. "You can finish this one off for me, since you're here."

"With pleasure." Raniero tossed a fireball at it and ended its sorry life. The demon pulled back his long dark hair, which had come loose from its tie. Because of their dark hair and their similar body size, many thought he and Gunnar were blood brothers. On closer examination though, Raniero had more of the look of a conquistador, with his dark eyes and olive skin. He never lacked for female companionship, despite the thin scar that ran down the side of his face. He had earned it in a fight with Vipers, their toxin preventing it from healing properly.

Gunnar turned to Nicole. "Are you hurt?"

"No." She scanned him from head to toe. "But you are."

"Superficial cuts," he shrugged, as Raniero walked over and eyed his arm. The puckered, raw skin had turned an ugly shade of red.

"That's gonna sting," the other demon remarked dryly.

"Says the Watcher who missed most of the action."

"I wouldn't want you to lose a chance to smoke as many Vipers as possible. You must miss them on Earth." His eyes slid over to Nicole.

Gunnar scowled. He loved a good brawl with any nasty creature, but there were a few that he'd only tangle with if his options were down to zero. He kept his eyes on his friend as he spoke. "Nicole, this ugly SOB is Raniero."

"It seems my comrade has forgotten his manners," Raniero said in mock affront. He reached for Nicole's hand and, with a glance at Gunnar's glare, stopped short of kissing it. He inclined his head slightly. "It's a pleasure to meet you, Nicole."

She smiled. "You showed up just in time."

Gunnar was about to retort that he had the situation under control but, in truth, he was glad to see his old friend. "It's good to see you, man."

"This bastard has saved my ass more times than I can count," Raniero said to Nicole. "You'll be safe with him." Hands on his hips, he turned to Gunnar. "What brings you to Torth? When I heard the sounds of the fight back there, you were the last person I expected to find."

"We're going to see Rosa," Gunnar answered.

"Rosa? Then you must have encountered a mystery that Rilan can't solve."

Gunnar nodded. "Nicole found something during a fight with some Skells."

Raniero snorted. "Those things are the rats of our world, and that's an insult to rats. But…you're working with the fae now?"

"She's not fae."

Nicole drew up her shoulders as Raniero regarded her expectantly. "Rilan says I'm a Solsti."

The olive skinned demon blinked. "They're a myth." He glanced at Gunnar and then back to her.

"Apparently, they *were* a myth." She held his gaze.

The other demon paused. "Ah, the arrows. That was you, no? I thought you were using some form of telekinesis."

She shook her head. "I was moving the air currents."

"I'll be damned." His dark eyes flashed with respect. "Well, Solsti, Rosa will certainly be interested in you, if not in the mystery you're bringing to her. Perhaps she was alive when the last Solsti existed."

"On that note, we should keep moving." Gunnar inclined his head toward the path.

"But what about your injuries?" Nicole protested.

"You won't make it to Rosa's before nightfall," Raniero said.

"You'll need a place to stay tonight. These woods are even more dangerous than when you were here last."

"No shit," Gunnar grunted.

"And," the other demon continued, "If you rest that arm, it will be back to full strength by morning. Alas, I cannot accompany you all the way to Rosa's domain. I can, however, bring you to a safe house."

Because the area that Raniero and the Torthian Lash demons monitored was so vast, they had several safe hideouts scattered throughout the area. When on wide patrols, it wasn't uncommon for them to find themselves too far out to return to the main house before dark. Even though the Lash were among the fiercest of demons, Arawn's Watchers usually patrolled in small groups, while some of the uglier nocturnal species that they watched tended to move in hordes. The hideouts weren't fancy, but they were safe and well-warded against detection.

"How far?" Gunnar asked.

"A couple hours' walk."

Gunnar nodded his agreement, but Nicole shook her head and put her hand on his chest. "You don't look like you should walk anywhere for the next two hours. Look at you!"

He couldn't help but allow a smile to tug at his lips. "Yes, look at me." He pulled up his ruined T-shirt to show her the cut from the Viper. Although crusty with dried blood, all that remained was a thin, nearly-healed red line.

Her mouth opened, then closed. She frowned at the mark and traced it gingerly with her fingertips. It was his turn to suck in a breath at the sensation of her warm fingers on his skin. She let her hand linger at his chest for an instant longer than she needed to, and raised her green, heated eyes to his. The tip of his cock tingled. Gods above, he wanted her soft hands all over his body.

Misreading his expression, she pulled her hand away and took a step back. "Does it hurt?"

"No," he said through gritted teeth.

"But how–"

"Accelerated healing." He yanked down his shirt. "Most supernatural creatures have it. You might, as well." He was furious at her for getting involved with the Vipers. At the same time he felt warmed by her worry over his wounds. With the exception of his fellow Lash, he couldn't recall anyone looking at him with such care and concern. He stepped closer to her and reached to smooth a lock of blond hair that had come loose from her ponytail. Gentling his voice, he said, "And I'm in no hurry to find out. You should have stayed down on the ground, not joined in the fight."

Nicole blinked, then looked past him to Raniero and blushed furiously. "I was just trying to help," she muttered.

Raniero cleared his throat and started back up the path. "If you're ready, then," he murmured, "Follow me."

Sunlight streamed into the room as Kai awoke to a quiet house. He was still royally pissed off about losing the Skell last night, but he would be able to think it through more clearly today. At least now he had a general direction.

His stomach let out a ravenous growl. He didn't need to eat every day, but he'd let it go too long. He almost never got to the point where he felt hungry. Rolling out of bed naked, he pulled on a pair of jeans and didn't bother with the top button. He headed down the stairs to the kitchen. The sounds of drawers opening drifted toward his ears as he rounded the corner, and when he reached the doorway, he stilled.

A woman peered into one of the lower cabinets. She had a sweet, round ass that was literally tilted up in the air as she bent down to retrieve a pan. Thick chestnut hair fell below her shoulders in waves. As she straightened, he noted her small waist, and saw she was rather tall for a female. His eyes travelled down her long legs and back up to her curvy hips. *Damn.* The unslaked lust from last night roared back to him, sending blood flowing to his groin.

He cleared his throat. "I'll take some sausage and eggs. Black coffee, too."

She gasped and whirled to face him. Holy hell, she was gorgeous. Pale gray eyes stared at him as her mouth opened and then closed. That mouth had lush red lips that instantly gave him ideas about what she could do with it on various parts of his body. Full breasts pushed against the fabric of her fitted, sleeveless top. Her face was heart-shaped, her skin like porcelain. Faint pink flushed her cheeks as her gaze lingered on his bare torso and low-hanging jeans. She opened her mouth again. "I... I'm not–"

"C'mon, baby. Kai's getting hungry." He moved a step closer.

She froze. Her expression changed from flustered confusion to cool assessment in a heartbeat. She raised her eyebrows. "You have two hands," she said sarcastically.

"Excuse me?" For a split second he was floored. Women didn't talk to him like that.

"Yeah. Excuse you. That was rude."

He let out a low growl and prowled into the kitchen, standing right in front of her. He could smell whatever soapy product she used in the shower, apple-scented something or other. "*What* did you just say?"

"I think you heard me."

He leaned down until his nose was inches away from hers. Standing this close to her, he was swamped with her sweet scent, almost making him forget her taunt. "Who do you think you are?"

Before she could respond, the back door opened and Brenin strode in. The other demon must have sensed the tension in the room and spoke in a voice laced with warning.

"'S'up, Kai?" Brenin leaned on the other side of the granite-topped island, standing in a pose that looked completely relaxed. But as Kai well knew, Brenin would vault over it in a split second if trouble started.

Was Brenin protecting her? Kai took a step back and blew out a breath, not taking his eyes off the female. "Who is this?"

Brenin spoke with a purposeful, slow voice that irritated

Kai. "Kai, let me introduce you to Brooke, Nicole's sister."
Turning to the woman, he said, "Brooke, this is Kai, the other
Lash demon who lives here. Looks like he woke up on the
wrong side of the bed today. He's not usually such an ass."

Nicole's sister. Shit. She had mentioned two of them, and
Rilan wanted to meet them. Because they were *fucking Solsti*. Kai
glared at her. It seemed he'd managed to offend a creature so
powerful and rare that she was supposed to be a myth.

"Fuck you, Brenin." Turning, he stalked to the basement
door and yanked it open. He needed to work off steam
somehow, and it looked like the training room was going to be
his best option. He wasn't going to apologize. This was his
territory and no one, not even a tart-tongued Solsti, talked to
him like that.

Nicole had never been so happy to hike through the woods.
What the heck happened back there? She'd do anything to keep
moving and to avoid talking to Gunnar right now. He was
obviously ticked at her, but she hadn't missed the blue flash in
his eyes when she touched his chest. His gaze had warmed her
skin the entire day, which only intensified the way her body
ached after last night's dream. She tried to make conversation
just to keep herself distracted. The run-in with the Vipers was a
definite distraction, but only a temporary one.

She had been transfixed watching Gunnar fight the snake-
headed creatures. All that raw male strength and the efficient way
he dispatched the Vipers made for a potent combination. His
powerful body ducked and swerved with a grace not immediately
evident in someone his size. The muscles in his arms rippled and
bulged every time he hefted that sword. It had to weigh half as
much as she did, but the way he moved made it seem like little
more than a sapling.

Then he had to go and taunt her with his gorgeous,
muscular chest, only to growl at her two seconds later. No one
told her that demons had super-healing abilities. Maybe it was
bold of her to touch him, but she was concerned about his

wound. That and the fact that she had been dying to get her hands on him, especially after last night. It wasn't just her dream, but the memory of his hands on her breasts that was making her a little crazy.

They walked along the path in a single line, with Nicole in the middle. True to his word, Raniero stopped a couple hours later and indicated for them to follow him off the path and into the dense bushes. After awhile they came to a very small clearing and Raniero smiled. "Here we are."

Nicole raised her eyebrows. "I don't see anything."

"We have very good wards," the demon said with a confident smile. He reached down to move a large branch on the ground, and Nicole noticed the outline of a door in the grass. The door itself appeared to be made of grass. Raniero tugged on a handle that Nicole thought was a rock, and the door opened upward. It looked like a storm cellar that was accessed from the outside. "After you," he murmured, inclining his head.

Nicole crept cautiously down the stairs. Motion-controlled lights flickered on as she descended farther. After two flights the stairs ended at a closed door. She waited, not knowing if this door was warded also. Raneiro reached around her to open it, saying, "Go ahead. It's not the Plaza, but it's safe."

She found herself in a large living room. There was a kitchen and a room that looked like an office off to the left, and a hallway to the right. The living room had a chair rail encircling the walls, the lower half painted a deep crimson and the top portion tinted with a warm tan. Sconces and small mirrors contributed to an understated sophistication. She spied marble counter tops in the kitchen, and was instantly glad that her newest friends took an interest in creature comforts. Glad, but a little bit confused. "You have electricity here?"

Raniero grinned at her. "Torth is not that different from Earth. It's as old as Earth, and has similar diversity in its geography and climate. And demons have been flashing back and forth between the two for centuries. Any modern conveniences have either been adapted to Torth or existed here first."

Her surprise must have shown on her face, because he added, "Of course, some of the conveniences on Torth may have a few supernatural modifications. Like electricity, for example. Torth doesn't have a power grid or power lines; instead, magic is used to channel power from the ley lines that cross the realm."

"Ley lines?"

"They're kind of like latitude and longitude, except they don't necessarily run north-south and east-west. They go where they want, connecting various places of concentrated magic or energy."

"Actually, Earth has ley lines, too," Gunnar added. "Though the ones here are more powerful."

"Okay." Nicole shrugged. That explanation was as good as any. Two-headed birds, angry snake-headed monsters, and magical power lines. *Don't over-think it.* She sank onto a soft red couch, the stresses of the day weighing on her. Her stomach picked that moment to growl, and she remembered she hadn't eaten anything since breakfast.

Both demons heard, of course. As they turned to look at her, she rose and walked to the kitchen. "I didn't realize how hungry I was! Do you guys want anything?" Then she paused.

She raised an eyebrow at Gunnar, who followed her. "I don't even know what you eat," she said softly.

He walked to the refrigerator and pulled out two bottles of water. "We don't need to eat as often as you do. These will be fine for now." Setting the drinks down on the counter, he turned to her. "Nicole, we were in a dangerous situation today. Vipers are among the most vicious creatures on Torth, and they ambushed us. I want to keep you safe, but I need you to listen to me."

She sighed. "But I was able to help you. I kept their arrows away from you. Well, most of them." She eyed the red, puckered skin of his arm ruefully.

"I can do a better job of protecting you if I know you're

not jumping into the fray."

"I can stay out of trouble and protect myself at the same time." She crossed her arms over her chest, and her stomach rumbled again.

"Actually, I don't think you can stay out of trouble. You attract it. You're stubborn." He grinned at her. "And you're hungry." He opened the freezer, revealing a large stash of frozen entrees. "Help yourself."

"Wow." She scanned the items inside and took out a frozen lasagna. She popped it into the microwave and waited impatiently for it to heat up as Gunnar joined Raniero in the living room. She was glad that he didn't seem too mad at her anymore. But staying away from the action? That would to be a challenge, especially after today. Being able to use her gift against those awful snake-headed monsters had been awesome and inspiring, and she couldn't wait to do it again.

CHAPTER 8

A COUPLE HOURS AFTER HER meal Nicole perched on the red couch, getting an earful of demon lore. The two men conferred while she ate, sharing details of their work and tales of altercations with creatures that she hoped never to see. She wiggled her toes as she listened, glad to be free of her socks and hiking boots. Despite her tiring day, she felt restless and edgy. Her mind swam with distracting memories of the soft, newly healed skin covering the muscled slabs of Gunnar's chest.

"Solsti." Raniero's voice broke into her thoughts, the word rolling off his tongue as if he was testing it out. "Simply amazing. It's still sinking in. Tell me about your sisters."

Raniero took a genuine interest in her talent and listened attentively when she described Brooke and Gin, hinting with a gleam in his eye that he'd enjoy meeting them. Although roguishly handsome, Nicole felt zero interest in the dark-eyed demon beyond friendly camaraderie. She was glad to have him as an ally.

Their impromptu host got up and stretched his brawny arms over his head. "I have enjoyed our conversation, but it's time for me to get some rest. I'll be up early tomorrow, tracking a trio of Serus demons. Bastards are robbing travelers along the western edge of the forest."

Nicole opened her mouth to thank Raniero for his hospitality, but stopped at the mischievous twinkle in his eyes. He flicked a knowing glance from her to Gunnar and murmured, "There are two bedrooms here—I'll take the smaller one...you two can decide about the other." And with a wink, he disappeared into the first doorway down the hall.

Nicole and Gunnar turned to each other. In a heartbeat, the air between them grew heavy and charged with anticipation. Everything faded from the room as his blue eyes locked with hers. Sapphire embers flamed. One bedroom. They would share a room tonight, or one of them would sleep on the couch. After last night, she knew what she wanted.

"I'll take the couch." His voice rasped like sandpaper.

She shook her head, rising to walk toward the large armchair he sat in, not breaking contact with the turquoise glow of his eyes. Awareness coursed through her body as she remembered his muscles rippling and flexing when he fought off the Vipers, and the way his fingers stroked her into a frenzy of need the previous night. She padded slowly over to him in her bare feet.

"No, you won't. Not after the way you teased me last night." She wasn't usually this bold, but Gunnar affected her senses like no man ever had. Leaning forward, she braced her hands on the arms of the chair. "You're spending this evening right next to me."

He stared at her, frozen. She thought he forgot to breathe. Did he need more convincing? "You're not kissing me senseless and then walking away, not this time—"

Her breath caught as he tugged her arms, tipping her off balance and tumbling her into his lap. He pushed her legs to either side of his so she straddled him. Gently, he cupped her face in his hands. "Hell no, I'm not going anywhere. But so much has happened in the last few days. I want you to be sure."

In response, she took one of his hands in hers and slowly brought it to her mouth. She pressed a kiss to the center of his palm, and then kissed her way down the length of one finger before drawing it between her lips. Blue flames flared in his eyes as he held her gaze. He had to hear the pounding of her heart as it crashed wildly in her chest. She had invited a demon to her bed, and every cell in her body was on edge with curiosity and aching need.

She swirled her tongue around his finger and scraped gently with her teeth. He inhaled sharply as she began to suck, his eyes riveted to her mouth. With his free hand on her lower back, he scooted her forward on his lap until her core came into contact with the impressive bulge in his jeans. Humming in pleasure as her hips cradled his, she was unable to keep from rocking against him.

That was all it took. He pulled his hand from her mouth and threaded it into her hair. His lips covered hers with a rough groan. Demanding and possessive, he held her in place, claiming her with his kiss. She twined her arms around his neck and slid her tongue along his, eager to taste him as he tasted her. She licked against him, savoring a bit of lingering sweetness from his drink.

Her fingertips caressed the sides of his neck, tracing the line of his massive shoulders, and moved down to explore his broad chest. His pectoral muscles were hard sinew under her curious fingers, his abs steel bands of strength. Gently hooking her fingers into his waistband, she felt his lower body clench as he growled and moved both of his hands to her hips.

The heat from his palms seared her, making her skin feel too tight. She craved his touch all over her body. He moved his hands up slowly, caressing her waist and ribs the way he had done at the club. But this time he didn't stop there. He cupped her breasts and rubbed her nipples through her bra and T-shirt, making them bead into tight points. Every nerve ending in her body exploded with need, aching for his hands, his teeth, his tongue.

He broke their kiss and she felt his hands at the hem of her shirt. In one swift movement he tugged it up over her head. He gazed at her for a moment before lowering his head to place teasing kisses along one side of her sheer black bra. His mouth was deliciously hot, his lips soft on her skin. He caressed the side of her other breast, then the top, before flicking his thumb across her straining nipple. She couldn't hold back a moan as her hips moved on his.

Not letting go of her, he stood, and she wrapped her legs around his waist as he walked them to the unoccupied bedroom. She vaguely registered a spacious room with walls painted a deep red, two chairs, and an enormous four-poster bed with black linens. Still holding her, he kicked the door shut and crossed the room to lay her on the coverlet. He followed her down, covering her body with his, infusing her senses with his warm skin and dark woodsy scent.

He caressed her arms, drawing them up above her head and holding them there while he lowered his head to her neck and traced teasing patterns with his tongue. She purred in pleasure when he scraped his teeth along her shoulders. Goose bumps erupted down her arms. He slid his hands under her shoulders to the center of her back, where he flicked open the clasp of her bra. She wiggled her arms out of it, loving the way he couldn't look away from her breasts. Impatient to explore his naked chest, she tugged on his shirt. "Off."

"Yeah?" he whispered. "And what do I get?"

A maelstrom of desire tore through her. She cupped her breasts and flicked the taut nipples, pushing them toward his mouth. "Taste."

"Deal," he groaned. His shirt was on the floor before she saw him touch it. Then his mouth found her breast, kissing and licking the soft underside. She couldn't hold back a moan at the warm, rough feel of him. He moved to her nipple, flicking it with his tongue before drawing it into his mouth. He suckled her tenderly, maddeningly, and brushed his fingertips across her other breast. Back arched, she pushed into his touch.

Knowing what she needed, he moved his hand down to her waist and popped the button on her jeans.

"Yes," she breathed, shimmying out of them. They were tight, so her damp panties came off right along with them. A tiny shiver danced up her spine when the cool air of the room hit the moist skin between her thighs. She stretched out, completely naked, watching him drink in every inch of her.

"So damn sexy," he murmured, tracing the line of her hip. He moved his finger across her belly and lower, drawing lazy circles on her skin. She shifted her hips, pushing them closer to him.

"You're killing me." She gasped as he cupped her and slid his fingers between her legs. When he brought them back up and just barely touched her most sensitive spot, her entire body jerked. "Gunnar," she breathed, "I'm really close."

Approval rumbled deep in his chest. "That's it," he whispered. "Come for me, baby." He lowered his mouth to her nipple. Pleasure short-circuited her mind, her breathing ragged. His hand continued to stroke her, once, twice, and when he circled her clit with his thumb, she couldn't hold back. Splinters of light exploded though her body as she rocked against his hand, her hips coming up off the bed.

Still floating on waves of pleasure, she realized he had moved down on the bed to position his head between her thighs. He didn't give her a chance to catch her breath as he licked the length of her center, lapping at the slickness that covered her. She tensed, thinking her flesh would be too sensitive, but he circled her tight bundle of nerves with his talented tongue. *Oh, yes.* She clutched the sheets as he coaxed her higher and higher, until she came again, her body convulsing with sensation.

She gazed at him through sated eyes as he moved next to her. He propped his head on one hand and splayed the other across her abdomen, leaning down to nuzzle her neck. She dimly realized that he still had his jeans on. She reached for his waistband. "Too many clothes."

"You're a demanding little piece." He grinned at her, standing up to shuck his jeans and boxer briefs. She watched, rapt, as he pushed them down, freeing his straining cock. Kneeling on the bed in front of him, she couldn't take her eyes from his heavy arousal. Huge and thick and proud, he made her mouth water.

She reached for him, wrapping her hand around his granite-hard length covered in velvety smooth skin. With slow strokes, she explored every ridge along his shaft. Looking up at him, she blinked at his clenched teeth and the corded muscles in his neck

"Gunnar?"

He grunted in response.

"I want to taste you."

Gunnar's head was going to explode. His body would be next, if Nicole kept her soft, slender hand on his dick for another second. And her mouth? He gritted his teeth at the thought. "Next time," he growled.

She pretended to pout as he nudged her back down on the bed. "Promise?"

He ignored her question, turning his attention to her dusky pink nipples. He had ached to taste her last night. How he held himself back, he didn't know, because the sweetness of her skin was as peachy and intoxicating as her scent. He laved one nipple while he brushed his thumb across the other one. She sighed and wriggled against him, running her hands across his shoulders and upper back.

He wanted to taste, touch, and explore every inch of her delectable body, but his cock throbbed with need. The feel of her exploring hands only pushed him closer to the edge.

"Gunnar," she husked. "Promise me I get to suck you."

"Or what?" How could she still be talking right now?

"Or I'll start describing, in great detail, exactly how I plan to use my tongue when I finally get your big, thick cock into my mouth."

He cursed long and loud, then muttered, "You can't be a Solsti." Her questioning gaze found his. "You must be a witch. Or a sorceress. Or something very wicked."

Her naughty streak entranced him. He flipped her to her stomach, deciding he needed to spend some time on her luscious ass. For the gods' sakes, he'd had his eyes glued to it *all day*. He brought his palm down against her bottom with a light smack, then followed it with kisses. She wiggled and purred like a contented cat.

He moved up her body, kissing the deliciously smooth skin of her back, until he reached her neck. With his flesh on fire everywhere that they touched, he let some of his weight settle on her as their bodies aligned. His cock rubbed against her butt, and she tried to wiggle beneath him. He didn't let her. Keeping her in place, he moved his mouth to the sensitive spot where her shoulder flowed into her neck, and he bit down.

She let out a small cry, and he kissed and licked the red mark. *His* mark. Something primal roared inside him. He nibbled his way up the dewy side of her neck, one of his hands holding both of hers tightly above her head. Then he rolled her to her back and gripped her hip firmly, meeting her gaze. Any trace of mischief was gone from her eyes, replaced by anticipation tinged with a hint of sensual nervousness. He traced one finger along the insides of her thighs, still wet from her release.

Letting go of her hands, he moved over her willowy, sated body. He took himself in hand, teasing her entrance with the blunt head of his cock. She let out a very feminine grunt and tried to lift her hips toward him, but he held her right where he wanted her. He continued to tease her until she whispered, "Gunnar, please."

Hearing his name on her lips as she lay hot and writhing beneath him was a drug to his senses. "Please, what?"

"I need you inside me. Now."

He meant to push inside her slowly. He groaned as his first inch slipped into her damp, delicious heat. But when she rocked her hips against him, his ragged control faltered and he plunged deep inside her. Gods, she was hot, tight, and so very wet. His mind fuzzed over until he was only aware of his desire to possess her. He drowned in the sensation of her soft body locked intimately with his. Her eyes, which had squeezed shut when he entered her, flew open to meet his.

"Hurt?" he rasped, a thread of concern weaving through the heat in his brain.

She shook her head. "Feels so good. So full."

He pulled out almost all the way, then plunged back in. He

was close to losing it. He had never met a more sensuous woman in his long life. Her curves, her skin, and her mouth all wreaked havoc on his senses, building his need to an unbearable level. Her peachy scent wafted up to him, and he started a pounding rhythm. She eagerly met each of his thrusts, and when he leaned down to tug one perfect pink bud into his mouth, she shattered.

The feeling of her inner muscles clenching his cock drove him over the edge along with her. With one final furious thrust, he bellowed her name, and his world exploded into white-hot shards of carnal heat. Head spinning with sensation, he allowed himself to collapse on her, pressing her into the mattress. His body felt sated, but not nearly close to being done with his beautiful, lithe Solsti.

After several minutes, he felt her body tense ever so slightly. "Gunnar." He pushed up a little, bracing his hands on either side of her head. Looking into her bright green eyes, he saw a tiny flash of concern.

"We forgot protection," she whispered.

He leaned down to kiss her pert nose. "We're not fertile right now. And we can't get human sexual diseases."

"What do you mean?"

"All the supernaturals I can think of are only fertile twice a year. Either at each solstice, or at each equinox. It depends on the species." He paused for a moment. "And even if you turn out to be able to conceive more often, I know I can't."

"I guess that's convenient."

"When you live a long time, you don't need to populate the planet as much as humans do."

She twined languid fingers through his hair, her brows knitted. "How old are you?"

"Just over two hundred years."

"What?" Her fingers stopped their delicious massage of his scalp, and her eyes widened. "Two...*hundred?* You look like you're thirty."

"Chalk it up to magic and good genes." He winked and kissed her nose again.

"Wow." She dropped her hands to his biceps. "Two hundred. And ley lines, portals, and witches. It all seems so…"

"New?"

"I was going to say unreal."

"Yet you've known about your own power for a long time." He brought one of her hands to his lips and kissed it. "And many here on Torth think the Solsti aren't real."

"True." She smiled. "You're cute for an older guy."

"Cute?" His voice was filled with mock indignation. "I'm not cute. Puppies are cute." Still semi-hard inside her, he rolled them so that she was on top.

"How about devastatingly sexy?" Her eyes sparkled playfully.

"That'll work."

She leaned down to kiss the muscles of his chest, lingering where the Viper had cut him earlier. No trace of the wound remained. Her soft hair brushed his skin as she moved across his body, licking and nipping with her little teeth. "You're even better than my dream," she murmured.

"What dream?"

She proceeded to tell him about the wet dream she had the night before. With every erotic detail she divulged, he grew harder inside her. Hell, everything about her was erotic. He couldn't have conjured up a fantasy hotter than her. She was beautiful, sexy, a little bit naughty, and he couldn't get enough of her.

Sitting up all the way, she undulated her hips as if reading his mind. He groaned as she moved up and then slowly lowered herself down his length. She did it again and stopped, obviously wanting to torture him.

"Witch."

In response she reached one hand behind her and down to cup his balls and massage them gently.

"*Nicole.*"

"I think it's my turn to play." She smiled down at him.

"You're either going to kill me, or make me embarrass

myself."

She only smiled again and leaned down. Bracing her arms on either side of him, she resumed kissing his chest. He felt himself twitch inside her when she gently scraped her teeth across his flat nipple.

"Enough," he growled, pulling her off him in a flash. He turned her to her belly and tugged her bottom up to where he knelt behind her. He placed one rough kiss to her spine before he gripped her hips and thrust deep inside. Keeping one hand at her hip, he used the other to push her shoulders down to the mattress, angling her body so that he could slide in even deeper. Then he slid his hand around to her front, making her whimper as he cupped her breast and teased her nipple with his thumb.

She took everything he gave as he pounded relentlessly against her soft sweet backside. His body built relentlessly to its peak, and he moved his hand to the sensitive apex between her thighs. She came suddenly, bucking against him, and he was helpless to do anything but follow her over the edge. As he collapsed, he rolled them both to the side and pressed her against his chest before falling into a deep, satisfied sleep.

Nicole drifted awake and froze, startled at the unfamiliar room. As her surroundings slowly registered and she remembered the events of last night, she smiled into the darkness. Her head rested on Gunnar's huge bicep, her back tucked against the warm wall of his chest. Her bottom fit snug against his hips. His arm draped over her side and across the front of her body, his hand cupping her breast as he slept. She had never woken up quite like this before. Every inch of her skin tingled where they touched.

She flushed, remembering how demanding he had been. She found herself wanting to give him everything he asked for, and was rewarded with more orgasms than she could count. Awareness surged through her body and she squirmed. *How can I want more right now?* She should be thoroughly sated. She liked sex, but Gunnar stoked her body to a new level of need.

She felt, rather than heard the rumble behind her. She made a soft sound in response, and felt his hot mouth against her ear as the hand on her breast squeezed gently. His erection nestled against her, insistent and ready.

His fingers brushed one nipple and then the other and she couldn't hold back a tiny grunt. She canted her hips and reached behind her to guide him inside, his girth stretching her sensitive flesh. He began an easy pace, holding her breasts in both his hands as he moved. She needed more, but his hands were deliciously occupied. Sliding her fingers down until she found just the right spot, she arched her back in pleasure.

He paused. "Naughty girl," he scolded. "That's my job."

"But I like where your hands are."

He pulled out and rolled her to her back. *Again.* She couldn't remember how many times he had flipped her, rolled her, or repositioned her last night. And all of it was beyond pleasurable. He lowered his head to her breast, drawing her nipple into his hot mouth and suckling her. His talented tongue tortured her, swirling and flicking her tight, puckered tip. His fingers tickled her other nipple, making her writhe and reach down for his cock, which hung thick and hard between them. He let her take him in her hand and rub him against her damp folds until she couldn't wait anymore. He drove deep inside her body, luminous blue eyes meeting hers in the dark.

Wrapping her legs around his waist, she hooked her ankles together behind him. She held onto his shoulders as he set a perfect, sensually slow pace. She moved with him, their pace building, reaching their climax together. As the waves of pleasure subsided, Nicole felt herself carried by another emotion entirely. She hadn't known what to expect from Gunnar, but she felt full of a rare contentment—a feeling of sweet, fulfilling bliss. Unable to process it, she simply accepted it as she fell asleep again in his arms, his length still buried inside her.

Gunnar awoke for the second time in as many hours with a warm, sexy Nicole entwined with him. He didn't know which god was looking favorably upon him, but he wasn't about to question it. He kissed her hair as she slumbered next to him. She must be exhausted, but she hadn't held anything back. Playful and responsive, she was the most adventurous bed mate he'd ever had. And when was the last time he'd had fun in bed? He thoroughly enjoyed the company of women, but when he bedded them, it was all about lust.

He glanced at his phone, his acute night vision allowing him to read the time across the dark room. Since this safe home was underground, no tell-tale sunlight streamed in to alert him to the new day. Grinning, he figured he had enough time to have a very thorough shower with Nicole before they had to resume their journey. He brushed her hair away from her neck, awakening her with kisses as he massaged her firm backside with his hand.

She stirred and stretched, mumbling something sleepily about mornings. "You know what the best thing about mornings is?" He kissed the tip of her ear.

"Breakfast?"

"Try again."

"Morning sex?"

"Close."

She blinked. "You think there's something better than morning sex?"

"Morning *shower* sex." He pushed back the covers and scooped her into his arms.

The standard size shower had no tub. Instead, the inner corners bumped out to form two small seats. Gunnar's cock twitched at the possibilities they presented. He set Nicole down in front of him, turned on the water, and grabbed a palmful of shampoo. Standing behind her, he worked the lather through her hair and murmured, "You know, the other day I couldn't stop thinking about this."

Her voice was a contented purr. "Thinking about what?"

"At my house, when you took a shower after we sparred."

"Oh, you mean after you took every possible opportunity to get me horizontal."

He nipped the tip of her ear. "All I could think about was fucking you."

She shivered under the spray and shot him a heated glance over her shoulder. "Yeah?"

"Yeah." He pulled her tightly against him, stifling a groan as her soft curves aligned with his hardness.

"I have some ideas about that," she murmured, green eyes wide with feigned innocence. "But I'm still dirty."

"Yeah, you are." He tapped her bottom. Reaching for the liquid gel and squeezing it onto a washcloth, he soaped her back. He skipped down to her calves and slender feet, washing each tiny toe, before moving back up to work on her thighs. He slid his hand between them, just barely grazing her damp curls. She shuddered and tried to push against him, but he turned her around to face him instead. Suds from the shampoo coursed down the front of her body, and he abandoned the washcloth in favor of cupping her perfect, round breasts in his hands. He massaged the soap into her soft skin, rubbing light circles along the sides of her breasts and up to her shoulders.

As the water rinsed her willowy frame, he bent to take her nipple into his mouth. He couldn't get enough of her sweet taste. Hell, he didn't seem to be able to get enough of *her*, period. He swirled and sucked her puckered tip, drawing her deep into his mouth. She made a contented, feminine sound and wound her fingers into his hair, tugging his head up to meet her hungry gaze.

She moved to the back corner of the shower, pulling him with her. As soon as she skimmed her hands down his sides to rest at his hips and perched her bottom on the small seat, he knew what she planned to do. His already-hard cock swelled at the thought of her warm lush mouth on him, and she grinned up at him with pure wickedness.

She pressed a kiss to his hip, then started licking her way across his abs. When she got to his other side, she nipped him before moving lower. He uttered a soft curse as he glanced down. Her sinful mouth was a mere inch from his throbbing cock, and her hands had come to rest at the very tops of his thighs. She seemed to take an eternity to move forward, and then his desire surged anew as she licked him slowly from root to tip.

He hissed in pleasure as she welcomed him into the warm cavern of her mouth. He hadn't even realized that he had been holding his breath. Damn, but she felt like heaven. She swirled the thick head with her tongue, then flicked its sensitive underside. He couldn't hold back from thrusting just a little. Unable to take his whole length into her mouth, she stroked. *Fuck, yeah.* He braced his hands on the shower wall above her head, groaning, as she made a humming noise deep in her throat that only added to the pressure in his groin. When she reached down to cup him, and started sucking him vigorously at the same time, he growled her name.

In response, she deviously sucked and stroked him harder. He wouldn't last another minute like this. Already he could feel his orgasm building. He reached down to pinch her nipple gently, making her gasp and release him. Grabbing her waist, he turned her to the wall and bent her down until she had to rest her hands on the seat.

One look at her bare, heart-shaped ass in front of him and he was undone. He entered her in one swift thrust, pausing to savor her tight heat before he reached around for her breast again. He closed his eyes, tilted his head back, and let the pleasure of her warm hot sheath and firm breast drown out everything else in his world. Then he lost himself to the furious rhythm of his lust.

Nicole pushed her hips back against him, meeting his thrusts. Surely she knew what she had done to him, knew how close he was to the edge. He was determined to hold onto his control long enough to bring his little vixen over with him. He flicked his thumb over her tight nipple one last time, then moved his hand lower to circle the tiny bud between her thighs. It took just a few strokes before she shuddered and shrieked his name, drawing him deep inside, her body pulsing with pleasure.

Her hips rocked uncontrollably, irresistibly, and he was helpless to deny his own release. With one last plunge, he jerked her hips hard against him and roared as he exploded deep in her body. He wrapped one arm around her torso and pulled her up to press her back to his chest. Burying his mouth in the crook of her neck, he nipped and licked the faint trace of red left from last night even as he continued to pulse inside her, not stopping until they were both thoroughly spent.

CHAPTER 9

NICOLE AND GUNNAR EMERGED FROM their room sometime later. With a grin, she smacked his ass before darting ahead to the kitchen. Gunnar found no trace of Raniero, not that he expected to. His comrade's duties would have him out the door early. Raniero's responsibilities here on Torth didn't include playing host and saving their asses.

He snuck a bite of the frozen breakfast sandwich she had microwaved.

"Hey!" she protested.

"It was just one bite," he said innocently. "I need to shore up my energy levels after the way you wore me out last night. And this morning."

"How about I make you a sandwich of your own." Her eyes roamed his body in a lazy caress. "That way, you'll be able to give me a repeat performance."

He snaked an arm around her waist and gave her one quick, searing kiss. "You got yourself a deal."

After they ate, they wound their way up the stairs to the concealed door of the safe house and stepped into the sunny clearing. They easily found their way back to the path. Rosa's home would be another hour or two ahead, providing that nothing slowed them down along the way.

Being more familiar with the area they were hiking through today, Gunnar changed their course. It wouldn't add any time to their journey, and there was something he wanted Nicole to see.

This route involved a little more climbing and he made her

go first, in case she slipped on the trail. "It's a good thing I'm in shape," she muttered.

"You're doing fine."

"You just like looking at my ass."

He grinned. She was right. "Just a little farther, I promise."

He caught up to her as they crested a ridge. "Wow," she whispered.

They stood at the top of a sheer rock wall overlooking a river. On the cliff opposite them, a waterfall cascaded hundreds of feet into the swirling current below. That alone was beautiful, but the creatures moving around and through the falls were the real treasure he wanted her to see.

Many water sprites made their home in the river. Beautiful and playful, they tempted males of all species to dally, and then divested them of valuables while they slept in a sprite-induced trance. But a rare sub-species lived here along with the common ones: sprites who spun rainbows with water and light and then wound their handiwork through the falls. As the water cascaded, it pulsed with bands of brilliant, shifting colors. The sprites also drew the rainbows back and forth across the current, so the river came alive with swirling rainbows and tiny dancing fairy-like creatures.

"It's amazing," she breathed.

"You had to see some of the ugliest things on Torth yesterday. I wanted you to see one of the prettiest as well."

"You know, underneath that tough-guy exterior, you're a big softie."

"Don't go telling anyone. I'll deny every word." He winked and flashed her a dimpled smile.

They followed the river's edge for a couple of hours before moving back to the woods. After a water break and another mile, they arrived at a small clearing.

Nicole halted. "No way."

He raised his eyebrows.

"This looks like a drawing from a fairy tale. Look, the chimney even has a perfect trail of white smoke coming out."

"I guess that's the look Rosa picked for today."

She cocked her head to the side.

"It's an illusion," he explained. "It's warded just like the safe house. The last time I saw Rosa, which was decades ago, her place looked like the homes in Englewood. And not the ones where Grandma tidied up the front porch."

Nicole's brows drew together. "What's she like?"

"To answer your question, we may as well knock on her door. If we're able to stand here and talk about her without getting zapped, then she already knows we're here."

"What do you mean, zapped?" Her fingers tightened on his biceps.

"I mean that Rosa is very powerful. No one bothers her. But don't worry." He dropped a swift kiss on top of her head. "I was serious when I said that she knows we're here. She's waiting for us. It'll be okay."

As if on cue, the top half of the square double-door opened and a petite figure called out, "Gunnar! Come here young man, and let me meet your friend!"

Nicole stared as they walked up the path. The home looked like a gingerbread cottage, minus the gumdrops on the roof. The top half of the door closed for a second, then both halves swung open together. The woman standing on the other side was tiny, just over five feet tall, with wide eyes as blue as a tropical sea. But her hair captured every ounce of Nicole's attention. It was true silver, not gray or white or salt-and-pepper. She'd never seen anything like it. She recalled Gunnar saying that Rosa was ancient, but she couldn't see even one tiny wrinkle on her porcelain complexion.

"Welcome, child," the witch said to Nicole. "Do come in." She wore a long gathered skirt in a shade of pale blue, and soft brown moccasins. A floral blouse topped with a beige cardigan completed her ensemble. She took Nicole's hand and led her to a small kitchen with an old wood-burning stove. They passed a living room with a braided rug in front of a fireplace, and a comfortable looking couch draped with an afghan crocheted in a familiar pattern of colored squares. *All she needs is a cat.*

"Tea?" Rosa asked, indicating that they should sit at her kitchen table.

"Thank you." Nicole was wary of this cozy illusion. For such a powerful being, Rosa had certainly chosen an innocuous setting. There was even a pot full of something that smelled delicious simmering on the stove.

"You look well, Rosa," Gunnar said gruffly. He shifted in the wooden chair, which seemed frightfully small beneath his bulk.

"You haven't come to see me in ages, my boy," she chided.

"I've been working on Earth."

"And now you're here, courtesy of your Elder." She poured tea from a kettle painted with yellow tulips. "What can I help you with?"

Nicole pulled the silver coin from her pocket. "I found this."

Rosa took it and rubbed her thumb over the symbol on the front. "I haven't seen one of these in years. Where did you come across it?"

"On...Earth," Nicole started awkwardly. She had never before needed to use a *planet* to describe her location. "There was a fight...with some Skell demons."

"And who else?"

Nicole swallowed. Would an ancient witch know about Chicago street gangs? Better to assume that the witch knew everything. "Some gang members."

Turquoise eyes locked with hers as Nicole felt the sudden prick of a hundred tiny needles along her arms, swiftly followed by the sensation of soft caressing feathers. She shivered at the touch of Rosa's power. "I won't bite you, child. Go on."

"My sister and I were involved. And two of Gunnar's friends. That's it." Nicole kept her hands wrapped around her teacup, absorbing its warmth.

"Ah, your sister. She is like you."

Nicole's eyes widened. "How..."

"I have seen much, child. I know what you are."

"So Rilan is right," Gunnar said.

"Rilan is right," Rosa agreed. "The Solsti have returned."

"But why?" Nicole's mind was overrun with an Alice-in-Wonderland feeling, and Rosa's story book cottage only added to it.

"The Solsti come when they are needed." The witch shrugged.

"But it's just me and my two sisters. Rilan told us the Solsti were supposed to be four?"

"There *are* four of you."

Rosa placed her hand on top of Nicole's, bringing with it a fresh wave of power. "I cannot say who or where they are, my dear. I can simply tell from touching you that all four exist. The elemental circle is complete."

Didn't Rilan say something similar? "So, somewhere in the world, there's a woman like me and my sisters, but we have no idea how to find her. And together we're supposed to prevent some great disaster?" She stared in confusion at Rosa. "I don't know where to begin."

"Ah, but you do, dear one. If you didn't, you wouldn't be sitting in my house right now." Her turquoise eyes flicked a knowing glance over to Gunnar, then back to Nicole. "And you wouldn't have a Lash demon for a... travelling companion."

Nicole stared at her tea, feeling as if the witch could see into her soul. And why shouldn't she, if she was as ancient and powerful as Gunnar said? Her witchy skills probably included things that Nicole couldn't even imagine, least of all picking up on the fact that she and Gunnar had been intimate. Unsure of what to say, she looked at Gunnar.

He chose to change the subject. "What can you tell us about the coin?"

"Oh yes. It's ancient. See the symbol in the middle here? This is the mark of the Gar demons. This is an actual piece of the currency they used."

"Gar demons," he said. "They're supposed to be a myth, too."

"That's because they haven't existed for a millennia. They were all killed in a fierce battle with the Domu demons."

"The Domu eliminated an entire species?"

"Yes, they had a lengthy war over territory. The Domu finally won and took everything the Gars possessed." The witch turned the coin over in her palm. "These do not carry much value anymore. It belongs to a Domu. But why one would bother with this old coin, I can't say."

"But when Nicole found it, there were Skells involved. No other demons. Our assignment is to investigate Skell activity. They've been causing more trouble with the humans in our city. Maybe they've allied themselves with a Domu?"

The witch smoothed her silver hair. "You know Skells are always looking to partner with powerful allies. And, with the exception of the Lash, the Domu are as powerful as they come."

"Couldn't a Skell have randomly stolen this from the… Domu demon?" Nicole broke in.

"And walked away with its life? Not likely," Gunnar replied. "The Skells are remarkably incompetent."

"So you need to find yourselves a Domu demon. And you need to tread carefully. There are some demons you can never underestimate." Rosa's eyes pinned Gunnar with a look that made a muscle tick in his jaw. He swallowed hard, and Nicole made a mental note to later ask him what that was all about.

"Are you offering advice?" he asked.

"I know of an item that will give you the means to defeat a powerful Domu. I can tell you where to find it…for a price."

Nicole looked to Gunnar, eyes wide. She shouldn't expect that any of these creatures would help them out of the kindness of their hearts. Raneiro had, but he and Gunnar were bonded through shared battles as well as decades of friendship.

"What price do you ask?"

Rosa turned her gaze to Nicole. "First, a lock of hair from

your lovely Solsti."

Nicole gulped. She didn't know anything about witchcraft, but from what she had seen on TV and in movies, a person's hair could be a powerful element in a spell. "My hair? What do you want with it?"

"Don't worry child. I mean you no harm. I will simply hold on to it until the time is right."

The witch had a point. She could have probably killed her a dozen different ways by now, if she had truly wanted to. Still, Nicole hesitated. In helping Gunnar, could she unwittingly put herself into a dangerous situation?

He seemed to be considering something also. "And the second?"

"You will bring your sisters to meet me."

Uncertainty flooded Nicole's veins. Despite her power, Rosa had been the picture of hospitality today. And who could blame her for wanting to meet the other Solsti, because they were apparently so very rare? Nicole looked to Gunnar.

Blue eyes twinkled and he nodded. "It'll be okay."

"It's settled, then." Rosa smiled, satisfied. "I knew I woke up feeling magnanimous this morning for a reason! Now then," she continued. "You need to travel to the wood nymphs of Rivkin. They hold the ashes of a dead Domu. Bring this ash into contact with the owner of this coin, and it will render him helpless."

"How did a group of wood nymphs acquire a weapon like that?" Gunnar asked incredulously. "They aren't exactly known for their fierceness."

"The ashes are not from just any Domu, but from Xarrek, the mage."

Gunnar's mouth opened and closed. "How—"

"Xarrek met his demise in the Rivkin Forest. The nymphs crept out after the other Domu left, and collected his ashes before the wind scattered them."

"Um, can one of you fill me in on the details?" Nicole interrupted.

"Xarrek was exceptionally greedy for power," Gunnar began. "He had the talent to cast basic spells, and he worked at building his skills. He wanted to achieve the sorcery level of a mage. He figured that if he could do that, he'd be invincible. But he wasn't subtle about it, and when the other Domu realized that he was getting stronger, they stopped him. A large group of them followed him into the woods one day and attacked. He fought back using both his physical strength and his magic, but he was outnumbered. After they killed him, they set fire to his body to ensure he wouldn't rise again."

"Why did they leave his ashes?" Nicole asked.

"The Domu were unaware of the potential danger. Normally, ashes wouldn't affect them. But since Xarrek had become a powerful mage, his physiology was altered."

"And the nymphs knew this?" Gunnar asked.

"The nymphs made a shrewd and accurate guess."

"So, a trace of him remains," Nicole said.

"Indeed it does," Rosa agreed. "And the nymphs will be happy to gain an ally like you. Both of you." She produced a pair of silver scissors from her pocket and, leaning over, snipped a lock of Nicole's blond hair. "Now then. You will eat with me. You'll need sustenance. The forest is half a day's journey from here."

As if on cue, the pot on the stove bubbled vigorously. Rosa stood, tucked Nicole's blond hair into a tiny silver box, and put the box back into her pocket. She pulled three large bowls from the cupboard and filled them with the contents of the pot. The delicious aroma that Nicole had noticed when they arrived intensified, making her mouth water.

"That smells divine," she said.

"It's my special recipe—rabbit stew." The witch placed the bowls on the table. *An ancient witch is serving us a home-cooked meal.* Nicole decided to stop thinking that things couldn't get any weirder. Every time she did, she ended up in a situation she could never have imagined. So she simply smiled and thanked Rosa. "Mmm." She breathed the steam in front of her.

After eating their fill, Gunnar and Nicole took their leave of Rosa and her tiny fairy tale home. The witch surprised her by giving both of them a warm embrace. As they left the clearing and entered the shade, Gunnar threw a huge arm across her shoulders and squeezed her into a hug. "Rosa really liked you."

"I'm glad she did, but I didn't do anything special. And she seemed so sweet. What were you talking about before? Can she really zap someone?"

"Yes. And you, my dear, must have some kind of innate charm. Rosa doesn't like many people. More like she merely tolerates them. If you cross her, she is fully capable of turning you into a toad."

"A toad? Really?" she gasped and shook her head. "I'm glad we didn't see that side of her today. How long have you known her, anyway?"

He paused and tilted his head as if mentally counting the decades. "I met her shortly after I started working as a Watcher, so it's been over a hundred years. She's very independent. She gets involved in conflicts only if she chooses to, but usually she stays out of things."

"I hope she chooses our side, when it comes time to fight whatever is out there."

"If this morning was any indication, then my guess is she will. She wasn't kidding about being magnanimous. She not only identified the coin, but she also volunteered the information about Xarrek's ashes. For her to do so, something pretty big is about to hit the fan."

His words unleashed a sudden memory of her favorite Shakespeare play, *Macbeth*, and she smiled. "By the pricking of my thumbs, something wicked this way comes."

"Yes." He frowned. "This is serious, Nicole."

"I didn't say it wasn't." She reached for his hand. "It's just a lot to absorb. I like to take things one day at a time, and the last few days have been a complete information overload. Although, today has been a pretty nice day so far. We had a good meeting with a witch, had a delicious lunch, and no one's attacked us.

And," she grinned. "I was woken up in the most *delightful* way. Twice."

In a blur of motion, she was whisked off the path and pushed against a tree, his big body pressed tightly to hers. Heat radiated from his skin straight to her core. "I'm glad you're so perky in the morning," he said before his lips covered hers in a kiss that was too short. "But as for the woods, don't speak too soon. You never know what's out here."

"Well, there are wood nymphs somewhere. Are they going to attack us?"

"No, not the nymphs. They'll put on a show of bravado, but they're quite far from here."

They stepped back to the path, shadowed by ancient oaks. This section of the forest had a healthy cover of purple flowering plants under their feet, and Nicole saw several more of those two-headed blue jays. Bees buzzed around the flowers, and sparrow-like birds flitted between the trees and bushes. "This looks so much like home," she murmured.

"Yes, this area is much like Earth. But not all of Torth is as nice as this."

"What do you mean?"

"Some parts are volcanic, dark and gloomy. And some cities are desolate. Imagine if all of Chicago looked like a fire-bombed, war-torn city. There are places where nothing grows. Everything is smoky, grimy, and polluted. Sometimes the sun can barely penetrate the haze." The grim set to his jaw spoke volumes more than his sober words.

"Have you...had to spend much time in those places?"

"Yes," he replied tersely.

"By choice?"

"No. And yes." At her quizzical look, he gruffly continued. "There were some years that I had no choice. And then I became a Watcher, and those visits were part of my duties."

"You didn't want to go back."

His only answer was a shake of his head, and she decided this wasn't the time to push him. Whatever had happened in his past must be a boxful of painful memories, and Nicole knew all too well how hard it could be to open that lid. Her fingers itched to hold onto his, to touch him somehow, but she knew he wouldn't want an attempt at comfort for something that had happened before he even met her.

They walked in silence under the oaks. Nicole was glad for the hearty lunch Rosa had provided. The path took them along the banks of a small river, where she glimpsed a few water sprites splashing in the crystal current. She didn't mind walking, but she hadn't realized that the primary method of transportation here would be her feet. Then again, she hadn't known what to expect. *Flying dragons? Magic carpets? More portals?* She had so much to learn about this new world.

She was about to suggest they take a break when Gunnar stilled, putting his hand on her arm. A rustling sound came from the path ahead of them. Silently, he tugged her into the bushes. Whatever was on the path wasn't making an effort to be quiet. In fact, she actually heard muttering.

The source of the muttering came into view. It was, of all things, a Skell demon. Smaller than the one she had seen in Chicago, this one walked alone, babbling to itself.

In one swift movement, Gunnar leapt onto the path in front of the Skell, blocking its way. The creature yipped and whirled to run back the way it had come, but Gunnar grabbed its spindly arm. "What is your business in these woods?" he snarled.

"J-just on my way home," the creature said with forced brightness.

"Quite a round-a-bout way to go home. Try again."

The Skell gaped at him, as if it had lost the ability to speak. Then it started thrashing about, trying to get free of Gunnar's grip. He leaned closer and growled, "Your kind has been causing a lot of trouble for me on Earth. How about you fill me in on what's going on?"

"I don't know anything about the ones on Earth," it protested, still struggling. "I don't get to leave Torth."

As the smaller demon twisted and flailed, Nicole saw a flash when something fell from its pocket. She darted from her hiding spot in the bush. Gunnar gave her a warning look, but she held up her hand. "Don't start with me," she warned. "This guy dropped something."

She knelt on the path, running her fingers through the carpet of leaves and flowers, and quickly found what she was looking for. A silver coin. Identical to the one she'd found in the city. Wordlessly, she held it up for Gunnar to see.

He gripped the Skell by its upper arms. "Who do you work for?"

"No one." The creature was a terrible liar.

"I'll ask you one more time before I start relieving you of your fingers," Gunnar hissed, and repeated his question.

Nicole gulped. Would he really start dismembering the Skell demon? Did he do this kind of thing often? She felt a sudden pang that despite the intimacies they had shared, she didn't truly know him as well as she should.

"No one," the Skell repeated in a barely audible whisper.

"Wrong answer," Gunnar grunted, and Nicole jumped as she heard the crunch of bone. Relief washed over her when she saw that he had merely broken its finger, not ripped it off.

The creature howled. Gunnar glared at it, waiting. He raised its hand as if to repeat the procedure.

"Wait!" the demon panted. "I don't know what the Skells on Earth are doing. Truly I don't. I don't have the ability to telepath."

"But you have this," Nicole said, still holding the coin.

"Those are rather rare," Gunnar growled. "Why don't you be a good little Skell and tell us where you got it?"

"I-I f-found it," the Skell stuttered. "In the forest. Just like you did, j-just now when you picked it up."

Nicole raised her eyebrows. These creatures really *were* incompetent.

Gunnar shook it by its arms again. "You try my patience, Skell. Where did you get that coin?"

"I don't know his name. He has a bunch of these."

"What's his name?"

The Skell shook its head.

"Then think harder," Gunnar hissed and broke another of the demon's fingers.

The Skell shrieked and tried to wring its hands, which were hanging limp beneath Gunnar's punishing grip on its arms. It hung its long gray head. "He'll kill me."

"Then it looks like you'll see hell soon, because if your master doesn't kill you then I will." Gunnar's voice was icy, calm, and loaded with menace. "Talk."

The Skell hesitated.

"If you don't feel like sharing then I'll find another one of your friends who will, and I'll still learn what I want to know." Gunnar's face darkened with rage barely contained. "I don't have time for your bullshit." He crunched another finger.

"Okay!" the demon wailed. "Okay, okay, I'll tell you. His name is Maeron."

"Maeron," Gunnar repeated. "Now was that so difficult?"

The Skell sniffled and squirmed.

"Tell us more about him."

"I don't–" the creature began, but changed his tone at Gunnar's menacing glare. "I only know a little about him. Just that he has a lot of these coins, and he's on Earth."

"What is his business on Earth?"

"I just know that he took a lot of Skells there. I don't know what he wants them to do."

"You don't know?"

"No," the creature said. "I really don't."

"You've said those words too many times today." Gunnar slammed one strong hand forward to connect with the demon's jaw. It immediately slumped in his grip. Gunnar looked at it for a second, then nodded, "He'll be out for awhile." He dropped the creature behind a clump of shrubs several yards off the path.

Nicole watched him wordlessly. She didn't know whether to be horrified or thrilled at the way he took charge of the situation. *He has a job to do.* He needed to gather information and keep her safe, both of which he did with remarkable ease. But this wasn't the first time she had glimpsed the fury that seemed to simmer painfully close to the surface. She itched to dig deeper, to peel back all the layers that made up the impossibly handsome and lethal male before her.

She knew instinctively that he would never harm her. It defied explanation, the certainty that she was safe as a newborn babe with him. But how much would he share with her? How close would he let her get to the thoughts that kept him up at night?

Aware that she was staring at him, and unsure of what to say, she blurted, "Are you okay?"

He looked at her as if she had grown another head. "Yes," he said evenly, holding her gaze. "Are you?"

"Yes. So, uh," she swallowed. "Breaking fingers is all in a days work, huh?"

He closed the distance between them and gently tilted her chin up. "Nicole, you saw me decapitate and burn several Vipers yesterday. Does this upset you more?"

"Not exactly. It's just that today, that...thing seemed kind of pathetic, like it couldn't actually hurt us. The Vipers were going to kill us, so obviously you had to...kill them."

"You're right. That Skell is pathetic. They all are. And it wasn't capable of harming us. That's why I didn't kill it. But we needed to get any information out of it that we possibly could. And if that involved breaking a few bones, then yeah, that's my job. And look what we learned—now we know the Domu's name." He lightly caressed her cheek, and it wasn't lost on her that his hand, now so gentle, had recently caused bodily harm to another. "Our world can be vicious, Nicole. Everything has its price. And there are those of us who do what we can to maintain the balance, to keep dark forces from having too much power."

Blue eyes gazed down at her. "I realize your introduction to our world has been rather abrupt. I wish it could have been easier for you, but I can't change it." He bent low enough so his lips brushed the tip of her ear. "I'll answer your questions and teach you what I know. And I'll keep you safe."

"I do feel safe with you," she whispered. She was burningly aware of just how much bigger he was than her, and the barest touch of his mouth sent tingles through her body. Images of their morning shower together flooded her brain. "I'm glad you found me."

He started to say something, but his words died on his lips as she tugged his mouth down to meet hers. She wound her arms around his neck and pressed her body against his, needing to feel his strength and heat. Tenderly, his lips moved over hers before she felt him smile.

He looked down at her with twinkling eyes, and she felt a flutter at seeing the adorable dimples framing his grin. He shouldn't be adorable. He was a demon, for heavens sake.

"Such a temptress," he said softly, tracing the contours of her lips. "But not here. You deserve better."

She smiled up at him. "I see the gentleman has returned."

"Yes, and the gentleman will have trouble walking for a bit."

"I'll make it feel better later," she whispered. That earned her a smack on her bottom and a sly grin.

"Let's go. And don't worry about the Skell. His bones will be healed by the time he wakes up."

They continued walking, the oaks giving way to a wide variety of trees that towered overhead. Small purple flowers, as well as pink roses on crawling vines, covered the forest floor. She stopped to take a closer look at the deep fuchsia petals, then jumped backward when the biggest cricket she had ever seen leapt out from the blooms. Gunnar chuckled at her and she tried to glare at him, but ended up smiling instead. Her body hummed with thoughts of what she was going to do to him later, when they were out of these beautiful but dangerous woods.

A sudden sense of foreboding pricked the back of her neck, and she realized her thoughts about the woods were too accurate. Gunnar whisked her off the path when she heard several thuds. It sounded like something—or several somethings—

had just landed all around them, trapping them on the trail. She stared at the beasts directly ahead of them and barely managed to stifle a scream.

There stood two red-skinned creatures, as tall and muscular as Gunnar, but with bulging eyes and horns protruding from their bald heads. They looked like some diabolical monsters from a comic book, but these were very real. As she stared in horror, one of them opened its mouth and hissed in a gravelly voice, "Lash and fae! Don't bother running." Its face broke into a sinister grin. "Or we'll shred your skin so slowly that you'll wish you hadn't."

CHAPTER 10

"SHIT. GHAZSUL DEMONS." GUNNAR SENSED two more behind them. Raniero was right about these woods being more dangerous than before, because Ghazsuls didn't live anywhere around here. The Ghazsul demons didn't fight as well as the Lash or even the Vipers. They had decent skills with a blade, but thankfully they didn't use arrows. Gunnar and Nicole were outnumbered. His heart hammered with the challenge to protect Nicole and fend off all four of them at the same time.

Gunnar pushed Nicole behind him and hurled a ball of demonfire at the nearest Ghazsul. It dodged to one side, avoiding a direct hit, but the fire singed and popped along its thick upper arm. It hissed and glared at the black streak of sizzling flesh on its bicep, then turned to Gunnar.

"Everything you do to us, Lash," it growled, "we will do twice as slowly and twice as painfully. To her."

"Like hell you will." Gunnar turned to Nicole. "Stay back. Use your dagger if you have to, but keep out of this!" He needed her to listen. The primal need to protect her filled him, taking over his senses. He vowed to keep her safe, no matter the cost to him. His life, though immortal, was expendable. Her life was extraordinary, a rare light brought into the world for the purpose of saving it.

Long-buried visions sprang unbidden into his head, making him shake with rage. *Ghazsuls grinning as throats were slashed. Screams heard and innocent blood shed as a sunny day morphed into a living nightmare. His family's anguished cries. A frightened child who lost everything.*

A familiar rush surged through his veins, filling him with the red haze of rage. His rational mind slipped under as the fury of a berserker took control, and his single focus became killing the red-skinned demons. He would end their lives, one after another, until he eliminated the threat to his female. Calm and logic would return when he destroyed the demons, and when Nicole no longer stood paralyzed with fear. Only then would he be able to pull back from the precipice of destruction on which he balanced. Only then would the man she knew be able to speak gently to her, to hold her in his arms.

With a snarl of fury he launched himself at the Ghazsul whose arm was still smoking. It leapt up at the last minute, his feet connecting with its chest. It stumbled back but didn't fall, and that gave Gunnar a split second to whirl and plunge his sword into its side. Black liquid spurted out, making the ground slick beneath them. The Ghazsul cursed loudly and swung its own blade at Gunnar, who had to duck low to the ground and roll to avoid it.

He paused, letting the Ghazsul creep closer even as its black blood continued to flow from its red body. At just the right moment, Gunnar drew upon his Lash speed and sliced upward, opening its belly completely. He followed it with a ball of fire, exploding the Ghazsul into burning bits of flesh and tissue along the forest floor.

The next demon sprinted toward him. Gunnar stood his ground.

"You would like to see her disemboweled, then?" It leered at him. "We'll keep you alive long enough to watch."

For a split second he was back in that awful place, frozen, watching the slaughter of those he cared for. But his childhood was far behind him. Gunnar roared and charged the demon. No longer capable of speech, he swung his sword mercilessly, landing blow after blow on the Ghazsul's torso. It grunted and drew ragged breaths at Gunnar's assault, its sword arm hanging low.

The tip of his sword sliced the demon's bicep. It let out a deafening, agonized bellow and howled something in another language to one of the Ghazsuls behind him. At the same time, Nicole shrieked.

He turned to see her struggling as one of the demons held her tightly against its chest, its claw-tipped fingers tearing the flesh of her bicep. Her arm reddened as the sweet scent of her blood filled the air. The demon's face contorted into a hideous grin as a set of black leathery *wings* appeared from its back. Gunnar stared, stunned. When the fuck had Ghazsuls gained wings, let alone the skill to magically hide them and produce them when needed?

Nicole's anguished cries snapped him back to the moment, just before the demon in front of him took another swing. He pivoted, avoiding its blade. Renewed fury burst through his body as he surged forward. The Ghazsul stumbled on the uneven ground of the path, and Gunnar took the opportunity to sever its head.

He looked up as the leaves in the trees rustled. The Ghazsul held Nicole in an iron grip, and it was rising off the ground, its wings beating slowly with the vertical take-off. Through the haze of rage, Gunnar's tactical mind sprang to life. Unless she had moved the dagger from its holster on her leg, Nicole wouldn't be able to retrieve it to stab the Ghazsul. But she could do something else.

"Nicole! Bring it down!" he bellowed. He didn't know if she would be able to understand him. His voice didn't sound the same, even to himself. His ears buzzed, red clouded his vision, and his body hummed with battle rage. Nothing about him would be familiar to her right now. He prayed she would trust him, that she would not be afraid of what he looked like. He only knew that if she could force the air around the demon's wings to bring it closer to him, then he had a chance to free her.

Pain seared Nicole's arm, radiating down through her entire

body. The nightmarish creature held her so tightly that her skin felt the prick of each one of its claws, and the more she struggled, the more they dug in. She was sure the ones that Gunnar had fought didn't have wings. Her heart hammered in her chest as she looked to Gunnar for help. His blazing eyes locked onto hers, his voice roaring a command that she couldn't understand. Her blood turned icy as the creature's wings pushed upward, creating air currents in their wake...

In a flash of clarity, she understood. *I can prevent this thing from flying!* She grabbed at the air currents with her mind, turning them into powerful gusts that rocked the demon back and forth. It grunted and pushed harder.

Nicole reached for the breezes that swayed the branches higher in the trees, turning them into gales and bringing them forcefully downward. Her arm was on fire, but she pushed aside the pain as determination sung through her blood. The Ghazsul demon's feet bumped the ground and it stumbled, nearly falling on her as it clutched her tightly. She continued to force the wind against its wings from behind. It let out a roar of rage as it struggled. She had precious few minutes and hoped fervently that Gunnar was right behind them.

A flash of silver confirmed her hopes as her warrior's blade sliced down through one of the Ghazsul's black wings. It screeched and released her. She ran for the area behind Gunnar, figuring that would be the safest spot, but the last of the red demons grabbed her before she got far. She yelped as it grasped her injured arm. Its wings were raised, their span even greater than that of its kin. Her fear turned to anger. Nicole mentally dared it to try to fly away with her.

She turned back to watch Gunnar, looking for a way to help him. Not that he needed it.

His blue eyes glowed with an inner fire brighter than any she had seen in him before. His gaze seemed simultaneously far away and resolutely focused on fighting the red-skinned demons before him. The angles of his face had grown harsher. His mouth curled into a vicious snarl and, inside, his teeth appeared longer and sharper. The tips of his fingers sprouted honest-to-goodness claws. He looked like a different, more frightening version of himself. The feral growls that came from his mouth sounded nothing like the sensual timbre she had been listening to for days.

His eyes shone as he struck relentlessly at the Ghazsul. It tried unsuccessfully to fold its wings, and now the injured wing hung at an odd angle, dragging on the ground like an unwieldy limb. The Ghazsul struck out, reaching for Gunnar's vulnerable core, but it missed and sliced its blade across his thigh. Blood spurted from the wound, but Gunnar only grunted and kept moving.

It seemed an eternity that Gunnar's sword clashed and clanged against the Ghazsul's. Neither one gave in. Riveted by the battle, Nicole worried that Gunnar's strength wouldn't last. He had already fought off two of the things, but the Ghazsul had incurred a more grievous injury to its wing. Then again, Gunnar seemed to have barely broken a sweat. Maybe whatever made his eyes glow so brightly, whatever had changed his features, gave him extra stamina.

As he swung methodically at the Ghazsul, she saw that in his other hand he held a shorter blade. He struck the red demon in the thigh, slicing through muscle and down to the bone, making the creature waver. In the instant that the Ghazsul hesitated, Gunnar plunged the dagger into its neck and dragged it lengthwise, then drew his sword along the path that his dagger had taken. Black blood flew as the Ghazsul's scream was cut short, its head already falling to the ground.

Gunnar whirled to face her and the last Ghazsul, who still clutched her upper arms. She had the fleeting thought that she should be feeling faint from blood loss, but she wasn't. Maybe Gunnar was right–maybe being a Solsti had given her some enhanced healing abilities after all.

Right now, her vision was captivated by the man before her. Blood covered his body, both his own and that of the three demons he had slain. Within the hard mask of his face, his eyes flashed an inhuman blue and he let out an animal-like roar. She had no idea what was happening to him, and yet, she had no fear of him. She knew that the big demon she had grown fond of existed somewhere inside that terrifying figure.

Her captor's wings were still extended, and Nicole focused her energy. She summoned a fierce gust that blasted it from behind, causing it to stumble and loosen its grip on her arms. Grabbing her dagger, she spun and hurled it at the demon's belly.

It lifted off the ground, avoiding her blade, only to screech and dive for her. She hit the ground as Gunnar jumped in front of her, landing in a crouch. With his sword pointed at the demon's soft underside, it had seconds to change direction. Breathing hard, it landed several feet away from Gunnar.

She rolled a short distance away and crouched near a cluster of thick shrubs, watching the two demons circle each other. This Ghazsul moved as fast as Gunnar, and in a flash it unsheathed its sword and thrust forward. Gunnar dodged the blow, but the Ghazsul repeated the strike, this time rising slightly off the ground as it struck. Gunnar's shoulder took the tip of the blade before he could pivot out of the way.

That bastard. Gunnar could probably take it down eventually, but she wanted so badly to help. And she didn't want him to garner any more injuries, accelerated healing ability or not. Since the creature hadn't folded its wings, it was as dumb as it was ugly, and it was fair game.

"Try that again," she murmured.

The two males parried back and forth. Gunnar managed to fling a few fireballs, but the Ghazsul dodged most of them. Nicole watched and waited impatiently for her chance. Finally Gunnar got the opening he needed, and tossed a ball of fire directly at the Ghazsul's belly. The red demon had to rise up a few feet to avoid being incinerated, and Nicole was ready for it. She instantly summoned a vicious vortex that caught the huge leathery wings and knocked the demon on its back. Swifter than she had ever seen him move, Gunnar released two fireballs. Flames consumed the Ghazsul in seconds, reducing it to ashes on the forest floor.

Nicole rose from her spot next to the shrubs. Gunnar turned to stare at her, his eyes travelling the length of her body before returning to meet her eyes. Blue fire pierced her with an expression she couldn't read as he stood there, still as stone. "Gunnar." She took a step toward him.

He opened his mouth, flashing those newly sharp teeth, and made a muddled sound.

"Don't try to talk." She stepped closer. "You're hurt. I want to check your leg and your shoulder." He rumbled something deep in his throat that may have been a warning, which she pointedly ignored as she walked within arm's reach of him.

Sharp features and unnatural turquoise eyes regarded her as he remained motionless. She still didn't understand what had happened to him or if he was going to stay that way, but she was compelled to draw nearer. "Gunnar." She put as much tenderness in her voice as she could, gingerly extending her hand. His eyes glanced to her open palm and then back up to her face.

To her surprise, he dropped to his knees in the grass, his head bowed. She instantly knelt in front of him, winding her arms around him, mindful of his injured shoulder. He shuddered and relaxed into her as she gently stroked his hair. She murmured his name, not caring that she was now covered in the same blood and demon guts that slicked his clothes. Finally he raised his head and looked at her.

Familiar blue eyes locked with hers. Big hands that were calloused—but not clawed—skimmed lightly down her arms. She reached up to caress his cheekbones, now softened into the gorgeous face she knew. Frowning, she put her thumb on his lower lip and peered inside his mouth. Yep—his teeth were back to normal, too. A smile of relief filled her face. "Welcome back," she whispered.

He wrapped his arms around her waist and crushed her to his chest so tightly that she could feel the pounding of his heart. He lowered his head and buried his face in her loose hair, her ponytail long gone. Drawing back suddenly, he cupped her face in his warm hands and gazed at her for a moment before covering her mouth with his. He kissed her tenderly, as if she was a delicate flower. She parted her lips to flick her tongue against his, reminding him that she was far from delicate, and he groaned as he deepened the kiss. He broke away to graze his lips across the tip of her nose, then he murmured her name. Or rather, he tried to. His voice crackled like broken gravel.

"Gunnar." She searched his face. "Are you okay?"

He nodded, and then came fully back into himself. His hand went to her arm, inspecting it.

"This cut *was* deep," he croaked as he gave her wry smile. "Looks like you're able to heal quickly, too." He scowled. "When that demon did this to you, I wanted to rip each of those claws out one by one. Through his throat."

She blinked. "Um, okay." Shaking off the violent image, she met his eyes. "Gunnar, what happened to you?"

He looked at her for a long moment. They were still kneeling, so he pulled her down to a sitting position and seated himself next to her. "I didn't mean to scare you."

"You didn't scare me. I mean, yeah, you *looked* scary...but I didn't think you were going to hurt me."

He took her hand. "I would never hurt you. I know I'm not capable of that, no matter what state I'm in."

"State?"

He ran a hand through his thick hair, then stopped, frowning as he encountered demon goop. Wiping his hand on the grass, he said, "Sometimes, when I'm in the middle of a fight, I...shift somehow. I become consumed by rage, and all I can do is kill my opponent. I can't snap out of it until the threat has passed. Or until I get killed."

Her brow furrowed. "But it didn't happen yesterday, when the Vipers attacked us."

"It doesn't always happen."

"What was different about today?" *Please keep sharing with me.*

"Ghazsul demons." His tone was clipped.

She opened her mouth to ask what was so special about the Ghazsuls, but he stopped her with a firm hand on her arm. "It's a long story."

She studied him, aware that he considered the subject closed, at least for today. *Time to change the topic.* "When you're like that, does it hurt?"

"No. Actually, I don't feel much of anything except fury. All my senses lock down. I was able to hear you scream, though."

"When you yelled, I couldn't understand you."

"I don't think I've ever attempted to speak while I was in battle rage before. But I was compelled to tell you what to do. I knew there was a way you could help yourself."

"So you can do more than kill, when you're in that state. You can think through the threat, find any weaknesses."

"Yeah, this time. I don't remember thinking about anything before. But today, I knew I had to protect you." He turned over her hand, tracing small circles on her palm. "You really weren't afraid of me? The way I looked, the things I did?"

She shook her head. "No. No fear. Not of you, anyway. I was just a little confused. I didn't know if, or when, you would go back to…to the regular you." She took in his sensual mouth and his handsome face before raising her eyes.

"You're amazing," he said softly, and leaned down to brush his lips across hers. She reached a hand up and wrapped it around his nape, keeping his mouth right where she wanted it as she kissed him tenderly.

He's worried that I think he's some kind of monster. But how could she? From the day they had met, his every word and action had been for the purpose of keeping her safe. She didn't care if he had to take on a more demonic appearance now and then. He was still the same man who was fair and just, and who mattered to her more than she ever expected. If he needed to know how she felt, she had told him as well as she could with words. And if he needed more convincing, she would show him with her body.

Still kissing him, he let her push him down on his back in the grass. God, the man could kiss. Suddenly the most naughty thought popped unbidden into her head. She sucked in a breath.

"What?" He ran a hand down her uninjured arm.

Her cheeks burned. "I just wondered...can you...I mean, would it be possible for you to...have sex while you're in that state?"

He stared at her, eyebrows raised, before flipping her to her back and grinning wickedly.

"If there was a river or lake nearby, I'd toss you in and we'd find out."

She covered her eyes with her hand. He must think she was a complete pervert. "I'm sorry. That was inappropriate."

He sat up, reaching for her hand and bringing it to his lips. "No, just a little surprising. You're full of those. I like that about you." He kissed her knuckles and grinned. "And to tell you the truth, I've never thought about it. Females don't usually stand around watching demon battles, waiting to jump the winner's bones."

She blew out a breath. "Well, good." She didn't want anyone jumping his bones except her. And now she was the one without words. They simply stared at each other for a minute, then she murmured, "We're both covered in muck."

"You could use a bath."

"So could you."

A devilish grin spread across his face he pulled her up and gave her a swift kiss. "On to Rivkin."

CHAPTER 11

As NICOLE AND GUNNAR WALKED, the lush forest gave way to sparse pines on rolling hills. Although tempted to ask if they were almost there, she didn't want to sound like a ten year old on a long car trip. The pines didn't appear to harbor nymphs, but she checked around the boulder when they stopped to rest.

"So, what are wood nymphs like?" She gulped from her water bottle, not caring that it wasn't cold.

"Small, good with a bow, and prone to tricks. They also enjoy sex, like all nymphs. And they don't have a lot of inhibitions."

No inhibitions? "What will happen when we get there?"

"We'll find out soon." He grinned. "We're almost there. And there's nothing to worry about."

Okay. He said not to worry about Rosa, and he was right about that. How bad could a group of nymphs be?

After a slow steady climb toward the nymphs' home, they crested a ridge. Trees grew thick at the base of the mountains. The creatures had chosen a perfect spot. They couldn't be surprised from the rear of the territory, and a river snaked across the open terrain in front of it. The sparkling water flowed between the nymph colony, and Nicole and Gunnar. The only access to the enclave was a wide wooden bridge stretching over it in an arc.

Nicole knew they would be seen well before they were even close to the bridge. "I hope they're friendly," she muttered under her breath.

"That won't be a problem. You may actually find them to be too friendly." His eyes roamed her body in admiration.

She shot him a sly grin. "I'll take that over those Vipers any day."

As they neared, a group emerged from the woods. They stopped on the bridge, one figure in front, the others behind in a defensive stance. Hands on swords, bows and arrows at the ready.

Gunnar strode forward, unconcerned with the display of weaponry. As he neared the foot of the bridge, the figure in front called, "Halt!"

Gunnar stopped and spread his arms. "We mean you no harm. We seek to discuss business."

"What business would that be, demon?"

"I hear you have something I may find useful. In return, I can offer you protection."

"Your name?"

"I'm Gunnar, of the Lash Watchers, and this my companion, Nicole."

"Gunnar," the leader said. "I've heard of you. The Lash have assisted us in the past. You are welcome here. I am Taszim, leader of Rivkin." Taszim's eyes narrowed as he took in their disheveled appearance and bloody clothes. "Are you injured?"

"We're fine now."

Nicole stood a few steps behind Gunnar, wary of the potential for all those arrows to fly at them. Now she moved next to him, getting a closer look at their newfound allies. Gunnar's description proved to be accurate. As the tallest nymph, Taszim stood a few inches over five feet. The group was made up entirely of short muscular males with hair in varying shades of brown. Their delicate faces held no battle scars, and they dressed in close-fitting brown tunics and pants.

Taszim inclined his head when he saw her. "Welcome to Rivkin, my lady." He gestured for them to approach, and the men behind him fell back to allow them to cross the bridge. As they walked toward the thick woods, Taszim said, "In the past, we sought you out, demon. I am most curious to hear what has brought you to us. But first, you will rest and eat."

At that moment Nicole's stomach rumbled. "Sorry," she mumbled in embarrassment.

"Has the demon not allowed you to eat, my lovely?" Taszim genially took her arm. Even though he was several inches shorter than she, his presence was commanding. He didn't seem to be put off at all by the fact that she had all kinds of nasty substances on her clothing. "I am confident that our kitchens will please you." He barked an order to one of his men, who jogged ahead. As they drew closer to the enclave's entrance, he named various trees along the path. Nicole was surprised to learn that this forest was full of many trees that were also found on Earth: copper beech, oak, maple, elm, and pine.

A figure emerged from the trees to glide gracefully toward them. Nicole couldn't help but stare at one of the most beautiful women she had ever seen.

"Taszim!" the woman called. "Stop jabbering. Our guests are probably dying to sit down and have a drink." Then she scrunched her little nose, looking up and down their bodies. "Shall I call our healer?"

She was tiny, not quite five feet tall, with huge green eyes and close-cropped dark chestnut hair. Her short haircut revealed ears with pointed tips, making her look like a genuine pixie. Like the men, she also wore a sleeveless brown tunic. Hers was fitted tightly, cut low in front, and her legs were bare. The fabric clung to her hourglass figure as she moved toward them, hips swaying, breasts bouncing.

Taszim stopped in front of her. "No, darling. They have already healed." He turned to Nicole and Gunnar. "Allow me to introduce my lovely wife, Larissa. She is truly my better half."

Did wood nymphs shake hands? Nicole opted for a simple nod of her head, saying, "It's nice to meet you. I'm Nicole."

Larissa pulled Nicole's arm from Taszim's and into her own. "You poor dear, travelling with this big creature and getting involved with something hideous along the way. You need to rest." The nymph's eyes raked over Gunnar's body appreciatively.

Nicole felt a flicker of possession, then confusion. She didn't have a claim on Gunnar. She remembered his words about the nymphs' lack of inhibitions and wondered if the other females here would also look at him as if they wanted to devour him.

"Nicole and Gunnar will be staying with us tonight." Taszim either didn't notice his wife's heated gaze, or he didn't mind it.

"Oh heavens, you're welcome to stay longer than that." Larissa tugged Nicole against her side and started walking toward the trees. She was surprisingly strong for such a tiny thing. "You will have a bath, then some tea, then we will get you ready for our evening meal. I think we can find something to fit you. You are so wonderfully tall, you know. Just like a willow. And the color of your hair is so golden, like the sun! We're all brunettes, you see. We're fascinated by new things. Especially when they're as lovely as you are."

Larissa chattered on, pulling her toward a towering tree and climbing into what looked like the basket for a hot-air balloon. "Come, darling."

Nicole glanced hesitantly over her shoulder at Gunnar, who walked a few steps behind with Taszim. His smile and wink put her at ease immediately. Clambering into the basket, she was startled when it began to move up.

"What—" Her eyes snapped to the edges of the basket, where sturdy vines stretched up into the canopy farther than she could see. She peeked over the side to see two males pulling the vines from the bottom. "Oh," she said sheepishly. "This is amazing."

The basket came to rest by a platform encircling a large wooden building, which could only be described as a tree house. *An enormous, breathtaking, fairy land tree house.* Intricate carvings on the doorframes mirrored the ones on the railing along the platform. This high up, the canopy was thick with intertwining branches, which allowed the structure to sprawl across several trees.

Larissa hopped out of the basket and, holding Nicole's hand, led her along the platform to a doorway well away from the lift. She opened the door and Nicole barely cleared the frame as she entered, suppressing a grin. *Gunnar will spend his entire time here ducking his head.*

Her attention veered to the huge bed in the center of the room. It was made of wood, of course, and had four actual tree trunks serving as posts. The posts rose to meet a smooth wooden canopy carved with more intricate details. Hanging from the canopy were yards of alternating silk and chiffon in varying shades of green.

It looked like it could sleep six adults comfortably. *Maybe it had.* She pushed the errant thought from her mind. The wood nymphs could do whatever they wanted behind closed doors. As long as they didn't do it with Gunnar, she amended. Nicole had the feeling that she was in over her head with the massive demon. Why did she care? She had only known him a few days.

She sighed, which Larissa misread. "Oh dear, is this room not to your liking? We have others, though they are smaller."

"No, no, it's perfect. It's amazing," Nicole assured her hostess. "I was just…lost in thought."

"You must be exhausted, my lovely. You've been tramping all over creation with that enormous demon. Let me take care of you." Larissa clapped her hands together and another petite, pretty brunette entered. She carried a tray of fruit and bread, as well as a pitcher of water. Another nymph behind her carried a basket with steaming, rolled up towels.

Larissa plucked one warm cotton bundle and handed it to Nicole, who gratefully wiped her hands, then repeated the process as Larissa gave her another towel for her face. Next, the nymph's strong hands on her shoulders pressed Nicole down into a cozy armchair. Handing her an apple, she ordered, "Eat." She settled on the ottoman in front of Nicole.

To her surprise, Larissa pulled Nicole's feet onto her lap, removed her shoes, and began to lightly rub her tired toes. She was definitely the most touchy-feely hostess Nicole had ever had. "You don't have to do that."

"Nonsense. We are honored to have guests such as you and your Lash."

Nicole recognized her cue to volunteer that Gunnar was, in fact, not hers. But she kept silent. Selfishly, she didn't want these lovely little creatures to throw themselves at his feet. Or give him lap dances. Or whatever wood nymphs did when they wanted to seduce someone. They were all gorgeous, and they probably didn't have to try very hard to get a man into their beds. She didn't want him to even look at any of them.

Squaring her shoulders, she smiled at her diminutive hostess. "We're grateful for your hospitality."

Larissa smiled back at her and instructed the other nymph to bring water for a bath. That's when Nicole noticed the large white enameled tub on the other side of the bed. Not one minute later, the female and several others returned carrying warm water to fill it. That seemed quaint, but the surprises weren't over. Next, a green dress and slippers were brought in. And *dress* was a rather generous term for the garment. It looked like it would hit just above the knee on a nymph, which meant that it would barely cover Nicole's butt.

"I think that might be a little short on me," she said as politely as she could.

"Hmm, perhaps. Your legs are so very long," Larissa murmured, her eyes appraising Nicole's limbs and then the dress. "We can add more moss."

"Moss?" Nicole took a closer look and realized that the dress was indeed made of moss. The fuzzy parts had been combed smooth and the fibers were woven tightly together. It did look a little sheer, though otherwise it was tasteful. It was short and fitted, with one strap stretching diagonally across the front from bodice to shoulder. "That's amazing," she breathed.

Still massaging her feet, Larissa looked up at her piercingly. "Would you like me to attend to your bath?"

"Um…" Nicole gaped at her, taken aback. Was Larissa

propositioning her? Did she help bathe all of her guests? She didn't want to be rude, but definitely preferred to bathe in private. *Unless I'm with Gunnar.* "I…I'm used to doing it myself. On Earth, we don't…I mean, I can…uh, no thank you."

Larissa only smiled at her, completely unfazed by her flustered response. "Of course, my dear. We shall give you some privacy and return later with the dress." She stood to leave and ushered the other females out. "Call if you need anything. We're close by." She smiled and closed the heavy door.

Nicole blew out a breath and sincerely hoped she hadn't just committed a huge faux pas. She stripped off her dusty clothes and lowered herself into the warm water. Like most tubs, it was too small to accommodate her long legs, but today she didn't mind. The water had been sprinkled with lavender, which made the whole room smell divine. Relaxation beckoned. Bent knees falling to one side of the tub, she leaned her head back and closed her eyes.

Her mind was instantly flooded with images of the last time she had bathed. She sighed and shifted as she remembered Gunnar's mouth at her breasts and his fingers teasing her cleft. She thought of his powerfully muscled thighs under her fingertips, and the sight of his enormous cock straining for her. She moved her hand beneath the water, stroked between her legs just once, and sighed again. Her slender fingers were woefully inadequate.

She'd wait for later, when she would have the chance to get him alone. At least, she assumed she would be alone with him later. No little wood nymph had better dare to flirt with her man. *Hers.* The thought startled her and at the same time felt very fitting. It didn't make sense, but there was simply no other way to describe the way he affected her. He was addictive.

CHAPTER 12

GUNNAR'S MIND WAS STILL REELING from the aftermath of the encounter with the Ghazsul demons. Not from the fight, or even from his spontaneous shift, but from Nicole's reaction to him. He had expected her to be terrified of the way he changed. For the gods' sakes, he hadn't even been able to speak. He was only able to bellow some unintelligible words at her. And she didn't break down. She didn't run. Instead, she tried to understand him, and she fought back using her ability in a way she had never done before, against a foe she had never seen.

Then there was her obvious concern for him, despite her bewilderment at his physical changes. He still felt the fury flowing through him for a few moments after he killed the last of the Ghazsuls. As he stood over its smoking body, her presence called to him. Two coherent thoughts formed in his mind: his female was safe, and the Ghazsul demons were dead. As he looked her over, seeing no severe wounds, the rage began to ebb.

He didn't know what would happen if she got too close to him. He wasn't sure that he could live with himself if he inadvertently hurt her in his altered state. But the beast inside him calmed to let her approach. It recognized that she was his, and as she boldly stood in front of him, murmuring soft words, the fury left him in a rush. He wanted to shout to the heavens with pride and relief that she wasn't afraid, but the crash from the adrenaline high brought him to his knees. His rational mind didn't understand, but his base nature did. His beautiful, brave

Solsti had wound her way into his very fiber, and there was no way he was letting her go.

Taszim's words broke into his reflections. "This way is our armory." He gestured ahead. The nymph had given Gunnar a thorough tour of the colony, partly to be gracious and partly to give Gunnar any logistical information that he may need in the future. The enclave at Rivkin housed many buildings, some on the ground and some in the air. They had yet to discuss the issue of the dead demon ash. That would come later, after a hearty meal and some nymphy entertainment.

Gunnar had first been shown to a room and taken a quick bath, then devoured a snack of fruits and nuts. He was dressed now for the impromptu banquet being held in honor of his and Nicole's visit. Nymphs loved a party as much as they loved company. And his state of dress was more of a lack thereof. All the males were shirtless. Growing up on Torth, he was accustomed to the preferences of the different species, including the nymphs' fondness for bare skin, but he could only imagine Nicole's reaction to the upcoming dinner.

He examined the impressive selection of bows and arrows. Like the Vipers, the nymphs had poison-tipped arrows, as well as wood, metal, silver, and iron. Other arrows were hooked or barbed. Their foes had different weaknesses, necessitating the variety of weapons. Swords and daggers, boomerangs and maces filled out the stock of battle gear. The nymphs knew how to put up a good fight, but some enemies would prove too strong for them. Their greatest weakness was fire. After all, they were creatures of the woods.

"You are well-armed," he told his host. For wood nymphs, the statement was true.

Taszim nodded. "We do our best to be vigilant, but we are aware of our limitations. Your help will be an asset."

"As will a certain item in your possession."

"Yes, of course. You have my word that we will soon speak of the reason for your visit. Would your lovely fae, Nicole, like to be present for that conversation?"

"Yes." Gunnar didn't know whether or not Nicole would want to be there when they discussed the ash, but he figured it was better to err on the side of caution. "And, Taszim?"

"Yes?"

"Nicole's not a fairy."

"Oh, my mistake! She is a sprite, then?"

Gunnar smiled and shook his head. "She, my friend, is a Solsti."

Taszim gaped at him. "But they are a myth."

"I said the same thing. But she's real. Rosa confirmed it."

"My stars…a Solsti. A great goodness necessitated by a great evil. And Rosa's rarely wrong." The nymph rubbed a hand over his jaw and leveled a look at Gunnar. "We are doubly honored, then, to be graced with the presence of such a rare creature."

They walked back to the large banquet hall on the lower level, the colony bustling with preparations. Delicious aromas wafted from the kitchens. Nymphs carried platters piled high with meats and breads. Swaths of bright fabric draped the walls. The music of stringed instruments emanated from the room, which was filled with long tables.

"Truly, friend, you did not need to go to all this trouble," Gunnar told his host.

"You know we love to celebrate. And now we have even more reason." Taszim spied his pixieish wife. "Larissa! My love, I have the most exciting news to share with you!"

Clad in a scant dress made of leaves and vines that wrapped around her curvy figure, she sashayed over to give her spouse an open-mouthed kiss. Then she turned to Gunnar, tugged his shoulders down, and did the same to him. Her actions didn't surprise him. Describing the nymphs as *friendly* would be an understatement.

Larissa gazed up at him. "Your fae has the longest and most lovely legs I have ever seen."

He couldn't suppress a smile, remembering Nicole's ankles hooked behind his back. "Yes, she certainly does."

"But that's just it, darling." Taszim didn't seem surprised at his wife's blatant admiration of Nicole. "Nicole isn't a fae at all. She's a *Solsti*."

"Taszim, dear, have you spent the last hour with Gunnar in the brew room? The Solsti are only a myth."

"You know, that's what *everyone* is saying these days."

Gunnar turned in the direction of Nicole's voice and froze. There she stood, endless legs on full display in a garment that he could only describe as lingerie. It was ridiculously short, with just one little strap running diagonally across her collarbone to hold it up. Moss-green in color, it matched her eyes perfectly...in fact, he realized as he took a closer look, it *was* moss. And because it was made of moss, it was almost sheer. Unable to draw his eyes from her figure, he could just make out the jut of her nipples beneath the "fabric." With a hidden reserve of strength, he forced himself not to look any lower down her delectable body. Even though he wanted to drink in every last inch of her, he had the sudden urge to cover her up so none of the other males could see her.

"What?" she asked, self-consciously smoothing a hand over her blond hair, which had been styled artfully atop her head.

"You look...beautiful," he said, searching for an adequate word.

"Thank you. You know, they had to add more *moss* to the length." She grinned at Larissa, who moved forward to embrace her. Nicole easily stood a foot taller than the nymph.

"It's still short," he said gruffly.

"Oh, never you mind what he says." Larissa playfully slapped Gunnar's hand. Nicole's eyes flashed at the contact. *Interesting.*

"My dear, I had no idea you are a Solsti," Larissa continued. "This is the most stunning and delightful news. Like most of us, I didn't think the Solsti truly existed. We're simply over the moon to have you here with us." Nicole smiled sweetly at their hosts.

"Please excuse us as we see to some last details." Taszim steered his wife toward the great hall. As they walked away,

Gunnar could hear him whisper to her about using the vines in her dress for another purpose later on that evening.

"Can you believe the way they dress here?" Nicole smoothed her hands over her hips. "Moss, for heaven's sake. And you, with no shirt. Not that I'm complaining." Her eyes drifted down his torso before moving back up to his face.

He stifled a groan at the movement of her hands and the appreciation in her eyes. "First, I'm not the only male here without a shirt. But I am the only one you should be looking at. Second, I've worked around nymphs before, so the dress code isn't a surprise to me. And third, that dress…" He trailed off, gripping her upper arm and leaning down to her ear. "It's going to drive me crazy all night."

"Hey, I didn't get to choose it. Larissa brought it to me. And she *did* have it made longer, so I couldn't refuse it. Not after…" she broke off and moved even closer, whispering, "She offered to *bathe* me!"

He raised his eyebrows. "She did? Well, she is a nymph after all. Remember what I said about them being friendly?"

"Yes, but, I didn't think they would…I mean, I hope I didn't offend her by saying I could do it myself."

"I'm sure she wasn't offended. That was probably her way of finding out what your preferences are."

"Oh my," she said. "I had no idea their hospitality extended that far."

"Actually, you may be in for another surprise tonight. Just wait for the entertainment portion of the evening."

Her green eyes widened. She opened her mouth, but before she could say anything, Gunnar felt a feminine touch on his arm. He turned to see a voluptuous nymph who barely reached his elbow idly running one finger along his forearm. Dark brown hair fell in waves to her waist.

"Welcome to Rivkin." the nymph gazed up at him with purposeful eyes. "I'm Diantha. Can I get you anything?"

She, too, had a "dress" made of vines and leaves, with heavy emphasis on the vines. She had only bothered to arrange a few leaves in strategic places along the front of her garment.

He diplomatically removed her hand from his arm. "It's lovely to meet you, Diantha. I'm Gunnar and this is Nicole."

Nicole looked ready to shoot daggers. "Hello. Your dress is so…artistic."

"Why, thank you." She didn't bother to look at Nicole. Her eyes were glued to Gunnar's chest. "We're so glad to have visitors like you. We want to make sure you're as comfortable as possible while you're with us."

"And we're so glad to be here," Nicole said with forced sweetness, twining her hand in his arm. "We were just going to speak with Taszim. It was nice to meet you."

She dragged him away from Diantha and into a corner of the hall near a great stone fireplace. As she walked in front of him, he had an excellent view of her ass, which was barely covered by the sheer moss dress. His groin tightened, remembering her firm little bottom pressed against him. "What was that all about?" she hissed.

"She's just a nymph being…well, a nymph," he said, feeling a burst of pride at her comments. "Honestly, that will probably happen again before the night is over. To you, as well," he added, before she could retort.

"Well then, I think that you and I had better stay joined at the hip," she muttered. "That dress was just strings and pasties."

Gunnar couldn't hold back a laugh at her indignation, and he pulled her close. "You're adorable when you're jealous." She started to protest, but he swiftly reversed their positions so that she backed up to the wall. Lowering his head so that his mouth hovered just above hers, he whispered, "I'd rather see that dress on you."

Taszim clapped his hands and the music quieted to a soft melody. His gaze landed on Nicole and Gunnar, and the nymph leader gestured for them to sit at the head table. "We are honored to have two special guests with us tonight." Taszim's eyes were merry.

The other nymphs smiled at them. Gunnar put his arm

around Nicole's waist and tugged her close as they approached the dais. Stepping up to the table, Taszim and Larissa embraced and kissed them. They all sat down and goblets of wine were immediately set at each place. The low beat of drums and trill of flutes filled the hall.

Gunnar sat next to Larissa, who chattered amiably while steaming bowls of soup were brought to them. As course after course was set on their table, he couldn't help but notice the female nymphs that stood just beyond the empty space next to him. A similar group of males stood on Nicole's side of the table.

"You know, Gunnar, you may partake of anything you like here at Rivkin." Larissa's eyes flicked to the females. "Truly."

He polished off his second braised turkey leg and glanced at Nicole who listened attentively, eating as Taszim spoke to her. Gunnar was only interested in the leggy blonde at the other end of their table, but he smiled and placed his hand over Larissa's. "Your hospitality is unparalleled, my lady."

"As is the radiance of your female. Have you known her very long? The return of the Solsti is wondrous, but I must admit it is also a little unsettling."

"You and I are in agreement again, Larissa. The Solsti are said to exist when there is a great need for their help. Right now, I don't know what we may be up against." He smiled as he glanced over at Nicole, listening intently to something Taszim was saying. "And I haven't known her long. You could say I just...found her."

"Aren't you the lucky one, then. If you don't mind, I'm going to whisk her across the room for a moment. I want to show her some of the treasures we have here in the great hall before my husband bores her straight to sleep." She turned to Taszim, wrapped an arm around his neck and pulled him close to kiss him, effectively ending his conversation with Nicole. "Darling, I'm going to borrow Nicole for a bit. I've been dying to show her how talented our weavers are. They are masters, and not just with moss." She winked at Nicole.

Nicole caught Gunnar's eye and shrugged. "I'd love to see them, Larissa."

The nymph took Nicole's hand and led her toward one of the beautiful tapestries that hung along the walls of the banquet room. It wasn't long before the two were surrounded by a bevy of males, who didn't seem the least bit bothered that they had to look up into Nicole's face to speak with her. Gunnar gritted his teeth, noting that most of them weren't looking at her face; rather, they let their gazes drop to ogle her lush, nearly naked body in that damn moss dress. He struggled to remind himself that they would be doing the same to any visiting female. And their own females, for that matter.

Speaking of female nymphs, Diantha appeared in front of the table. She had lost the few leaves that covered the tips of her breasts and the neat curls at the juncture of her thighs, so with only vines wrapped around her body, she stood practically naked before him. Given her earlier reaction to Diantha, Nicole would probably unleash a tornado if she looked their way right now. He kept his eyes on her face as she murmured, "I came to make sure you were enjoying your evening, my lord."

She was pretty, Gunnar had to admit. And before Nicole had come into his life, he would have accepted Diantha's offer without hesitation. But there was only one female on his mind now. He purposely gentled his words. "You honor me, nymph. But I must decline."

Diantha pouted. "I see. Let me know if you change your mind." She turned to join a group of males, taking one on each arm and walking to the other end of the room.

"Lovely girl." Taszim eyed Diantha's virtually bare backside. "As is your Nicole."

Gunnar nodded as he watched Nicole across the room. She chatted comfortably with the many nymphs surrounding her. Her eyes shifted over the bevy of brown-haired creatures, then sought him out. She winked like she'd expected him to be looking at her. *Damn.* His chest clenched at her loveliness. Her hair shimmered like a golden halo, and her smile exuded a sunburst of warmth.

At that moment the music changed to a pulsing, sultry beat. The mood in the great hall changed. Gunnar stood up to go to Nicole, but she was already making her way through the nymphs to join him. She pressed up against his side, whispering, "What's going on?"

"I think this is the entertainment," he replied in her ear, wrapping his arm around her waist.

They sat down at their table and looked toward the center of the room. Several female nymphs came forward and began to dance. They had abandoned their leafy attire and swayed slowly, completely naked but for the shimmery veils they twisted and twirled around their own bodies and each other's. Their limbs intertwined languidly as they came together in the middle of the floor. With one quick flash of silk, they drifted apart, each wrapped in another's veil. Their sensual movements of together and apart, covered and bare, continued in perfect rhythm to their primal music.

After a few moments they were joined by a number of males who were also nude. Gunnar knew where this "dance" was headed, but he was fairly certain it would be a first for Nicole. He glanced down to see her watching, wide-eyed, as the males each took a female and tied a veil over her eyes. Still moving to the sultry beat, the men held the women in their arms and began to dip them, lift them, and bend them into various graceful but blatantly sexual poses. Some of the females untied their veils and used them to caress their partners, or to give them a turn at being blindfolded.

Nicole watched raptly. He couldn't resist tracing the back of his hand down her side, deliberately brushing his knuckles along her breast. She gave a small gasp and turned to him, emerald eyes huge. "Are they going to…have sex? Right there?"

He nodded.

She sucked in a small breath. "Are we supposed to stay and watch?"

He nodded again.

She went on in a barely audible whisper, "Are we supposed to join them?"

This time he couldn't suppress a smile. "We certainly can if we want to. But we don't have to."

"Oh." She looked back at the dancers. "This is a new one for me." The nymphs' movements grew bolder, their hands and mouths moving over their partners' bodies. Nicole rested her hand on his thigh, sending a delicious warmth straight to his groin. She squeezed his leg as the nymphs abandoned the concept of partners and began to kiss and caress the skin of any others they could reach.

All of the males were visibly hard as they suckled at the taut nipples of whichever female was before them. Around the edges of the room, other nymphs had found partners and continued the activity of the dancers. Nicole tilted her head as she stared at the center of the room. A female nymph—he realized it was the friendly Diantha—was on all fours as she took one male into her mouth, a second male below her suckled her breasts, and a third male entered her from behind. It looked like Diantha's passion would be slaked tonight, despite Gunnar's rebuff.

Oh, he loved that his Solsti was curious. Still staring at the foursome, she tilted her head the other way and shifted in her seat. The scent of her arousal pierced his nostrils, making his mind go fuzzy. *Spicy, sweet, and utterly intoxicating.* Moving his hand up from where it rested at the curve of her waist, he cupped her breast. Her entire body jerked as she tore her gaze away from the nymphs and looked at him.

Pleased by her responsiveness, he drew her tiny earlobe between his teeth and released it, making her shiver. He traced the tops of her breasts just above the neckline of her dress. The pulse at the base of her neck beat a frantic tempo. With his lips a bare fraction away from hers, he whispered, "So what do you think of your first live sex show?"

Her eyes widened and her breath came faster as she watched him, her green gaze full of a raw sexual hunger that drew him like a magnet. His tongue flicked out to trace her lower lip and he dragged his fingers up her thigh. Her bare skin was soft as silk, and from the glimpse of her perky ass he had gotten earlier, she wasn't wearing anything under the dress. She grunted sweetly on a sharp exhale and swiftly pressed her lips to his. As her tongue darted into his mouth, he pulled her onto his lap and covered her breast again, his thumb teasing her nipple to a hard peak.

Her dress had ridden up, and he cupped her bare bottom with his hand. With her fingertip, she slowly traced a line down the center of his bare chest. She kept going when she got to his trousers, lightly skimming his hard length. He groaned, remembering the attention she had given him earlier with those hands and with her sinful mouth.

Urgency flowed through her kiss. She tangled her tongue with his, one soft hand on his jaw. Dragging his fingers along her bare ass, the thought of her damp heat made his cock swell even more.

She squirmed on his lap, her breathing uneven. "Can we go somewhere else? They won't mind?"

He glanced to the other end of the table. Taszim had unwrapped most of the vines and leaves from his wife's body, save for one that he used to bind her wrists behind her. Sitting on her husband's lap, Larissa's head was thrown back as Taszim pleasured her breasts with his mouth.

"They won't even notice." Gunnar picked Nicole up and carried her from the banquet hall. "Your place or mine?"

"Mine has a really big bed," she murmured, her mouth licking and tantalizing his neck. "But I don't remember how to get back there."

"I do." He had made a point to know where she was at all times, and he knew exactly which room she had been given. His long strides ate up the ground quickly, her silky hair brushing his shoulder, her arms wound around his nape. After a swift basket ride, they were alone in her room. He raised his eyebrows at the enormous bed. "You weren't kidding."

Still holding her, he started to walk toward it, but she

stopped him with a tug of her arms. Eyes dark with desire, she whispered, "Right here."

With a growl, he turned and pressed her against the heavy door. He hardened even more with the knowledge that she wanted him this very second. One swift tug of his hands and the flimsy dress disintegrated in downward swirls of moss.

She rubbed her bare breasts across his chest and circled her hips against his, her spicy-sweet scent filling the air. Her wild need shredded his control. They would have time to go slow later; now, he just needed to be inside her. He quickly freed himself from his pants and lifted her by her hips, then lowered her onto his raging erection with one deep thrust.

He cursed softly at the sensation of her sweetly hot sheath surrounding him. *Fucking amazing.* She moaned and rocked her hips, snaking one naughty hand between them to flutter against herself. *Again with those fingers.* Through his haze of lust, he made a mental note to make sure she couldn't use her hands on herself next time.

He bent his head to her breasts, taking one puckered pink tip into his mouth, and that was all it took. Her body bucked wildly against him with the force of her release. He raised his head to watch the ecstasy on her face as she shrieked his name. Her body squeezed him, flooding him with more of her delicious warmth, and then he came apart with her, pounding into her, pushing her even harder against the door.

CHAPTER 13

THE AFTERSHOCKS COURSING THROUGH NICOLE'S sated body were the only things keeping her from turning into a puddle of goo. She couldn't have lifted her head if she wanted to. The smooth wood at her back dimly registered. But her front...*mmm, yes.* Her front was all wrapped up in Gunnar's heat.

"Now will you let me take you to bed?" he murmured in her ear.

"Sure," she sighed, as Gunnar shifted their positions to cradle her against his chest. As if she weighed nothing, he carried her across the room to the huge tree-poster bed. He lowered himself down on top of her, leaning his weight on his strong arms, gazing at her.

"I think..." His grin radiated sex. "That I should take you to nymph shows more often."

"You'll kill me." She smiled in lazy satisfaction.

"It'll take a lot more than this to kill you."

"Then I guess we'll have to watch another one." She gazed up at the visual feast that was his body. Smooth skin covered rock-hard muscles everywhere. The solid wall of his bare chest, with its light dusting of dark hair, had tempted her all night. Every time she glanced at him she'd wanted to kiss her way across those thick slabs of muscle.

Apparently, so had others. Nicole took complete feminine satisfaction that he barely glanced at the pretty, curvy nymphs flitting around his elbows all night. She hadn't known what to expect here at the colony, with all the females being so willing and eager, but she needn't have worried.

Watching the nymphs have sex had been unexpectedly arousing. When she first realized what was going to take place, she wanted to leave the great hall. But once they started, she couldn't look away. *When did I turn into a voyeur?* Maybe it was just being here on Torth, literally a different world, which made her so interested. Or maybe it was just being among the touchy-feely, hyper-sexualized nymphs. Either way, she wasn't complaining. Gunnar certainly hadn't minded her reaction.

She looked up now in appreciation at his biceps, sculpted by years of fighting. He was long and lean. Not one spare ounce of flesh graced his powerful body. Her gaze trailed down his long torso to the hard ridges that made up his abdomen, and she couldn't resist reaching her finger up to trace them lightly. His muscles clenched at the contact, but he let her explore. A shiver of awareness shot through her as she paused at the top of the line of fine hair that trailed down lower, to his magnificent, thick penis, which was still semi-hard. For her.

As she stared, it twitched and grew. She looked up at him with wide eyes.

"That's what you do to me, Nicole." He leaned down to kiss her, his lips slowly exploring hers. The rough stubble on his cheek teased her when he broke away to nuzzle the sensitive skin between her breasts. He licked the soft undersides, then drew achingly close to one pebbled nipple.

"You have a bad habit," he whispered.

"I do?" she practically squeaked. *What is he talking about? And why is he talking at all?*

"Mmm-hmm." A quick flick of his tongue.

She jerked. "What's my bad habit?"

"Touching that sweet little clit of yours." He took her other nipple between his thumb and forefinger and then simply held his hand still. She shifted, trying to create the friction she needed. He nipped her shoulder and she shuddered.

"I thought men liked to watch women pleasure themselves."

"Wicked woman." The fingers on her nipple pinched ever

so gently. "You can do that for me later. But now, I intend to drive you out of your mind, until you can't move those little fingers except to wrap them around my cock. And," he paused, finally rubbing her nipple between his fingers. "I'll make sure of it."

"How?" Her legs shifted on the bed and heat flushed her skin as she tried to push her hips up to his, but he had other ideas. Reaching into the pocket of the pants he had dropped on the floor, he produced one of the veils from the dance.

She sucked in a breath and felt her eyes widen. "How did you get that?" She didn't remember him being near the dancers.

"I have my ways." He gave her a sly wink.

"Now who's the wicked one?"

"You have no idea." His eyes roamed her naked flesh. He took her hands in his and brought them above her head. Winding the veil around her wrists, he secured her to the tree-branch headboard.

He caressed his fingers down the length of her arm, across her collarbones, and down to her breasts. He traced circles, getting oh-so-close but not touching the sensitive tips. She wriggled in frustration. "Impatient already?" He made a tsking sound. "You may as well settle in. I intend to take my sweet time with you."

"You're torturing me."

"I'll make it feel so good though." He covered her body with his, and for the briefest second she felt the delicious brush of his chest against hers before he lowered his weight onto her. As he aligned their bodies she felt his hard length pressing against her belly, and she took a small measure of satisfaction in knowing he was as aroused as she was.

He lowered his face to hers and kissed her like he owned her. His tongue thrust inside her mouth, flicking the roof, sweeping into the deepest recesses. She angled her head to allow him to go deeper, eliciting a murmur of approval from him. When he finally drew back slightly to let her take a breath, she sucked his full bottom lip into her mouth, nipping it gently.

"That's right, Nicole. You're gonna feel my teeth, too." He dropped his head to her neck, nuzzling her throat, then moving to the sensitive spot where her shoulder began. He licked and scraped her with his teeth, and then he bit down. She jerked at the small pain of his sharp teeth. He held her there, teeth on her skin, licking and pressing her down. Shivers fired through her body at the dark eroticism of being bitten and restrained in such a primal way. And yet, there was a tenderness to his actions; he wasn't being gentle, exactly, but he was marking her, making her his.

His. The thought had barely formed in her mind when he moved down to focus on her breasts. Letting his weight rest on her legs, he traced one finger across each stiff peak. She couldn't hold back a moan. "Want your mouth," she rasped.

"Hmm." He held each tight bud between his fingers again, driving her insane. "And what do you want with my mouth?"

"Suckle me."

Thank goodness he obliged, swiftly taking one engorged nipple deep into his mouth. He sucked hard, swirling her with his tongue, while his fingers teased her other tip. If he wasn't pinning her in place, she would be writhing with need. But she knew he would make good on his promise to take his time. He released her, blowing a breath across her damp nipple, before attending to her other side.

His touch drove her crazy. She felt a rush of liquid heat between her thighs and knew she was more than ready for him again. By his smug grin, she guessed his enhanced sense of smell had picked up on it as well. He teased his finger down her belly and lower. Her muscles clenched in anticipation.

"You're so beautiful," he murmured as his wicked fingers deliberately skipped over her neat curls to caress her inner thighs. He bent his head to place kisses along the line he had just traced, then moved to her side and nipped her hip.

He moved lower still. "Your scent is intoxicating." He cupped her mound, then caressed her slick folds with his fingers. She writhed in earnest, seeking release, but his hands clamped down on her thighs. "Not yet." And then his mouth was on her, licking her up and down slowly, tortuously.

She squirmed against her restraints. "I need more, Gunnar."

With a low growl he indulged her need, circling her clit with his tongue and flicking it gently. He slid one finger inside her entrance, then two, pumping her in a sensual rhythm that matched his tongue. She rocked against him, unable to stop. Suddenly he sucked her clit hard, and she came on an explosion of sensation, her body convulsing against him.

She was still shuddering as he reared up. He pulled her ankles to his shoulders and dragged her hips to his cock. He filled her so completely, she felt as if he was nudging her womb. Not bothering with slow and easy, he thrust furiously with a need that matched hers. Blue eyes bored into hers. With a sly grin, he flicked her most sensitive spot with his finger. She came again, her body arching off the bed as she cried his name. He exploded right after, his hot seed filling her.

He collapsed on her sated body. *So big and heavy.* But she liked the feeling of him covering her. "I think I'm dead," she murmured.

He lifted his head long enough to nip her neck. "You can't die yet, remember."

"But this would be a good way to go. Having you fuck me to death."

Growling at her coarse language, he lightly slapped her thigh. "Devilish female." He shifted his weight and shook his head. "That settles it. You're the wicked one."

"You're the one who tied me up."

He glanced up at her bound wrists. "I think you've fulfilled your penance." He untied the veil.

She immediately rolled on top of him, stretching her body along his in the same way he had done to her. "Damn right." She rested her head on his chest, listening to his heartbeat as it slowed to a normal pace.

He rested one big, warm hand on the curve of her butt. "It was torture seeing the bottom of these perfect cheeks all night, under that damn excuse for a dress. You have such a sweet ass," he whispered.

"So do you." They lay like that for a few moments. Nicole wondered how her ability, something she once thought may be a curse, could have brought her to this powerful, sexy demon. She had never known anyone as fierce and dangerous as Gunnar, or as roguishly virile. The way her body responded to him was intense and out of control, like her mind had been left completely out of the equation. He had been both rough and tender with her, and she craved all of it. Lying on his muscular body, she knew she would never be the same. No man could elicit the same response from her. Ever.

Her neck throbbed where he had bitten her. "You marked me."

"I did."

"What does that mean?"

"It's a warning to all other males to back off."

She pondered his words. Was she supposed to do the same to him? She definitely wasn't interested in any other men, and she didn't want Gunnar to even look at any other women. But something niggled at the back of her mind.

Sure, their bodies were eager to be permanently joined, though she had only known him a few days. She cared for him, but she knew there was much more that she didn't know about him. Like when he had "encouraged" the Skell demon to divulge information earlier. She sensed a darkness in him and wished he would share it with her. She wanted to understand her demon on all levels. Wanted him to open his heart to her.

She also didn't want to lose the sweet intimacy of the moment. "I think they'll get the message." She lazily kissed his chest. "I've been wanting to do this all night."

He grunted his approval and stroked her ass. Her hair had freed itself from the nymphs' handiwork, and she let its loose length slide across his skin, nuzzling her way to one of his flat nipples. She kissed it, then flicked her tongue across it. "Does that feel good?"

"Yes," he rasped. "But keep it up and you'll find yourself on your—"

"No." She pushed up on her hands. "I want you like this, on your back. Let me explore you." She traced his lips with one finger. "Let me ride you."

A scoundrel's grin spread across his handsome face. "Yes, my lady. You can have your wicked way with me."

"Be a good boy or I'll tie you up." She leaned down to kiss his sensuous mouth, loving the feel of his soft lips and plundering tongue. She languidly moved down his throat, stopping to savor the woodsy, musky scent at the base of his neck. Her eager mouth found his chest again, licking every thick band of muscle. He tasted slightly salty, earthy, and wholly masculine.

She shifted to sit beside him on the bed, her hands caressing his huge biceps before moving down to his fingers. Bringing one hand up to her mouth, she kissed each knuckle. She licked the tip of one finger before lowering her mouth to cover it completely. He sucked in a breath, eyes locked on her mouth. She swirled and teased him like she had last night at the safe house, humming deep in her throat. His cock stood at attention, rigid and ready for her.

She released his hand and bent down to roam his abdomen with her lips, learning every hard ridge and sculpted dip. *God, he's perfect.* He may as well have been carved from granite and then come alive for her benefit. Her own personal Pinocchio, she thought wickedly, but with an entirely different body part capable of growing. When she got to his hip, she nipped him as he had done to her. He groaned and thrust a hand into her hair. He trailed it down her back and slapped her when he reached her bottom, then he nudged at her hip.

"Uh-uh," she murmured. "Not yet. Isn't that how you put it?"

He growled again but dropped his hand. She knelt between his legs. "You're huge." Her hair slid off her shoulder and tumbled across his thigh.

"You're a tease."

"But you know I'm a sure thing." She moved closer and licked him from root to tip, pleased to see a single drop of liquid had squeezed out. She lowered her lips and drew the shimmery bead into her mouth. His hands clenched the sheets.

She cupped and cradled his sac, enjoying the feel of his soft flesh in her hand. A soft curse left his lips.

Deciding to have mercy on him, she took as much of his length as she could. She sucked and flicked, loving his earthy taste. Knowing this battle-hardened warrior had turned to putty in her hands filled her with a heady rush. She brought him to the edge of his control and he held on, barely. *Because I asked him to.* Giving his balls one last massage, she moved her hand to his shaft and stroked below her mouth. She pressed her lips tighter around him as she pumped up and down, squeezing and milking her demon.

She moved to straddle him, leaning over him so that her breasts brushed his chest and his erection grazed her folds. Pressed against his warm body, she was ready for him, so wet that his hard cock slipped along her cleft. She knew he ached as much as she did when he rasped her name in frustration.

Giving into their mutual need, she lifted up enough to guide him just inside her entrance and lowered herself down. She sighed and let her head fall back as he filled her inch by delicious inch. *I'll never get enough of this.* Leaning forward, she braced her hands on either side of his shoulders.

"Touch me," she whispered and before she had even gotten the words out, his hands were on her breasts, cupping her, flicking his thumbs across her nipples.

She moaned as the sensations he created shot in a straight line to her core, and her hips rocked against him. Teasing him had been delightful erotic fun for her, and now she perched on the brink of another orgasm. His body rubbed her just where she needed it. His hands teased her breasts, caressing the sensitive undersides, and when he pinched her aching nipples, she shattered. She cried out as she ground hard against him. He gripped her hips as he pistoned beneath her, bellowing her name as his release shot hot and deep within her body. She collapsed onto his chest in a haze of sated bliss, her breathing ragged, her body surrendered.

CHAPTER 14

NICOLE WOKE UP TO SUNLIGHT streaming in the window and hungry kisses along her bare bottom. She raised her head from her bent arm and looked over her shoulder. "Mmm," she murmured drowsily as Gunnar's mouth moved to the tops of her thighs, continuing to nibble her sensitive skin.

"Morning." His voice rumbled against her flesh.

"You sure know how to wake a girl up." She couldn't hold back a sleepy giggle.

"I can't get enough of your perfect little ass."

"Good." She stretched out on her belly. Dropping her head, she savored another minute of his delicious attention. She was still so blissed-out from last night that she didn't think she could get any more relaxed.

He brushed the hair from her neck and sucked the spot where he'd bitten her. "Time for a bath."

Nicole rolled over and blinked. Were her eyes playing tricks on her? A second tub sat next to the one she had used yesterday, and lavender scented steam wafted from the water. She thought about asking him how and when this had all happened but decided that it didn't matter. Meeting his gorgeous blue eyes, she smiled. "You think of everything."

"I do my best." He scooped her up and settled her into the closest tub.

She dipped her head back until her hair was soaked, and then he proceeded to wash it. His fingers on her scalp felt divine, his warrior's hands touching her hair gently, as if it were fine silk.

"You're good at this," she murmured.

"I've taken an interest in making you feel good." He picked up a cloth and gently washed her skin. When he was done, he instructed her to stay put and soak while he took his own bath.

She watched him unabashedly from half lidded eyes. His body was so finely sculpted and powerful that she could look at it all day. She watched his muscles ripple under his skin, remembering the taste of him on her lips. "Another time, I'll bathe you."

"I'll remember that." He climbed out of his tub and flashed a roguish grin at her.

They dressed in the clothing they had worn yesterday, which had been washed and lay neatly folded on a chair. Gunnar held her hand as they walked through the busy colony in search of Taszim.

All the nymphs were fully dressed today, though for the females, the *usual clothing* was nothing more than a short, clingy tunic. The males all wore tunics and pants, mostly in shades of brown. Everyone they passed greeted them warmly.

They found Taszim deep in conversation with one of his sentinels, hand on his jaw as he listened to the other man. As they approached, he smiled and gestured for them to join in his conversation. He took Nicole's hand and kissed it. "Well, don't you look as content as a cat relaxing in the sun, my lovely. I trust you slept well." He winked at her.

Nicole smiled and bit her lip, feeling heat rise in her cheeks. She looked up at Gunnar, who stroked his hand down the curve of her spine. From the way they had left Taszim and Larissa, she guessed the nymph leader's night had been spent in a similar manner.

Taszim clapped Gunnar on the back and nodded to his man. "Tomas here was just giving the morning's report. Things are quiet…unusually quiet." He frowned and turned to his sentinel. "Keep me updated. I'll be in my study." The other nymph nodded, shaggy brown hair swinging around his head, and walked back toward the colony's entrance.

Taszim offered Nicole his arm and she took it, then the three of them walked a short distance to a low building near the center of the colony. Taszim's study was paneled in dark wood and contained several pieces of mahogany furniture and two overstuffed armchairs.

"So, my friends." Taszim swept his arms wide. "What can I do for you?"

He leaned against the edge of his desk and indicated that Nicole and Gunnar should sit. Nicole settled into one of the cozy armchairs while Gunnar stood near her.

"You have something that will be of great use to us against one of our enemies," Gunnar replied. "We have reason to suspect a Domu on Earth has organized a number of Skell demons to commit crimes for him." Gunnar then related the details of the attacks in Chicago and the coins they had found on the two Skells. "We still don't know what he plans to do with the blood he's collecting, but we need to stop him before his plan can be fully realized. We need Xarrek's ashes."

Taszim's brows furrowed. "For what purpose?"

Gunnar folded his arms across his chest. "Rosa said it will help defeat him. She didn't go into specifics."

"Rosa." Taszim huffed out a breath. "Of course, the witch knows we have the ash. She—"

The door burst open. "My lord!" The sentinel from earlier gripped the sides of the doorway, out of breath. "Vipers, my lord Taszim! We are under attack!"

Both Gunnar and Taszim raced for the door. Gunnar looked back at Nicole. "Stay here!"

"No way." Nicole stood. "I want to help."

He gripped her upper arms and glared down at her, but she didn't miss the flicker of worry that crossed the blue fire in his eyes. "You could get yourself killed."

"If they use arrows, I can deflect them. *All* of them. You know I can."

"Goddamn it, Nicole!"

"We don't have time for this, Gunnar. There's a reason that

I'm here. Maybe this is part of it." She marched out of the study.

He reached out to grab her arm.

"If you try to stop me, I'll just find a way to get there. I am a Solsti. I *will* help."

He growled but didn't stop her as he jogged beside her. "Just stay back. Use the trees to protect yourself. Or stay behind the nymphs' archers. I don't like this, Nicole."

"I'm not crazy about it either, but I'm not going to sit back and hide when I could be helping."

Gunnar looked at her as if he wanted to say more, but they were almost at the edge of the trees. He hauled her close and placed a searing kiss to her lips. "Don't you dare get hurt," he warned, and then he charged toward the front line of nymphs.

The scene before Nicole was so different from the previous day that she barely recognized the field in front of Rivkin. Battle cries and the clang of metal rent the air. The near side of the river was filled with nymph archers launching their arrows from behind rocks, trees, and shrubs. On the far side of the river stood dozens of Vipers. Most had bows, and she assumed they were using the poison-tipped arrows. But she realized that at least half of the archers had arrows tipped with flames.

Flames.

Anger heated her blood. The vipers would burn the nymphs' home and then, once getting them out in the open, poison them.

She gritted her teeth. *That won't happen today. I won't let it. No way.* She crept closer to a group of nymph archers that were concealed behind thick shrubs. Other nymphs engaged the Vipers in swordfights as they tried to protect the bridge. But because of the nymphs' much smaller size, not many of them succeeded. She cringed as one nymph tumbled beneath a Viper blade, then another.

She looked for Gunnar. In the center of the chaotic field, he fought one Viper with his sword while flinging a ball of demonfire at another. His size made him an imposing figure on a normal day; now, in the midst of battle, he looked ferocious. He moved like a savage god, in control of his opponents, lethal and powerful. His strikes were calm and precise, years of experience and training having forged him into a bastion of insurmountable force. She marveled again at his hands, so tender this morning, now dispatching the evil demons with ease.

Nicole focused her energy. She directed a gust of wind at the next volley of arrows, sending them all into the river with a sharp hiss. The Vipers bellowed and reloaded, glancing around. She guessed they sensed her energy. Calling up a gale force wind on their side of the river, she sent loose twigs, rocks, and leaves into it to throw them off in any way she could.

She raised one hand to steady her power as she maintained the furious wind on the opposite side of the river. Manipulating an air current from the nymph side, she put extra force behind the nymph archers' arrows. The arrows flew toward their targets with a velocity that stunned both sides. The Vipers fell as the nymphs whistled their approval and reloaded. Nicole helped them do it again, and again.

With a hiss and a thud, a flaming arrow sank into the trunk of a tree next to Nicole. Slivers of bark shot into the air and a tendril of smoke curled skyward from the licking fire.

"Oh, yeah?" she whispered. Extinguishing it with a forceful draft of air, she refocused on the incoming round of arrows. She blasted them end over end flying backward toward their source. A Viper howled as an arrow landed in his eye. Others slumped to the ground, their own weapons protruding from their thick necks. As the Vipers' scaly flesh burned, a stench like burning rubber drifted across the river.

Nicole's power surged through her blood. She felt oddly detached, as if watching herself from afar, feeling no remorse for the taking of lives. The Vipers intended to kill the nymphs— she was glad to defend them. And at the same time she felt exhilarated. She felt like she had found her true purpose. She wasn't odd, she was rare and helpful and *needed*.

The Vipers' strength waned. Gunnar had slain a dozen at least. Because of Nicole's talent and the skill of the nymph archers, scores more lay lifeless on the ground. The handful that remained fell back into a tight group and unleashed one more round of flaming arrows, which Nicole easily sent into the water. The snake-headed beasts turned and fled.

The nymphs standing next to Nicole turned to her and let out a joyful whoop. Then they sobered and murmured, "My lady." They all knelt before her.

Surprised and a little uncomfortable with the display of gratitude, she whispered, "Please, stand." She looked for Gunnar and saw him still on the field, walking among the Vipers, making sure they were truly dead. "Nymphs." Nicole looked at the grassy expanse. "Your work is not quite done."

They stood and rushed to aid Gunnar in his grisly task. She leaned against the nearest tree, muscles wobbly. Whether it was from the extended use of her power or from the adrenaline rush of the battle, she wasn't sure. Letting the trunk support her, she watched her big demon as he handled the aftermath of the attack. Even now, he made sure they were safe. Her heart swelled with the knowledge that he would stop at nothing to eliminate every potential threat to her.

The bright flash of his blue eyes swept the tree line, searching for her. His gaze locked with hers across the field and he charged toward her, a blur of churning muscles and raw male power. In a heartbeat, he crushed her to his warm chest, caressing her hair, murmuring sweet words. He pulled away to look into her eyes, a range of emotions flickering across his own. Admiration, possession, relief, and something more that she couldn't name.

Leaning down, he covered her mouth with his, tenderly at first and then more urgently. He gripped her upper arm with one hand and wrapped her hair around his other one, kissing her senseless.

He finally let her go and looked at her. "You're safe."

Gasping from his kiss, she managed to speak. "I stayed behind the trees, just like you ordered me to."

"I gave you orders because I need to protect you. But

Nicole, today…" he shook his head. "You were amazing. You turned the tide of the attack."

"I don't need to be protected anymore?"

"You're not getting rid of me that easily. There are many other foul creatures out there that may not be as susceptible to your skills."

Taszim jogged off the field and bowed to her. "My lady, we are in your debt."

Nicole smiled, unsure of what to say.

Gunnar wrapped an arm around her shoulders and spoke to Taszim. "Let's meet in one hour. Bring any of your men that need to be there."

"Of course." The nymph turned to walk into the colony.

Nicole spied Larissa hurtling headlong down the path and into her husband's arms. Their passion and devotion to one another touched her heart, and she looked away, not wanting to stare at their intimate moment. *Why does this seem more private than what went on last night?* She looked up into Gunnar's piercing blue gaze as he tugged her toward the elevator basket and saw the same mix of emotions crossing his rugged features. She longed to dig deeper, but at this minute it seemed there were more important things at hand.

CHAPTER 15

GUNNAR DIDN'T BREATHE UNTIL HE had Nicole behind the closed door of her room. He hadn't let go of her as they walked through the colony. They'd offered to help move the wounded nymphs to the infirmary, but Rivkin's healer insisted that she had more than enough volunteers. Some nymphs looked dazed, and others looked at Nicole with a new, awe-filled adoration.

He didn't want to think about what could have happened to Rivkin if he and Nicole hadn't been here today. Her display of power had astonished both sides of the battlefield, and word of her existence would spread like wildfire. That was one more reason to not let her out of his sight. Although many would not believe that the Solsti had returned, others would jump at the chance to capture a creature as rare as she.

He hated knowing that she was close to the action on the field, but his strategic battle instincts won out over his protective instincts. Though she had yet to develop her ability to its fullest potential, she could still help the nymphs. And as he had stated before, she wasn't defenseless. Having only watched her tussle with a few ignorant criminals in tough human neighborhoods, he never imagined how much power she could wield in a true battle. Seeing her courage today, her utter determination to help the nymphs only heightened his feelings for her. When she had turned the Vipers' own arrows against them, the creatures weren't merely shocked, but were confused and afraid. And that had sealed their fate.

Still holding her upper arms in his hands, he gazed down

into her green eyes. "I am so proud of what you did today."

She smiled. "Me, too. I mean, I'm glad I could help. I...I didn't know exactly how things would turn out."

"With Vipers, you never do. Remember that." He cupped her chin and tilted her mouth up to meet his lips. She kissed him hungrily, no doubt the heat of the battle still flowing in her veins. He indulged her for a minute, then pulled back reluctantly and studied her. "You looked a little pale out there. Are you sure you're okay?"

"I'm always pale," she murmured. "But if you get me all revved up, I won't be pale anymore. I'll be nice and—"

"Stop, vixen." He laid a finger on her lips, and then remembered the things she had done to his fingers with that mouth. He caressed her silken cheek instead. "Have you ever used your ability for so long, and in that capacity? Directing multiple air currents at the same time?"

"Not really. I did it in practice a few times, but only for a few minutes." She pouted at him. "I'm fine, Gunnar. More than fine." She started to trace circles on his chest with her fingertip, and then stopped and made a face. "What on earth is that?"

Some Viper's blood and a bit of tissue was stuck to him. Well, he thought wryly, he did want to change the direction of her thoughts, for the time being anyway. There would be time later to thoroughly examine his Solsti and make sure she was truly okay.

He looked down at his chest and frowned. "I need to get cleaned up and make a call."

"You have a phone here?" she asked in surprise. "Cell phones work on Torth?"

"Not a cell phone." He pulled a small device from his pocket. "On Torth, we have gem phones."

She held out her hand and he gave it to her. "Wow." She gazed at the small device. "I don't remember seeing any cell phone towers around here."

Gunnar chuckled and kissed the top of her head. "Ley lines, my dear."

They had been so occupied in the last few days that he hadn't thought to show it to her. The gems were, like their namesake, saturated with deep colors. His happened to be a rich garnet. Any creatures on Torth could find them, usually in the cities, and always for a price. They were used in much the same way as cell phones were on Earth, but his had the addition of an energy-recognition feature. With hundreds of different species roaming around, it helped to have a virtual encyclopedia on hand to identify different creatures' strengths and weaknesses.

"I need to call Raniero and let him know what happened."

She handed the gem back to him. "Of course. We need to go home, but we can't leave Rivkin undefended." She paused. "Do you want me to leave? Do you need to speak privately?"

He grinned at her politeness. "Stay. Anything regarding today is your business as well as mine. And I'm not letting you out of my sight."

She smiled and collapsed on the huge bed. "Good. I'm going to take a nap, since I didn't get much sleep last night." She winked at him, then curled up into a ball on top of the coverlet and closed her eyes.

Raniero sat high in a tree, surveying the clearing below. The Serus demon would be coming through any minute to get up close and personal with one of his custom-made barbed arrows. He normally didn't use anything special, just a quick strike to eliminate his targets. But this mark had pissed him off with his uncanny ability to avoid his fate. When Raniero had a job to do, both his colleagues and his enemies considered it done. Not that he had many enemies; at least not many who were still breathing. His official responsibilities among the Lash Watchers, as well as his unofficial and covert one as a conscripted killer, made certain of that.

His demon hearing picked up the snap of a twig a hundred yards away. He readied his bow. There was no way the Serus would anticipate Raniero's presence here. As the creature lumbered through the trees and into view, Raniero let the first arrow fly, swiftly followed by a second, just to make sure the demon was incapacitated.

The Serus' bellow was cut short as both arrows sank deep into its flesh. It tried to pull them out but only succeeded in aggravating the wounds. Raniero leapt down from his branch and hurled a ball of demonfire at it, finishing it off.

He stood a short distance away and watched the burning corpse. Finally. That bastard had been a pain in the ass to kill. Luckily, his fellow warriors hadn't had any reason to question his absences; they assumed he was entertaining female company or on an extended patrol. Which he frequently was. Raniero always covered his tracks.

He hadn't always been so guarded. But decades ago one man's cruelty had forced him into a lifestyle of secrets and shadows soaked in death. It had been a century ago. The meeting stood in sharp relief in his mind, vivid brush strokes that no amount of time could fade.

Raniero paused in his briefing when the conference room's heavy door opened.

"Father, I—" echoed in the quiet. The voice, dulcet and husky, caressed his skin. The female that it belonged to peeked around the door, stopping Raniero's heart.

"Later, child. We're not finished here." Cale gestured for her to leave.

But not before she looked toward Raniero, rendering him speechless. Huge, luminous green eyes gazed at him from her heart-shaped face. Straight ebony hair cascaded around her shoulders and down her back. Her toffee-colored skin was warmed by the summer sun, and a diaphanous pale coral gown clung to her sweetly curving breasts and hips. Her eyes darted from his to glance back at her father, and then she backed out of the room.

Later he sought her out. Ashina. Her name rolled on his tongue like fine wine, his senses overloaded with the melody of her voice. The image of her standing in the doorway, bright colors and feminine curves, called to him.

He spotted her standing at a window, her back to him. Closing the distance between them, he stood close enough to inhale her sweet scent. He leaned in, lips at her ear, and said, "I've been looking for you."

He anticipated her gasp and whirl, catching her upper arms to steady her. The look of joy on her face was a sunrise in the desert: bright, shining, not a cloud to cast a single shadow.

"You wanted to talk to me? Not my father?" Her voice came out higher than it had earlier, but by the smile that reached her eyes, it was from excitement and not nerves.

"You." He smiled and released her arms, only to reach for her slender hand. "Walk with me?"

They strolled in the vast, sprawling gardens for hours, talking and laughing. Though he had known her for less than a day, his soul reverberated with the sense that she was different from any woman he had met. A mix of emotions built as he walked at her side: the desire to touch, to claim, and to protect her. His body also roared with the urge to tuck her against his side. Forever.

"Looks like the first oranges are ready." He pointed to the ripe fruit hanging from several trees in a nearby grove. The tropical scent filled the air as he led her into the trees. He plucked one and scored it with his dagger, removing the peel in one long strip.

"I love oranges," she whispered.

He raised a segment to her lush lips and she bit into it, giggling as a tiny trickle of juice ran down her chin. She went to brush it away but he caught her hand.

"Let me." He traced his finger along her jaw and down her throat, capturing the drop. The smile faded from her gaze, replaced with startled wonder. Lips parted, her eyes tracked his hand as he brought it up and sucked the droplet into his mouth.

He released his finger and extended it to trace the contours of her lips. A shaky breath escaped her, and his control abandoned him. He pulled her close and covered her mouth with his.

She tasted like oranges, her lips soft and giving under his. And inexperienced. He processed the thought with a flare of satisfaction. He would be the one to bring her pleasure one day. She was young enough that her father still saw her as a child, but old enough that no one else did. Her innocence melted his heart.

In the days after, he requested an extension of his assignment at

Ashina's enclave. But a nest of marauding Neshi demons marched relentlessly on Torth's Western Forest. All available Lash demons were needed to fight. Forced to leave, he held her and kissed the top of her head.

"I'll be back as soon as I can," he promised, stroking her hair.

It took longer than expected to subdue the Neshis. Weeks passed before Raniero retuned, his heart bursting as she rushed through her doorway to greet him. Being away from her was one of the hardest things he had ever endured.

They planned to meet in the gardens later that night, when everyone else had gone to bed. Arriving first, he waited in the orange grove, acutely aware of her delicate steps growing ever closer. She tiptoed into his line of sight. Their eyes locked as she broke into a run and leapt into his waiting arms.

He savored her sweet kisses, the scent and taste of her a balm to his soul. And when she unexpectedly licked the seam of his lips with her tongue, his world went black. He opened for her exploration, her tentative forays driving him wild.

With a growl, he set her down and guided her deeper into the gardens, to a section that had been allowed to grow more wild. Finding a secluded copse of silver birch, he backed her against one pale trunk and kissed her with raw possession. A soft moan escaped her lips, sending fire through his veins. His muscles shook with the need to claim her, but he forced himself to go slow. She was his. They would have a lifetime together.

He pulled her silky blue dress over her head, sucking in a breath at her exquisite form. Clad only in white lace panties that stood out against her toffee skin, she bit her lip and looked down.

"Sweet Sheena." He captured her face between his hands. "You're beautiful." He kissed her lips reverently, shaping them with his, until her boldness returned. She opened for him and he swept his tongue inside the warm cavern of her mouth, tasting honey sweetness that made his body harden in anticipation.

He lowered her to the soft grass and stripped off his clothes. She watched him, radiance lighting her face, arms stretched toward him.

"I love you." It came out as a husky growl as he prowled up her body, kissing every inch of baby-soft skin.

"I love you, too." She tugged him up for another delicious kiss.

He covered her body with his, claiming her mouth with slow, deliberate strokes. She met his tongue with her own, proving to be a quick learner. Her eager passion ignited his own as she arched toward him in encouragement. She fit him perfectly. He nipped at her throat, unable to hold back the waves of love and desire. Lying under the stars, she exuberantly gave him her innocence, forever marking him with her devotion and trust. She owned his soul.

The night was as perfect as anyone could ask for, and they lay watching the moon rise high overhead. Foreboding prickled along his skin just as a crashing in the trees tore their world apart.

"What the fuck is this?" bellowed Cale, bursting into the copse with two of his men.

Raniero pushed Ashina behind him, but the men grabbed him, dragging him several feet away.

"Whore!" Cale's face turned red with rage as he drew back his arm for a brutal backhand that sent Ashina flying to the ground.

Raniero lunged for her, but the men held him in a vise grip. Cale's sword was already at his neck when she landed in the grass.

"I have every right to kill you," Cale hissed. "But I have another use for you. If you want her to live, you'll agree."

Another of Cale's men stepped from the trees and picked up Ashina's sobbing form, holding a dagger to her throat.

"No!" Raniero surged against his captors' arm, but only brought his neck against Cale's blade. The tangy scent of blood wafted up to his nose.

"She dies right now unless you agree to work for me," Cale said, his voice full of menace. "One hundred years. You will do what I ask. And you will never lay eyes on her again. Ever. Or I will kill her."

Blood boiled in Raniero's veins. The need to kill Cale, or anyone who would lay a hand on Ashina, filled every fiber of his body with rage. But he could never cause her harm. In one beat of his heart, the hardest choice of his life morphed into the easiest one. He would sacrifice everything to keep her safe.

"I agree," he said, though the words tore his heart as jaggedly as Ashina's soft weeping.

Eventually, her father would soften his stance. Eventually, Raniero would find her. Eventually...

Raniero cursed the smoking corpse in front of him. His contract of one hundred years' service was nearly up. At first he had searched continuously for her. In every city and forest, in his work for the Lash or as Cale's mercenary, he inquired as to her whereabouts. He was able to discover that her father had banished her to another realm; but which one, he didn't know. He had no idea if she was still alive, if she still loved him, or if she had mated another and moved on with her life.

The uncertainty began to drive him mad, and after a few decades the part of his heart that belonged to her had been buried under the weight of his frustration and grief. Being forced to work for her father was constant salt on the wound, but he learned to hide all emotion when dealing with the demon. He completed each assignment and then waited impassively for the next one. And if he ever had any free time, he spent it buried between the willing thighs of beautiful females. He never had to look hard to find them; in fact, they seemed to stumble upon him wherever he went. He gladly let his reputation as a ladies' man grow to precede him, because then the twin darknesses of his past and his present would remain unseen and unsuspected. As if the man he had been, as well as the woman he had loved then, ceased to exist.

He looked down and saw that the Serus was nothing more than a pile of ashes. Pulling his gem phone from his pocket, he notified Cale of the completed task. He turned and broke into an easy jog as he headed for a nearby safe house.

His thoughts turned to the call from Gunnar he'd received earlier. The Vipers' unprovoked attack on the peaceful wood nymphs pissed him off. It didn't make sense. The vicious snakeheads already occupied a decent amount of territory in the area. Perhaps they wanted to tip the delicate balance of power that the Lash demons strove to protect. Perhaps it was a harbinger of the reason for the reemergence of the Solsti.

He had been shocked to learn that they were real. As would most residents of Torth, he surmised. After all, the legends had been passed down for so many centuries that most creatures weren't even sure if the Solsti had ever existed. But meeting Nicole and seeing her power first-hand had been exhilarating. He knew she had yet to develop her potential to its fullest, but she and her sisters would be truly formidable one day.

His friend Gunnar was a lucky bastard, he thought wryly. Raniero wasn't exactly sure what was going on between his comrade and the pretty Solsti. But if the lingering looks they had been giving each other were any indication, Raniero could guess. That and the fact that when he had departed the safe house early in the morning, Nicole's T-shirt had been on the living room floor and they had been tucked away in the other bedroom.

Raniero grinned, knowing he would find his own fair company among the wood nymphs. He and a few other Lash Watchers would take the first several days of guarding Rivkin. The nymphs' reputation for delighting in the pleasures of the flesh well exceeded even his own. Coming to the aid of the nymphs would be among the most coveted of assignments, despite the threat of Vipers.

"Anything further?" Taszim asked the group. Sunlight filtering through the trees shone through the glass walls of the conference room, lending it an open air feel. The rays also illuminated Nicole's blond hair with a soft light, making her look like an angel.

My angel. Gunnar pulled his attention away from her to respond to Taszim. "I think we've covered everything. Tomas and I ran a wide perimeter patrol earlier. You'll continue those at regular intervals. More sentries round the clock. And Lash guards will arrive tomorrow."

Taszim glanced around the table at his sentries, then nodded. "We implement the changes immediately. That is all." He stood, and the rest of the nymphs followed suit.

As they filed out the door, Taszim laid a hand on Gunnar's shoulder. "Come with me."

Gunnar took Nicole's hand as they followed Taszim through the trees to his nearby office. The nymph leader gestured for them to go inside and entered behind them.

"I believe we have business to finish." Taszim crossed the room and walked to a colorful tapestry hanging on the wall. Drawing it to the side, he revealed a door secured with a silver lock. He unlocked it and reached inside, pulling out a small glass jar. It was round, with a raised circular corked opening on top. "Rivkin is in your debt. The ash is yours."

Gunnar took the jar and studied its contents. The fine gray granules seemed so innocuous, something that could've been scattered on a gentle wind. Not what he would expect to bring down a warrior-turned-mage. "Thank you, my friend. Now we just need to find this bastard."

The nymph tapped a finger on his chin. "I don't think I can assist with that particular search, demon. But I have something else that may help you. Being a more peaceful species, we must take every advantage possible." He reached back into the safe and removed a small, leather-bound booklet. "We managed to take this grimoire from Xarrek's cloak before he was completely incinerated."

"Nice work." Gunnar turned it over in his hand. He raised his eyebrows and traced his finger over the cover. "Here's the same symbol that's on the coins."

"None of us can read a word of it, so I hope you can get something out of it."

Gunnar flipped it open. "That's because it's in old demonish. Lucky for us, Rilan spends entire days translating this stuff."

"We will continue to aid you in any way we can. You're welcome to stay at Rivkin as long as you like," Taszim replied. "Not every night is equal to last night in terms of revelry, but we have excellent food and entertainment. And tonight, we'll honor you."

"Tonight?" Nicole asked.

"Tonight." Taszim smiled at her. "My wife is planning quite

a banquet for you."

CHAPTER 16

NICOLE'S BELLY RUMBLED AS SHE and Gunnar made their way to the great hall. His arm wrapped around her waist, holding her close as they walked through the trees.

He kissed the top of her head and leaned close enough to nuzzle her ear. "You look stunning tonight. Even though that excuse for a dress is killing me."

She tugged at the hem of the new moss dress Larissa had given her. "Can't help it if I left all my party dresses at home. I didn't know you were taking me anywhere fancy." She smiled up at him, shivers racing across her skin as his blue eyes twinkled at her.

"Neither did I." He stopped in the middle of the path, pulling her close to his bare chest. His sensual lips captured her mouth in a quick, searing kiss before he patted her bottom. "Let's get you some food."

It seemed they were the last ones to arrive at dinner. The lively strains of wind instruments filled the room, accompanied by one horn and one drum. She was grateful that the skills of the nymph musicians masked her growling stomach.

Though more subdued than last night, the nymphs were still feeling festive. This time, when she and Gunnar entered the room, no whispers floated on the air. The room quieted to an awed silence. Some of the nymphs met her eye before inclining their heads. Some bowed, as Taszim had in the woods. Still unsure of how to handle their adoration, she kept a peaceful smile on her face as they walked to the head table.

Two female nymphs brought platters piled with huge slabs of steaming ham, making Nicole's mouth water. Bowls of roasted potatoes followed, as well as warm bread, soup, and vegetables. She dove into her dinner, listening as her hostess chattered next to her.

Larissa brought her up to speed on the health status of the injured nymphs. Nicole was heartened to see that several had been well enough to come to dinner and told her as much.

"Oh, darling," Larissa murmured. "*You* are the main attraction, not the food."

"What?" Nicole smiled and tried not to look shocked. "What do you mean? If they're not well enough to be here–"

Larissa touched her arm. "Then they wouldn't have gotten past our healer. But even if they are able to eat only soup or bread, they'll be here tonight. Having you here is an honor that none of us ever expected. You're not supposed to exist. And not only do you exist, but you defended us today. I speak for everyone here in telling you our feelings for you go far beyond adoration."

"Oh." How did one respond to that? Nicole decided to be honest. "I've had a wonderful time here, and I'm delighted that I was able to help. It felt good. I've never done anything on that scale before."

"Well, my lovely, you could have fooled all of us." Larissa dabbed delicately at the corner of her mouth. "And, just for you, we have a different sort of entertainment tonight."

"Different?" Nicole's eyebrows shot up. She couldn't imagine how the nymphs could possibly top last night's festivities.

"Oh yes. You're in for a treat, my dear." Her petite hostess beamed at her. "Look, here comes Niles now!"

Nicole's attention shifted to the center of the room, where a nymph made his way toward them. He looked much like the other males: shirtless, trim, slight figure, brown hair left a little long. He approached the head table and Nicole could make out the faintest of lines etching his face. Bright eyes shone with confidence as he glanced at each of them, murmuring their names and inclining his head. When his gaze reached Nicole, he bowed deeply and intoned, "My most venerable lady."

Nicole stuck with her routine of *smile-and-nod* to whoever was lavishing such attention on her. It seemed to be the right thing to do so far.

Niles straightened and addressed the room in a resonant voice. "As you know, there are two species of nymphs here on Torth. Our dearest cousins, the water nymphs, are much like us, except that they have no choice but to live half their lives in the rivers and seas." His gaze swept the room. "It was not always thus. Our two species were once one. Tonight we will hear the tale of the lovers Lia and Idris, and the jealous river goddess Mara, who changed not only their lives but the lives of all nymphs from that point forward.

"Tens of centuries ago, nymphs lived cheerfully on Torth. They lived in colonies much like this one, and they set up their homes wherever they wanted. They swam in the rivers and climbed the trees as they pleased. They were not physically bound to one place or another.

"Among one of the colonies lived two lovers, Lia and Idris. They had been friends since they were wee children, stealing sweets from the kitchen when the cook's back was turned. Now on the verge of adulthood, they realized that their long friendship was but a precursor to something much greater. They fell deeply into romantic love and wished to bind to one another forever." Niles walked to the center of the room, his voice becoming grave as he continued.

"One day as they frolicked along the banks of a river that flowed across the edge of the nymphs' territory, a river goddess happened to glide by on the current. Now this was Mara, who was bitter, jealous, and spiteful. As she floated by, she spied the lovers sitting together in the grass. She watched as handsome Idris fed his beloved a grape and tenderly caressed her hair. Mara couldn't look away. She had never seen any creature that was as handsome and perfectly formed as Idris. He was strong, young, and virile, and the goddess instantly wanted him for herself.

"Rising naked out of the water, she perched atop the moving current and beckoned to him. When he did not run into her arms, she grew angry and demanded he come to her. Lia and Idris were rightly fearful and turned to run from Mara, but she bade the water to rise up and overtake them. Lia was pushed aside as the river formed a terrifying watery arm that grabbed Idris and dragged him down into the water. He was a gifted swimmer, but even his strength was no match for a goddess." The storyteller paused, his arm rising toward one of the tapestries on the wall.

Nicole sucked in a breath, for the scene depicted the force of Mara's rage. Chills ran down her arms as Niles spoke again.

"Lia had climbed a tree whose thick branches extended far out over the river. She tried to reach Idris, tried to extend her hand to him, but Mara held him firm in her grasp. Mara bestowed upon Idris the ability to breathe under water, and they disappeared below the surface. Lia shrieked and cried for her lover for hours, laying in the tree's sheltering branches, her tears mixing into the river's flowing waters.

"Her cries were heard by the other nymphs, who tried desperately to help. Many of them leapt into the water to search for Idris, but this so incensed Mara that she altered their lungs as well. She turned them into creatures who, although they could breathe both air and water, were not capable of spending any length of time out of the current. Thus, they were not able to return to their lives, homes, or families in the nymph colony.

"When the rest of the nymphs realized what Mara had done, they cursed the goddess and mourned their losses. And all this time, Lia would not leave her tree. She continued to watch the river for a sign of her beloved Idris. The rest of the colony decided, out of deference to her, that they would also make their homes in the trees. They, too, would continue to watch for their lost ones, in the desperate hope that Mara would return them one day.

"That day never came. Lia lived a long life, never leaving her tree, her heart forever bound to her lost love. Idris and Mara were never seen again. Generations passed, and the nymphs that had been taken into the river gave birth to young ones with lungs just like the ones Mara had given the parents. The nymphs who lived in the trees needed the woods for shelter, lest they grow weak. Over time, the nymphs evolved into two closely linked but different species: the wood nymphs and the water nymphs."

Silence hung in the room for a few seconds before the nymphs wildly applauded Niles' story. Whistles and catcalls filled the room. Nicole was stunned but delighted by the tale. The nymphs were so full of joie de vivre, it had never occurred to her that their history would have some dark moments. She clapped with the rest of them and gave Niles her biggest smile, which he returned as he bowed deeply to her.

"That was amazing," she murmured to Larissa as the music started up again. "Thank you."

"Niles is one of the best, if I do say so myself," Larissa replied.

Gunnar got up from his seat next to Taszim and came to stand next to her. "Hell of a tale, Larissa. Rivkin has quite a fine storyteller."

Their tiny hostess smiled and patted Gunnar's hand. "I'll tell him you said so but, by all means, feel free to speak to him yourself as well." With that she scooted over onto her husband's lap, cradling his head for a languid kiss.

Nicole glanced around the room for Niles, and saw that she and Gunnar weren't the only ones who appreciated his skill. He was surrounded by several scantily dressed females who were stroking his arms and fawning over him. She looked at Gunnar and grinned. "Maybe we'll tell him tomorrow."

He nodded and took her hand. "C'mon. I have something to show you." He tugged her through the colony, its paths nearly empty because most of the nymphs were in the great hall.

"That was quite a story. Have you heard it before?"

"No. Although, I always thought it was interesting that there are different kinds of nymphs. I never knew why."

"It's so sad." She shook her head. "Is it real?"

He shrugged. "It may as well be. They believe it to be, and it happened so long ago that no one can verify it. A lot of myths are like that."

"Except the myth of the Solsti." She hesitated as she realized he was taking them along the walkway that led out of the safety of the dense canopy. "I thought you said it wasn't safe to be outside at night."

"We're not going far. And extra watchmen have been added. I'll keep you safe."

Nicole had the fleeting thought that one day she'd be saying the same thing to him. Energy still buzzed in her veins from using her ability to help defeat such a heinous enemy. She wondered what would have happened had Brooke been here with her. What magic would they have been able to work together? There was that river nearby. Brooke would've been able to do a lot with–

Her thoughts broke off abruptly. She hadn't seen or talked to her sister in days. She missed her and was bursting to tell her about every second she had spent here on Torth. And one day Brooke would see this place for herself. After all, Rosa had requested it. Nicole wasn't about to go against any of the old witch's requests.

Gunnar led her out of the colony and along the edge of the field, but stayed on the nymphs' side of the bridge. He re-entered the trees a little ways down and stopped after a few feet. "There's no path here, but it's not far." He scooped her into his arms.

She would never tire of being in Gunnar's arms. And since she was so tall, not many men had ever carried her around like he did. She smiled and rested her head against his shoulder as he navigated his way through trees and brush. It seemed only a minute had passed when he announced, "We're here."

She looked up and felt her jaw drop in wonder. The most exquisite flowers she had ever seen covered the ground. Small and delicate like pansies, the petals held the lustrous tints of pink, purple, and yellow, and they *glowed* with a soft inner light. There had to be hundreds of them climbing up the trees that surrounded the tiny open space. It was like being surrounded by tiny botanical Christmas lights.

"What are these?"

"Phos-blooms. Their flowers naturally contain high amounts of phosphorous." He set her down on the carpet of soft, downy grass.

"They're exquisite." She couldn't tear her eyes from the softly glowing petals that surrounded them. Not wanting to step on a single one, she picked her way carefully to one edge of the clearing. "This looks like a dream."

"Hopefully it's a good dream and not a nightmare like this morning." He moved closer to her, crowding her against the nearest tree.

"This morning wasn't a nightmare. It was a lesson. One which the Vipers failed miserably." She reached up to link her hands behind his neck.

"You did well," he whispered. "But that won't be the last battle you see."

"I'll be ready. Brooke will be ready too. I know you want to keep me safe, but you can't put me in a bubble. We both know I'm here for a reason." She caressed his nape and stood on tiptoe so that her lips gently brushed his. "Did you bring me out here to talk?"

"No. But if there was a bubble that could hold you, I'd find it," he growled, and with one tug of his hand, her leafy dress ripped open and fell to the flower-covered ground. Like last night's almost-sheer dress, there was no way to wear panties under this garment without looking ridiculous. A couple of days with the scantily-clad nymphs had made underwear seem unnecessary, anyway. She ran her fingers through his silky black hair and circled her naked hips against him.

His lips covered hers tenderly, gently shaping her mouth with sweet kisses. She opened to let him in, feeling the rush of adrenaline from this morning surge back into her. She didn't want him tender right now. She wanted the warrior she had seen out on the field, easily cutting down the enemy as if he could do it in his sleep. With his steely strength and her innate gift, they had battled *together* to defeat the Vipers. Licking into his mouth insistently, she wanted to tangle with him, wanted to possess him. She clutched his shoulders, her nails digging in to his skin, making him hiss.

Need uncoiled low in her belly, sending shimmering waves across her overheated skin. Her nipples hardened into tight points as they rubbed against his bare chest. She ran her hands down to the waistband of his trousers, hooking one finger inside and dragging it slowly back and forth. With her free hand she reached around to cup his ass. His muscles clenched under her touch.

He groaned into her mouth. "So aggressive tonight, Nicole. Is that how you want it?"

"Yes." Her breath was ragged. She nipped at his lip. "Now."

"And here I thought I'd be all romantic, making love to you tenderly among the phos-flowers," he chuckled. His hand covered her breast.

Why is he still talking? "Next time." She popped the button on his fly.

With the tree at her back, he nudged one of his thighs between hers. She hooked one ankle around his calf, sliding it up. His pants were gone, his erection huge against her stomach. The blue fire in his eyes was brighter than the flowers around them. He lowered his mouth to her neck and tugged her marked flesh between his teeth. She gasped as little jolts of pleasurable pain shot straight to her core.

With a growl, he turned her around, and lowered her to the soft grass. His big hand on the center of her back pushed her shoulders down. She turned her head to one side, her cheek on the carpet of glowing flowers, and looked at him. He was so powerful, so huge and masculine, and he delighted her on every level. Her butt was up in the air, her sex hot and wet and exposed to his hungry gaze. Her position was completely submissive, yet she felt potent, knowing her warrior would give as much as he took.

He licked her once, tantalizing and teasing from her rear all the way down her slick folds. She moaned in response, fingers clutching blades of grass. He grabbed her hips and with a snarl he thrust his cock deep, tilting her body to give him complete access. She'd probably have bruises tomorrow from his tight grip, but she didn't care. He let go of one hip, only to bring his hand down hard on her ass.

A whoosh of air left her lungs. Just like the first time he had spanked her in the hallway of his house, it felt naughty and erotic. She had no idea why, and this wasn't the time to start ruminating on her new-found sexual pleasure. She only murmured, "Do it again."

He spanked her other cheek, then reached around to find her nipple and tease it with his fingers. Leaning down, he bit her shoulder. She cried out, his teeth sending shivers all along her back and around to her chest. Her skin tingled everywhere as need built inside her, and she pushed back to meet his body.

He thrust harder and deeper, making her breasts bounce against the grass. With one last gentle pinch, his hand left her nipple and trailed down her belly. She gasped as his teasing fingers found her clit and began slow, tortuous circles.

"Faster," she moaned, and he obliged her with a growl. She braced one arm against the ground to keep from sliding forward from the force of him as he pushed deeper inside her. She relished the night air on her skin. The sensation of being naked outside, with him buried inside her, made her pleasure build until her world exploded into white heat.

When she could breathe again, she realized he was still pounding against her backside. Then she decided turnabout was fair play, and reached her own hand back to cup his balls. He cursed and pumped her harder. She continued to massage him until she felt his body detonate as he roared her name.

He slumped forward, leaning his weight on her for the briefest moment. Then he swiftly flipped her to her back and set upon her breasts with his mouth and hands. He sucked, licked, tickled and teased her nipples and the tender skin around them until she writhed in the grass.

Keeping his lips closed around one achingly hard nipple, he moved one hand down to stroke between her thighs, which were soaked from their combined fluids. One stroke, then two, then he fluttered his finger devilishly against her clit. She cried out as her body rocked against his hand, her vision hazy, the sensations seeming to go on and on.

She rode out the last of the aftershocks and gazed up. Through her fog of delight, she could see his handsome face framed by the endlessly glowing blossoms. It would be so easy to believe this was some sort of Eden, that she had been transported straight into a dream she didn't want to leave. All of Torth seemed that way so far. Even though they came here to gather information and had run into their share of trouble, the journey had been magical. They had found such a wealth of pleasure in each other's arms that she knew she would never get enough of him.

But Eden had its snake, and so did Torth. The Vipers and Ghazsul demons had shown the vicious underside of life in the demon realm. And she and Gunnar were here to prevent another ugly evil from taking hold on Earth. She reached up to caress his jaw and he leaned into her hand, kissing it.

"This place is amazing," she whispered. "It still feels like a dream."

"A very wet one," he murmured teasingly. "But yes, you look like some kind of dreamy sex goddess, lying here on the ground, sated from my touch, with your hair full of crushed phos-blooms."

"What?" She reached up to touch her hair and couldn't suppress a giggle. So much for not crushing any of the delicate flowers. Deciding to just leave them there, she said, "Lie down."

He obliged, and she curled up next to him with her head on his shoulder, her arm thrown across his chest. She wanted to steal just a few more minutes in this magic place with him. They lay quietly entwined as the moon shone high overhead, its pale light adding to the soft glow of the phos-blooms and sharpening the edges of the tree trunks.

Today had been a momentous day for her. She felt closer to him than ever, but still, she knew he harbored a dark secret. She wanted to break down that last barrier between them. Something haunted the big dangerous demon in her arms, something that he hadn't wanted to share with her. *Is he hesitant because he's not sure what I'll think?* She pressed a kiss to his shoulder, the knowledge growing in her that she cared for him with a surprising protectiveness. Whatever had happened was in the past, and nothing could alter their connection. She wanted so badly to understand him, to know every single thing about him, that tonight she felt bold enough to push him.

"Gunnar?" She traced his collarbone with tentative fingers. *Please don't shut me out.*

"Mmm?" His rumbled response made her belly flutter.

"What happened between you and the Ghazsul demons?"

CHAPTER 17

THE ENTIRE WORLD FROZE. GUNNAR went utterly still. The wind held its breath, as Nicole held hers. Even the crickets quieted their soft chirping.

She propped herself up on one elbow to look into his handsome face. His eyes shone with an azure luster, but his gaze hardened as he stared up at the moon. She gently cupped his cheek and whispered, "Please tell me."

He lay silent for so long that she doubted he'd confide in her. Disappointment chilled her veins at the thought that he didn't trust her or didn't care enough about her to share this painful part of his life. Then she felt instantly chastened, worried she'd pushed too far. Unwelcome tears gathered and she closed her eyes, her heart beating in dull thuds of regret.

Her emotions tumbled to a halt as he nudged her down to the soft grass, reversing their positions so that he leaned on his elbow beside her. He gazed at her, his eyes glowing and soft. "It's not easy to talk about."

Afraid to speak for fear she'd ruin the moment, she reached for his hand and held it between both of hers. Tenderly she rubbed small circles along the back.

"I haven't spoken of it in a long time." Breaking her gaze, blue eyes looked off at some distant point in the trees. He seemed a million miles away. She continued to caress his hand, trying to convey the overwhelming devotion welling in her heart. His internal struggle painted on his face, she waited. Then he spoke.

"My family lived near a city called Halice. We had a house just outside the city limits." His voice was rough. "It wasn't huge, but it was nicer than most of the homes in the city. My sister was a year older than me, and we played games constantly. She and I looked alike enough that many people thought we were twins. Our mother taught us at home, and we always tried to get out of our studies.

"One day we were playing hide and seek. We had the perfect house for it–there were lots of rooms and closets. We even had a secret passageway; although my sister and I made up a rule that it was off limits. It was too obvious to hide in there.

"We convinced my parents to join us. Our mother played our games with us sometimes, but it was my dad who took more coaxing. He loved us, but there were a lot of demands on his time.

"We decided that since there were four of us playing, we would use the entire house and yard. My mother was "it." I was hiding in a closet in one of the bedrooms when it seemed like it was taking a long time for her to find me. I didn't hear my sister either, and she always made a lot of noise when her hiding place was discovered."

A sick feeling filled Nicole's stomach. She couldn't look away from Gunnar as raw emotions fired across his beautiful eyes. Her fingers stilled and she squeezed his hand tightly.

"Then I heard screams coming from downstairs. I tiptoed to the second floor landing and looked down to see our foyer full of Ghazsul demons. I didn't know it then, but it turns out it was a group of thugs who had broken into some homes in the city a few months back. They had never been caught, but things had been quiet for a while, so everyone thought they had moved on.

"Being Lash demons, my father and mother were both excellent fighters, but they were vastly outnumbered. My mother was on the floor, trying to protect my sister who was cowering and crying underneath her. But they pulled her away."

Gunnar broke off, his face a mask of painful memories. She

wanted to reach for him, but she was afraid to move. At this moment he wouldn't want her comfort. He was finally sharing with her the burden of his past, and she sensed he would do it by finding the strength within himself to get the words out.

His voice dropped to a whisper. "Two of them held my sister. Three each held my mother and father. They slit their throats, one by one. First my sister, then my mother. They forced my father to watch. Then it was his turn.

"I didn't know what to do. I couldn't move. I was frozen in a nightmare, watching my family being murdered. Then someone yelled to search the house, and I ran for the secret passageway. I stayed there as the Ghazsuls ransacked our home. Then they were gone."

Nicole bit her lip and tears again brimmed in her eyes. She ached to hold him, to embrace the dark-haired boy she saw in her mind's eye. But that boy was gone, replaced by the dangerous man who'd finally opened his soul to her. She swallowed hard and waited.

"I stayed in the passageway for hours, scared that one of them might have stayed behind. Finally I got too hungry to stay put, so I came out. I crept through the house as quietly as I could, but there was no sign of the Ghazsuls. They had just left my family there on the floor. I couldn't move them–I was too little. I sat down next to them and cried. Night came and I stayed with them. I almost wished the Ghazsuls had killed me, too, because I didn't know what to do. We had no other family.

"I took some bread from the kitchen, took some bedding from my room, and went back into the secret passageway. I did that for a few days, until there was no more food. Then I had to find a way to eat.

His expression darkened. "That's when I became a criminal. I stole food and slept in the street. If I got caught by the shop owners I got beaten, so I learned how to sneak through the shadows undetected.

"On the streets there were other young feral demons like me. Most were looking for food or a fight. Most were stronger, so I had to be careful. The bigger ones slept in the better places, the alleys that weren't full of piss and biting rats. I was small and alone, and I had my dinner taken away from me more than once. But as I grew older, I grew bigger. A lot bigger than the others, since most of them weren't Lash. I learned how to fight any way that I could, even if it meant fighting dirty. I made a lot of enemies.

"My anger only grew stronger. If I came across a Ghazsul demon, I killed it. No questions asked. If anyone stole from me, I killed them. Whenever I thought of my family, I was filled with rage. I wanted to avenge them. Deep down, on some subconscious level, I knew I wasn't going about it in the right way. My father wouldn't have wanted me to live like that. But I didn't know anything else. At that point, I didn't know who I was. I was nothing more than a thief and a killer.

"One day I came across a group of demons fighting near the waterfront. Some were Lash, and some were Domu. They were the two most powerful species that I knew of, and they were fighting to the death. It was like watching a macabre ballet— the way they leapt, dodged blows, and sliced with their swords. The ground was soaked and slippery with spilled blood, but they never lost their footing. Heads flew into the water as they were separated from their bodies. I hid behind some barrels and watched as the Lash eventually defeated all the others, finishing them off with demonfire from their palms.

"Watching members of my own species fight like that gave me an idea. Maybe I could fight with them; channel my anger into something productive. I felt like I already had something in common with them, and joining them would be my way out of the hellish way I'd been living. If they would let me in.

"I came out of my spot behind the barrels. I didn't know if they would kill me, and at that point I didn't care. My pathetic existence wasn't helping anyone. I knew I would either fight with them or I would die, and either option was fine with me."

He turned to her and gave her a wry smile. "Obviously they didn't kill me. They brought me to Arawn, the leader of the Lash demons. He remembered my parents, but no one had ever known the whole story of what happened to them. He accepted me into the Watcher ranks and I began to train with them. That was nearly two centuries ago."

Blue eyes locked with hers in the parti-colored clearing. "To this day, Ghazsuls make me angrier than any other foe. I don't always shift into the thing you saw yesterday. But I can't control it. When it happens, it needs to run its course."

Nicole reached up to caress his stubbly cheek. Her heart broke for the child he had been. The horrors he witnessed had hardened him and taken his innocence, but he retained a resolute sense of fairness. Like her, loss had shaped his life but didn't define it. She stroked his face and whispered, "I'm so sorry."

He gazed down at her. "I was a criminal. Then a warrior. At one point," he paused. "I didn't imagine I'd live to see two centuries pass."

"You did what you had to. No child should have to endure the things you saw. But you never stopped fighting."

He shook his head. "And now, by some twist of fate, I find myself in the arms of a Solsti. I thought the gods hated me. But I must have found favor with at least one of them."

She smiled up at him, her heart swelling as she realized that a piece of it would forever belong to him. The massive demon at her side had lost one family and gained another, and bore the scars on his very soul. She wanted to kiss the hurt away, but knew from her own life that it would always be there. The sadness would remain, but it would exist next to new, buoyant memories. He had come through his own fiery trial as she had hers, not unscathed, but forged into something altogether different and stronger. "Come here." She tugged his face down to hers and kissed his mouth tenderly, then dotted his jaw with tiny kisses. "I'm so glad you found me."

"That makes two of us." He rolled them so that she lay atop him, their bodies aligned.

Her hair had to be a tangled mess of grass and glowing petals, but she let it fall around their faces like a curtain. She studied him, never wanting to forget how he looked beneath her in the moonlight, his body, mind, and soul open to her. Resting her head on his shoulder, she nuzzled his neck and inhaled his dark, masculine scent. She was flooded with the realization that one lifetime with him would never be enough.

With the steady beat of his heart at her ear, she lay pressed against him, his hand at the small of her back. An unfamiliar sense of blissful, contented joy mixed with fierce possession washed over her. She adored her scarred and lethal demon, and she luxuriated in the knowledge of him that warmed every fiber of her being. She didn't know how much time had passed before he slid his hand down to pat her bottom, a gentle reminder that they needed to return to the colony.

She pushed herself up to a sitting position and, out of habit, looked around for her clothes. Huffing out a small sound of frustration, she realized that her leafy dress lay in hopeless shreds on the grass.

He quirked an eyebrow.

"We have to walk back into the colony, and I'll be naked."

"Trust me, none of the nymphs will be offended."

She glared at him. "Other males will see me."

"They'll look the other way if they want to avoid bodily harm." He got up and ducked behind a tree, only to come out holding something. "I left this here earlier today."

She beamed as she recognized one of his T-shirts. It would be huge on her, but she would be covered. "You think of everything," she sighed softly. "Do you do dishes and cuddle, too?"

He frowned. "Hmm. I can't make any promises about dishes, but we did just cuddle, so that's a definite yes." He closed the distance between them and said against her lips, "Besides, cuddling leads to fucking."

"I thought cuddling happened after fucking."

"It's both." he growled. "And hearing your pretty mouth say 'fucking' is really hot."

She grinned as she pulled on his enormous T shirt and

raised her arms. "Then let's start cuddling again right now. You can carry me back to the colony."

Chapter 18

MAERON PACED IN HIS UNDERGROUND lab, mindful of the bare light bulbs, his head nearly reaching the ceiling. He towered over the Skells, who scurried to complete their tasks and stay out of his way at the same time. Only a few of them had returned with blood this evening, no doubt due to the interference of the blasted Lash demons. They considered themselves to be some kind of white knights for the entire immortal realm, and now they had spilled over to Earth. Picking up an empty glass jar, Maeron hurled it across the room, satisfied as it shattered against the concrete wall.

With shuffling feet and downcast eyes, the last of the night's successful Skells descended to the deepest part of the lair and crept toward the work table. It carried a plastic container, which it held up for him to see. Just a few precious drops, but it would do. He only needed one drop from each pathetic human.

"Pour it in!" he snarled. "Carefully!"

Shaking, the Skell walked to the end of the table where a vat lay beneath a large beveled opening in the stone surface. Flush with the opening, the top edge aligned so none of the blood could be spilled by the clumsy Skells. This one actually managed to be careful as it overturned its container into the vat, which was more than half full.

Its contents more valuable than gold, the vat would soon be filled with the blood of five hundred human souls. The more destitute and down-trodden, the greater the despair of the souls, the more powerful the blood. Hence, he sent the Skells into the worst areas of the city. Not only did the residents provide the perfect ingredient, but no one would give credence to their claims of being cut up by gray-skinned creatures. Maeron watched the crimson blood drip into the vat before barking at the Skell to leave.

The pathetic Skells had some ridiculous claims of their own. A few nights ago, several had received telepathic messages from three of their kin. They bungled their job and, in the middle of a human gang fight, met a quick demise at the hands of the Lash demons. His Skells claimed to see two female fae in the middle of the ruckus. They fancied the females manipulated both air and water, causing harm and distraction to the humans. Maeron snorted his disgust. The Skells would believe in anything, even creatures that didn't exist.

His icy heart swelled a little as he regarded his crimson treasure. Kept at a warm simmer by magic, the vat maintained the blood's viability until he attained the necessary amount. He had all the other ingredients ready. Maeron would collect the blood himself if not for his decidedly demonic appearance. The Skells at least bore a slight resemblance to the human form. Being a Domu had great advantages, but looking human was not one of them. He stood nearly seven feet tall, with dark charcoal gray skin, yellow eyes, and claws that tipped long spindly fingers. His figure was too distinct to move freely on Earth, but soon that would change.

One of the benefits of this spell was the ability to create changes in his own appearance, as well as illusions of an individual's environment. And that was only the beginning. A grin cracked his dry, charcoal face. The spell, hidden for so long, was one of the most powerful in existence. He would be able to teleport, erase memories, and conjure demonfire, among other things. Once complete, he would finally receive his due respect.

He'd searched for centuries to find something just like this. He was tired of the supposed balance of power in the world; instead, he saw a void that needed to be filled by one being. And he decided that being would be him. He combed every realm for every spell he could find. He amassed an impressive library of grimoires plucked from every remote corner of the world. And thanks to one of his ancestors, he had his plan in place.

But unlike his ancestor, the Domu Xarrek, he moved his base of operations to Earth to avoid the inevitable scrutiny of his kin. They would recognize a power play immediately. But they couldn't recognize one if they weren't around, and not many of the Domu travelled to Earth. Their appearance alone would cause too much of a sensation among the humans, and then the Lash demons would get involved.

All of his frustrations circled back to the Lash demons. They would be sorry they'd interfered. He looked forward to crushing them with a flick of his littlest finger.

Gunnar and Nicole stood with Taszim on the bridge. The morning sun warmed their backs as they scanned the horizon, watching for Raniero. A small group emerged along the ridge far across the field. Gunnar froze, scrutinizing them, then nodded. "That's Raniero."

A few moments later they all stood together, introductions complete. Raniero took Nicole's hand, winked at her, and kissed it, partly to annoy Gunnar, she guessed. Certainly he could see the mark on her neck. Everyone could.

"It's a pleasure to see you again, Nicole," he said. "I hear you were a great help to Rivkin."

"I'm sure you'll be even more helpful than I was. I'm sorry that we can't stay longer. Taszim is an excellent host."

"The nymphs are known for their hospitality." Raniero's eyes twinkled. Here was one demon who she doubted would turn down any offers of comfort from Rivkin's females.

They headed inside the colony for a meeting to discuss strategy. The new group of Lash demons attracted covetous stares from most of the females they passed. *Yep, these demons will enjoy themselves while they guard Rivkin.* It seemed like a win-win situation.

All too soon it was time to leave. Larissa and Taszim stood with the other demons, as well as a large contingent of nymphs, to see them off. Larissa hugged Nicole, kissed her on both cheeks, and ordered her to return one day soon. Like Rosa, she also instructed Nicole to bring her sisters. If she got that request again, she'd be giving Brooke and Gin a guided tour of Torth soon. *Just add "enchanted realm tour guide" to my resume.*

Gunnar held her hand in one of his, and with the other he produced the amulet that would take them home. He muttered a few words in demonish, and a shimmering giant ring appeared in the air next to them.

"Ready?" he asked.

She nodded and waved one last time to her new friends. He wrapped his arms around her, pulling her close, and then stepped into the portal.

Once again she experienced the sensation of tumbling through the air. *Will I ever get used to this?* It was like swinging high on a swing set and then jumping off, except that it took much longer to land. She was glad to have Gunnar's strong arms around her.

They fell on the grass with a soft thud. She raised her head from Gunnar's chest to see that they were lying in the back yard of the Evanston house. Gunnar had maneuvered so that he was under her, taking the brunt of the fall.

"Are you okay?" she asked.

"Are you kidding? You're on top of me. There's no way that I wouldn't be okay."

She narrowed her eyes at him. "Rogue."

"Vixen." He leaned up to steal a kiss.

A voice carried across the yard as a short figure hurried over. "Gunnar! Nicole! I was beginning to wonder if you planned to stay on Torth for good," Rilan chided as he reached them.

Standing up, Gunnar towered over the Elder. So did the three other Lash demons that had emerged from the large house. Nicole remembered meeting them all, but it felt like it was months ago.

"We made a side trip to Rivkin," Gunnar said. "I'll tell you all about it inside."

At the mention of the nymph colony, the other three warriors whistled and mumbled appreciatively. Rhys nodded and grinned. "Aw, man. Nymphs."

Gunnar shook his head. "Raniero and his friends are keeping them safe at the moment."

"Safe?" Kai asked. "From what?"

"It's a long story." Gunnar rubbed the back of his neck.

"Wait, where's Brooke?" Nicole glanced around the yard. Was it her imagination, or did Kai scowl at the mention of her sister?

"Not here at the moment. She said something about a business trip that she couldn't get out of," he muttered.

"That's right. Her big account in Florida." A few times a year, Brooke had to go to South Beach for some face time with her most lucrative client. "She'll be back Friday night." She furrowed her brow. "It's Wednesday, right?"

Gunnar smiled and took her hand. "Yes. Time passes the same in both realms."

"Well I, for one, can't wait to hear all about your trip." Brenin stood with his hands on his hips. "I hope your last few days were more successful than ours."

Nicole opened her mouth to ask what he meant, but stopped when Gunnar cupped her cheek. "Inside." Wrapping an arm around her shoulders, he tugged her to the back door of the house. The rest of the group fell in step behind them. "We'll sit down and go over every detail of what we found over the last few days."

They settled into the great room for Gunnar and Nicole's account of their adventures on Torth. The others listened and nodded. Brenin grimaced when Gunnar described the meeting with Rosa.

Nicole looked back and forth between the two men. "What? She was nice."

"Yeah, I'm sure it was." Brenin folded his arms over his chest. "She has my respect, but *shit*. That witch's power is intense."

Nicole shrugged. She wasn't about to question Rosa.

Gunnar went on to detail the attack by the winged Ghazsul demons. The men froze, eyes locked on their comrade.

"Fucking *wings*?" Rhys narrowed his eyes. "What the fuck?"

Gunnar nodded grimly. "My thoughts exactly. The good thing is," he turned to Nicole, "Our little Solsti's talent comes in quite handy against flying creatures." He squeezed her hand and she smiled. He then went on to explain the surprise raid on Rivkin yesterday morning.

The other Lash demons stared at Nicole. "You turned the tide against the Vipers." Brenin's blue eyes studied her intently.

Nicole dropped her gaze to her hands. "The nymph archers were really accurate."

"That's true, but the outcome would have been different without you. The nymphs fought hard, but they would've lost many more lives. And possibly their home." Gunnar gave her hand another warm squeeze.

"What the hell is headed our way?" Kai's tone was pissed. "What fucking nightmare necessitated the return of the Solsti?"

"And here I thought you liked me, Kai," Nicole said, trying to lighten the mood in the room.

"Yeah, *you're* okay," the blond demon grumbled.

"It's more important than ever that you and your sisters are prepared," Rilan said. "Now that you have made an appearance on Torth, word will travel. Although not many will believe it at first, so you may have some time." He paused. "Can't you bring your other sister here?"

Nicole shook her head, sighing as she said her sister's name. "Gin. If there was a book about being stubborn, Gin would've already written it. She thought Brooke and I were crazy to go out and practice using our gifts the way we did. She doesn't want anything to do with her ability."

"She's the one who can conjure fire?" Brenin asked.

"She can't conjure it, if it isn't there to begin with. But all she needs is a lighter, and she can build a flame into an inferno. Kind of like how Brooke only needs a few drops of water to create a deluge."

"Hmm." Brenin frowned. "Maybe if she sees how we shape and control our demonfire, she'll be more comfortable."

"I'll talk to her, but I can't make any promises."

Kai stood up, anger rolling off his tall frame. "Yeah, well, she needs to understand this isn't all about her. We all have to make sacrifices."

Gunnar tensed. "Watch your fucking mou–"

"It's okay," Nicole said. "I agree with you, Kai. It's just that Gin will take some convincing."

Kai stalked to the window and folded his arms across his chest. He glared out at the September sunlight. "I followed one of those maggots as far as I could before it got into a fucking car. Headed south on I-57. I couldn't run it down."

"We'll keep searching the area, man," Rhys offered. "And now, we know the bastard's name. Maeron. Whoever the fuck that is."

"Yeah, and that he collects old coins," Brenin mused. "Although, he's not being very careful if the Skells are running off with them. Unless he's letting them."

"So other demons know that they're allied with this guy?" Rhys balled up a piece of paper and tossed it across the room. It landed with a soft swish, dead center in a small garbage can by the computers.

"Perhaps," Rilan said. "We'll search the south suburbs and along the interstate. Nicole, I want you and your sisters to keep honing your skills. If you need me, just ask." He held the old grimoire from Taszim carefully in his hands. "I'll begin translating this as soon as we're done here."

Gunnar turned to her. "I don't want you going out at night, playing hero." He placed a finger on her lips at her look of indignation. "It's too dangerous, now that word is out about you. I know you want to help people, but think of everyone you'll help if you can repeat what you did at Rivkin."

Remembering the vicious Vipers shifted her disgruntled mood into perspective. *What will happen if they come here?* She shuddered at the thought of the carnage they would cause. "Okay," she said softly. He seemed almost surprised at her acquiescence. "What about you?"

"Kai and I will look for Skells tonight."

"Rhys and I will search the areas south of the city," Brenin said.

"Rilan will be translating," Gunnar continued. "You'll be safe here. You should get some rest."

She nodded, and her stomach rumbled as if on cue. This was getting embarrassing. Gunnar grinned at her. "Eat first, then rest."

She rummaged in the kitchen's huge freezer and found a frozen deep dish pizza from a local restaurant. Evidently even demons agreed with her that nothing could compare to Chicago style pizza. Smiling, she preheated the oven and searched the cabinets and pantry. Frozen items were fine, but if she was going to spend more time here, she would need to stock up on fresh foods. Especially with several huge and hungry demon males around. Gunnar said that they didn't need to eat often, but the aroma of cooking food seemed to attract them like bees to honey.

Gunnar sat with her as she ate and polished off the two thirds of the pizza that she couldn't finish. They shared a lingering kiss after they'd cleaned up the kitchen, with Nicole insisting that he be careful and Gunnar insisting that she get sleep. Then he and Kai went to the training room to prepare for the evening, and she went upstairs alone to his bedroom.

I could be sleeping here for a while. A smile crept across her face at that thought. Gunnar's décor could only be described as sparse and masculine. Several pieces of dark mahogany furniture occupied the room, including a king-sized poster bed and a large armchair. A huge old-looking double-bladed sword hung on the wall. *I bet there's a story behind that.* She made a mental note to ask him about it later.

Picking up her phone, she dialed Brooke's number. She had texted her sister earlier in the day to tell her she arrived home safely, and that she'd call when she got a chance. Brooke would be busy with her client until after dinner, anyway.

"Nic!" The relief in her sister's voice was palpable. "Where are you?"

"Here in Evanston, at Demon Central. And don't worry, I'm not going out tonight. I'm going to do something unusual and get some sleep."

"I'm sure you need it. But first I want details of your little excursion."

"I think I have to tell you most of it in person. Torth is an amazing, beautiful, dangerous, wild place. It'll take days to tell you everything. But you'll see it for yourself one day."

"Oh, really? I'm going there? Did you just decide this for me?"

"No, a very old witch did. Your presence has been requested." Nicole couldn't hold back a laugh at Brooke's screech on the other end of the line. She gave in and told her all about Rosa and her fairy tale cottage. Before she knew it, an hour had slipped by. Talking to Brooke was like a balm. She hadn't realized quite how much she had missed her sister. Finally they agreed to hang up, with the promise of much more conversation in two days' time. Eyelids suddenly heavy, she washed up quickly in the adjoining bathroom and slipped into Gunnar's bed. Her last thoughts were of how his sheets smelled deliciously like him: clean and woodsy, masculine and brawny, and *hers*.

CHAPTER 19

KAI ITCHED TO GET OUT of the house and into the city's rough neighborhoods. He needed to vent his pent-up frustration on some unfortunate creature. It had been two days since Brooke left for her business trip, and he could still smell her sweet scent in the house. Especially when he passed the guest room where she'd slept. At least it was finally dissipating enough that he didn't get hard just walking by the door anymore.

He did his best to avoid her for the twenty-four hours following their little confrontation in the kitchen. The house was big, but not big enough. He'd left for a few hours, only to return to find her in the back yard with Rilan, trying out some trick near the birdbath. Kai went out to watch, thinking maybe he could set things right.

"Nice. I knew a water sprite once who could do that. Among other things." He studied the thin stream of water that shot skyward before splitting in two graceful arcs. He didn't see the point of that particular exercise. How could she do anything with a trickle of water?

She looked at him like he was a bug stuck to the bottom of her boot. "Good for you."

"Everyone's gotta learn sometime. You know, start with the basics..." He broke off as she narrowed her eyes and glared at him. She opened her mouth as if to say something, then closed it and turned away.

He stalked through the back door and into the kitchen, muttering under his breath. "S'up?" he said to Rhys, who stood juggling three apples in a swirl of red flashes.

Rhys stopped, tossed Kai an apple, and retrieved a water bottle from the fridge. "She's been out there all afternoon with the Elder." He rested a hip at the counter and nodded toward the window.

Kai rolled his eyes and sank his teeth into the crisp fruit. Great, two insults in less than sixty seconds. *How soon is she leaving?*

The next day he went downstairs to work out in the training room. Her lilac scent enticed him as soon as he started down the steps, caressing his skin and firing his blood. He gritted his teeth. No reason he couldn't get through a fucking workout just because she was in the room. But when he opened the door to see her running on the treadmill, he froze.

Every drop of blood in his body shot straight to his groin. All he could do was stare at her, transfixed by her rounded ass and full breasts bouncing as she jogged. She had earbuds in, a music player resting on the display, and she wore a black tank top and shorts. A light sheen of sweat covered her creamy skin, nearly all of which was displayed nicely thanks to her skimpy outfit. Thank the gods she didn't see him, since he was now sporting a hard-on the size of a rocket. He silently backed out of the room and closed the door.

He avoided her the rest of the day, knowing she had to leave to catch her plane that evening. If she walked into a room, he walked out of it. To hell with being nice. She unsettled him. He wanted to return her every glare and prickly comment. And he wanted to pin her sweet curves against the nearest wall, fucking her until she screamed his name.

Now he perched silently with Gunnar on a rooftop in a gentrifying west-side neighborhood. Fast food bags and used napkins drifted down the street, past gleaming new condos mixed in with shabbier buildings. Only years of training kept Kai from fidgeting. His sexual frustration and general bad mood were turning him into a ticking time bomb, and he really needed to smoke some Skells.

Gunnar glanced at him from his position several feet away. "What's up with you?"

If Kai had to be stuck with someone tonight, Gunnar would be his first pick. He'd push Kai, but he knew when to shut the hell up. "Just ready for a fight." *Enough about me.* "So, you and the blonde, huh?"

Gunnar grunted but couldn't hold back a grin. "Yeah. Me and Nicole."

The bright eyes and look of pure contentment on his friend's face was one Kai had never seen on him before. "Fuck." Kai stared at him.

"What?"

"Dude, you've got 'whipped' written all over your face."

Gunnar didn't say anything at first. He raised his eyebrows and his smile widened. "I have no argument with that."

Kai snorted. "Never saw that one coming."

"Neither did I."

"Yeah well, better you than me. Just don't get soft out here, man." Kai scanned the street below. *Good for Gunnar.* Kai didn't do commitment.

"I can still take your ass down—"

"G. There." Kai's fight instincts jumped to life as he saw a small shape dart into an alley across the road. "Showtime."

Kai didn't wait for his friend as he made the three-story drop to the ground. In a blur of movement, he sprinted to the other side of the street and into the alley. To his acute eyes, the dark space was bright as day. He quickly spotted the telltale gray skin of the Skell as it turned the corner at the other end of the block. Kai grinned as he chased it. It didn't have a prayer of escaping him.

He emerged from the alley onto a side street used primarily for deliveries. Warehouses loomed like concrete sentries, and debris littered the sidewalks. The Skell scrambled toward a dumpster and ducked behind it. A soft thud above, audible only to Kai's demon hearing, let him know that Gunnar was perched on the roof.

Kai ran to the dumpster and shoved it aside, revealing the quaking Skell's hiding place. He grabbed it by its scrawny neck and shook it. "Time to talk, maggot."

A small plastic bottle fell out of its pants pocket.

"You're gonna tell me what that's for," Kai snarled.

"I don't know," the Skell gasped through Kai's chokehold.

"Try again." Yeah, the Skells were incompetent, but with this many of them involved, someone was bound to know something.

"No, I really don't." It flailed its arms.

Gunnar's footfalls sounded behind him, ready for backup duty. Not that he would need it against one of these things. He already knew his friend would let him take the lead on this little interrogation.

"I'm really tired of getting that response," Kai said with feigned disinterest as he drew a dagger from his thigh and studied it. Then raising it in silver arc, he brought it down, severing the Skell's hand. It shrieked and howled.

"Ready to talk now?"

It clutched its bloody wrist with its good hand. "H-he just keeps making us go out and get more. We don't know what he's going to do with it."

"With what?"

"The b-blood. From the humans."

"He makes you guys bring it back to him?"

The Skell nodded pitifully. "He m-makes us put it into a big container. That's all. We haven't seen him do anything with it. He just says he wants more of it. He says he's almost ready."

"Ready for what?" Kai lifted it to his eye level. The bumbling demon hovered two feet off the ground.

"I don't know! None of us do. We don't know," it whimpered, before its speech dissolved into incoherent mumbles.

"I think that's about all he's got to say," Gunnar muttered from behind him.

Kai nodded in agreement. He released the creature and took

a step back, then summoned a ball of demonfire and tossed it at the Skell. Its pathetic life winked out in an instant.

"You're so sexy when you're killing one of those things."

Kai whirled at the velvety purr behind him. "Miranda." He locked eyes with the sultry Deserati demon. "What are you doing here?"

Full red lips pouted. "I'm being punished." Her mouth curved into a smile as her gaze roamed him from head to toe. "But I didn't know you were in the area. Punishment is looking more fun already."

He lowered his dagger and raked a hand through his hair. "What'd you hit this time?"

"Just because I put a hole in a mountain trying to kill one of those." She nodded at the smoking Skell. "They sent me to the flattest land they could think of." Swiveling around, she said, "Hi, Gunnar. You know I think you're cute, but I've always had a thing for blondes." She turned her appreciative smile back to Kai.

Kai snorted. "He's off the market now, anyway."

She raised her eyebrows. "*You* had better not be."

Kai met Miranda some twenty years ago, when their paths had crossed tracking down a troublesome band of dark elves. The Deserati demons were almost always on the same side as the Lash demons, if they bothered to get involved in a conflict. One of their special skills was scrying. It helped to have someone who could tell you what would happen next, or where your target was going to be the next day. Of course, their services came with a high price.

Like all the Deserati, Miranda had pointed ears and small horns, which she usually kept hidden beneath her mane of thick, wavy auburn hair. She also had a long, elegant tail that she could hide much the same as the Ghazsul demons hid their wings. Kai had vivid memories of the deviously carnal things she could do with that tail.

Every time they'd run into each other over the years, they ended up in bed. Miranda had a sinfully curvy body, and she was as voracious as she was talented. But by mutual agreement, it was all about sex between them, and nothing more. She was as opposed to settling down with a mate as he was.

His gaze travelled over her now. Dressed from head to toe in black leather, she had some kind of corset top that bared her midriff and pushed her full breasts up. Her green eyes filled with heat as she watched him study her body. *Yeah, Miranda might be exactly what I need tonight.*

"You took out a mountain, huh? That takes a lot of power." A small percentage of Deserati could call upon lightning. Unfortunately Miranda's talent, despite years of training, was as inconsistent as it was rare. As a result, she was prohibited from using it unless specifically ordered to.

She blew out a breath. "I'm getting stronger. Just not more accurate." One arched eyebrow quirked as she took in the Skell, now just a pile of ash, and the desolate street. "What're you guys doing here, anyway?"

Kai summed up the situation with the Skells. As much as he could, anyway. It seemed like they had been searching for answers for weeks and getting nowhere. He was tired of this fucker Maeron and his band of Skells making the Watcher brethren run in circles.

As he wrapped up his explanation and the facts they had, Gunnar broke in. "You know Miranda, we could use your assistance."

The demoness raised her eyebrows and nodded. "You do seem to be hitting a lot of brick walls. I can help you." She tilted her head. "What are you willing to offer?"

"Protection."

"Am I going to need it?"

"Some major shit may be hitting the fan soon," Kai muttered.

"Oh? Do tell, Kai. Or do you want me to coax it out of you?" she murmured, her gaze dropping to his crotch.

"We don't have any specific threats. It's just...that something's coming," Gunnar said.

Kai guessed his friend didn't want to share the news of the return of the Solsti. Too bad Miranda could be relentless when she wanted something.

"You both know I'm not going to let that vague threat slide by. Now, spill it." She folded her arms under her breasts, pushing them up even more.

The two males exchanged glances. Kai gave Gunnar a pointed look and gestured to Miranda. "Go ahead. Enlighten our lady."

Gunnar turned to her. "I don't know if any of your kin foresaw this, but...the Solsti have returned."

Miranda's eyes widened to the size of saucers. "I know the Solsti are a myth. They'll supposedly return when their powers are needed to fight against a great evil." Her gaze darted between the two Lash. "And I know you well enough to know you're not shitting me. Have you seen them?"

"He's more than seen one of them," Kai muttered under his breath, just as Gunnar continued.

"Yes, we're working with them."

"Hmm." She tapped a crimson fingernail against her chin. "Not many are alive now who remember when the Solsti were last here. No one knows how diabolical the coming threat will be." Green eyes flicked up, studying the charcoal sky. "Yes, my family will ally with the Lash. You can have the honor of protecting us. That is, when I'm not doing it myself and knocking down the Himalayas." Her sensual lips pulled into a grin.

"You'll get more precise." Kai winked at her.

"Okay boys, let's see what's going on here." She knelt on the pavement and started pulling objects from her leather jacket. Always prepared to work, Miranda produced a pint-sized water bottle and a small bowl that folded nearly flat. Next came a tiny vial. She squeezed one drop of liquid from the vial into the bowl, muttered some words under her breath, and poured the water in. Looking toward the ashes of the Skell, she asked, "Is there anything left of that guy?"

Kai shook his head, then remembered the severed hand. "Here." He tossed it to her.

"Nice," she mumbled as she picked it up and popped off a dirty fingernail. She dropped that into the bowl as well, then watched the shimmering surface.

Gunnar and Kai crouched down behind her, peering over her shoulders. A fine mist chased lazy circles over the top of the bowl, only to dissipate in a few seconds. The smooth surface revealed a dilapidated old farmhouse.

"Where is that?" Kai asked.

"Let me try something." Miranda held her hand over the bowl and spoke a few more words.

Kai didn't know what she was saying, but it sounded like ancient Demonish. As they watched the scrying bowl, the image got smaller and the surrounding area came into view, like zooming out on a map. Unfortunately, the fields around it looked deserted and completely nondescript. Kai scowled.

"There. A river." Gunnar pointed to the lower curve of the circle.

Miranda spoke more Demonish and the view shifted slightly to show them a greater portion of the river. But other than clusters of trees, no significant landmarks became visible.

"I'm afraid that's all we're gonna get tonight, my dears." Miranda sat back on her spiked heels. "I trust that helped?"

"Yes, Miranda, thank you. We're in your debt," Gunnar said.

"You sure are," she agreed cheerfully as she dumped out the water and began putting her things away.

"So we're looking for a run-down farmhouse somewhere south of the city, near a river. That's kinda vague. There's probably a lot of those out there," Kai grumbled.

"That's more information than what we had a few hours ago." Gunnar stood with his hands on his hips. "We should reconvene when Rhys and Brenin get back to the house. And maybe by then Rilan will have translated the grimoire from Taszim."

"You were at Rivkin? I'm jealous."

Kai met her piercing gaze. "*He* was."

"Oh. Well, good. I can show you a better time than those little wood nymphs any day." She straightened from her perch on the ground, unfolding long, shapely legs.

Gunnar cleared his throat. "On that note, I'm going to head home."

"It was nice seeing you again, Gunnar," Miranda called as he melted into the shadows. Abruptly, she turned to Kai and curled her hand into his T-shirt, pulling him close. She had always smelled of roses, and her promise-filled scent hit him now as her lips hovered inches from his. "What do you say, Kai? Watching your big, strong body is getting me all hot and bothered. Want to go someplace more private? Or do you want to dance with me right here?"

"Decisions, decisions." He folded her into his arms and closed the distance between their mouths. She molded her curvy body to his, reminding him of hot nights spent all over the realms. Feeling her lips move under his, thinking about burying himself in her tight warmth should have had him painfully hard. But he couldn't get another face out of his head. Porcelain skin, arresting gray eyes, and silky chestnut waves passed by his closed eyelids.

Miranda knew it, too. She pulled back, her eyes searching his face. "What's going on? Are you involved with someone?"

"No," he muttered, rubbing the back of his neck. "Ah hell." She deserved better than for him to play mind games. He took her hand. "I'm not involved with anyone, exactly, but..."

"That's okay, warrior. I know when you've got something on your mind. Or someone." Slender fingers brushed his cheek. "Just don't go and get mated or anything." She smiled and squeezed his hand, then her cell phone chirped. Tugging it from her impossibly tight pants pocket, she glanced at the number. "Looks like I'm being called away anyhow." Her soft hand clasped his for another second. "Stay safe, my friend."

"You too," he called as she vaulted to the nearest rooftop and disappeared, leaving him to ponder what the hell just happened.

CHAPTER 20

GUNNAR ENTERED THE HOUSE SILENTLY, figuring that its occupants would be asleep. A quick check with his senses confirmed this, and also told him that Rhys and Brenin hadn't returned yet. The car they had driven wasn't parked with the rest of the vehicles, but that didn't always indicate their location. Sometimes the men ended up hoofing it home. Or spending the night with fairer company.

He thought of his own pretty female as he padded up the stairs to his room. Cracking open the door, he paused, noting her slow, even breathing. Her peach scent assailed his nose, and his heart swelled with possessive satisfaction as he took in the view. *Nicole in my bed.* Curled on her side under the sheet, she faced away from him. With his acute vision, he could easily see every strand of pale blond hair splayed across his pillow.

Crossing the room, he pulled his T-shirt over his head. He hadn't gotten covered in Skell blood tonight, instead letting Kai do the dirty work. Gunnar could sympathize with the need to vent his anger through a good brawl. And now, he wouldn't have to turn on the shower and risk waking Nicole.

She should be exhausted after their eventful days on Torth. It hadn't even been a week since she had learned that she wasn't human, and the things they'd been through could've made her run for the nearest bus to anywhere-but-here. But she handled things with a grace and level-headedness that awed him. Although she did seem too eager to jump into battle…but hell, how could he fault her for that? As a Solsti, she would have to fight one day. And if not for her sense of justice, he wouldn't have found her facing off with thugs on the city's meanest streets.

He stripped completely—he usually slept nude. Seeing her in his bed and inhaling her sweet fragrance had him semi-hard, but he was resolved not to wake her. They'd have time in the morning, especially because she was so damn perky at that time of day. He pulled back the sheet to slide in beside her, admiring her long, bare back, small waist, the slight flare of her hips, and her perfect ass.

Which was clad, barely, in a pair of red bikini panties that revealed more of her rounded cheeks than they covered. But the words printed along the top edge, just below the waistband, made all the blood in his body rush to his straining cock. In bright silver block letters, they read "Wake Me Up."

Good gods. In a heartbeat, he climbed in next to her and tugged her tightly against him, her back to his chest. He needed to be skin-to-skin with every long inch of her. Burying his face in her hair, he nestled her sweet bottom on his now-throbbing erection and reached around to cup her breast. She wanted him to wake her up? Good, because he couldn't stop thinking of things to do to her. He couldn't quite believe that he had found a female so perfect, and then she sighed and tried to turn into him.

He didn't let her. Holding her close, he traced circles on the velvety skin of her breast. He moved his thumb back and forth over her nipple, rubbing and circling until the soft skin turn hard and pebbled under his touch. She whispered his name and wiggled her barely-covered ass against him. "You're back."

"You're naughty."

"What'd I do? I was just sleeping."

"In naughty panties."

"They're not as messy as writing on the mirror with lipstick." She moved her free arm up and back, around his neck, bringing her other breast tantalizingly close to his face. He leaned down and closed his lips around her puckered nipple, flicking her with his tongue. His fingers teased under the edge of the red panties.

"I like these. I'll try to not rip them off you."

"There's more where they came from. I have a whole collection." She giggled as he groaned and released her nipple.

His fingers wandered further down, pushing her panties aside to stroke her.

"Be a good boy and you'll get to see the rest," she managed to gasp out before her words disintegrated into a whimper, and her body went completely pliant in his hands.

"Wicked woman." He knelt and pulled her onto her back, then slid off the red, taunting scrap when she lifted her hips. Still kneeling, he kissed his way along her inner thigh, inhaling the spicy-sweet scent of her arousal. Unable to resist, he put his hands under her ass to raise her to his mouth.

Her scent was a drug to him. It was her "tell" that she was ready for him. *No way she can fake that.* The need to claim her grew to a crescendo. Claim not just her body but her very soul. He didn't want any other man to touch her, to caress her silky skin, ever again. She was *his*.

Holding her body in his hands, he paused. Let her feel his warm breath on her mound. "You're mine," he murmured. She squirmed in anticipation.

He licked her slowly, running his tongue up and down her slick folds. She tasted earthy and wild, and she moaned as he kept up his teasingly slow pace. Tonight, he wanted to pleasure her thoroughly, even though his cock was aching to plunge deep inside her. He slid two fingers into her tight entrance and pulled them back out, dripping with her sweet juices. He licked them slowly, eyes meeting hers in the dark as she wriggled beneath him.

"I want you," she whispered.

"Mine." He dipped his head once again to taste her. Resuming his slow teasing licks, he built her need to the brink and then backed off again and again. His hands wandered up her smooth belly to her breasts, teasing her nipples with his fingertips. Finally, knowing she was close to her limits, he sat up and let his eyes rove over her. A light sheen of sweat had broken out over her pale skin, and she tossed her head back and forth on the pillow. Her gloriously long body shifted restlessly around on the bed, her hands fisting the sheets.

"Gunnar, please."

"Please, what?"

"Stop torturing me. I need your cock. Now."

With a low rumble of approval, he moved up her slender body, stopping at the valley between her breasts where her scent concentrated. He drew a breath and made a satisfied sound deep in his chest as her essence washed over him. Moving to one breast, he nuzzled the stiff, pink tip before taking it deep in to his mouth. He repeated the process on her other side and a soft cry of frustration escaped her lips. His eyes never left her face, watching her desire build as her hips sought his. Bracing his hands on either side of her head, he leaned down and nipped her ear. "You're mine."

She mumbled something and tried to reach for him. He took both her hands in one of his and pinned them above her head.

"Mine," he repeated, gently holding the delicate lobe of her ear in his teeth.

"Yes, Gunnar," she finally gasped. "Yours. I'm yours."

Growling in satisfaction, he positioned himself and nudged his blunt head inside her. Frantic with need, she grabbed for him, pulling him down as she locked her ankles around his hips.

"God, you're perfect." He sank into her fragrant heat. Leaning down to kiss her, he thrust his tongue into her mouth as he thrust his cock into her eager, willowy body. She came almost instantly, shuddering and arching off the bed. He kept going, pounding into her, feeling her shatter again beneath him. His orgasm built like a monstrous wave, driving him to push deeper inside her, to possess her completely.

Sitting back on his knees, he jerked her hips up roughly, deepening his angle until he was buried hilt-deep in her tight sheath. He looked down into the luminous green pools of her eyes, which gazed up at him with a mixture of wonder and sated bliss. *Mine.*

He had brought that look into her eyes. He had made her breath ragged and her skin flushed. His woman. The building wave suddenly crashed over him and he exploded, a primal roar ripping from his throat. His body pumping wildly, his seed shot deep into her warm channel as she clutched his legs. When her body had finally wrung the last drop from him, he collapsed on top of her. "I think this time *you* fucked *me* to death," he groaned.

"You're immortal, remember?" She nipped his ear.

He shifted his weight so that he lay at her side with one leg draped over hers and one hand on her ribs.

"And anyway, turnabout is fair play."

He gave her a questioning grunt.

"You were the one teasing me into a frenzy." She propped herself on one elbow and ran her fingers through his hair. "And now you're the one who's too sated to move."

He eyed her beautiful, perky breasts, which hovered mere inches from his mouth. *Damn. She's right.* That had been the most intense orgasm of his long life. And, for the moment, his limbs felt weighted down. "Just give me a minute," he mumbled.

"Take your time, baby. We've got lots of it." She lay back down on her side, facing him and snuggled one arm under her pillow. Her face lit with a dazzling smile, and then her eyes slowly drifted shut. In minutes, she was sound asleep.

He gently untangled his limbs from hers and lay facing her. He could gaze at her physical perfection for hours, but tonight a deeper feeling wouldn't allow his eyes to look away. Something in his world had shifted tonight. She mattered to him on a profound level, one that he hadn't experienced before. Sure, she was beautiful and her body was a carnal playground he never wanted to leave, but this was something else.

He admired her bravery and her determination to help others. *Even though she can be so stubborn.* He smiled and caressed a wayward lock of her hair. Accepting both his past as well as the rage-filled demon it provoked, she hadn't been afraid of him when he shifted, and the beast that took over his mind had in turn accepted *her*. She was so much more than a beautiful creature who needed his protection. He knew her power would continue to grow and would one day become stronger than his, but she was still vulnerable in many ways. He burned with a fierce need to do anything to keep her safe, even if it meant laying down his life.

He would die for her.

His heart stuttered as he gazed at her in the inky darkness, recognizing her as his mate. Possession and peace sung through his veins in harmony, as the depth of his love for her bathed his battered soul.

Raniero drifted to consciousness, letting his hearing and nose alert him to his surroundings. He tensed, realizing he was pinned down. Then he opened his eyes.

A lazy smile spread across his face as he took in the sprawled limbs and full breasts of two of Rivkin's most talented and energetic females. He closed his eyes again, feeling their soft warmth on either side of him, remembering their boundless enthusiasm from the night before. Yes, he would enjoy every minute of his time protecting the nymphs.

Though sorely tempted to rouse them for another round of delectable sex, he knew from the angle of the sun that he had already lingered in bed too long. He could find them later on. He disengaged himself from their silky skin, eliciting sleepy feminine protests, and rose to wash his face and get dressed.

The colony bustled with morning activities as he made his way along the paths. The kitchen clanked with sounds of dishes being cleaned from the morning meal. Soldiers carried weapons as they walked toward the main entrance and the open field beyond. Taszim had ordered extra practice sessions for all able-bodied nymphs.

Finding one of his men, he learned that the night had

passed without incident. He had expected as much. It was doubtful that the Vipers would attack again so soon, but one could never tell with those creatures. He decided that a wide perimeter search was in order, but he wanted to find Taszim first.

He turned when he heard a soft voice at his elbow.

"Would you like some water, my lord?" purred a curvy female. Like most of the females, she wore a simple short brown tunic that was tight enough to show that she wore nothing under it. Her hair was thick and long, a pretty mahogany shade. He took the glass she held out to him and gulped it down, his eyes never leaving her figure.

"Thank you, love. What's your name?"

"Jaina, my lord. Can I get you anything else?"

"Yes, Jaina, I might need something later on." He ran a finger down her bare arm. "But right now, I need to speak with Taszim. Do you know where I can find him?"

"I saw him in the armory a few minutes ago, my lord."

"Thank you kindly, my love." He leaned down to whisper in her ear exactly what he was going to need from her later, and left her giggling in the middle of the path.

Striding toward the armory, he ran into Taszim. The nymphs' leader clapped him on the back in a warm greeting. "I trust you slept well, my good man?"

Raniero chuckled. His unfailingly polite host knew exactly what went on in his colony. "I had a wonderful night, my friend."

Taszim's eyes twinkled with mirth, then his expression sobered. "Last night passed uneventfully, if you haven't yet heard."

"Yes. There's something else I wanted to discuss with you."

"Of course. Let's go to my study. It's much quieter there."

Raniero nodded and fell into step with his host. "Rivkin seems to be prospering," he said as he noted the activity around them.

"Yes, things have worked out well," Taszim agreed as they

stepped inside his study. "The tree harvesting, of course, makes up the bulk of our income. But the nut breads and pastries are doing surprisingly well."

"Pastries?" Raniero raised his eyebrows.

"My wife is quite creative in the kitchen. She came up with a few recipes and brought some of the bakery items to the market at Bearen, and they were a runaway success."

"I'll have to try some of those later." Raniero rubbed a hand along his jaw. "And speaking of business, I'd like you to think back on your recent transactions. I've been speculating on who would retaliate against you. Perhaps the Vipers were simply hired muscle. We've already talked about potential enemies who may have instigated the attack. But what if there are others we have not considered? What if it's business related?"

"Someone who wants Rivkin's assets?"

"No, someone who resents that Rivkin conducted business with another. An enemy, perhaps."

"An enemy of my allies," mused Taszim. "Most of our partners are creatures we have dealt with for decades. The water nymphs, sprites, sorcerers, and many of the fae. Then there are some of the predatory demons, like the Lash and Deserati." He met Raniero's gaze. "I did sell some rare wood to a new Lash acquaintance recently. His name was Cale."

Holy shit. Raniero's heart leapt into his throat, but years of practice allowed him to remain expressionless at the mention of his employer. That demon had scores of enemies. Raniero knew for certain that the Vipers were among them. Because a month ago Cale had ordered him to carry out a hit on one of the Viper's high-ranking leaders. And Raniero had successfully completed his assignment.

Because Cale was wealthy, powerful, and capable of quashing anyone who dared to cross him, the Vipers would be understandably hesitant to strike him directly. Attacking the wood nymphs would be a cowardly choice, but one that could prevent Cale from getting something he wanted.

"Rare wood? What kind?" Raniero asked, bringing his

thoughts back to the business aspect of the deal.

"Silver birch. We have so few of them that we only cut down a handful each year. It's our most expensive wood." Taszim paused and smiled slightly. "The demon was complaining that he had been requested to find that particular wood for his porter."

"He has a porter?" Extremely rare, only a handful of porters existed. They could be found in any species, their ability to travel anywhere being the common thread between them. They could go to any realm at any time, with no need for spells, amulets, or assistance from Elders. And they could bring others with them. They were often wealthy, being able to charge any fee for their uncommon services. He hadn't realized that Cale had a porter on his staff; then again, he shouldn't have been surprised. The demon had everything, and he obtained it using any means necessary. Raniero wondered if this porter had been unwillingly conscripted, as he had.

"Yes," Taszim said. "Of course, Cale didn't come here himself. He sent an associate to negotiate the deal. And after several rounds of our copper beech ale, the man became quite chatty."

Raniero raised an eyebrow, not bothering to hide his curiosity. Any details he learned here may lead to the reason behind the attack. Anything that was of personal use to him would be a lucky coincidence. "Go on."

"It seems this birch wood was part of his porter's fee. She planned to bring it to her family on Evena."

Raniero blew out a breath. "This story gets better and better, my friend." Evena was a wasteland of a realm. Hardly anyone could go there, and he had never known anyone who wanted to. Amulets and spells wouldn't allow for travel to its decimated lands, and none but the very oldest of Elders could find it. And, of course, porters.

Evena didn't have much to offer anyone. Centuries ago it contained bustling villages that harvested a rare black lily. The lily contained an essence that, when properly extracted, mended any wound. Its restorative powers stayed active in the body for months, giving the receiver a boost of strength. It had been a highly coveted and expensive export.

Four centuries ago, two predatory demon species fought over control of Evena and its lily extract. One of the species, the Serus demons, was capable of releasing clouds of toxic fog from their mouths. The battle raged for weeks because their opponent, the Kentini demons, only needed to breathe a miniscule amount of oxygen to survive.

Eventually the Serus demons won. But their victory was short lived. Extended use of their fog had irreparably harmed some of the native flora and fauna. The lilies remained intact, so the Serus initially gloated over their coup. But they soon realized that Evena's humble brown bee had been completely eradicated in the battle. And this particular bee was the only insect capable of pollinating the black lily.

Because of the fog, Evena's once fertile landscape had been altered from lush green to dingy, barren gray. Some plants still grew, but without the bees, the lilies eventually died out. The Serus demons, along with many other species, tried unsuccessfully to grow the black lily on Torth and other realms. No one had been able to do it. The Serus left, and the rest of Evena's population dwindled.

Even today, no one wanted or needed to go to Evena. Full of empty buildings, many of which had fallen into disrepair, just a few hardy souls had stayed on to call it their home.

Raniero had never been there, had never had any motivation or means to go. But if Cale had a porter, he could travel to Evena. And anywhere the porter could go would become a potential hiding place for Ashina.

Raniero's head reeled with the possibility of a new place to search for her, but he mustered the strength to bring his mind back to the matter at hand. "I've heard of this Cale," he said carefully. "He's a gangster with his hand in a lot of pies. He has a lot of enemies."

"Would the Vipers be among them?"

"I wouldn't be surprised." Hell, he knew for certain that the Vipers were Cale's enemies, but divulging that information would give away his unwilling association with the corrupt demon. He gritted his teeth in angry frustration. *Almost free.* He could taste it.

Fury shot through Raniero's blood at the thought that his assassination of the Viper lord may have led to the attack on the gentle wood nymphs. And he seethed with the thought of Ashina being shuttled off to a desolate place like Evena for all these years. As always, when he thought of her, old familiar doubts crept into his mind. Could she forgive him for the choices he made in the last hundred years? Was there a chance that she still loved him? Was she still alive?

He needed to get outdoors and clear his head. Focus on that wide perimeter patrol. "This conversation has been helpful, my friend," he said to Taszim. "I'd like to dwell on it a bit. Some of my men and I are going out to check the perimeter."

The nymph leader nodded and turned to the books on his desk. "As long as I'm in here, I may as well go over my ledgers. Definitely not as interesting as a patrol." He waved Raniero out.

Anxious to get out into the untamed woods, Raniero's strides ate up the colony's paths. A run outside would help him focus. But not even a hundred years could push aside the image of toffee-colored skin and bright green eyes gazing sweetly up at him from among the orange trees.

CHAPTER 21

NICOLE AWOKE FEELING RESTED, EVERY muscle relaxed and blissful. She opened her eyes to spy a scrap of red on the floor and, realizing it was her panties, stretched in lazy satisfaction. She reached for Gunnar, her hand gliding across the expanse of crisp cotton sheets. Empty sheets. She blinked, raised her head, and scanned the room. No Gunnar.

He's probably busy. He'd said he didn't need much sleep. She dropped her head back down to the pillow. It had only been a few days, but she was already used to waking up wrapped in his warm embrace. She liked the ways he found to wake her up... she smiled, thinking of how relentless he had been last night. Her own energizer demon.

So determined, like he had something to prove. But exactly what had been going through his head, she wasn't sure. She hadn't realized how tired she had been. She didn't even remember much after they made love. But she did remember how he reacted to her message panties. Grinning, she debated which pair to wear for him next. She really did have a whole collection, which she'd bought at a lingerie party and never worn.

She took a quick shower, dressed in a pair of jeans and a bright pink tank top, and went downstairs. *I need a jolt of caffeine.* Walking into the kitchen, she stopped in front of the fancy coffeemaker. She found a mug in a cabinet, and stood at the counter examining the machine when she sensed a change in the air pressure behind her. Gunnar.

She tried to turn to kiss him, but he pressed his big body

flush against hers, wedging her between him and the countertop. A small gasp escaped her mouth as his muscular chest warmed her back, sending tingles through to her breasts. He brushed her damp hair aside and bent to kiss her nape, his lips moving languidly across her skin. Her body melted into his sinewy strength.

"Good morning," she murmured.

"Good morning," he whispered, moving his hand up to close over her throat as he continued to nuzzle her neck. His other hand slid down to her hip, gripping her tightly. His hold was proprietary and dominant, and yet she felt safe and utterly adored as he lavished affection on her. Her thoughts returned to last night, with him huge and hard and demanding as he loomed over her. *Mine.* His words echoed in her head, and she recalled their conversation from days earlier. Immortals didn't marry, he'd said, they mated. He never explained quite how that worked. But his words and his body language screamed that she belonged to him.

His hand on her hip worked around to her abdomen with fingers splayed wide, then moved down between her thighs. She gazed with unfocused eyes at the white numbers marching up the side of the glass coffee pot. Last night, with her heart ready to stop from the delicious agitation of his skillful hands, she would've done anything he asked. Last night, with her hands pinned above her head and his teeth gripping her earlobe, she whispered the one word her mouth had been able to form. *Yours.*

Goose bumps erupted down her arms, and not just from the velvet strokes of his tongue on her skin. She craved him with a fierce possessiveness. She'd been ready to drop kick any of the nymphs at Rivkin who would have dared to flirt with him. She wanted him all to herself. Was he… *hers?*

She reached both arms up and back to twine around his neck. The length of his cock, thick and heavy in his jeans, pressed into her backside. *Forget the coffeemaker.*

She turned and gazed up into his handsome face, tracing his jaw and cheekbone, remembering how his face had altered in the midst of the battle rage. The sharp-toothed, savage creature inside him had sought to help her, had calmed down for her.

And Gunnar had finally opened up to her about his years of scraping by as a lonely, lost child. She didn't know if he would ever be able to be free of the battle rage when it came to Ghazsul demons, but it didn't scare her. He was strong and lethal, but he was just.

She looked into his blue eyes, glowing slightly from desire, and tried to read him. She'd never stopped to think about what was blooming between them. What with running around Torth and trying not to get killed, there hadn't been much time to think. She only reacted, and her body responded to his in a way that it never had with anyone else. The sexual heat between them had never been in doubt. Even now, with questions running in circles around her head, she felt a rush of heat at her core as his hands kneaded her bottom.

What was he to her? 'Boyfriend' seemed like a ridiculous term after what they had been through. Lover? Partner? She wasn't sure, but she knew she wasn't going anywhere. Especially since she was somehow supposed to help save the world, a venture he was fully vested in. If they were going to fight some heinous foe, she wanted to be at his side. And when it was time to take refuge from the evils they had faced, she wanted to be in his bed. She wanted to be wrapped tightly in his arms, forgetting everything but how he made her feel.

A shiver ran through her at the rather permanent direction her thoughts seemed to be taking.

"Are you okay?" he murmured.

Unable to give voice to her emotions, she only nodded. She'd never expected to find someone who would accept her strange ability. She assumed she'd be single forever, that she would never fully open herself up to another for fear of ridicule or exploitation. But Gunnar recognized her gift immediately, and saw it for what it was: something extraordinary. *He* was extraordinary. She leaned up to press her lips to his sensuous mouth, needing to tell him with her body the feelings that she couldn't speak.

His lips were so soft, his tongue enticing as it tangled with hers. She deepened the kiss, pushing against him, exploring every delicious part of his mouth. Knotting her hands in his hair, she felt the urge to rub herself against him just so he would smell like her. She pulled back a bit, wondering where the heck that had come from, when Rilan rushed into the kitchen.

"I've translated the old grimoire," he said excitedly.

The other three males walked in behind the Elder. "Everyone in the great room, stat," Kai barked.

Nicole was still wedged between Gunnar and the countertop.

"Get a room," Rhys joked as he brushed past them.

"I was just saying good morning to my girl," Gunnar replied, not taking his eyes off her.

Rhys snorted. "Heard you two saying 'good morning' the whole damn night."

Nicole gave Gunnar a tiny smile and shrugged. He wrapped an arm around her as they walked to one of the massive couches in the great room, where he sat and pulled her onto his lap.

They all turned to Rilan. "This spellbook contains what Xarrek considered to be his masterpieces. It contains warding spells, locater spells, and spells to increase one's power. And one of these power spells requires human blood." Rilan looked around the room, his gaze landing on each member of the assembled group. "The interesting thing is, this spell doesn't call for a large volume of blood from one or two humans. It requires just one drop from each of five hundred human souls. And," he paused, "the more destitute and downtrodden the human life is, the more power will be transferred in the spell."

"That's why none of them have been drained." Kai looked at the ceiling and blew out a breath.

"And that's why they're working the drug addicts and the gang-ridden neighborhoods," Nicole added.

"So say he collects all of this blood. What will Maeron be able to do?" Gunnar asked.

"Almost anything he wants." Rilan shook his head grimly. "He'll be able to teleport virtually anywhere. He'll be able to summon demonfire, create illusions, and even assume another form temporarily."

"Shit. Last night that maggot we caught said Maeron was 'almost ready,'" Kai growled.

"Why don't you fill us in on last night, bro?" Brenin asked.

"We only found one Skell, but he didn't know why Maeron was collecting blood. Only would say that he was 'almost ready.' Then we ran into an old friend–a Deserati–and she was able to show us Maeron's hideout. Wait." Kai held up a hand to quiet the burst of shouts to go after the Domu. "She showed us what his lair looks like. But we don't know exactly where it is."

"Some help," Rhys muttered.

"She didn't have an iPad, dude. She couldn't zoom out and give us a fucking map." Kai glared at the other Lash. "Her scrying bowl showed us a virtual snapshot of his location. It's an old beat-up farmhouse. Looks like it's about to fall down. It's near a river. That's what we have to work with."

Rhys jumped over to the computer and his fingers tapped out a staccato rhythm. "Thank the gods for satellite photos."

"So, we have no idea how close Maeron is to having all that he needs for his spell," Nicole said.

"Man, why has this fucker been so hard to catch?" Kai snarled as he paced the room.

"He's very smart," Rilan replied. "And Skells are expendable and easy to come by. There will always be more of them to do his dirty work."

"Yeah, since he can't show his ugly mug around here." Brenin raked a hand through his long blond hair.

"You know what he looks like?" Nicole asked.

"Well, we know what Domu demons look like, and my guess is Maeron fits the general description pretty well." Gunnar went on to describe the physical traits of the Domu species.

Nicole made a face. Yes, a seven foot tall, charcoal skinned, yellow-eyed creature would cause quite a stir walking around

Chicago. No wonder he utilized the Skells.

"We have to find him before he can alter his appearance," she said.

"We have to find him, like, yesterday," Rhys grumbled as he scrolled through screen after screen of images. "Hey, check this out."

Everyone crowded behind his chair to peer at the computer screen. "If you head south of the city on I-57, after about ninety minutes or so you start getting close to the Kankakee River. It has all these little streams that feed into it, here." He gestured to a maze of tiny blue lines on a map. "And, in that area, there are three of the shittiest looking buildings around." He pulled up the first image.

"That's not it," Gunnar said right away.

Kai agreed. "The one Miranda showed us didn't have a barn that was still standing."

"Okay, how about this one?" Rhys closed the first image and opened another. Gunnar and Kai looked at each other and frowned.

"That could be it," Kai said. "It's worth checking out. Is it occupied?"

"Real estate records show that all of these are foreclosures. If anyone's there, they'd be a squatter." Rhys minimized the second page and opened the third one.

"Could be that one, too," Gunnar said. "Are there more?"

"Hell, yeah." Rhys hit a button and the gray printer on the table whirred into action. "These were just the first three I found, moving south from here."

"I say we take a closer look," Gunnar said. "Let's split into two teams and check out these two houses. Surveillance only—we wait to move in until we can regroup. We know he has Skells, but he probably has other creatures around his headquarters for security."

"I'm going with you," Nicole told Gunnar.

"No you're not. It's too dangerous."

"I'm not helpless," she reminded him, as the other demons

drifted out of the room.

"True. But you'll be safest right here." She opened her mouth to protest and he laid a gentle finger across her lips. "I need to focus on recon today. Maeron may have some fiendish guard dogs. We're going to have to get in and get out quickly, without him knowing we've been sniffing around. I can't be as effective if you're there because I'll be worried for your safety."

She glared at him, pissed and hurt at the same time. Hadn't she proven herself during their time on Torth? *I held my own against the Vipers and the Ghazsul demons.* She narrowed her eyes and started to tell him that, but he stopped her again.

"Nicole, if you use your power anywhere near him, he'll know it. He may not know what you are, but he'll sense your unique energy, and he'll come after you. He's a crazy, power-hungry bastard. He'll want you. Who knows what kind of shit he'd try if he could use you?"

She blew out a breath. "Who knows what kind of shit *I* could do to *him*? I'm here for a reason, and I want to start fighting with you. You know that one day my sisters and I are supposed to battle something nastier than your worst nightmare."

"We'll worry about that when it happens. And you can use this time to practice. Today, you stay put."

"You can't keep me in a cage!"

"I won't have you taking a foolish risk." His tone brokered no argument.

She gritted her teeth and clenched her fists. "I wasn't foolish at Rivkin."

"Rivkin was different. We were on friendly turf, with an army of archers. I don't know what we'll walk into today."

She glared at him, her hands still balled into fists. She wanted to scream at him or punch him. Maybe fling him across the room with her mind. Her muscles trembled with rage, but also with the niggling thought that his actions and words were rooted in concern for her. *Then why can't he care enough to let me grow?*

"Hey." He took her chin in his fingers and turned her face toward his. "I can't risk your life. You're too important."

"That's right, the Solsti are here because the world needs them," she recited numbly.

"And I need you," he said before hauling her up to his mouth for a rough, demanding kiss that stole her breath. The anger racing through her blood turned to heat as the sweet demands of his tongue coaxed her lips apart. She planted her hands on his chest and pushed, but she may as well have pushed a brick wall. With one of his hands resting at the small of her back, and the other at her nape, her traitorous body softened against him.

She mentally cursed him and fought hard to suppress the moan rising in her throat. Right now she didn't want to give him the satisfaction of knowing how badly her body craved him.

Giving him another shove, she broke the kiss and took a step back. Still glaring at him, she drew a reluctant, ragged breath. *Damn it.* There was no hiding the way he affected her.

His eyes radiating blue heat, he flicked his gaze to her lips and back up to her eyes. Turning, he stalked away without a backward glance.

She blinked as she watched him go, shaking her head to clear it. A faint echo of his voice reverberated in her mind. But how could that be? One word that she not only heard, but felt deep in her heart. *Mine.*

CHAPTER 22

NICOLE KNEW SHE COULDN'T STAY in that house all day waiting for the four demons to return. She decided her first order of business was to stock up on fresh foods. The men had driven off in two black Escalades, leaving a white Tahoe and two plain looking Honda sedans behind. She eyed one of the Hondas. That was more like the car she shared with Brooke. Her gaze swept the kitchen, finding a pegboard pierced with hooks near the back door. Flipping through the dangling keys, she found the ones she needed and headed out.

A surreal feeling washed over her as she pushed her cart through the aisles. All the other shoppers bustled about their business, checking their grocery lists and selecting vegetables, having no idea that the world was full of creatures who weren't supposed to exist. A week ago she was having the same out-of-body experience while walking around Torth; now, being back in the "regular" world seemed even stranger.

All the things she had thought were "normal" had been turned upside down. She had always secretly hoped the talent that ran in her family wasn't a fluke, that there was a reason behind it. Now she had her reason and she was thrilled to have a purpose. She could only dream about what she, Brooke, and Gin would be able to accomplish together.

She sighed, thinking of her younger sister. Gin thought she and Brooke were crazy for doing what they did in the city at night. She preferred to forget that her ability even existed. Convincing her otherwise would be a major feat.

Nicole finished up her shopping, hurried home, and unpacked the groceries. A huge Denver omelet sounded excellent, and she went looking for Rilan to see if he wanted one, too. Not seeing him, she went upstairs to check his room. The door was closed and she gave a quick knock. *No response.* She shrugged and returned to the big kitchen.

Soon the spacious room was filled with the aroma of eggs, cheese, and bell peppers. She polished off her omelet and sipped her coffee, contemplating what else to do with her time. Two days until Brooke came back. Nicole's fingers drummed a bored pattern on the smooth granite breakfast bar.

Gunnar had told her to practice, so that's what she would do to keep from going stir crazy. She quickly washed her dishes, grabbed the car keys, and paused. Scrawling down a quick note so no one would worry, she placed it on the island and left.

It felt good to drive out of civilization, as Brooke called it. She was leaving the strip malls and gated subdivisions behind and getting out into flat fields that stretched as far as the eye could see. Heading southwest, she passed row after neat row of corn and wheat. Grain elevators occasionally punctuated the flat Illinois horizon.

After about an hour of driving, she left the interstate behind in favor of a rural highway that passed through small towns. Pulling onto a tiny dusty lane, she spotted what she wanted: a wide field of prairie grasses with clusters of oaks and other large trees scattered along one side. And most importantly, no people. She didn't need an audience for the gales she was about to summon. *Especially since I'm still working on my control.*

Finding a nice clump of sycamores, she parked the car so that it couldn't be seen from the road. She got out and stretched limbs that were stiff from sitting for so long, and walked out into the knee-high grass. Eyes closed, she inhaled the scent of sweet meadow and clean air, letting her power build and coil.

Flush with energy, she summoned a breeze to push down the grass on her right. She smiled. But she wanted to split her mental focus, as she had done with the Vipers at Rivkin.

Keeping the current constant, she tried to call another breeze to sway the grass on her left.

She ended up with a face full of dust and coughed, breaking her concentration. Maybe she needed more distance between the two areas of activity.

Determined to master the dual forces, she called the wind to blow the grasses low to the ground again. Then she looked to the tops of the trees and summoned a gust to rattle the leaves in the highest branches. This time she was successful. She worked on different skills, like parting the grass in front of her to form a narrow path. She extended it as far as she could see, a thin dark line like a snake arrowing away from her to the other side of the field.

The fights with the Vipers and the Ghazsuls popped into her mind, and she tried to think strategically about what would have helped them. She practiced moving her air currents around in different ways, doubling them back on themselves and changing directions quickly. Her body hummed with so much energy that, too late, she realized she had an audience.

She froze as two hands clapped together slowly and deliberately. "Quite impressive, little fae," a low voice rasped.

Fear rooted her feet in place, even as it turned her blood to ice. She whirled, but it seemed like moving in slow motion. *No!* Standing in the shade of the towering oak trees stood two Ghazsul demons.

The one who had been clapping stopped and tilted his ugly red head at her. "Although, you're a little tall to be a fairy."

Nicole gulped as questions shot though her mind. What were Ghazsul demons doing on Earth? Had they been looking for her? Did they want revenge for the battle in the woods on Torth? Or was this a sick coincidence?

"You're a pretty thing, whatever you are," the second one said. They didn't seem wary; in fact, they looked cocky, like she couldn't possibly hurt them. Maybe they didn't know anything about her little adventure on Torth.

"So." The second demon licked his lips. "Care to divulge

your heritage? Your energy is rather unusual." His black eyes roamed every inch of her body.

She gulped again. There was no way she was going to tell these creatures that she was a Solsti—*they wouldn't believe me anyway*—but she wasn't sure what she should pretend to be. She hadn't exactly thought up a cover story for situations like this, and didn't know enough about the different types of fairies to fake it.

I'll dodge the question. "Who are you?" she asked.

The first demon got in her face so fast that she didn't even see him move. "I asked you first, little fae." He leaned in close enough that she could see a sparse coating of wiry hairs along his muscular, red, bare arms. Grabbing her upper arm, he inhaled, then frowned and turned to his friend. "You smell her."

Nicole jumped and cringed as the other Ghazsul stood way too close on her other side. He took a deep breath, his nose brushing the shell of her ear. "I don't recognize her scent, either." She felt like a lab rat alone with two evil scientists.

"You get one more chance to tell us your true nature, little one. Or we'll all take a trip to see our master. He'll be intrigued with you. He likes unique things." The first demon spoke with a laugh that sent chills down her spine.

She fought her rising panic. They were stronger than her. She hadn't even brought her dagger, because she never would have anticipated needing it in an open field. On *Earth*. Peering at their shoulders, she tried in vain to see behind them. These Ghazsuls either didn't have wings or they had them tucked away. If she could get them to fly, even if they were holding her, then she could get them to fall.

She turned as if to run, knowing that she wouldn't be able to break the demon's hold on her arm.

It chuckled eerily. "Now, now, the party's just getting started."

She let her body go limp, and when he relaxed his grip a little, she twisted free, spun around, and aimed a high kick at him. Her strike should have landed a blow to his jaw, but he was so tall that she didn't make it that far. He grunted as the top of her foot snapped near his shoulder. Before she could recover he grabbed her ankle and flung her to the ground. He did it with as little effort as Gunnar had the day they sparred in the training room. The Ghazsul was much rougher, and she wheezed, trying to get back the breath that had been knocked out of her. Thank goodness the Ghazsul didn't jump on her to keep her down.

She got up slowly. "I don't see a car other than mine. What'd you do, fly here?"

"She's trying to be funny." The second demon laughed.

Anything to stall them. "Well, if you guys had wings, it would make sense that you were able to sneak up on me."

"We were able to sneak up on you because we're predators, little fae," the first Ghazsul growled. This one was clearly playing the bad cop. "And if you had ever seen one of us with wings, you wouldn't have lived to tell anyone about it. Our winged brethren are the most elite and vicious fighters in the realms."

Okay, definitely a good idea to keep quiet about the little incident on Torth. These two probably wouldn't take well to hearing about how she and Gunnar had eliminated several of their "elite" fighters.

Gunnar. Her heart tugged with a desperate longing for his presence. The two Ghazsul demons would already be smoking corpses on the ground. She was completely in favor of doing her part, but she knew she was in over her head. If these creatures didn't have wings, she wasn't sure how she could escape them.

This mess was her own fault. Then again, he hadn't told her not to drive around. And no one had mentioned seeing Ghazsul demons on Earth. Maybe they didn't know the Ghazsuls were here. And if the Lash demons didn't know Ghazsuls were hanging around, they wouldn't know how much trouble she was in.

Who was this master of theirs anyway, and why was he here in Illinois? If they took her to another location, her chances of this situation having a good outcome went from slim to almost nonexistent.

Her eyes snapped to the towering trees. They were old, stately and beautiful, and sturdy as hell. She could eventually use enough wind gusts to knock one down, but it would take too long. She'd lose the element of surprise and be unable to defend herself while doing it.

She spied some branches on the ground beneath the nearest elm tree. They must have come down in a recent storm because their leaves were still green, their exposed bark rough and pale. She aimed her energy at the largest branch, causing it to pitch end over jagged end along the ground. When it picked up speed, she focused a sharp gust at it, causing it to become airborne. Nicole concentrated on that branch, imagining it was a flying sword, and sent it straight into the chest of the first Ghazsul.

The demon howled as black blood spurted from its front. The wound wasn't fatal. Unfortunately, she knew just how hard these things were to kill. She had probably just gotten him really pissed off.

Nicole turned and bolted for her car, hoping she could drive faster than they could run. Or at least if she got near a store or post office, maybe someone could help her. Maybe the Ghazsuls wouldn't show themselves around humans.

Hands trembling, she fumbled the unfamiliar keys in both her hands. She set one hand on the roof of the car to steady herself and yanked it back, shrieking in pain. The surface of the car had to be five hundred degrees. Behind her, she heard the second Ghazsul laugh. "Fair's fair, little fae."

Suddenly he was right next to her. She looked up at him in terror as she cradled her burned hand. He leaned on the car as if it wasn't hot at all. Maybe he had magically cooled it down, or maybe Ghazsuls were immune to heat. She didn't know and she sure didn't want to ask him about it.

He bent and took a deep breath. "I can smell your fear," he whispered. "And you're feisty. That's a good combination. Our master will be beyond pleased to make your acquaintance." He spoke casually, as if they were friends chatting in a coffee shop.

Nicole didn't know whether his demeanor was supposed to

encourage her to talk. It certainly wasn't working, and only made her feel more creeped out.

"If you'll remember, we told you that you had one more chance to talk to us before we brought you to him. You just blew that chance. Say goodbye to your little vehicle." He plucked the keys from her fingers and dropped them on the ground next to the car. "You won't be needing these anymore." Then he chanted in a language she didn't recognize.

Maybe it was old Demonish. Maybe it was the same tongue that the Ghazsuls on Torth had spoken. Either way, she was in even deeper trouble now. The demon's eyes were open but slightly glazed as he muttered the words to a spell.

Paralysis crept through her feet, then her legs. She tried to move, but her muscles weren't responding. The numbness spread up her body until she stared, frozen, at the demon. Gravity's hold dragged her down and there was nothing she could do about it. Her head hit the ground with a thud, and her vision faded to gray and black swirls of nothingness.

Nicole awoke to total darkness, blinking into pitch black. *Where am I?* She lay on a dirt floor, that much she could tell. It was so dark that whether her eyes were open or closed didn't seem to make much difference. She tried to move her head and then wished she hadn't, as a wave of dizziness washed over her. Her hand burned. Her head throbbed and felt like it was full of cotton.

What happened? Memories flashed into her mind in short bursts. *I was fighting the Ghazsul demons and I wasn't doing so well.* One temple ached and she felt a lump under her hair, probably from when the first Ghazsul had flipped her to the ground in the field. Or maybe from when she had fallen down next to her car, when the second Ghazsul had put that paralysis spell on her.

*Paralyzed…*she shifted her legs, relief flooding her veins, though her limbs were heavy as lead. *I can move!*

Trepidation accelerated her heart rate. *Don't panic. That won't help. Think…* Forcing deep breaths, she calmed down enough to assess her surroundings. She slowly recalled the situation with the Ghazsul demons. Remembered being unable to do much to help herself. She needed to figure out where she was and how to get as far away from here as possible.

Tracing a finger through the dirt, she noted that it was soft and grainy, not muddy or packed down. Her ears picked up a faint noise and she strained to identify it. Barely audible, its high-pitched tone reminded her of a train whistle. And it sounded muffled, like there was a wall between her and the sound. She guessed she was inside some kind of building, and if the floor was dirt, her black hole could be a basement or cellar.

Another wave of dizziness washed over her when she tried to sit up. She stretched her legs out instead and met resistance in what she hoped was a wall. Scooting on her side until she was close enough to pat it with her good hand, she discovered the roughness of brick. *Brick means a wall.* Awkwardly, she wiggled and pushed until she leaned against it. She still couldn't see anything and felt like she had the mother of all hangovers, but at least nothing could surprise her from behind.

She sat silently for several minutes, listening for any sounds or voices. Nothing. Fighting the dizziness and the unsettled feeling in her stomach, she stirred to explore her confines. Crawling was her only option, because there was no way she could stand or walk yet. On hands and knees, she crept along the wall of the room until she bumped into a perpendicular wall, then turned to follow it. Her basement idea was nearly confirmed as she realized there were four walls, and the room wasn't large. But where were the stairs?

Looking up into the darkness, she saw nothing. The possibility of digging out through the floor crossed her mind. But who knew what was on the other side of those walls? Not to mention her hand still felt like it had been through a meat grinder on the sun. She closed her eyes and settled against one of the walls. Her thoughts drifted to Gunnar.

The last words he said to her echoed in her head. *I need you.*

Infuriated at the way he ordered her to stay home, she'd pushed his voice from her mind. Now, alone in her dark prison, she allowed her emotions to surface. She wanted him here. Every time she had been in a tight spot in the last few days, he'd been there for her. Would he find her now? Was he looking?

She touched her lips, remembering his scorching kiss and the fire in his eyes. *God, those eyes.* She wanted to sink into those blue pools and never come up for air. Why had she pushed him away? She'd give anything to feel his mouth on hers again, to be clutched in his strong embrace.

He wanted to protect me. That's nothing new. And, heaven help her, she understood his reasons. Understood them on a level so deep that their souls found solace in their shared losses.

She thought of his big arms around her and the electricity that zinged between them from the moment they met. But with him it was more than lust, more than scratching an itch. She'd felt so possessive toward him when they were at Rivkin. She hadn't wanted to share him with anyone then. Now, she realized, she didn't want to share him with anyone, *ever*. He was hers. *Will I get the chance to tell him?*

They fit together like two pieces of a puzzle, both incomplete until they snapped together. They had both lost much, but chose to focus their energy on a greater good. Warmth bloomed in her chest as the knowledge dawned that there would never be anyone so perfect for her. She needed him. She loved him. Dear Lord, she had fallen for him, head over heels.

Footsteps overhead jerked her from her warm thoughts. They stopped directly above her, and she heard the scraping sound of metal sliding against metal. A door in the ceiling opened, revealing a square of dim light about three feet across. She squinted even though the light wasn't that bright. A wooden ladder descended into the square opening.

"Time to come out, little female," called a voice that she recognized as the Ghazsul demon who had heated up her car and put that spell on her. So much for him being the good cop.

She wasn't sure which was worse—staying in the dark basement or getting near him again.

He didn't give her time to think about it. "We know you're awake, female. We heard you moving around. We can also hear the sound of your breathing. It's different when you're unconscious, you know." He was back to that chatty, casual demeanor. She didn't know if it was supposed to make her agreeable to their plans, but it only disturbed her more.

"And," he continued, "If we have to drag you out, I doubt you'll enjoy it. Unless you like pain."

There was no way she wanted anything to physically pull her out of that basement. Suppressing a shudder and favoring her injured hand, she grabbed the ladder and started climbing.

CHAPTER 23

GUNNAR AND KAI CROUCHED SILENTLY a hundred yards away
from the farmhouse that matched their first coordinates.
Concealed in thick, overgrown trees for several minutes, they
watched and listened. Their Escalade was parked off to the side
of the quiet road a mile away.

Gunnar glanced at his friend. This place truly did look
abandoned, but the need for certainty screamed in his head. *End
Maeron.* It was non-negotiable.

They crept closer, sticking to the line of trees that ran up to
the rear of the silo. A few wooden beams remained of the once-
shingled roof, and rabbits hopped in and out of the ripped up
sides.

"No wards," Kai muttered.

Gunnar had noticed the same thing. They were close
enough to sense if the building was warded against intruders.
And if a power-hungry Domu demon was preparing a life-
altering spell in here, he would most definitely have wards in
place.

"Let's go in and make sure," Gunnar said. The wind rustled
the leaves of a towering oak as they approached the silo, which
had one side caving in on itself. *Empty.* Then they moved to the
house, entering cautiously. A quick sweep of the rooms
confirmed their hunch that the place was deserted.

Gunnar called Rhys on his cell phone and found that the
other two demons had run into a dead end as well. But Rhys,
true to form, had printed out a list of other locations before

they had all left the house. With a new set of coordinates to search, Gunnar and Kai strode back to their SUV.

Back in the car with Kai driving farther south, Gunnar tried to reach Nicole on her cell phone. It went straight to voice mail, and he didn't feel like leaving a message in front of Kai. Not that his friend was fooled by anything.

As if reading his thoughts, Kai asked, "Is she your mate?"

It hadn't even been a day since he had been hit with that stunning revelation. "Yeah."

"You tell her yet?"

Gunnar shook his head.

"Maybe you should, dude. She was raised in the human world. She may be expecting a diamond ring or a big white dress or something."

"She can have those if she wants. And when did you become an expert on relationships?"

Kai shot him a grin. "I watch Dr. Phil re-runs."

Gunnar snorted and checked the GPS. "We're almost there. Let's pull over."

They parked the car, jogged the remainder of the distance on foot, and repeated their surveillance procedures. Gunnar let out a string of foul curses when they came up empty a second time. The last thing he wanted to do was sneak around derelict buildings out in the boondocks on some wild goose chase. But everything else had either been a dead end or yielded no decent results.

His phone vibrated and he saw Rhys' number on the caller ID. Picking up, he barked "What did you find?"

"Nada, dude," Rhys drawled. "You?"

"Same."

Rhys gave him another set of coordinates and hung up. Gunnar knew they had to find this guy fast, and this slow-ass method made his skin feel too tight. He itched for a fight.

The next location wasn't far. The two-lane rural road followed the river. Wide fields lay fallow, punctuated with an occasional towering elm or linden. Drivers that passed them in the oncoming lane raised their hands in friendly waves, causing the two demons to look at each other and shrug. A hand gesture of a completely different sort was more common on Chicago streets.

Finding an area thick with brush, they hid their car and began yet another jog to the newest location. Gunnar absentmindedly rubbed the center of his chest, where a dull throb had set in.

Kai looked at him with narrowed eyes. "That's the third time you've done that in the last few minutes. What's up?"

Gunnar shook his head. "Not sure. It's like an ache."

"We don't get aches. You get hurt last night?"

"No."

Kai scowled. "Fuck."

As the drawn-out curse lingered, the ache turned into a sharp pain that sliced through Gunnar's chest. Falling to his knees, his lungs squeezed and he fought for air. Intense, piercing agony ripped through his torso with every breath. He may as well be on the receiving end of a chest strike from an evil Deserati's tail.

Kai crouched beside him. "What the fuck? Is it some kind of dark magic?" His brown eyes scanned the area. "Any mage or sorcerer would have to be close, and we're the only ones here."

His friend's words registered like they were far away. Gunnar braced himself with one hand on the ground. He pressed the other to his chest, where the striking pain turned to a burn.

What the hell was this? Gunnar felt like a pansy. His insides stung and twisted like some psychotic supernatural chef was filleting and roasting them. He'd faced countless monsters in his two hundred years, and never experienced anything like this. Well, he thought, if anyone had to see him fall down like a little girl, he would choose Kai. His friend was the most loyal Lash he had ever met. He might have a short fuse sometimes, but Kai wouldn't leave anyone behind–literally or figuratively.

In a flash of understanding, the cause of his pain

crystallized. "It's Nicole," he rasped.

"How is Nicole doing this to you?"

Gunnar shook his head. "She's not doing it on purpose. She's in trouble. I can feel her panic. Something's happened to her." With trembling fingers, he reached for his phone, but his hand wouldn't do what he wanted.

"I got it." Kai grabbed Gunnar's cell and hit redial. "Straight to voicemail. Shit, man. I'll call Rilan." Kai barked orders when the Elder demon answered. Thanks to his enhanced hearing, Gunnar listened to the entire conversation.

Dread filled his stomach like a lead balloon as Rilan relayed to Kai that Nicole wasn't in the house and that one of the sedans was missing. "Goddamn it, I told her to stay put," Gunnar muttered.

"You told her to practice," Kai reminded him. "Stay with me, man. We'll find her. Rilan's going to look up her location."

All of the demons' vehicles had GPS trackers installed, in case anyone failed to return from an assignment. They had never actually had to use them before, and Gunnar would never have expected that the first time would be to locate his own mate.

He listened with increasing frustration as Kai talked Rilan through the steps of the computer program. Though grateful the Elder was home to do it, Gunnar knew computers were far from Rilan's specialty. Maybe he should just cast a locator spell instead, Gunnar thought grimly. Not that he knew if Rilan could manage one.

"No, no, close that option. Now click on the box that says..." Kai said into his phone.

Gunnar forced himself to breathe. He clenched and unclenched his fists. The slashing pain had dulled, the fire banked to a vexing ember. His heart beat in rapid thuds as he pushed the last ragged edges down to a teeth-gritting discomfort. He pictured Nicole's wide green eyes and the radiant smile she'd given him before she fell asleep last night. The need to locate her pulsed through his veins. *I will find you.*

After several minutes Kai repeated the coordinates that

Rilan had been able to look up. Gunnar punched them into their GPS and groaned. She was more than an hour away, far from any towns. He didn't know whether he should be relieved that she wasn't in some blighted city neighborhood. Then at least he would have some idea of what she was up against. Out in the middle of nowhere, he had no idea what could have happened to create such fear in her that it physically affected him. Back on his feet and running for their SUV, he ignored the chest pain and breathing issues.

Kai tore past him. "Let's go find your girl. And you're definitely riding shotgun."

The sun sank below the tree line, lengthening the shadows as they neared the location of the Honda Nicole had driven. The last vestiges of fear and pain had stopped, and that worried Gunnar more than anything. Was she okay now? Had she escaped? Was she unconscious? The beast inside him paced furiously, desperate to get out and fight for his female, but Gunnar had no idea who they were up against.

Their coordinates led them to an open field with a few trees, and yes, there was the car. Gunnar was out the door and bolting for it before Kai stopped the Escalade.

She wasn't there. Only faint traces of her peachy fragrance remained. How long had it been since she'd been here? One hour? Two? He stood next to the car in an agonized silence as Kai walked up next to him.

"Car's intact. Keys, here." Kai nudged the keys on the ground with his boot. He set a hand down on the roof of the car and quickly pulled it back. He looked at his hand and then at the shiny metal. "Something's off here..."

They both scented the air and caught the same faint tendril. "Another demon," Gunnar said. "Not Skell."

"The Domu?" Kai asked, but then shook his head immediately. "Doesn't stink like they do. Let's take a look around."

"How many other fucking demons have been hanging around the heartland?" Gunnar muttered.

They stepped into the field cautiously, but a quick scan with their heightened senses confirmed they were alone. Whoever had been here with Nicole was long gone. Gunnar's heart constricted, this time not from fear, but from his own frustration and pain at the thought that Nicole was alone and hurt. He meant his words this morning. He needed her. He just hadn't been able to articulate all the details at the time.

The tender possessiveness he felt for her was so new and surprising to him. He had never fallen in love before, had never cared so strongly for a female that he would bare the darkest secrets of his soul to her. Speaking eloquently had never been his strong suit anyway. As soon as he found her, he would tell her in whatever words he could that he loved her and wanted her to be by his side forever.

Walking in step, both males caught the tangy smell at the same time. It was blood, recently spilled. *Demon blood.* Shit. What in the world had Nicole stumbled into?

Gunnar spied the black substance in the grass in front of them and knelt to touch it. He brought his fingers up to his nose, but he already knew what creature it had come from. He held his hand out to Kai, who confirmed Gunnar's guess.

"No. Fucking. Way. Ghazsul demons here?" He looked around the immediate area and saw a large jagged branch on the ground. "There's Ghazsul blood on that branch, too. But no human blood anywhere." Kai rested his hands on his hips. "How does a Ghazsul end up hurt by a huge tree branch? They're good fighters, and it's not exactly an ideal weapon."

Gunnar looked at his friend as realization dawned on him. "It is for a Solsti."

Kai frowned at him, then started speaking in a tone that meant to be reassuring but that indicated to Gunnar that his friend thought he was nuts. "I know she works out a lot, dude, but I'm having a hard time picturing her lifting up a massive tree branch and stabbing a Ghazsul demon."

Gunnar closed his eyes. "She didn't lift it with her arms. Remember what she did with the Vipers' arrows on Torth?"

After a long pause, Kai muttered, "Holy fucking shit."

The two demons stared at the bloodied tree branch for another minute as reality sank in. Nicole had been here recently, and so had at least one Ghazsul demon. Probably more, since they liked to work in packs. There had been a struggle, Ghazsul blood had been shed, and now the area was deserted.

"What do you want us to do?" Kai asked.

"We need the Elder." Gunnar gritted his teeth. "Call Rhys. We need to regroup. Now."

Nicole cautiously pulled herself up far enough so that she could let go of the ladder and scoot onto a linoleum floor. She sat in a dirty, dusty old kitchen that looked like no one had prepared any meals there in decades. Layers of grime coated the scuffed, scratched floor. Standing near the basement opening she had just climbed out of was the second Ghazsul demon, as she had guessed. With him were two other Ghazsuls that she had never seen before, as well as a few Skell demons.

"Well, hello there," the Ghazsul said in that eerily pleasant voice, as if he watched people climb out of basements every day. Heck, he probably did.

She eyed him warily. "Where am I?"

"You're in the master's lair, little female. He is most anxious to meet you. Come now."

Meeting this master was the last thing Nicole wanted to do, but she was outnumbered. There could be even more demons scattered throughout the rest of the house. She stood up and slowly walked toward the Ghazsul. A subtle shifting in the air alerted her that the other demons had fallen in behind her. *Nowhere to run, nowhere to hide.*

Dark wood cabinets hung on walls covered with peeling, faded floral wallpaper. Most of the cabinets had lost their doors, revealing mostly empty shelves, a few dishes, and ancient-looking coffee cans. Chipped yellow laminate counters were bare except for layers of dust, and one small table stood forlornly under a window.

The Ghazsul headed to a hallway that branched off the kitchen. Opening the first of several doors, he disappeared into it. Nicole followed him and stumbled on what she belatedly realized was a staircase going down. She grabbed for the railing with both hands, biting back a gasp as the rough wood chafed her injured skin. The staircase itself had no lights, but she could see a dim glow at the base of the stairs. She clutched the railing with her good hand and shuffled her way down. Reaching the bottom, she followed the Ghazsul and then froze.

They stood in a large room with cement floors and walls— clearly a newer basement. Maybe the tiny room she had been initially dumped in was an old fruit cellar. This room had several bare light bulbs hanging from the ceiling. Metal shelving units crammed full of books lined two of the walls. Peering at the nearest shelf, she saw that these weren't modern books, but thick tomes that looked centuries old. Some were bound with leather loops, and sheaves of paper stuck out at odd angles. They reminded her of the collection in Rilan's study.

She gave a little jump when the Ghazsul who had come down the stairs behind her nearly bumped into her. "Keep moving, female," it growled.

Inching further into the room, she noticed the other walls had shelves lined with odd equipment. Flasks and scales stood next to small stone bowls and tiny vials. Then she spotted the work table in the center of the room. The top was a huge stone slab with a large square opening in the center. The beveled edges slanted toward a vat containing a dark substance that she really didn't want to identify. Staring in morbid curiosity at the table, at first she didn't notice the huge creature standing across from her. Until it took a breath.

She couldn't hold back a sharp inhale. The thing had to be seven feet tall. Its bare head brushed the low ceiling of the room. Its skin was dark gray and ashy, like charcoal. But the most unnerving thing about it was its large almond-shaped eyes, which glowed a sickly yellow as they bored into her. The pupils narrowed into reptilian slits. She gulped and jerked her gaze from those hideous orbs, only to feel a jolt of fear as she noted sharp claws at the ends of long gnarled fingers.

Big and powerfully built, it looked at her like she was dinner. Silence hung in the room as she waited for it—or anyone else— to speak. There was no way she was going to interact with that thing if she could help it. There were more Skells down here, shifting awkwardly in the shadows as if they were waiting too. Nicole shot furtive looks around the room, taking mental notes of her surroundings and also trying to look anywhere but at the thing across from her.

She sneaked a glance at the last wall and then wished she hadn't. Four heavy metal chains hung from bolts in the concrete. Clenching her fists, she fought the rising panic. She still didn't know if the huge yellow-eyed thing was the "master" that the others had referred to or simply another hired muscle, but she had a feeling she was about to find out.

"Female," it rumbled in a low and gravelly voice. Its yellow eyes never left her face. "I hear you put up quite a fight against two of my associates today."

Nicole stared mutely at those claws. What was she supposed to say? She could agree and then have him think she was more powerful than she actually was. Or she could disagree, which seemed like the worst idea ever. This thing didn't look like it tolerated anything that disagreed with it. So she swallowed hard and remained silent.

"One of them is still recovering over there." He gestured to a corner, where the other Ghazsul demon sat on the floor.

She recognized the one she had flung the tree branch into. Blood covered its chest, and its eyes were closed.

"Normally I wouldn't have let him live, after he let you get the jump on him. But I was most intrigued with the story of how you injured him." The creature paced slowly along his side of the table. "Now, little female...how, exactly, did you do that to my Ghazsul demon?"

Nicole stood, frozen to the floor. She couldn't open her mouth to speak.

The tall being stopped his pacing and his yellow eyes pierced her. "What kind of creature are you, that you have the ability to use your mind to fling a tree branch at such a powerful fighter?"

Nicole looked at her feet. Ice shot through her veins and her head swam with questions. *Who are these creatures?* How had her innocent drive out to the country turned into such a mess?

"I am not a patient demon, female. Answer me. What are you?"

Oh, shit. She had to come up with something fast. She couldn't deny her ability, since the Ghazsul demons had witnessed it and the very evidence of her skill sat on the floor drenched in blood. So she did the only thing she could, and fell back on the story that had defined her life until a week ago. "I'm just a person," she said quietly.

The tall demon in front of her burst out laughing, and it wasn't a happy laugh. It was a nice-try-now-stop-bullshitting-me laugh. "You can't possibly expect me to believe that, female."

Nicole thought back to the first conversation she'd had with Gunnar. She remembered her confusion when he implied she wasn't human, and that the world was full of creatures that were supposed to be myths. "I grew up near the city. I don't know what I am, other than a human who has a special...talent."

"Oh, you aren't human, little one. And with what you did today, I think you know exactly what you are."

"But I *am* human," Nicole pleaded with the creature. "What else would I be?"

"I grow tired of this talk. Let's find out if you're telling the truth." He nodded to the second Ghazsul demon, who still stood slightly behind her and to the side. "Draw some blood. Her arm will do nicely."

"Yes, Maeron," the second Ghazsul demon murmured. He stepped toward her.

Maeron? Nicole's head spun. *This* was the Domu demon they had been searching for? If this was his lair, it made sense that there were Skell demons hanging around. But why did he have Ghazsuls with him? And why had they brought her to him? She still didn't know if they had tracked her to the field on purpose or if this was all just a sick coincidence.

The Ghazsul grasped her arm and she tried to pull away, but he held her in a vise-like grip. One black claw arched out from a fingertip, and she had a flashback to the woods on Torth.

"No!" she screamed, but his claw sank into her upper arm, dragging downward in a slow line. She gasped as crimson blood streamed down her skin. He reached for a small glass jar and held it below the wound, allowing a few drops to fall in. Then he released her.

She cradled her arm and glared at him as he walked close to the center of the table. He bowed and extended his hand to Maeron, who plucked the jar from his grasp. Slitted yellow eyes never left her face as he raised it to his wrinkled lips and tilted it back.

Bile rose in her throat. *Did he just drink my blood?*

Nicole didn't think it was possible for her to get any colder, but she felt as if every cell of her being was encased in ice as realization dawned. The vat in the center of the table held blood. *Human blood.*

This room, this crazy laboratory, must be where the Skells brought the blood they gathered. How many human blood donors were needed? She thought Rilan had said five hundred. She fought the urge to gag at the thought of all that blood being stored right there in front of her.

Maeron flung the jar across the room, where glass collided with concrete in a shower of tiny splinters. "You lie, female." He raised his yellow eyes to her, seeming angry but not surprised. "I can identify many species by the taste of their blood. And although I don't know yours—yet—I know you're not human." He resumed his restless pacing. "I will ask you again. What are you?"

"I don't know," Nicole whispered. "I was raised human. How can I not be one?"

Maeron looked at the Ghazsul who had clawed her. "Other side."

"No!" Nicole shrieked as the Ghazsul grabbed her good arm. Her other arm still stung from his claws. She wasn't about to sit around and play pincushion. She twisted free, only to slam right into Maeron's hard chest. She hadn't even seen him move around the table. Up close, she realized that his skin didn't just look like ash; it actually was ashy, like she could trace lines in it. She couldn't hold back a shudder.

"I'll do the honors, then." His voice was menacingly quiet as he held up one long gray finger tipped with a jagged claw. "Unless you'd like to stop lying."

"I'm not lying. I can just...move stuff sometimes."

"You can move stuff," Maeron repeated slowly, mocking her. One of his huge bony hands closed around hers, and he dragged her toward the wall with the chains. She dug her heels into the ground, but physically she was no match for him. They reached the wall and he slammed one cuff around her wrist.

"Stop! Why are you doing this? What do you want with me?"

He leaned down so that his face was close to hers. "I want to know what you are. I want to know the extent of your powers. And then I'll decide if I'll let you live and work for me, or if I'll kill you."

"Work for you?" She shrank from his hideous countenance. "Doing what? Who are you?"

"Ah, female, soon everyone in the world will know the answer to that. I am Maeron, and it will behoove you to be on my side when I'm running the show in every realm. Because you will have to choose. And everyone who chooses against me will die." He snapped the other cuffs into place on her ankles and her other wrist. "Now, female. Give me a demonstration of your ability."

Nicole swallowed and thought about lying again. She could

tell him that she couldn't always call upon her power. But that would lead to another lie, and she would have to make up reasons why her power wasn't always available. Using her skills on command for Maeron was the last thing she wanted to do, but she also wanted to stay alive. Her life was not going to end in this crummy basement, not when she and Brooke had just figured out the purpose behind the gifts they had been born with.

And she had to stay alive so that she could tell Gunnar she loved him. It didn't matter that he had simply told her that he needed her. Well, she needed him, too. She would be his mate or whatever he wanted to call it. The terminology wasn't important to her; she wouldn't let another day go by without telling him how she felt. He and the other Lash demons were out there searching for Maeron right this minute. She saw the images Rhys had pulled up on the computer this morning. Of all the dilapidated buildings he had found, surely this was one of them.

She looked around the room, eyeing the various objects on the shelves. She'd never tried to call up a strong gust indoors before, because she had never wanted to trash any of her friends' homes. But this place could go up in flames for all she cared. Flames. She grimaced at the thought of Gin and the havoc she could wreak here.

The heaviest things in the room, besides the work table, were some of the books and a few large stone jars. She spotted a book that had been shoved carelessly on the highest shelf and stuck out into open space. Just like with the Ghazsul, this would probably piss Maeron off, but she wasn't going to meekly follow every order the Domu barked at her. She concentrated her energy on the lifeless air in the room and began to coax it to viability.

A swirl, then a breeze, then she had a strong current moving around the basement. The Skells inched as close to the wall as they could, and the Ghazsuls shifted their weight from side to side. She directed the wind at Maeron, then focused on the book. The shelving unit swayed and groaned, and as its weight shifted, the book flew off the shelf. Nicole put as much force as she could into her wind and into the tome, and sent it flying straight into the base of Maeron's skull.

He roared in anger as he stumbled to his knees. "Bitch!" he bellowed as he reached out and raked his claws from her hip to her ankle, shredding her jeans into ribbons.

A scream tore from her throat. Blood streamed down her leg. The last thing she saw was his other hand, formed into a fist and hurtling toward her face with demonic speed. She heard a sharp crack, which she dimly registered was her head hitting the wall, and everything went black.

CHAPTER 24

GUNNAR HAD BEEN PACING FOR nearly an hour. His skin felt too tight, his muscles jumpy. He whirled at every rustle of leaves or whisper of a bird's wing. While he'd prowled around empty rundown farmhouses in the middle of nowhere, Nicole had vanished. And from the echoing arrows of her pain that tore through him earlier, she'd been injured as well. A thought ghosted around the edge of his mind. *How could it get any worse?* But he refused to let it fully form, because as he knew too well, things could always get worse.

Kai had stopped telling him to relax and left him alone. *Thank God.* Gunnar barely kept the battle-rage at bay. The only thing helping to contain it was the lack of an immediate enemy to fight. He didn't know exactly who had Nicole, so the beast inside him had no one at which to strike out. It howled its agitation for its mate.

Finally, Gunnar's keen ears picked up the eight-cylinder roar of an SUV, spitting pebbles up from the road in its speed. Its light came into view first as tiny points, then grew to illuminate the inky black Illinois field. Brenin hopped out, followed by Rhys with his tablet computer in hand.

Brenin laid a hand on the sedan that Nicole had driven. "They used some kind of magic on the car. Since when do Ghazsuls cast spells?"

"Or visit Earth?" Kai muttered.

"I did some research in the car." Rhys opened a window on his tablet. "Check this out. There's one foreclosed house about two miles west of here, and it's right on a small river. There're more old farmhouses in this area, but they're all further out and not near water." He tapped his screen and looked to Gunnar. "I say we start with this one."

All the other Lash would defer to him on this mission. Even though the others were unmated, they recognized the depth of feeling Gunnar had for Nicole. There was no need to spell it out for them. They could see the glow of barely contained rage in his eyes. They knew that his inner beast had decided she was his. And they would do anything they could to help him get her back.

Gunnar nodded. They needed to go in carefully. If Ghazsuls were involved, then other predatory demons might be as well. His beast calmed down slightly as his tactical mind plotted their course of action.

They drove the first mile together in one of the Escalades, then covered the last mile on foot. They split up as they got closer, with Rhys and Brenin circling around to approach from the north. Kai and Gunnar had just taken cover in thick, overgrown brush a hundred yards from the house when Gunnar felt the unmistakable zing of Nicole's power. It prickled over his skin and through his muscles in a warm electric current, driving his beast to the brink. *She's fighting.* The beast bellowed to join her, to save her.

Kai's head whipped around to Gunnar. "Holy shit!" He rubbed his hands along his forearms. "Your girl's got game!"

"Almost there, Nicole." Gunnar's muscles urged him to bolt for the building, when his mind exploded in pain. He grabbed his head and doubled over, fighting to control the nausea flooding his body. He couldn't allow himself to vomit or cry out. They were too close to nabbing this bastard. *Nicole.* Her name became a mantra in his mind, repeating on an endless loop as he willed her to hang on. Gunnar would shred the muscle and bones of whatever creature dared to harm her.

Kai crouched next to his friend and scanned the area. "Fuck. We gotta get her out of there"

Gunnar nodded. "No shit. I'm gonna skin every last one of those motherfuckers."

"Save one for me, man. The good news is, looks like she got off a shot at one of them."

And then, as quickly as the pain had started, it ceased. Gunnar blinked. "It just…stopped."

"Is that good or bad?" Kai asked.

"I don't know." Gunnar straightened up.

They crept closer, advancing silently through the brush until Gunnar was hit with the odd feeling that it didn't make sense to go any further. Their plan suddenly seemed ridiculous, their mission futile. The best course of action right now would be to turn around and leave. One look at Kai confirmed that his friend felt the same way.

"Wards," Gunnar muttered, his warrior's mind cutting through the magically-enhanced fog of doubt. They had been expecting as much.

Rilan had discovered several warding spells in the old Domu's grimoire. The Lash demons figured that Maeron would use at least one of these to fortify his edifice. Because they knew the basis for the original spells, Rilan spent the morning working on a few counter spells, and relayed them over the phone to Kai while they waited for Rhys and Brenin to arrive. Kai then made sure all of them knew the counter spells, just in case they ended up going in separately.

Gunnar muttered the words now, and was infinitely grateful for Rilan's skills as the heavy feeling of futility lifted from the air. They were close enough to see the house; their acute night vision noting every detail of the crumbling structure.

The roof sagged low over what had once been a garage. Many window panes had long-ago shattered, giving the home a gap-toothed appearance. The few gutters that were still attached to the eaves hung askew, swaying in the night air. Paint peeled from the siding and the front porch steps were rotted. As they watched the house, a flash of movement caught Gunnar's eye.

A Skell. Unaware that it was being observed, it navigated the rotting steps and disappeared inside the house. Gunnar knew only too well that other demons' sense of hearing equaled theirs, so he signaled Kai to wait. As they continued to watch, a Ghazsul demon came around the side of the house. It stopped near the porch and stood motionless, scanning the surrounding area.

Gunnar's beast clawed at him, desperate to get out and fight the other predator. His blood boiled as he mustered the strength to hold it back. *Soon.* They needed to wait a few more minutes, to survey and try to gain every advantage they could before mounting their attack.

A faint yelp echoed from the other side of the house. Gunnar smiled. Rhys and Brenin had made their move. The Ghazsul at the front ran around the side, leaving the porch unprotected.

"Now!" Gunnar and Kai sprinted toward the house. There was no point in stealth. They had almost reached the house when three more Ghazsul demons came at them from the other side of the building.

The urge to fight rushed through Gunnar's veins like lightning. He let his beast take control as he engaged the first Ghazsul, his sword swinging with a vicious urgency. Familiar rage engulfed him. His vision took on a red haze. His rational mind slipped under, buried by the fury of his beast unleashed. He moved faster than his opponent, slashing at him with unholy speed until he raised his sword for the killing blow. Slicing cleanly through the creature's neck, Gunnar didn't even stop to watch its head hit the ground.

Kai held his own with one of the Ghazsuls, so Gunnar turned to the third. It struck first, landing a blow to his shoulder. Gunnar grunted. Blood poured down his arm.

The Ghazsul lunged for him and Gunnar dodged out of the way, losing his balance in the process. The other demon was fast, and it leaped on top of him and rammed the huge ball of its fist into his face.

Gunnar looked the Ghazsul in the eye. This is what he'd

been waiting for. *Bring it, motherfucker!*

He moved his head out of the path of the demon's clenched hand before it could land a second blow, and then he rolled them both across the ground and into the rotting steps. Jumping up, he grabbed the Ghazsul by its arms and slammed it back against the packed earth. It groaned but got right back up, only to get smacked across the face by a wooden board that Gunnar had ripped from the stairs.

Still it came at him, producing a small dagger from a holster on its leg. Gunnar twisted to the side, avoiding a wound to his belly, and the blade caught his thigh instead. He grabbed the demon's wrist, yanked the knife out of his own leg and turned it toward the Ghazsul.

The Ghazsul growled through clenched teeth, muscles shaking as the blade inched closer to its face, pushed ever closer by the strength of Gunnar's rage. Gunnar gave a final mighty shove, and the dagger sank securely into the Ghazsul's neck. Black blood spurted from the severed artery. Gunnar raised his sword and decapitated the Ghazsul, ensuring he was truly dead.

He looked up in time to see Kai finishing off his Ghazsul with a ball of demonfire. A Skell that had been peering out one of the front windows turned and ran when it caught Gunnar's eye.

"He knows we're here now." Kai nodded toward the door. "I've got your back. Let's go get Nicole."

Gunnar vaulted up the porch steps and burst inside the doorway. The inside of the dingy house contained a minimum of furniture. A small decorative shelving unit hung perilously on a wall above a worn orange couch. Holes dotted the plaster throughout the room. There was no sign of the Skell that had peeked out at them, but he heard a noise from the back of the house.

He and Kai crept through the front room and paused next to an open hallway. Stairs led up and two doors hung off their hinges, but no other demons were in sight. They continued moving to the rear of the dilapidated house, which contained a kitchen and what had once been a dining room. The kitchen sat empty. A forlorn, shabby door opened to the back yard. Striding to it, Kai looked outside.

"Rhys and Brenin are doing fine. Two down, two to go." He twisted to take in the dirty kitchen.

Gunnar paused just inside the room as the familiar scent of peaches hit his nose. He and Kai noticed the square trap door in the floor at the same time, and rushed over to peer down into the space. Nicole's scent saturated the air, but the little cellar was empty.

Turning around the room, Gunnar noticed a second hallway. Motioning to Kai, he moved toward it without a sound. A swift check of the open doorways revealed only empty rooms, so Gunnar kicked open the last remaining door.

The scent of peaches and Ghazsul blood assaulted his nose. And the tang of human blood and...another predatory demon. His beast roared as it recognized both its mate and its enemies in the same space. He rushed down the steps with Kai right behind him.

A deafening bellow of rage escaped his lips as he took in the sight that greeted him. Nicole drooped, unconscious, her limbs chained to the wall. Blood covered her leg.

One Ghazsul demon guarded her. Numerous Skells lined the walls, attempting to hide in the shadows of the basement. A bloody Ghazsul slumped on the floor. A work table held some kind of container, reeking of human blood. And in the center of it all, grinning a sadistic grin, was a Domu demon. Maeron.

"Ah, the Lash demons have come to save the day," he called out with false cheerfulness. "What took you so long?"

"Release her." The words Gunnar meant to say came out as a series of snarls.

Maeron seemed to know the intent behind Gunnar's rough voice. "Oh, I don't think so. This little female has caused me quite a bit of trouble today. Besides, I want her to work for me. She has a most unusual talent."

In one swift move, Gunnar leapt toward Nicole. He swung

his sword at the Ghazsul in front of her, severing one of its arms. Gunnar wanted to roar that its head was next, but he was no longer capable of speech. Only a furious, deafening sound came out of his mouth. The Ghazsul screeched in pain, but still managed to lunge for Gunnar.

Gunnar growled in victory, knowing that the lunge would put his opponent off balance. He spun in a circle and swung his sword up in a flashing arc, decapitating the Ghazsul. Its head thudded dully as it hit the cement floor behind him.

Standing in front of Nicole, he hissed at the sight of her bruised and filthy face. Her jeans hung on her hips, half of the denim gone. At least the claw marks on her leg seemed to be clotting. He tried to say her name, but could only manage a low rumble.

He turned to Maeron, releasing a bellow that shook the glass on the shelves, and charged. The Domu was prepared for him and blocked Gunnar's sword, but Gunnar was the faster fighter. And he was in the throes of battle-rage.

His senses flared as they registered the presence of another male in the room. *Brenin.* Gunnar struck out at Maeron, carving a long line into his chest.

The Domu cursed and jumped back, and then muttered something under his breath. Gunnar realized he was casting a spell and lunged at him to stop the flow of words.

Maeron finished too soon, smirking. "Ah, ah. I wouldn't be so quick to wound me now."

Behind him, Nicole let out a sigh and a tiny moan.

What did you do to her? The thought pounded in his head, his voice reduced to jumbled, animalistic sounds. Terror for his mate fought through the fury in his mind, forcing him to pause.

"I can just about see the wheels turning in your little brain," the Domu sneered. "What could I have done from over here? Why don't you take another swing at me and see?"

His beast was beyond tolerating the Domu's jeers. The pause over, Gunnar lashed out with his sword and connected with the thick muscles of Maeron's shoulder. A second too late, he understood that the Domu allowed the strike, though he dodged just far enough to ensure it was non-lethal. He heard an agonized shriek behind him as blood poured from Maeron's wound.

His own shoulder burned white hot. Looking down, he saw no wound. He blinked, but his confusion was buried under a surging wave of concern for Nicole.

Turning to vent his rage on whoever had hurt her, he froze as he saw the fresh wound on her shoulder. It was identical to the one he had just inflicted on the Domu.

And no one was near her.

"Fuck!" Kai shouted. "He linked his pain, his wounds, to her with that spell!"

"Oh, the blonde gets points for having brains," Maeron jeered.

"You cocksucking piece of shit!" Kai rushed the Domu, but Brenin grabbed his arm and clamped a brawny hand just above his elbow.

"Watch it, Kai!" Brenin shouted. "Hold off until we reverse that damn spell."

"You won't succeed, Lash. I've amassed a collection of spells, amulets and magic that is beyond anything you can comprehend. Some of the most ancient and powerful evil that ever existed has contributed to my personal grimoires."

Gunnar couldn't move. The rage-filled demon inside him howled at seeing its mate hurt. Its desire for revenge on Maeron licked at his soul like an inferno. But the rational part of his mind fought its way to the forefront, staying his hand. He couldn't risk harming Nicole. Kai's words rolled around in his head as he stood there, torn.

"Gunnar." Nicole's whisper broke into his thoughts.

He rushed to her side, trying to tell her not to speak, but the sounds that came out were muddled. One side of her face was swollen and turning purple, and blood flowed from her shoulder. Her arms dangled in the chains, her weight balanced between her uninjured leg and the wall.

Gently taking one of her hands in his, he grasped the metal cuff to snap it in two, but it didn't budge. He grunted, low and frustrated. Of course Maeron wouldn't have put her in ordinary manacles; he would have ensorcelled them.

She blinked up at him. "You're here."

He opened his mouth to speak, but words wouldn't form around his sharpened teeth. Her eyes opened wider as she registered the scene before her and then settled back on him. "Oh," she sighed, "I know you can't talk. But I knew you'd find me."

She smiled and gazed at him, her green eyes radiating relief and hope. His beast backed down from its seething rage, basking as her strength flooded him. Good gods, she shouldn't be trying to talk right now, but her coherent words eased his heart.

Finally his voice started working again, coming out as a throaty croak. "We'll get you out of here," he rasped, rubbing his thumb over the back of her hand.

"Well, isn't this a pretty scene," Maeron chuckled behind them.

Gunnar turned, standing in front of Nicole, and saw that Rhys had made his way down to the basement. That meant that any demons who had been upstairs were now dead. Kai motioned to the other two Lash, and spoke in a low, quick tone

"Ah, one more Lash joins the party. You all better get used to these walls. You're going to be looking at them for a while." Maeron's eyes flared with yellow light, and his lips moved with rapidly murmured words.

Gunnar's skin prickled with warning, his eyes drawn to movement at the base of the stairs.

A pale blue fog took shape, snaking along the perimeter of the basement. It stretched and rose until it was as tall as the Lash demons.

The fog pulsed and sighed like a living creature. Vertical lines of a darker blue ran up and down it, like the warp threads on a giant loom. All of them, including the injured Ghazsul and the Skells, stood trapped within the misty barricade.

Dark magic rolled off it like a slap of humid July air. Beads of sweat formed on Gunnar's brow, and he fought the pull to let it envelope him. In his long years of fighting, he'd encountered this sentient mist once before. It was an enticing trap as well as an impenetrable wall. Weaker-minded creatures tended to fall prey to it sooner rather than later.

One of the Skell demons chattered to itself, transfixed by the mist. Its mouth formed soft cooing sounds, its eyes growing wide. Gunnar could guess what would come next, but couldn't look away. As if drawn, the Skell moved forward in a flash, all gangly gray limbs, and dove into the barrier.

Its shriek filled the room and cut off, ending on a pop. A small flash of light shone from within the fog and the smell of burning flesh spilled into the room.

Nicole gasped behind him. "What–"

Maeron's chuckle rumbled through the room. "You see? And when the last of my Skells returns to me tonight, I will have everything I need to crush you. I'll make you sorry you ever existed. And that female will be mine."

"Never!" Gunnar roared and started to lunge for him, but he was stopped by the combination of Kai's loud protest and Nicole's soft whisper behind him. "Be careful, Gunnar. He's so dangerous."

"I know, love." He turned to her, aching inside at the sight of her bonds and wounds. "Don't worry. He won't hurt you again."

"Of course I won't," Maeron said. "You'll do it for me."

CHAPTER 25

YOU'LL DO IT FOR ME? Nicole sucked in a breath. *What the hell does that mean?* After seeing a Skell demon get vaporized by the blue fog, she wasn't about to put *anything* past Maeron.

Don't worry. Gunnar had said those words to her before, and each time everything had turned out okay. The difference was during those times she hadn't been chained, beaten up, and in the presence of a psychotic demon who could cast spells and who laughed when other creatures went up in smoke.

The searing pain in her shoulder had jerked her back to the realm of consciousness, the burn fading as she took in the view of Gunnar. She knew he was caught up in his battle rage. His eyes radiated an unnatural turquoise, the planes of his face sharp and defiant. And when he opened his mouth...it was like when they had been on Torth. Not words, but instead a vicious rumble had torn out.

She sensed his agony at not being able to free her. Standing before her now, he radiated savage fury, but it was coiled and ready to strike, rather than unhinged delirium. *Because of me.* She knew this on an instinctive level that she couldn't explain. And when he spoke to her, his rough cadence full of tenderness, she fell in love with him all over again.

"Gunnar," she whispered. "Do you have the ash?"

"Yes." His voice was still gritty from rage. "But anything we do to him, also happens to you. I won't risk it."

Being this close to Gunnar while he was all raged-out was giving her a powerful burst of strength. *Funny, it didn't feel this way on Torth.* It was like her own energy had been infused with high-octane fuel. Not about to question it, she let the new feeling zip through her veins. Her eyes landed on the blue fog.

She gazed at the dark blue vertical lines as they moved and swayed. An image flashed in her mind of the tall slender grasses she had parted earlier in the day. Invisible sparks danced down her arms, an idea crystallizing in her mind.

"Goodbye, creepy fog," she murmured, focusing on one blue line directly opposite her. She didn't have to summon the forceful blast of air. It simply sprang from her body, shooting across the room like a cannonball.

An eerie shriek echoed in the room as a ragged hole appeared in the pulsing mist. Nicole couldn't tell what had made the sound—the mist or Maeron. The tear widened until the wispy, cloud-like fingers separated, leaving a gap several feet wide.

Every creature in the room stared at her. No one moved as her heart thudded once…twice. Gunnar's bright blue eyes rounded in surprise, and she thought she saw him fight back a smile.

He whirled around and bellowed, "Go!" Rhys and Brenin darted through the opening and ran up the stairs. Kai moved to stand beside Gunnar.

"I'll kill you all!" Maeron's ashy face contorted with fury. He raised his hand and hurled a ball of blue fire from his palm, followed by another and another.

Kai blocked them with his sword, sending some of them flying into the Skells. A couple of them shrieked and collapsed right where they stood. "Is that all you got, Domu? Because I can do this shit all night." He continued deflecting the blue fire. "You need some more human blood for your spell. But none of your little slave laborers are coming home. Not tonight. Not fucking ever."

"Gunnar," she whispered urgently as Kai distracted the huge Domu. "Use the ash."

"Not until we get you untangled from him." His ragged tone was absolute.

"It may be the only way to stop him. You have to try!"

"The only thing I have to do is keep you safe." His eyes glowed blue as he took her hand in his.

"But your assignment was to find out what he was doing and stop him."

"And finding you was an important side note to my assignment." His azure gaze locked with hers. "You're more important than you can ever know, not just to the world, but...to me."

Her heart skipped at his words. She knew that he was still fueled by rage, and knew that the fury-drenched demon inside him accepted her as well.

"Gunnar...I need to tell you something."

He reached a claw-tipped hand toward her face, turning it so that his knuckles brushed her cheek. "You should save your strength, love. Rilan is working on a counter spell. Rhys is talking to him right now. I promise we'll get you out of this."

"I feel stronger than I ever have. And I know you'll do whatever it takes to get rid of Maeron. But," she paused, *just in case things go wrong*...She needed to tell him how she felt. "Gunnar, I love you."

He stared at her and sucked in a breath.

"I'm yours. I'll be your mate, or whatever you call it. I love you."

He raised his other hand toward her and opened his mouth to speak, but a ball of blue flame blasted the wall near her head.

"You may as well savor this moment of domestic bliss, Lash, because it will be your last." Maeron raised his hand. This time a white fiery line arced from his palm toward Gunnar, who darted to the side just in time.

Gunnar roared and charged the Domu, tackling him to the ground and pinning him face down. Kai shouted at him to stop, but Nicole sensed Gunnar's inner beast had reached its limit with Maeron's antics.

His frustration seething in her own blood. She understood that even though he held the larger demon trapped beneath him, he was doing it with care. She felt the iron grip of his arms as he kept Maeron motionless, but no pain.

The Domu laughed, the unearthly sound echoing around the room. The blue fog shifted and pulsed, but hadn't knit itself back together. "Well, what shall we do now? It seems as though we're at an impasse. I've got your female, and you plan to kill all my Skells. We may as well settle in and get comfortable."

Feet thudded on the steps, then Rhys barreled down the stairs and leaped across the split in the mist. "Fuck you, Domu." He closed his eyes and chanted in a language she couldn't understand. Everyone in the room paused, except Maeron. He twisted sharply to one side, trying to get free of Gunnar.

"What is this?" he shouted. "Do you think you possess any magic as great as mine?"

The air in the room swirled gently. Everyone else was quiet, waiting for something to happen.

Rhys paused and opened his eyes. His dark gaze shot to Gunnar, who looked like he wanted to introduce Maeron's head to the concrete floor about a hundred times. Instead, Gunnar grabbed the larger demon's hand and started to bend one finger backward.

Nicole gasped and let out a small cry at the ache that shot up her own hand.

"It didn't work." Kai let out a string of foul curses.

With a snarl, Gunnar released the demon's hand but didn't shift his weight from Maeron's body.

Maeron cackled, his voice full of wicked glee. "That was certainly entertaining. Lash demons speaking spells. You all could perform somewhere, maybe go on tour. Of course, it would be better for business if your spells actually worked." Then he began chanting, and Gunnar was thrown off the Domu and slammed hard against the stone work table.

A jolt rocked her, the raw force of it reverberating in her bones. The impact was so strong that she felt Gunnar's rational mind slip away, replaced by his beast. She shook her head, uncertain how her mind and body registered all these new sensations.

Kai bellowed and rushed toward them. Skells shrieked as Rhys towered over them, herding them all into one corner of the room. In all the commotion, no one but Nicole saw the small flash of falling glass as it reflected light from the bare bulbs.

Her eyes darted toward it. The tiny jar from Rivkin lay uncorked on the floor. It had fallen out of Gunnar's pocket with the impact of Maeron's magical blow, and rolled a few feet down the length of the table. A bit of the ash spilled out, but most of it remained in the glass.

Now. This is my chance.

The tiny hairs on her arms stood straight up as newly amped-up power tingled along her skin. None of the males would agree with her, but they were all engaged in other things at the moment. She stared at the ash and felt the power within it. Her own energy built, vibrating with untapped potential.

All the activity and tension in the room worked in her favor as the air crackled, creating its own gusts. The atmosphere held back. Ready. Primed. Waiting for her command.

She pulled an air current down from the eddies around the surging demons, and pushed the small glass upside down. The fine gray ash spilled onto the floor.

Gunnar was the first to sense her power growing in the room. He turned to her and opened his mouth to protest, but only a garbled roar came out. She wasn't planning on listening to him anyway. Not this time. If she had the opportunity to rid the world of this crazy-ass demon, she would take it.

Keeping her focus on the dead Domu's ashes, she coaxed another small breeze down to the work table. The ash lifted gently, as if being cradled by two invisible hands. She brought another current to her aid, positioning it near the suspended ashes.

She glanced over at Kai and Maeron, who circled each other with death stares in their eyes. Kai was probably pissed as hell at not being able to use his sword on the Domu, and at Maeron's resulting glee. There was enough space between them that she had a clear shot, and she didn't hesitate.

Using her second air current, she packed more power into it and directed it straight toward Maeron. The ashes zipped across the room and flung against Maeron's face, exploding in a soft cloud that filtered down into his eyes and mouth. It coated his gray cheekbones and dusted the top of his head. His jaw dropped open in shock, then his yellow eyes widened in disbelief. He howled as he fell to the ground, doubled over in pain.

Kai and Rhys gaped at her. The manacles on her wrists and ankles clattered to the floor as an unholy shriek filled the room. Nicole clapped her hands over her ears. *Where is it coming from?*

Maeron huddled on his knees, arms wrapped around his broad chest. His eyes flitted around the room, pausing as he gazed toward the wall. He looked back at Nicole and short, pained bursts of laughter tore from his mouth.

She blinked in confusion. *What's going on?*

A chill enveloped her body, driving deep into her bones. The furious shrieking continued, but it didn't originate from any of the demons. Her veins turned frigid, her blood slowing as she saw the blue mist pulsing like a heartbeat. It sucked itself in, then pushed its sides out. In, out. Over and over, and it howled. Its cold rage drenched her skin.

Slender, curving tendrils swirled out from it, as if examining its surroundings, and then they drew back into the cloudy mass. The hole she had torn fused itself together and the fog once again encircled the room. No gaps. No way out. It tightened in one beating pulse, closing in around her.

"Gunnar!" she screamed, but the mist moved faster than he could. It bent and dipped, dissipated and rematerialized, avoiding the demons and coming for her. *Oh, God.* Visions of the unfortunate Skell demon popped into her mind. She drew her arms in close, hands clenched under her chin. She saw nothing but blue. She heard nothing but the high-pitched screech.

No, no, no. I'm not dying in this hellhole! She shoved at the mist with her mind.

Nothing happened. The god-awful noise continued, and a tendril reached out to coil around her leg.

No! It took her a second to realize she hadn't poofed into the ether. The bitter cold ribbon of fog cut into her jeans, releasing more mist, freezing her skin. She couldn't hear anything. *Where is Gunnar?* She screamed his name in her mind. Another subzero tendril curled around her other leg.

A shot of adrenaline cut through her terror, warming her blood. She recognized the beefed-up version of her power, and understood that she was somehow able to link to Gunnar's raw vitality. She focused her energy, trying to blast a hole in the mist as she had earlier.

It didn't work. *What the hell?* She drew a ragged breath. Her ears were ringing… but the shrieking had stopped.

"Gunnar!" she yelled again. Her voice sounded high-pitched and muffled, like she had been standing in front of a speaker during a rock concert.

She didn't know how, but she felt his palpable fear for her, mixed with his boundless strength. Dark and formidable, he loomed somewhere near, enraged at not being able to get to her. His beast was ready to rain fire.

More misty arms wrapped around her body, and she couldn't contain a cry of pain. She'd never felt so cold in her entire life. *No!* She had to beat this thing.

Concentrating on her ability, she opened her heart to the all-consuming love she felt for Gunnar. She visualized their bond as a steel cable. Unbreakable. Sustaining unfathomable weight. All the fibers of their losses and joys woven together into something new. Together, they would fight whatever hell was on its way. And this pathetic mist would be just a footnote.

Every cell in her body rallied as she drew on their combined strength. She gritted her teeth and pushed. Shivers wracked her body even as sweat streaked her face. She envisioned the mist dissipating into nothingness. *Not…gonna…let…you…win…*

Her face collided with the concrete floor. Her body shook from cold and pain. Her ears buzzed. Time stilled.

She felt herself lifted and tucked against something warm. Tears streamed down her cheeks. Her limbs and shoulders burned with a fire that hurt as bad as those arctic foggy tendrils.

Looking down at the hands that held her, she saw claws. Gunnar. His love poured through her and a new wave of tears spilled from her eyes.

She looked around the room, seeing no blue fog. Kai and Rhys held Maeron to the ground. They stared at her with a mix of concern and admiration.

"What happened?" Her hoarse scratch was barely audible.

A low, rolling sound came from Gunnar's throat.

"You beat the mist. We, ah…weren't sure you'd make it. Are you okay?" Kai's eyes assessed her in a swift, clinical manner. "Ah, shit, your legs."

Nicole looked down and wished she hadn't. Ugly red welts wrapped her legs where the misty tentacles had touched her. "God, it was so cold." She didn't want to leave the shelter of Gunnar's arms, but her skin burned all over. "I need to stand now."

He set her down in front of him. Her limbs wobbled like a newborn colt's. He grunted something unintelligible that she knew was meant to be soothing, and she sank into his strength.

Dimly, she heard Rhys and Kai talking, the fallen Domu tackled to the floor. To her still-buzzing ears, their voices sounded miles away. Then she realized they were calling to her, urgently asking her something.

"Can you feel that? Nicole? We need to know if your shoulder hurts," Rhys said.

"The bone, not your skin!" Kai added.

She had to stop and think for a minute. Why did they want to know about her shoulder? Her legs had taken the brunt of the mist's numbing touch. She peeked around Gunnar's massive shoulder to see Kai bending Maeron's arm behind his back, twisting it at a wrenching angle. "No," she managed to respond. Whatever they were doing still didn't register with her. "My shoulder is fine."

Kai and Rhys exchanged a grin. "Showtime," Kai stated triumphantly. He turned to Nicole, who still clung to Gunnar. "We're all clear. Do either of you want the honor?"

"Honor?" she asked.

Gunnar's voice, raspy and rough, finally broke through the battle rage. "We can kill Maeron now. He can't hurt you. The spell is broken."

"Oh." The meaning of their question became clear. "Uh, no. No thanks."

Gunnar tilted her chin so that their eyes locked. "I would avenge you."

Nicole nodded, gazing up into the bright blue of his eyes, and shivered as she took in both sides of her deadly male. She caressed his sharp, high cheekbone and traced a finger down to his jaw. Deep in her heart, she understood his need for retribution. Her scarred demon's feelings stemmed not only from vengeance, but from love. His need to kill for her neither thrilled nor horrified her. It simply existed as a part of him. And she loved all of him.

"Close your eyes, love." He kissed the top of her head. Easing her backward until she leaned against the wall, he turned and stalked toward Maeron, still pinned under Rhys and Kai. The other two Lash moved back to flank her.

Eyes shut, she heard two pops in rapid succession, followed by sizzling. A flash of light registered behind her closed lids, and the smell of burning flesh wafted across the basement. She coughed and covered her mouth and nose. *God, that smell is awful.* She called a gentle breeze to blow the stench to the other side of the room.

Two heavy hands landed on her shoulders and she opened her eyes. His claws rested lightly against her skin, but his voice was almost back to normal. "You took a huge risk. You had no idea how tossing the ash would affect you. Don't you ever do that again."

"But it worked," she said softly. He only stared down at her, his eyes unreadable. "You're mad at me, aren't you?"

"Extremely," he barked. "Thank the gods you're safe."

He lowered his head to claim her mouth. He kissed her gently at first, his lips moving softly over hers. She moved her hands up into his hair and let him in, welcoming the warm probe of his tongue. Her body went limp, grateful that this nightmare had ended, and she gave herself over to her lethal warrior. He bent her backward, kissing her with a deep hunger, marking her soul for himself. She was faintly aware of pops of demonfire in the room, but at that moment all she cared about was Gunnar's huge body surrounding her.

A slight cough drew her attention from her man. Gunnar released her and she straightened up to see several piles of smoking demon remains scattered around the room. Rhys, Kai, and Brenin stood there, preparing to overturn the stone work table.

"You may want to get to the stairs so you don't have to walk through this stuff," Kai told her.

"Oh. Right." She started to walk across the basement and made it about two feet. Stumbling forward, she was caught once again in Gunnar's strong arms. He picked her up and carried her to the lowest step, then turned to his friends.

"You got that?" he asked.

The three nodded, then together gave one huge push and flipped over the table and the vat of blood. A deafening crack echoed in the room as the stone slab snapped in half. The floor and all its demonic remnants turned a deep crimson.

"I'd say it's time to blow this popsicle stand." Kai strode toward the stairs.

They all headed up to the first floor and outside. Gunnar, still carrying Nicole, walked a good hundred feet away from the old house before gently setting her down. She sagged against him, her arms wrapped around his waist, and watched the other three demons.

Circling the house, the males aimed balls of demonfire at key points in the crumbling frame. It lit up the dark night in a brilliant starburst before the flames settled down to consume every inch of the rotting structure. Relief and victory shot through her. Maeron and his evil spell were gone.

She felt the weight of Gunnar's stare as she watched the old farmhouse burn. Nicole tore her eyes away from the blazing fire to look at her demon. His gaze held only the faintest glow of blue luster, his breathing had calmed, and the ragged traces of rage had faded. She couldn't suppress a smile as she traced her finger along his jaw. "You saved me."

"As you saved me." He kissed the top of her head. "Let's go home."

CHAPTER 26

NICOLE LAY ACROSS THE BACK seat of the Escalade with her head in Gunnar's lap. *My mate.* Through the still-forming bond, he felt the pinches and pulls of her skin healing, as well as waves of relief that their ordeal had ended. But overriding everything else, he felt love. It bubbled up from her soul, caressing and soothing his own. Gunnar held one of her slim hands in his, and his free hand gently stroked her hair. Her eyes shone bright and expectant, never leaving his face, but something hung unfinished in the air between them.

And that "something" wasn't about to be discussed in the SUV. Iron Maiden's "Number Of The Beast" pounded from the radio. Kai sang as he drove, probably trying to give them as much privacy as possible. Even though his friend knew how he felt about Nicole, Gunnar didn't want to have that conversation here. They'd be home soon.

He gazed into the emerald pools of her eyes. He was angry she'd taken a risk. The thought of losing her had been an icy fist around his heart, and seeing her subjected to Maeron's sadistic whims had sent him into full battle-rage. *And that hellacious fog.* When it engulfed her, he'd felt the terror in her mind as strongly as the icy burns on her skin. He'd wished with every fiber of his being that he could trade places with her. Instead, he'd breathed his strength into their bond.

She loves me.

He hadn't gotten the chance to tell her he felt the same way. He moved his hand from her hair to her face, tenderly stroking the back of his knuckles across her downy cheek.

She watched him as the car rolled north. As they reached more populated roads, shadows and light from the streetlamps flickered across her delicate features. Nothing could detract from her beauty, not even the now-healing bruises along one side of her face. Nothing seemed to be able to shake her grace under fire, and that made his heart swell with pride.

They pulled into the driveway at their house, followed by Brenin driving the other Escalade and Rhys driving the sedan Nicole had taken earlier. Though they were covered in blood, with bruises and lacerations decorating their skin, their Elder couldn't have looked more pleased to see them. He came out the back door to meet them as the cars pulled around. Rhys and Brenin hopped out, grinning from ear to ear.

"Now that's what I call a party!" Brenin hollered. His long blond hair swung across his back as he pumped one brawny arm. "Let's do that again!"

"I think I'll skip the next time, if you don't mind." Nicole eased out of the car. She seemed steady enough to walk, though she didn't let go of Gunnar's hand.

"Seriously, Nicole, you did good." Rhys gave her a lop-sided grin.

"I'm the reason we all ended up in that basement."

Gunnar brushed a wayward lock of hair from her face. "We planned on ending up wherever Maeron was hiding his sorry ass–basement, cave, whatever. Although you being there definitely wasn't part of the strategy." He turned to his fellow warriors. "You can stay up hashing out the details with Rilan if you want. We're going to get cleaned up." Draping an arm across Nicole's shoulders, he tugged her through the door.

She didn't protest as he led her up the stairs to his bedroom and closed the door behind them. As it clicked shut, she melted into his arms, burying her face in his grimy T-shirt. "We did it," she said against his shoulder.

"*You* did. I'm so proud of you." He slid his finger under her chin, tilting her head up so he could look into her bright eyes.

"Nicole, what you said before, in Maeron's lair…"

Her tender gaze swept through him like a soft breeze, enticing his soul and caressing his heart. He almost couldn't believe she was his.

"You know that the mate bond is permanent?"

She took his hand in hers and raised it to her mouth, kissing his knuckles. "I think you mentioned that."

He would never get enough of her sweet lips and her playful spirit. "Then I belong to you."

"And I belong to you." She tugged his face down to her.

God, but he loved hearing those words. Every nerve tingled, ready to burst with the deluge of love and devotion she poured into him with her kiss. Her mouth was tender and sweet and ripe with promise.

She pulled back and looked at him for a moment, her eyes searching his face. "Now what?"

"I say we get cleaned up."

"No, not that. Are we mates now?"

"The bond has been forming for a few hours. That's how I knew you were in trouble. It's the reason I was able to lend you my strength when you were fighting the mist. But it won't be fully complete until we do one more thing." He gave her a slow wink and dropped his eyes to her mouth.

"What's that?"

"It involves getting naked." He smacked her bottom and she jumped. "Shit. We can wait–"

"No, I'm okay." She smiled and glanced at her arms. The criss-cross pattern of angry welts had faded to pink. "It may not look like it, but I seem to be healing even faster."

She trailed her hands down his arms, tangling their fingers for an instant, then let go and walked to the center of the room. Turning, she shot him an expectant look. Dirt and grime covered her hair and her clothes. Her face looked like Maeron's punching bag, although the bruises had already changed from purple to yellow. Lingering pink burns from the fog painted her skin. Dried blood caked her arm and one of her legs, which was barely covered by her shredded jeans. But she had never been more beautiful. She was home. She was safe. She was *his*.

Her eyes travelled the length of his body, which was even filthier than hers, and flashed with a wicked gleam. "I feel dirty."

She kicked off her boots, and gave her jeans a sharp tug. They met the floor in a crumple of denim. Her pink tank top followed suit. She turned to walk toward the bathroom door, unhooking her bra and dropping it. "Wanna help me wash my back?" she called over her shoulder as she disappeared. He heard the hiss of the shower a second later.

Still standing against the door, Gunnar grinned broadly. He couldn't wait to join his Solsti, in every possible way. Once they were mated, he would never again have to wonder how she was feeling. He would be able to sense her emotions all the time and hear her thoughts if she was near. She would be able to do the same with him. And right now, he caught a faint, impatient echo from her mind.

He walked to the bathroom, divesting himself of his clothing as he went. Pulling back the curtain, he stepped in behind her. She leaned forward, her hands braced against the wall under the spray, head bowed, letting the water pound against her shoulders.

Ribbons of pink twined around the length of her legs. *Fuck.*

"I'm okay," she said over her shoulder.

Had she realized that he hadn't spoken out loud? He closed the small space between them and pulled her close, placing tender kisses down her neck and shoulder. "Mine," he whispered, and sucked the mark on her neck.

She sighed and wriggled her hips, pushing her ass against his erection. He had been hard ever since she'd tenderly kissed his hand. And now, skin-to-skin with her, inhaling her scent, his cock throbbed in anticipation.

He grabbed the soap and washed her back, massaging her muscles through the billowing lather. Turning her, he inspected the cut on her arm. Only a thin red line remained. *Thank the gods.* He lowered his head to kiss it and she sighed contentedly.

"Can you wash my hair, too?" she murmured. "It feels so good when you do it."

"Hell, yes." He reached for the shampoo.

When she was thoroughly sudsy, he knelt to wash her long legs. He rubbed the soap in small circles from her ankles to her sexy ass. Kneeling in front of her, he gripped her hips and kissed the smooth skin of her belly. He moved his hands around to her backside and kneaded, sliding his fingers between her cheeks. She inhaled sharply and he rumbled his approval against her skin. He kissed her again, and this time he caught the unmistakable scent of her arousal mixed with the clean smell of soap.

He'd go to his knees before her any day, but she tugged at his shoulders, urging him up. He stood and crushed her to his chest, one hand at her waist and the other in her hair. Growling, he kissed her deep and rough.

She responded by nipping and sucking his lower lip. Fierce need ripped through him as he felt her passion on a new level. The sensation was curiously both new and familiar...then he recognized the ache of her lust rising along with his own. *My mate wants me.* He'd heard about this aspect of the mate bond.

Nicole rocked her body against him, moving her hands up along his neck and into his hair. She stopped abruptly, paused, and then he felt her smile against his mouth.

He pulled back slightly. "What?"

She slowly brought one hand down to eye level. Between her fingers was a black glob of demon goo. He grimaced. But she only grinned as she flicked it down to the drain. "Been there, done that. Looks like it's your turn for a shampoo."

He must have looked mortified, because she kept smiling. "I still think you're totally hot. And I'll wash demon guck out of your hair any day. Especially if it means we get to share a shower."

I love this woman. He bent his head so she could shampoo him. And was rewarded with the sight of her soft, round breasts moving in the most enticing way as she reached up and massaged his scalp. He watched as rivulets of water slid along her shoulders, across her collarbones, and down to the puckered tips of her pink nipples. He groaned, unable to resist, and traced one droplet's path with his finger. She gasped as he rubbed her nipple with his thumb, then moaned as he repeated the process on her other side.

She shoved him under the spray. "You're clean enough, demon."

Chuckling, he turned around, quickly making sure anything else that may be considered a biohazard was rinsed from his body. He twisted the faucet to turn off the water, grabbed a blue bath towel, and began to dry her off. No longer in the mood to be pampered, she reached for a second towel to dry him. When he pressed the soft terry cloth to her breasts she made a most unfeminine sound of aggravation.

Yanking the towel from his hands, she threw her arms around his neck. "Now, Gunnar. I can't wait."

He'd wanted to take his time with her tonight, after the ordeal they had been through. But her urgent desire only stoked his need higher. He picked her up and she wrapped her legs around his waist. She nuzzled his neck as he walked them across the bedroom and lowered her down to his bed. *Our bed.*

He knelt before her and caressed her hips, her abdomen, and the tops of her thighs. Impulsively he leaned down to swirl his tongue around her navel, and inhaled a fresh burst of her spicy-sweet scent. *Intoxicating.* His cock twitched.

She writhed under him and reached for his shoulders. "*Gunnar.* I need you inside me. Now."

A growl escaped his throat and he positioned himself at her slick entrance. He nudged inside her heat, and she arched her hips up to take him in all the way. She caressed his shoulders and moved her hands to his back, dragging her nails down his skin. He hissed in pleasure, beginning a steady thrusting inside her.

She cupped his ass and pulled him even closer. "Harder."

He grunted his approval and leaned back, tilting her hips up so that he could drive in deeper. Her breathy little moans made him crazy. Her body was so soft under him, so open, her need a beacon to the primal male in him. He would pleasure her every day for the rest of their long lives. He would be hers to command.

Her hands clutched the sheets and her breasts bounced as he slammed his hips against hers. An urgent sound escaped her lips as she gazed up at him. "I'm so close. Make me come, Gunnar."

His balls tightened. He moved his thumb to his lips and moistened it, then trailed his hand down her body to her core. Finding her most sensitive spot, he circled her and applied a steady pressure. Her body bowed, and her shoulders came off the bed as the orgasm swept over her. She dug her fingers into his biceps, holding on for dear life.

His own release built at the base of his cock, and as her inner muscles squeezed him, he exploded inside her. Unable to stop, he pounded into her until his last drop was spent and he collapsed next to her on the bed.

He stared at her lying beside him. Her eyes were closed, lips parted, her breathing ragged. She was so beautiful, so sexy, so brave and determined. *Mine*. His heart swelled with adoration and joy, and the words spilled effortlessly from his mouth. "I love you."

Her eyes snapped open and she propped herself up on her elbow. A huge smile lit her face. "And I love you," she murmured, leaning down to kiss him. Her lips brushed along his, then moved to place tiny kisses along his jaw. "Tell me again."

"I love you, Nicole."

She beamed at him, then her expression sobered. "Gunnar...I know you'll always want to protect me and keep me safe. I understand that it's part of who you are. But..." A ghost of sadness flickered across her emerald eyes.

"You're right. I'll kill anyone who tries to harm you." He stroked his hand down her arm. "But...what?"

Her eyes shone with steely resolve. "I spent my life feeling like I was the odd one out. And now I've discovered my true purpose, the reason behind my talent. I'm a Solsti, and I'm here for a reason. Gunnar, I won't hesitate to fight if I'm needed. If I can tip the balance in our favor, or if I can help someone who's weaker, I'll do it. Can you...accept that? Can you accept that about me?" She looked so fragile at that moment, so unsure.

"I accept you, Nicole. All of you." He took her hand in his. "Hell, your bravery is part of who you are. As much as my protective instincts are part of who I am. You've made me so proud over the last few days. Even though you nearly gave me a heart attack every damn time," he added wryly. "But I love you. And I'm not letting you go. Just don't go running into a battle if I—or our allies—have things under control."

She lay back down on the bed, facing him. "I promise not to do anything crazy." The love in her eyes melted his heart. She rubbed her thumb absently over the back of his hand. "I was afraid I had jumped the gun back in that basement today."

He raised an eyebrow and she continued. "By telling you that I love you."

Caressing her side, his hand stopped at her hip. "I had already realized that I felt the same. I just didn't know how to tell you."

A playful smile curled across her face. "When did you know?"

"The other night, when I came home to find you sleeping in my bed. That's when I realized you were my mate. That's when I realized I didn't want to live without you."

A question flared in her green eyes. "Are we mated now?"

I think so, he answered silently.

She shot up in the bed. "What?"

He grinned broadly. *Oh yeah, we definitely are.*

A look of cautious wonder and surprise crossed her face. "What's going on?"

He spoke the words aloud this time. "Mates can hear each other's thoughts when they're near."

She opened her mouth and then closed it. *No way.*

Way.

Her eyes widened to the size of saucers. "We're...mated." She stared down at him with the goofiest, most adorable grin he had ever seen.

"We can also sense each other's emotions. We don't have to be in close proximity for that."

She tilted her head to one side. "Anything else?"

Yeah, there's one other thing.

"What?" She clutched his hand, squeezing it tightly.

"A lock of your hair will change color to match mine. And one of mine will change to your color."

She frowned and looked at him as if he had sprouted a second head. "That's crazy."

He nodded. "It's true."

"How come Taszim and Larissa didn't have that?"

"First of all, the wood nymphs all have brown hair, so it may not have been obvious. Also, it may not happen in the nymph species. But it most definitely happens for demons."

She bolted off the bed and ran to look in the mirror over the dresser. Peering at her reflection, she said, "I'm still blond."

He loved that she was so comfortable running around his room—their room—stark naked. Folding his hands behind his head, he soaked up the view of her perfect ass, hips thrust backward as she leaned over his dresser. "It may take a few hours."

"What if a person tries to color it? Or cut it off?"

Are you trying to get rid of me already?

"No!" She returned to the bed, settling next to him. "I'm just curious. I never would have imagined this."

"Hair dye won't take to the mate lock. And if it gets cut, it'll grow back within a day."

"Oh." She laid on her side, facing him and smiling, her fingers drawing slow circles on his chest. Joy saturated the air between them.

Through the window, gray streaks of dawn shot across the autumn sky. The longest day of his life had become the best day of his life. And he couldn't imagine another sunrise slipping by without this woman at his side. He stared into her luminous green eyes and threaded his hand into her hair before kissing her again. "I will always love you," he whispered against her lips.

Nicole slowly drifted awake in Gunnar's big bed. Happiness uncurled as a contented smile that tugged her lips up, and her mind registered his presence in the house. She snuggled deeper under the sheet, blocking the bright light streaming in the window, remembering what they had done in this bed not too long ago.

She thought sex with Gunnar was hot and intense, addictive even. But nothing could compare to how it changed after the mate bond formed. She could feel his desire and love—heck, his orgasms too—right along with her own. It was sex on steroids, with a nuclear fallout of erotic heat. They'd consumed each other in a hurricane of bliss as night surrendered to dawn's insistent rays.

So much had happened over the last several days that she was still trying to process it all. *There's no rush—I've got time.* And right now, all she wanted to think about was her new mate.

She rolled back the other way, about to kick off the sheet, when she saw Brooke sitting in the big armchair across the room. Her sister glanced up from her smart phone and grinned. "About time you woke up."

"You're back! What time is it?" Nicole bolted upright, forgetting she was naked beneath the sheet.

Without missing a beat, Brooke tossed a pile of fabric at her. Nicole fist pumped the air when she saw that they were fresh clothes from their condo. "You stopped by our place! You're the best."

"Yeah, I violated direct orders from Demon Central." Brooke rolled her eyes. "I knew that if I needed more things, you probably did too. And it's almost five in the afternoon."

"Five?" *How did I sleep the whole day away?* She shrugged, deciding that she deserved it after everything that happened.

"How was your trip?" She wiggled into the panties and bra, then pulled on the short sleeved black tee and jeans.

"Completely uninteresting. But I hear you had quite the adventure yesterday. I mean, I leave for a few days and you get kidnapped, chained in a basement, and...*married?*"

Nicole's expression fell and she turned to face her sister. "Don't be mad, Brooke. Things happened really fast, I'll admit, but everything will be okay. And we're not married, exactly. We're mated."

Brooke was staring at her as if she had just spoken Greek. Her gray eyes narrowed and she said in a low voice, "*What* did you do to your hair?"

Nicole gasped and rocketed off the bed to peer into the mirror once again. There, on the left side of her head, falling straight down from her side part, was a lock of hair as dark as a moonless night in central Illinois. It stood out in sharp contrast to the rest of her blond hair. She felt her jaw drop in wonder as she touched it, tugged at it, and finally tucked it behind her ear. "The mate lock," she said softly.

Behind her, Brooke huffed out a breath. She sat back in the chair and crossed her arm over her chest. "Okay, Nic, you've got some explaining to do."

Nicole fought the desire to run through the house looking for Gunnar to see if he was now sporting his own blond lock of hair. She owed her sister an explanation. Or twenty. Since Brooke had already heard about yesterday's events with Maeron and his minions, she started by explaining the mate bonding process–and its ancillary effects–as best she could.

"I still don't understand how you didn't know it was going to happen," Brooke grumbled.

"Well, it wasn't like we said vows or anything. I guess all it took was both of us realizing that we were truly meant to be together. And then after we told each other, and knew we both felt the same way, the bond just...took over. I love him, Brooke."

"Then I'm happy for you. I mean, he seems like a nice guy.

And he's nuts about you. I guess I'll just have a little less sister time now. But…" she paused. "Hmm. I'm gaining a brother-in-law. Do you think he can change that ugly light fixture in our dining room?"

Nicole walked over to tug on her sister's hand. "You won't have less sister time. Now that we know our purpose, we'll be working on new skills all the time. We have to get ready for the mysterious Armageddon that we're supposed to stop."

"Yeah, that little matter. The one where we're supposed to get Gin on board." She shook her head. "These guys have no idea what they're in for."

Nicole smiled and touched her newly dark lock. "I guess I'll be doing a video chat with Gin tonight. Wanna back me up?"

"Oh, I'll sit with you for the chat, but you have to do the explaining." Brooke gave her a big grin. Then her expression turned pensive. "I was wondering…are you going to live here now?"

"Gunnar and I haven't talked about it yet. But I guess I will."

"Well, I would prefer not to." Brooke held up a hand when Nicole opened her mouth to protest. "Look, I know it's a beautiful house, but it's not our home. I'm not one of the guys, even though they're nice enough. And you're in the throes of honeymoon bliss. I'll feel like the third wheel. So…I want to keep our condo."

"Brooke, you won't be safe there. You heard about the demons that attacked me yesterday. And the ones that attacked us on Torth. What if they come here? They're vicious. And we aren't invincible."

"I know safety is an issue. But I had an idea. I heard about the old grimoire that Rilan is translating. I've already talked to him about it…he said there are some good warding spells in there. He can ward the condo. He can even put some mild, generic wards on the whole building. It'll be the safest place in the city."

Nicole pursed her lips. "I just worry about you."

"The feeling's mutual," Brooke replied. "I hated watching you go through that portal. I didn't know if you'd ever come back."

Nicole pulled her sister into a hug. "I know our world has just turned upside down. I love you. Nothing will change that."

"Okay, big sis. Love you, too." Brooke stepped back but held onto one of Nicole's hands. "Now, let's go downstairs and find your man. You can stop glancing at the door already."

Nicole scrunched up her face. "Was I that obvious?"

"Chica, you may as well have a neon sign." Brooke pulled her through the door and they started down the steps. "And, just so you know, he gets the *sappiest* grin on his face whenever your name is mentioned. Which, during the story about yesterday's adventures, was constantly."

Nicole beamed. "Brooke, I'm so happy."

"I know. I'm happy for you. Just don't make me an aunt right away. I don't do diapers."

"No, no! There won't be any baby demons for a very long time!" She laughed and shook her head. They rounded the corner to the kitchen, and Nicole stopped short when she spied Gunnar standing in the great room with the rest of the Lash demons.

He had been waiting for her, she realized, and rather impatiently. But he'd known that she and Brooke needed to talk. Her heart swelled in her chest as she spotted the bright blond lock on his head, nestled among his glossy black hair. It stood out like a beacon, telling the world that he was mated. To her. She ran to him and jumped into his strong arms. He spun her around once before setting her down and kissing her senseless. When he pulled back to let her breathe, she reached up and reverently touched his blond mate lock.

His eyes glowed with possession and love as he gazed down at her, taking in her newly darkened lock. He took her left hand in his. "I have something for you."

She sucked in a breath as she felt the cool press of metal against her finger. Looking down, she felt her jaw drop as she stared at the large round diamond set in a band of gems. "Oh my gosh," she said in breathless surprise. "It's beautiful." The facets mirrored each other endlessly, the depths of the diamond glowing with a rainbow of colors.

"Not as beautiful as you. Take a closer look."

She complied, peering at the band. The other stones were emeralds, two on each side of the diamond. "I love it."

"I chose emeralds because of your eyes," he explained, "And there are four of them to represent you and your sisters."

Her jaw dropped again, and this time tears of joy welled in her eyes. "I love you."

"And I love you." He lowered his head to kiss her again. "Always."

Need to satisfy your Lash demon craving?
Read on for an excerpt from WICKED WAVES.

WICKED WAVES
Book Two
The Solsti Prophecy Series

KAI CROUCHED ON THE ROOF of the gleaming Lincoln Park condo building, all of his enhanced senses on alert. Through the concrete and metal below his feet, the smell of lilacs wafted up to him, reassuring him of Brooke's presence. He focused on the unit below, listening for the steady beat of her heart and the even rhythm of her breathing. Satisfied that she was sound asleep, he relaxed and inhaled, letting her scent wash over him. He could drown in that seductive, soothing fragrance.

Brooke would kill him if she knew he was here. Most days, she looked ready to hurl a dagger between his eyes. If his brethren found out, he would never hear the end of it. The other Lash demons stationed in Chicago would fall on their asses laughing, and that would be after giving him shit for three days straight. Kai, who took pleasure in bedding as many women as he wanted, was stymied by one willful brunette.

But Brooke wasn't just any brunette. The entire supernatural world believed her existence to be a myth. One day she would wield devastating power. Until she grew into her talents, her vulnerability made him edgy.

It gnawed at him that she stayed alone in her condo, though protective wards were placed on it by their Elder. So every night when he completed his patrols, he stopped by her building. He made it his private mission. *Private* being the operative word.

He couldn't explain his need to ensure her safety. She hadn't been threatened and held no affection for him. He snorted. *Ice Princess*. Cold as hell. That's when she wasn't shooting him a death glare or looking at him like he was a bug stuck to her shoe.

He cast a glare at the wispy clouds drifting across the dark sky. It never turned jet black, not with all the lights blanketing the city. The quiet streets gave him no cause to linger, yet he found himself thinking of reasons to stay. He watched the few souls walking down her tree-lined street, most returning from trendy neighborhood bars. There was no dark magic here. No need to hang out on her roof.

Straightening to leave, he heard her cry out. Adrenaline surged through his veins and a switch flipped in his mind, his body changing from observer to protector. Her unit was on the top floor of the building, which he could reach via her balcony. After dropping down outside the sliding glass door, he paused to take a deep breath. He didn't detect any other scents inside her rooms.

Tugging on the door, he was pleased to find it locked. He would've been furious if she had been so careless as to leave it unlocked—then again, he wouldn't be able to do anything about it. *Since I'm not supposed to be here.* She wouldn't listen to him anyway.

He would've shattered the large glass pane if necessary, but she'd left a window cracked open next to the sliding door. *All the better to not wake the neighbors.*

Removing the screen, he shoved the frame open as far as it would go and climbed inside. It was tricky squeezing his six-and-a-half-foot body through, but he had been in tighter spaces. With a calculated drop, he landed soundlessly in a tidy living room.

He paused again, hearing nothing but her breathing, no longer as steady as it had been a few minutes ago. The fragrance of lilacs drew him through the living room and down a hall. He passed an empty bedroom, a bathroom, and then came to her open door.

She lay on her side, sheets twisted around her body. Alone.

As he crept into the room, he let out a breath. *Must've been a dream.* She slept soundly.

Or maybe not. She exhaled sharply, letting out a grunt before rolling onto her back. Her arm came up as if swatting something away, then dropped to her pillow. She sighed, and the fluttering behind her eyelids slowed. Gradually, so did her breathing.

Kai stood in the center of her room, unable to tear his eyes away from the most beautiful woman he had ever seen. And in his nearly two hundred years of existence, he had seen—and fucked—hundreds of females. Watching her now, slumbering peacefully, utterly relaxed, she looked innocent and delicate. No icy glare shone from her pale gray eyes. No snide comment fell from her lush red lips. Chestnut waves, wild from her fitful sleep, splayed across her pillow. This was simply Brooke, unguarded.

Had she fought with someone in her dream? He wondered if her subconscious wrestled with the role she and her sisters had been thrust into. They'd been raised human, oblivious to the immortal world that paralleled theirs.

He studied the flush that colored her ivory cheeks and extended down her neck, to the tops of her full breasts. *Ah, hell.* He could dream about her breasts all day long. And right now, her pajama top gave him quite an eyeful.

She wore a pink tank top, which had gotten twisted as she tossed and turned. The skimpy thing pulled tight across her body, revealing the heavy side curve of her breast. The cursed scrap of fabric barely contained all that creamy flesh. If it twisted half an inch lower—God, he'd be able to see her nipples. Stiff and taut, they pushed at the stretchy cotton, begging for his touch.

Kai closed his eyes and willed the blood to return to his head, as it all seemed to be pooled in his groin. *She's safe.* It was only a dream. The last thing he needed was for her to wake and find him ogling her.

Stealing one last glance, he walked out of her bedroom and retraced his steps to the living room window. He climbed out, put the screen back in place, and glanced around. No one milled about the back of the building at this hour. He vaulted over the balcony railing to the pavement four stories below and sped home, hoping the ten-mile run would douse the heat racing through his veins.

WICKED WAVES is available NOW! Start reading today!

About Sharon Kay

Sharon Kay writes award-winning fiction and can never get enough reading time. She loves paranormal romance, with romantic suspense following close on its heels. She loves winter and black coffee, and is endlessly inspired to write kick-ass heroines and the men strong enough to capture their hearts.

Sharon lives in the Chicago area with her husband and son, and didn't expect to write one book, let alone a series. But WICKED WIND and the Solsti series formed in her head one weekend and refused to stay quiet until she put pen to paper. Her characters tend to keep her up at night, as they banter, fall in love, and slay endless varieties of power-hungry demons.

Sign up for Sharon's newsletter to keep up with her demons, see early cover reveals and be entered in periodic giveaways.

www.sharonkaynovels.com
www.facebook.com/sharonkaynovels
Twitter: @sharonkaynovels
Pinterest: www.pinterest.com/sharonkaynovels
www.tsu.co/sharonkaynovels

A NOTE FROM SHARON

I sincerely hope you enjoyed reading WICKED WIND. Please take a moment to leave a review. Yes, I know I raised a few plot questions that I didn't answer here, but I promise they all get answered as the series unfolds. All four books, plus a bonus novella that can be read as a stand-alone, are available now. Thank you!

Printed in Great Britain
by Amazon.co.uk, Ltd.,
Marston Gate.